Switch

MEGAN HART

Switch

HARLEQUIN®
entertain, enrich, inspire™

SWITCH

ISBN-13: 978-0-7783-1520-9

For questions and comments about the quality of this book, please contact us at CustomerService@Harlequin.com.

www.Harlequin.com

Printed in U.S.A.

To my trusted crit partners, you know who you are.

To my family, for your support and love.

To my readers—without you, I'd have no success. Thank you.

I don't write books without music. My thanks to the artists and musicians who make it possible for me to sit at my computer day after day and make worlds and the people who populate them. Please support their work through legal sources.

Don McLean, "Empty Chairs"; Joaquin Phoenix and Reese Witherspoon, "It Ain't Me, Babe"; Joshua Radin, "Closer"; Justin King, "Same Mistakes"; Lifehouse, "Whatever It Takes"; Meredith Brooks, "What Would Happen"; Rufus Wainwright, "Hallelujah"; Sarah Bareilles, "Gravity"; Schuyler Fisk, "Lying to You"; She Wants Revenge, "These Things"; Tim Curry, "S.O.S."

Chapter 01

Sometimes, you look back.

He was coming out. I was going in. We moved by each other, ships passing without fanfare the way hundreds of strangers pass every day. The moment didn't last longer than it took to see a bush of dark, messy hair and a flash of dark eyes. I registered his clothes first, the khaki cargo pants and a long-sleeved black T-shirt. Then his height and the breadth of his shoulders. I became aware of him in the span of a few seconds the way men and women have of noticing each other, and I swiveled on the pointed toe of my kitten-heel pumps and followed him with my gaze until the door of the Speckled Toad closed behind me.

"Want me to wait?"

"Huh?" I looked at Kira, who'd gone ahead of me. "For what?"

"For you to go back after the dude who just gave you whiplash." She smirked and gestured, but I couldn't see him anymore, not even through the glass.

I'd known Kira since tenth grade, when we bonded over our mutual love for a senior boy named Todd Browning. We'd had a lot in common back then. Bad hair, miserable taste in clothes and a fondness for too much black eyeliner. We'd been friends back then, but I wasn't sure what to call her now.

I turned toward the center of the shop. "Shut up. I barely noticed him."

"If you say so." Kira tended to drift, and now she wandered toward a shelf of knickknacks that were nothing like anything I'd ever buy. She lifted one, a stuffed frog holding a heart in its feet. The heart had MOM embroidered on it in sparkly letters. "What about this?"

"Nice bling. But no, on so many levels. I do have half a mind to get her one of these, though." I turned to a shelf of porcelain clowns.

"Jesus. She'd hate one of those. I dare you to buy it." Kira snorted laughter.

I laughed, too. I was trying to find a birthday present for my father's wife. The woman wouldn't own her real age and insisted every birthday be celebrated as her "twenty-ninth" along with the appropriate coy smirks, but she sure didn't mind raking in the loot. Nothing I bought would impress her, and yet I was unrelentingly determined to buy her something perfect.

"If they weren't so expensive, I might think about it. She collects that Limoges stuff. Who knows? She might really dig a ceramic clown." I touched the umbrella of one tightrope-balancing monstrosity.

Kira had met Stella a handful of times and neither had been impressed with the other. "Yeah, right. I'm going to check out the magazines."

I murmured a reply and kept up my search. Miriam Levy, the owner of the Speckled Toad, stocks an array of decorative items, but that wasn't really why I was there. I could have gone anyplace to find Stella a present. Hell, she'd have loved a gift card to Neiman Marcus, even if she'd have sniffed at the amount I could afford. I didn't come to Miriam's shop for the porcelain clowns, or even because it was a convenient half a block from Riverview Manor, where I lived.

No. I came to Miriam's shop for the paper.

Parchment, hand-cut greeting cards, notebooks, pads of exquisite, delicate paper thin as tissue, stationery meant for fountain pens and thick, sturdy cardboard capable of enduring any torture. Paper in all colors and sizes, each individually perfect and unique, just right for writing love notes and breakup letters and condolences and poetry, with not a single box of plain white computer printer paper to be found. Miriam won't stock anything so plebian.

I have a bit of a stationery fetish. I collect paper, pens, note cards. Set me loose in an office-supply store and I can spend more hours and money than most women can drop on shoes. I love the way good ink smells on expensive paper. I love the way a heavy, linen note card feels in my fingers. Most of all, I love the way a blank sheet of paper looks when it's waiting to be written on. Anything can happen in those moments before you put pen to paper.

The best part about the Speckled Toad is that Miriam sells her paper by the sheet as well as by the package and the ream. My collection of papers includes some of creamy linen with watermarks, some handmade from flower pulp, some note cards scissored into scherenschnitte scenes. I have pens of every color and weight, most of them inexpensive but with something—the ink or the color—that appealed to me. I've collected my paper and my pens for years from antique shops, close-out bins, thrift shops. Discovering the Speckled Toad was like finding my own personal nirvana.

I always intend to use what I buy for something important. Worthwhile. Love letters written with a pen that curves into my palm just so and tied with crimson ribbon, sealed with scarlet wax. I buy them, I love them, but I hardly ever write on them. Even anonymous love letters need a recipient…and I didn't have a lover.

Then again, who writes anymore? Cell phones, instant messaging and the Internet have made letter writing obsolete, or nearly so. There's something powerful, though, about a handwritten note. Something personal and aching to be profound. Something more than a half-scribbled grocery list or a scrawled signature on a premade greeting card. Something I would probably never write, I thought as I ran my fingers over the silken edge of a pad of Victorian-embossed writing paper.

"Hey, Paige. How's it going?" Miriam's grandson Ari shifted the packages in his arms to the floor behind the counter, then disappeared and popped back up like a jack-in-the-box.

"Ari, dear. I have another delivery for you." Miriam appeared from the curtained doorway behind the front counter and looked over her half-glasses at him. "Right away. Don't take two hours like you did the last time."

He rolled his eyes but took the envelope from her and kissed her cheek. "Yes, Bubbe."

"Good boy. Now, Paige. What can I do for you today?" Miriam watched him go with a fond smile before turning to me. She was impeccably made up as usual, not a hair out of place or a smudge to her lipstick. Miriam is a true grande dame, at least seventy, and with a style few women can pull off at any age.

"I need a gift for my father's wife."

"Ah." Miriam inclined her head delicately to the left. "I'm sure you'll find the perfect gift. But if you need any help, let me know."

"Thanks." I'd been in often enough for her to know I liked to wander and browse.

After twenty minutes in which I'd caressed and perused the new shipment of fine writing papers and expensive pens I couldn't afford no matter how much I desperately wanted one, Kira found me in the back room.

"Okay, Indiana Jones, what are you looking for? The Lost Ark?"

"I'll know it when I see it." I gave her a look.

Kira rolled her eyes. "Oh, let's just go to the mall. You know Stella won't care what you give her."

"But I care." I couldn't explain how important it was to…well, not impress Stella. I could never impress her. To not disappoint her. To not prove her right about me. That was all I wanted to do. To not prove her right.

"You're so stubborn sometimes."

"It's called determination," I murmured as I looked one last time at the shelf in front of me.

"It's called stubborn as hell and refusing to admit it. I'll be outside."

I barely glanced up as she left. I'd known Kira's attention span wouldn't make her the best companion for this trip, but I'd put off buying Stella's gift for too long. I hadn't seen much of Kira since I'd moved away from our hometown to Harrisburg. Actually, I hadn't seen much of her even before that. When she'd called to see if I wanted to get together I hadn't been able to think of a reason to say no that wouldn't make me sound like a total douche. She'd be content outside smoking a cigarette or two, so I turned my attention back to the search, determined to find just the right thing.

Over the years I'd discovered it wasn't necessarily the gift itself that won Stella's approval, but something even less tangible than the price. My father gave her everything she wanted, and what she didn't get from him she bought for herself, so buying her something she wanted or needed was impossible. Gretchen and Steve, my dad's kids with his first wife, Tara, took the lazy route of having their kids make her something like a finger-painted card. Stella's own two boys were still young enough not to care. My half siblings got off the gift-giving hook with their haphazard efforts when I'd be held to a higher standard.

There is always something to be gained from being held to the higher standard.

Now I looked, hard, thinking about what would be just right. Don't get me wrong. She's not a bad person, my father's wife. She never went out of her way to make me part of their family the way she had with Gretchen and Steven, and I surely didn't rank as high in her sight as her sons Jeremy and Tyler. But my half siblings had all lived with my dad. I never had.

Then I saw it. The perfect gift. I took the box from the shelf and opened the top. Inside, nestled on deep blue tissue paper, lay a package of pale blue note cards. In the lower right corner of each glittered a stylized *S* surrounded by a design of subtly sparkling stars. The envelopes had the same starry design, the paper woven with silver threads to make it shine. A pen rested inside the box, too. I took it out. It was too light and the tiny tassel at the end made it too casual, but this wasn't for me. It was the perfect pen for salon-manicured fingers writing thank-you cards in which all the *i*'s were dotted by tiny hearts. It was the perfect pen for Stella.

"Ah, so you found something." Miriam took the box from me and carefully peeled away the price sticker from beneath. "Very nice choice. I'm sure she'll love it."

"I hope so." I thought she would, too, but didn't want to jinx myself.

"You always know exactly what someone needs, don't you?" Miriam smiled as she slipped the box into a pretty bag and added a ribbon, no extra charge.

I laughed. "Oh, I don't know about that."

"You do," she said firmly. "I remember my customers, you know. I pay attention. There are many who come in here looking for something and don't find it. You always do."

"That doesn't mean it's the right thing," I told her, paying for the cards with a pair of crisp bills fresh out of the ATM.

Miriam gave me a look over her glasses. "Isn't it?"

I didn't answer. How does anyone know if they know what they're doing is right? Until it's too late to change things, anyway.

"Sometimes, Paige, we think we know very well what someone wants, or needs. But then—" she sighed, holding out a package of pretty stationery in a box with a clear plastic lid "—we discover we are wrong. I'd put this aside for one of my regular customers, but he didn't care for it, after all."

"Too bad. I'm sure someone else will." I wasn't surprised a man didn't want the paper. Embossed with gilt-edged flowers, it seemed a little too feminine for a dude.

Miriam's gaze sharpened. "You, perhaps?"

I waved the flowered paper aside and shoved my hands in my back pockets as I looked around the shop. "Not really my style."

She laughed and set the box aside. She'd painted her nails scarlet to match her lipstick. I hoped when I was her age I'd be half as stylish. Hell. I hoped to be half as stylish tomorrow.

"Now, how about something for yourself? I have some new notebooks right here. Suede finish. Gilt-edged pages. Tied closed with a ribbon," she wheedled, pointing to the end-cap display. "Come and see."

I groaned good-naturedly. "You're heartless, you know that? You know all you have to do is show me…oh. Ohhh."

"Pretty, yes?"

"Yes." I wasn't looking at notebooks, but at a red, lacquered box with a ribbon-hinged lid. A purple-and-blue dragonfly design etched the polished wood. "What's this?"

I stroked the smooth lid and opened it. Inside, nestled on black satin, rested a small clay dish, a small container of red ink and a set of wood-handled brushes.

"Oh, that's a calligraphy set." Miriam came around the counter to look at it with me. "Chinese. But this one is special. It comes with paper and a set of pens, not just brushes and ink."

She showed me by lifting the box's bottom to reveal a sheaf of paper crisscrossed with a crimson ribbon and a set of brass-nibbed pens in a red satin bag with a drawstring.

"It's gorgeous." I took my hands away, though I wanted to touch the pens, the ink, the paper.

"Just what you need, yes?" Miriam went around the counter to sit on her stool. "Perfect for you."

I checked the price and closed the box's lid firmly. "Yes. But not today."

"No?" Miriam tutted. "Why is it you know so well what everyone else needs, but not yourself? Such a shame, Paige. You should buy it."

I could pay my cell phone bill for the price of that box. I shook my head, then cocked it to look at her. "Why are you so convinced I know what everyone else needs? That's a pretty broad statement."

Miriam tore the wrapper off a package of mints and put one into her mouth. She sucked gently for a moment before answering. "You've been a good customer. I've seen you buy gifts, and sometimes things for yourself. I like to think I know people. What they need and like. Why do you think I have such atrocities on my shelves? Because people want them."

I followed her gaze to the shelf holding more porcelain clowns. "Just because you want something doesn't mean you should have it."

"Just because you want something doesn't mean you should deny yourself the pleasure," Miriam said serenely. "Buy yourself that box. You deserve it."

"I have nothing to write with it!"

"Letters to a sweetheart," she suggested.

"I don't have a sweetheart." I shook my head again. "Sorry, Miriam. Can't do it now. Maybe some other time."

She sighed. "Fine, fine. Deny yourself the pleasure of something pretty. You think that's what you need?"

"I think I need to pay my bills before I can buy luxuries, that's what I think."

"Ah. Sensible." She inclined her head. "Practical. Not very romantic. That's you."

"You can tell all that from the kind of paper I buy?" I put my hands on my hips to stare at her. "C'mon."

Miriam shrugged, and it was easy to see how she must have been as a young woman. Stubborn, graceful, beautiful. "I can tell it by the paper you *don't* buy. When you're an old lady, you'll be wise like me, too."

"I hope so." I laughed.

"I hope you'll come back and buy yourself that box. It's meant for you, Paige."

"I'll definitely think about it. Okay? Is that good enough?"

"If you buy the paper," Miriam told me, "I guarantee you'll find something worth writing in it."

Chapter 02

Shall we begin?
This is your first list.
You will follow each instruction perfectly. There is no margin for error. The penalty for failure is dismissal.
Your reward will be my attention and command.
You will write a list of ten. Five flaws. Five strengths. Deliver them promptly to the address below.

The square envelope in my hand bore the faint ridges of really expensive paper and no glue on the flap, like the reply envelope included with an invitation. I turned the heavy, cream-colored card that had been inside it over and over in my fingers. It felt like high-grade linen. Also expensive. I fingered the slightly rough edge along one side. Custom cut, maybe, from a larger sheet. Not quite heavy enough to be a note card, but too thick to use in a computer printer.

I lifted the envelope to my face and sniffed it. A faint, musky perfume clung to the paper, which was smooth but also porous. I couldn't identify the scent, but it mingled with the aroma of expensive ink and new paper until my head wanted to spin.

I touched the black, looping letters. I didn't recognize the handwriting, and the letter bore no signature. Each word had been formed carefully, each letter precisely drawn, without the careless loops, ticks and whorls that marked most people's writing. This looked practiced and efficient. Faceless.

The paper listed a post-office box at one of the local branch offices, and that was it. Since moving into Riverview Manor five months ago, I'd received a few advertising circulars, requests for charitable donations addressed to two different former tenants and way too many bills. I hadn't had any personal mail at all. I turned the card over again, listening to the soft sigh of the paper on my skin. It didn't have a name or address on the front. Only a number, scrawled in the same languid hand as the note. I looked closer, seeing what in my haste I hadn't noticed before.

114

That explained it, then. This note wasn't for me at all. The ink had smeared a little, turning the one into a passable version of a four, if you weren't paying close attention. Someone had stuffed this into my mailbox, *414,* by mistake.

At least it wasn't another baby shower or wedding invitation from "friends" I hadn't seen in the past few years. I wasn't a fan of being put on a loot-gathering mailing list just because once upon a time we'd been in a math class together.

"What's that?" Kira had come up behind me in a cloud of cigarette odor and now dug her chin into my shoulder.

I don't know why I didn't want to show her, but I closed the card and slipped it back into the envelope, then found the right mailbox and shoved it through the slot. I peeked into the glass window and saw it resting inside the metal cave, slim and single and alone.

"Nothing. It wasn't for me."

"C'mon then, whore. Let's get upstairs. We have a threesome with Jose, Jack and Jim." She held up the clanking paper grocery sack containing the bottles.

Every woman should have a slutty friend. The one who makes her feel better about herself. Because no matter how drunk she got the night before, or how many guys she made out with at that party, or how short her skirt is, that slutty friend will always have been…well…sluttier.

Kira and I had traded that role back and forth over the years, a fact I would never be proud of but couldn't hide. "It's not even eight o'clock. Things don't start jumping until at least eleven."

"Which is why I stopped at the liquor store." She looked around the lobby and raised both eyebrows. "Wow. Nice."

I looked, too. I always did, even though I'd memorized nearly every tile in the floor. "Thanks. C'mon, let's grab the elevator."

She had to have been as equally impressed with my apartment, but she didn't say so. She swept through it, opening cupboard doors and looking in my medicine cabinet, and when it came time to eat the subs we'd bought for dinner she made a show of setting my scarred kitchen table with real plates instead of paper. But she didn't tell me it was nice.

It was almost like old times as we giggled over our food and watched reality TV at the same time. I hadn't forgotten what a bizarre and hilarious sense of humor Kira had, but it had been a long time since I laughed so hard my stomach clenched into knots. I was suddenly glad I'd invited her over. There's something nice about being with someone who already knows all your faults and likes you anyway…or at least doesn't like you any less because of them.

She had a new boyfriend. Tony something-or-other, I didn't recognize the name. Kira had never mentioned him in her text messages or occasional e-mails to me, but the way she dropped it casually into our conversation now meant she wanted me to ask about him.

"How long have you been going out?" I leveled a shot of Cuervo and studied it, not sure I wanted to take it. Once upon a time I'd been able to toss them back without fear of the consequences, but I hadn't done much drinking lately. I pushed it toward her, instead.

Kira drank back the shot with a practiced gulp. "Since just after you moved. A long time."

I didn't feel as if it had been that long, but anything longer than three months was a record of sorts with her. "Good for you."

She wrinkled her nose. "Whatever. He's good in bed and buys me shit. And he has a fucking awesome car. He's got a job. He's not a loser."

"All good things." I had slightly higher standards, or at least now I did, but I smiled at her description of him and wrapped up the papers from our food.

Kira got up to help me. "Yeah. I guess so. He's a good guy."

Which said more than anything else she had. I shot her a look. Times did change, I reminded myself. So did people.

When it came time to get ready to go out, though, the Kira I knew faked a gag. "Gawd, don't wear that."

I looked down at my low-rise jeans. They were boot cut. I had boots. I even had a cute cap-sleeved T-shirt. The hours of working out I'd been putting in lately were paying off. "What's wrong with what I have on?"

Kira swung open my closet door and rummaged around inside. "Don't you have anything…better?"

High school was a long time ago, I wanted to say, but looking at her short denim skirt and tight, belly-baring blouse, I figured my comment would be lost. I shrugged, instead.

"I know you have hotter clothes than that." Kira reappeared from my closet with a handful of shirts and skirts I remembered buying but hadn't worn in a long time. She tossed the clothes onto my bed, where they spread out in a month's worth of outfits.

I picked up a silky tank top in a pretty shade of lavender and a stretchy black skirt. I held them up to myself in front of my full-length mirror. Then I put them back on the bed.

"No, thanks," I said. "I'll wear what I've got on. It's comfortable."

Kira shook her head. "Oh, ew. Paige, c'mon."

"Ew?" I looked at myself again. The jeans clung to my hips and ass just right, and my T-shirt emphasized how flat my stomach was becoming. I thought I looked pretty damn good. "What's ew?"

"It's just, you know…" Kira trailed off and pushed her way next to me to hog the reflection. "You gotta show off a little bit."

I looked her over. Even in my stack-heeled boots, I stood a few inches shorter. She'd grown her natural red hair into long layers that fell halfway down her back. She never tanned, so her dark eyeliner looked extrablack and the fuck-me red lipstick even redder.

I looked in the mirror again, turning my chin to one side, then the other, to catch my profile. My hair's blond. And it's natural. My eyes are blue, but dark, almost navy. I look a lot like my dad, which is one reason, maybe, why he never bothered denying I was his.

"I think I look fine," I told her, but the faint sound of longing slithered into my voice.

I spent my clothes budget on simple, brand-name pieces I picked up off-season or in discount stores. I'd spent the past few years building my wardrobe. Clothes for work and casual wear that looked expensive enough to pass as classy. I paired them with shoes I couldn't always afford. I wasn't going to be Clarice Starling, giving away my background with my good bag and my cheap shoes.

I looked again at my reflection and thought of the whisper of satin on my skin. Going without a bra, how my nipples would push at the fabric and force a man's eyes straight to my breasts. Every man's eyes.

I picked up the tank top again and held it up. I smoothed the fabric over my stomach. Kira gave me an approving nod and slung an arm around my shoulders and bumped me with her hip. "C'mon. You know you want to."

I did want to. I wanted to go out and get shit-hammered drunk and dance and smoke and rub up on half a dozen boys. I wanted to feel a hot, hard body against mine and look for lust in a pair of eyes I didn't know.

I wanted not to worry about proving anyone right about me.

I pulled my tank top over my head and after a second's hesitation, unhooked my bra. The satin tank top slithered over my head and fell to my hips. My breasts swayed under the smooth fabric. My nipples tightened at once, and I shivered.

"Let me get you some makeup," Kira said.

She lugged her huge purse over to me and pulled out pots

and tubes and brushes and glitter. I love glitter. I hadn't worn glitter in forever, either. No place for it here, in my new life.

"I'll do it." I wouldn't dream of sharing makeup that had been on her face. No telling what germs could be passed on that way. I waved her away and went into my bathroom, where I rummaged beneath my sink.

I pulled out my own box of tricks and treats. Lipsticks in berry shades, eye shadows in rainbow hues. Lots and lots of half-used black-eyeliner sticks and a few bottles of liquid eyeliner. I shook one, thinking it must have dried up after all these years, but when I unscrewed the cap with its built-in brush, the makeup inside was still smooth.

I painted a mask. It looked just like me, only brighter. Bolder. More. Once, I'd worn this face every day. Once, it had been the only one I had.

My makeup finished, I squeezed into the tight black skirt. I left my legs bare. I'd be chilly on the walk from the parking garage to the bar, but hot enough inside once I started dancing. From my closet I pulled out a truly fucking fabulous pair of pumps.

Kira had been bent over her phone, fingers stabbing out messages, but her eyes widened and she reached for the shoes. "Oh, wow. Steve Madden!"

"First pair I ever bought." I stroked the smooth black patent leather. Four-inch heels. Most men couldn't have told the difference between a Steve Madden shoe and a Payless pump, but they looked twice when I wore them. Sometimes more than twice.

I slipped into the shoes and stood, adjusting to the way my center of balance shifted. My mother had taught me the art of how to walk in heels this high. I used to raid her closet as a kid and parade around the house in her shoes.

I smoothed the silky shirt over my belly and hips and turned around to look at myself one last time in the mirror. "Ready to go?"

"I guess so," Kira said sullenly. "Except now you look awesome and I look like shit."

"You look hot," I promised. What were friends for?

She was convinced, more because she wanted to believe it than because I'd tried hard. "Okay, let's go get shit-hammered!"

I saw him again, that dark-haired man. This time, he was coming in as I was going out. We passed each other not so much like two ships, as much as one ship passing while the other crashes into an iceberg. I couldn't be offended that his gaze slid over and past me, taking in the short skirt and high heels without a second look. He had his head down and was talking urgently into his cell phone. He didn't have attention to spare me. And it wasn't his fault I was trying so hard to pretend I wasn't looking back at him that I ran into the edge of the door frame hard enough to leave a bruise.

"Smooth move, Ex-Lax." Kira smirked. She hadn't even noticed it was the man from earlier that day. "Nice to see you can hold your tequila."

I shrugged off the sting in my shoulder and didn't reply. His sleeve had brushed my bare arm as he passed, and the hairs on it all the way up to the back of my neck had stood at that brief, simple touch. A slow, tumbling roll of sensation centered in my belly.

He lived in my building.

Chapter 03

I shouldn't have been so surprised. I saw a lot of Riverview Manor tenants at Miriam's shop, and in the Morningstar Mocha, the coffee shop at the end of our block. I ran into them in the post office and parking garage and at the grocery store, too. Harrisburg's a small city.

Even so, I couldn't shake the memory of those dark eyes, that thick, dark hair. The brush of a shirtsleeve on my bare skin. Fuck. I was horny, no two ways around it, and no wonder. It had been ages since I'd had sex with anyone but myself.

We had our choice of places downtown, but I wanted to go to the Pharmacy. We took a cab since I wouldn't drive after drinking, and the walk that was fine on a Sunday afternoon in sweatpants would be too long to make at night in heels…and shit-hammered.

The bar was packed, even for a Friday night. We pushed through the crowd toward the bar, Kira leading. She stopped abruptly and I ran into her. Someone ran into me. Someone also grabbed my ass, but when I turned to see who it was and possibly haul off and smack the shit out of them, all I could see was an ocean of possible culprits.

"Hey, Jack," Kira said, and I turned.

Shit. Jack had been the love of Kira's life our senior year, when he transferred in from another school. She'd plotted and schemed for months to get him to ask her to the prom, determined to get in his pants. It hadn't worked, so far as I knew. I only knew that once Kira had keyed one of his girlfriends' cars.

Kira didn't know Jack and I had fucked each other senseless for about two months straight a few years ago. I doubt either of us even cared anymore. But Kira would have, so I tried to pull her away before things could get ugly.

Besides, he wasn't alone. The woman with him had a beer and she tipped it to her mouth, eyeing us with a smile. I yanked Kira's elbow to pull her away.

"Ow," she said when the crowd closed behind us, cutting off the view of him. "What did you do that for?"

"Don't cause trouble," I told her. "C'mon. Drinks."

"I wasn't going to cause trouble." She frowned and tossed her hair, not caring she'd whacked some dude across the face with it. He looked pissed. Not the way I wanted to start the night.

"There will be other guys here," I told her.

Kira just sniffed and crossed her arms over her chest. "Oh, I know that."

The Pharmacy was almost always a total sausage party—three guys for every girl, easy, and all of them horny and looking to hook up. Chivalry had nothing to do with them pulling out their wallets and plying us with booze. It was all about getting laid.

"Oh, look," Kira said from beside me. "Talk about trouble."

She was right. Trouble with a capital *T.* I stood taller in my sexy shoes and lifted my chin, straightened my shoulders. "Hello, Austin."

Once upon a time, Austin and I had fucked like tigers. I was willing to bet he still had the scars. I did.

"Paige." His hair was longer, but he had the same grin, the one that parted thighs like the Red Sea. He didn't look surprised to see me.

Austin wore a blue-striped shirt and faded jeans that hugged his ass just right and hung down, ragged, at the hems. Jeans like that should be outlawed on men like Austin. His buddy, some guy I didn't know, wore an almost identical shirt, but with brown stripes. He didn't look half as good.

Behind me, Kira dug her fingernails into the skin of my elbow. It stung, and I shook her off. "How are you?"

"Good. I'm good." His eyes shifted to Kira and back to me. "Haven't seen you in a while."

"Haven't been home," I said, though home to me now was an apartment on Front Street, not a trailer or a rented house in Lebanon.

"Yeah. I know. Hey, Kira. I made it."

My insides froze. I glared at her, but Kira gave me her best dumb look. "What?"

She'd told him we'd be here. I knew it. I could see it on both their faces, their conspiracy, and I wondered how he'd convinced her to tell him. I thought about walking out, and the only reason I didn't was because he was looking at me. Not her.

Kira saw it, too, and she gave me a narrow-eyed glare. I wouldn't have put it past her to have set this up purely to see the throw down between me and Austin, but I wasn't going to do it. I was past those days. She rallied when Austin's friend gave her a grin. It helped that he was cute. Not as cute as Austin, but then really, who was? Who had ever been?

"What're you drinking?" Austin was already pulling out his wallet to pay.

I wasn't going to turn down a free drink, not even from him. "Margarita."

"I'll take a Slow, Comfortable Screw." Kira made sure to lean in close so he could hear her. Her lips brushed his ear.

Austin leaned away a little, not enough that Kira would notice. But I did. He introduced us both to his friend, Ethan, who managed to tear his gaze away from Kira's tits long enough to nod toward me without a trace of recognition. Well, what had I expected him to do? Say, "Oh, so *this* is Paige?"

"So what are you up to now?" Austin asked me as Kira and Ethan eyed each other.

"I work for Kelly Printing." The last time we spoke I'd still been finishing the degree I'd started when we were together and taking care of some rich couple's kids. I didn't ask him what he was doing, not for work and not here in Harrisburg. I didn't want him to think I cared.

"What about your mom?" Austin moved closer, his arm on the bar. "She still working for Hershey? I haven't been to the shop for a while."

My mom owns a tiny sandwich shop she inherited from her dad when I was in high school. I'd worked in that shop almost my entire life, running errands as a kid then graduating to making subs and running the cash register. Now I only helped if she had a big order to fill and deliver, or a party to cater.

"She still has it. She was working for Hershey but got laid off."

Austin nodded. "I'm working for McClaron and Sons."

I had no idea who or what McClaron and Sons was, but the fact he was working for someone other than his dad surprised me into a reply. "What about your dad?"

Austin shrugged, then grimaced, and only because I'd once known him so well it had been like knowing myself did I catch his hesitation. "It was time I got out of that job."

"But you're doing the same thing, right? Construction?" Kira popped into the conversation and drew both our attentions.

"Yeah, and some other stuff," Austin said, but didn't elaborate.

Interesting. Austin had worked for his dad's business the way I'd worked for my mom's—summers and after school since he'd been old enough to carry a hammer. It had always been the assumption that he'd take over the business when his dad retired, and become a full partner some time before that. I'd figured he already was.

"What about you?" Kira sipped her drink, eyes on Ethan. For someone with a boyfriend, she certainly seemed interested in him, but then Kira was just one of those girls.

You know. The slutty ones.

"I'm a mechanic," he said. "For Hershey."

"Oh, that's a good job!" Kira sidled in between Austin and Ethan.

"It is a good job," Ethan agreed and drank from his cup while his eyes wandered everywhere on Kira's body but her face.

It was so easy, really. They wanted to seduce us. We wanted to be seduced, for a few hours anyway. I knew what we looked like to them. Two girls in slinky outfits, sucking back drink after drink and letting the crowd push us closer and closer. There's no such thing as social distance in bars. The music makes conversation impossible unless you lean across to shout in someone's ear. The crush of people means you have to fight for your own small space, and sharing it doesn't seem so bad after a drink or four.

When Austin's hand ended up on my ass, I didn't even blink. It felt good there. Heavy, warm. He had strong fingers to go along with those biceps. He smelled good. Drakkar Noir. Despite myself and everything that had happened with us before, I'd missed him.

Austin said into my ear, "Wanna dance?"

Our bodies had always worked just right together, whether we were dancing or fucking. I was ready for both. Leaving Ethan and Kira, he took my hand and pulled me up the stairs to the third floor, where the songs ran into one another without stopping and all sounded the same. We found a spot in the middle and started dancing.

The booze had made me soft and melty, but the music wasn't. I wanted to slow dance. Austin wanted to grind. We compromised with a little hip action that brought us groin to groin, but when he tried to flip me around and get up on me in the back end, I pushed away with a smile.

"You don't answer my messages," Austin said.

It was easy to pretend I didn't hear him with the music so loud. I smiled and shook my head. He took me by the arm, up high in the soft part that bruises easily. His fingers closed all the way around it.

He moved in to brush his lips against my ear. "I've really missed you."

I inched away from him, but Austin grabbed my wrist just as

a bazillion watts of supernova bright light lit the entire dance floor. Austin still looked good. I must not have looked like Frankenstein, because he reached to brush my hair from my forehead. He smiled again as the lights went down and the beat of the music started its rapid *thump-thumping,* the same as my heart.

It was different when he kissed me. I felt different. His mouth opened and I let him inside me. His tongue stroked mine as his hand came up to curl in my hair. He didn't pull it, though my body tensed in anticipation.

Austin nuzzled at my earlobe. "You still taste the same."

Fortunately, I remembered the reasons I'd broken off our relationship. Unfortunately, I still remembered all the reasons we'd ever hooked up. When Austin ran a fingertip down my bare arm along the sensitive inside flesh to press his fingertip just over the pulse at my wrist, I knew he felt the way my heart sped up at his touch. Time hadn't changed that. Maybe it never would.

Maybe that was okay.

"Come home with me," Austin said.

"It's too far." Forty minutes I'd have driven in a heartbeat back in the day, just to get in his pants. It wasn't too far. Just too long.

"Paige," Austin said with a grin like a shark. "I moved to Lemoyne."

Just across the river. Fifteen minutes, tops, if you drove really slow or got stuck in traffic. The world fell out from under my fuck-me pumps, but Austin was there to catch me. The crowd moved and danced around us, but we stayed still. I looked deep into his blue, blue eyes, made bluer by the strobe lights.

"What the fuck," I said evenly, "did you do that for?"

"New job," he reminded. "Remember?"

I tried to recall if he'd said where McClaron and Sons was, and couldn't. He should've told me, I thought, and hated myself for being irrationally angry. I tugged my arm from his grip. "I have to go check on Kira."

"She's fine. She's with Ethan."

I tried to level him with a glare, but I'd never been able to level Austin. He'd laid me out cold a thousand times with a look, but though I'd practiced and perfected my steely-eyed look of cold disdain, it slid off him like oil. I bit my lower lip and lifted my chin.

"If he's anything like you, I'd better make sure she's okay."

"Paige." Austin's hand snagged my wrist. Pulled me close. "If she's anything like you, she can handle him."

The night it ended between us, we'd fucked up against the wall of our shitty, third-floor apartment on Cumberland Street in Lebanon. The red-blue lights of a cop car outside on the street had painted the ceiling and wall over our heads. He'd torn away my panties, tossed them to the side, used his body to pin mine to the wall while his hands held my ass.

I bore the marks of that last encounter on my back for a few weeks where a nail from a fallen picture had gouged me. I hadn't noticed the pain or the blood while we were going at it. I never had found my panties.

It had ended but wasn't over. The plain truth is, with a few drinks in me there was little chance of my resisting Austin. Not drunk. Not sober, either. Why else had I moved so far away?

"Hell, no," Kira said when I found her downstairs and brought up the subject. She shook her head and looked over my shoulder to where I was sure Austin was watching. "You told me to never, never, never let you fuck him again!"

I made myself stare at her, not look back at him. "I know. But that was before."

"Before what?" Kira's lip curled.

"Before you thought it would be fun to invite him out with us. I haven't talked to him in months. Since before I moved here. But now here he is."

"And looking utterly fuckable." Kira didn't lose the sneer, but her gaze flickered back and forth to my face and over my shoulder. "You know, Paige, I've known him as long as you have. He moved up here, wanted to know where the good places to go were. I told him we were coming here. I didn't know you were going to go home with him. I thought you were over him."

"I am over him!" I looked over my shoulder and caught his gaze, then turned away with hot cheeks and fast-beating heart.

"Whatever."

"I'll give you my key." I looked back at Austin, now bent in conversation with Ethan.

"Fuck, no. I'll get Tony to come pick me up!" Kira shook her head and stumbled a little bit.

I reached to steady her and she clutched at my hand. "Will he come for you?"

"He will if I fucking tell him to." Kira straightened, then swiped at her hair.

"I'll wait with you until he comes."

"Don't do me any favors," Kira said, then slung her arm around my shoulder. "Paige. Don't forget what happened."

As if I ever could. "I'll be fine!"

"Don't let your pussy get you into trouble," she continued, warning me off what she'd fallen prey to many times herself. "He made you cry."

"Yeah." I let Austin's gaze catch mine when it turned toward me and didn't look away. "Well, he won't make me cry anymore."

"He'll always make you cry," Kira said. "But go. Whatever. He's got a magic cock. I get it."

Remembering the times she'd left me stranded so she could go home with someone she met in a bar, I didn't feel nearly as bad as she wanted me to. "I'll wait until Tony gets here."

I could do that, at least.

Going to Austin's place was one thing, driving with him another. I wasn't going to get in the car with him after he'd been drinking, for one, and for another, I wasn't going to be stuck at his house without knowing for sure I'd be able to get home.

He grinned when I went over to him, but I fended off his kiss. "I have to wait for Kira to get picked up. I'll meet you there."

Austin pulled me close and nuzzled my neck exactly how he knew I liked it best. "Just come with me."

"No." I pushed him slightly away. Drunker, I'd have given in. More sober, I'm sure I'd have gone home alone. Stuck in this midway point where I wanted to taste him again and knowing lust is never as pretty the morning after, I shook my head. "I'll meet you there. Give me the address."

Maybe things were different, after all.

Austin kissed me again, harder, and this time I let him. He knew just how to do it, where to put his hands and his tongue and how to bump me with his groin to make my breath catch in my throat. My nipples throbbed, poking the silk of my shirt.

"Don't take too long." He stepped back, steady on his feet and not slurring his words. He reached as I turned and at the last moment, captured my wrist with his fingers. I let him tug me closer. "You're not going to bail on me, are you? Like last time?"

Last time I hadn't had Kira to remind me that I'd vowed never to go to bed with Austin again. Not that it was stopping me. Last time I'd called him just after two in the morning and told him I wanted to come over, but when I hung up the phone, good reason had won over the desire for his hands on me. That had been months ago, before I moved here.

"Are you still angry about that?"

"I wasn't mad. Just disappointed. Do it again, I'll be mad." He grinned and dipped his head to kiss me but stopped short of my lips, just brushing them. "And disappointed."

His blue eyes bore deep into mine, and for half a minute nothing else mattered. I felt Kira at my elbow, but I didn't turn to look at her. I looked right into Austin's eyes when I replied. "You won't be."

He let me go with another kiss and a nuzzle that sent shivers marching along every nerve. I found Kira waiting for me by the door. Oblivious to the crowd buffeting her, she held her place instead of stepping aside until I showed up to pull her by the elbow onto the sidewalk.

"You sure you'll be all right?" The chilly night air had done a pretty good job of sobering me up, but I wasn't reconsidering my rendezvous with Austin. At least not yet.

Kira nodded. "Fine."

She didn't look fine, she looked pissed off. I glanced out onto the street. Lots of cops. No cabs. I'd only turned away for a few seconds, but when I turned back to face her, Kira's expression had turned stormy.

"You asshole!" She took a couple of steps forward, her heel catching on a crack in the sidewalk, and stumbled.

Jack.

With an inward sigh, I went after her. Jack was with the same woman from earlier and he did his best to ignore Kira. I saw him give his date a pained glance she answered with a shrug, and they started walking.

"Hey, Jack! Jackass! Don't you walk away from me!"

"C'mon, Kira, don't." I didn't blame him for ignoring her. I was a little less pleased he was also actively ignoring me, even though I knew it was really for the best, all around. "He's not worth it!"

"Fuck you, Jack!" Kira couldn't let it go, apparently.

Jack grimaced and pulled his cap from his back pocket. He put it on, but didn't look at her. We hadn't gone more than another few steps down the sidewalk when Kira launched herself at his back.

Jack stumbled forward as she slammed into him, her legs and arms flying. She didn't actually manage to hit him more than once or twice, but the spectators leaped out of the way of her drunken tornado performance. She was shrieking insults, mostly stupid and incoherent ones.

Jack gave me an angry look that pissed me off. It wasn't like I'd told Kira he and I had hooked up or anything. Her issues with him were his own problem and had nothing to do with me. He pushed her off him firmly and grabbed her arm at the same time so she wouldn't fall. She kept trying to hit him and missing.

"Stop it," Jack told her and gave her arm a little shake before letting her go. When she flew at him again she managed to knock his cap off. I stepped forward, wishing I'd gone with Austin and left Kira to her theatrics alone. This was a scene I really didn't want to see.

"I hope your Prince Albert fucking rips out and you have to piss through three holes!" Kira screamed.

"Kira, c'mon." I reached for her.

Kira allowed herself to be led away, still shouting insults. By the time we got to the parking garage the crowd had thinned and we had a better shot at hailing a cab. I rubbed my bare arms and shivered, but Kira had anger as her cloak and she danced back and forth on the nubbly pavement, waving her hands and muttering curses.

"He's not worth it," I repeated. "Jesus, Kira. What's wrong with you?"

"He's a jackass," she said sullenly. Her makeup had smeared, her hair tangled. She needed to be in bed.

Fuck. I wanted to be in bed, and not alone. Yet here I was, instead, babysitting her while she had a tantrum about some guy she'd had a crush on a million years ago but had never even dated.

I didn't correct her, even though I didn't agree. "You're drunk. Call Tony. Go home."

She sniffed and crossed her arms. "Oh, you don't care! You're going to screw Austin. What difference does it make to you if my heart is broken?"

I laughed and knew I'd made a mistake by the way her brows pulled low over her smeared eyes. "Your heart's not broken. You didn't even go out with him. He doesn't even have the Prince Albert anymore."

She glared at me. I thought suddenly she was maybe way less wasted than I'd thought. "Did you fuck Jack?"

"It was ages ago."

"You fucked Jack?" Kira's fist clenched at her sides, then opened as her shoulders slumped. "I thought you were my friend!"

"Kira, it was years ago, and you weren't—"

"That doesn't matter!" she cried, and I knew she was right. "You knew how I felt about him! I loved him!"

I'd never loved him. At least there was that. "I'm sorry."

Kira whipped her phone from her purse and stabbed the buttons with her fingernail. She turned her back to me. I should've counted myself lucky she didn't try to punch me in the face the way she'd done Jack. As it was, I was cold and my stomach had begun to churn.

"Your sorry is shit." Kira spoke into the phone next. "It's me. Come pick me up. Yeah, I know what time it is. I'll be waiting at Tom's Diner on Second Street. Harrisburg, you 'tard."

She hung up and stalked off down the sidewalk without looking back.

"Kira!" She flipped me the bird without even pausing. There was no way I was going to run after her, not in my four-inch fuck-me pumps. I managed a hobble, though. "Kira, c'mon. Wait."

"You're supposed to be my friend," she said, and the quiet affront in her tone was worse than an insult or a punch. "God, Paige. Just because you can doesn't always mean you should, you know? This isn't high school anymore."

I stopped trying to follow her. "No shit, really? And calling out some dude on the street when he's with another girl, that's not straight out of high school?"

"That's different!"

"How is it different?"

"You knew how I felt about Jack!" Kira shouted.

We'd have attracted more attention if it wasn't Friday night just after the bars all closed, but as it was we were just two more drunk sluts fighting over a guy. In high school I'd have shouted back at her, maybe even done a little hair pulling.

But as we'd already established, we weren't in high school anymore.

I trapped my tongue between my teeth to stop myself from shouting back, but even then my voice came out clipped and sharp. "I said I was sorry. You weren't with him. You never even dated him. And you weren't even speaking to me at the time."

She faltered for a moment, her lashes batting and her mouth working as though she meant to say something really awful but could only come up with "...Yeah, well. You shouldn't have."

I didn't point out the number of boys I'd liked that Kira had fucked, or tried to fuck, or lied about fucking just to needle me. I said nothing, just stared, and she at last had the grace to cut her gaze from mine. She shrugged instead of speaking.

If you're lucky, the friends you make when you're sixteen stay with you for the rest of your life. If you're smart, you know when it's time to let them go. I stopped walking. I watched her walk toward the diner, where drunk and hungry people would order eggs and stiff the waitress and steal the silverware. I let her go there, even though she'd been drinking and she needed a ride home and I couldn't be sure the person she'd called would come to get her.

Yeah. Some friend.

Chapter 04

"I'm really glad you came," Austin said this as soon as he opened the door.

I said nothing.

He closed it behind me as I moved past him and into his living room. I recognized the chair and the couch. It had been mine, once. The chair had been his and he'd been welcome to it, but I'd paid for that couch.

The couch didn't matter.

"You want something to drink?"

I turned to look at him, this boy grown into a man. "No. I didn't come here to drink."

Austin smiled. "So, what did you come here for?"

I pulled him forward by his belt. Two steps. He didn't stumble, but he did put his hands on my upper arms. I must have caught him by surprise. I looked up, up into his face. But when he bent to kiss me, I turned my head.

"Let me guess," he said into my ear. "You didn't come here for kissing?"

"You can kiss me." I took his hand off my arm and put it between my legs. "Here."

I looked at him, then, and his expression gratified me immensely. His fingers curled experimentally against me and pushed at the soft cloth of my skirt.

Austin blinked, slowly. His smile didn't fade so much as leak away. "Paige?"

"We both know what I came here for." I curled my fingers around his wrist and moved his hand down to the hem of my skirt, then up again to replace his palm against my panties. "Let's not pretend anything else."

I thought, for one brief, strange second, he was going to turn me down. The heat of his hand seeped through my panties, but the flash of ice in his eyes left me cold. Suddenly I had no trouble remembering why I'd left him.

He didn't let me pull away. "Fine. I'm not pretending."

"Good."

"Good," he said. His fingers slipped inside my panties and found me already wet. Again, his gaze flickered. "Fuck, Paige."

"Yes, please," I said.

He'd always been bigger than me, but in the years since we'd broken up he'd gone from a bulky football player's build to the harder, leaner muscled frame of a man who made his living working with tools. He might have quit the construction job with his dad's company, but whatever he was doing kept him in tight, hard shape.

At first I thought he might not kiss me. We'd done it before, fucked without kissing each other on the mouth. We'd fucked angry, rough. We'd done it tender-soft, too, and sweet.

So when Austin pulled me closer and brushed his lips across mine, I was already tense and waiting. He kissed me softly and pulled away. He looked into my eyes.

"I was sure you'd bail on me."

I frowned, not wanting to talk, and when I opened my mouth he took my words away with another kiss and the restless stroking of his hands. I'm not ashamed to admit I stretched under his touch, so familiar no matter how long it had been. We kissed for a long time, all the way up the stairs and down the hall to his bedroom. I kissed him with my eyes closed, trusting him to lead me so I wouldn't stumble. We kissed the way we always had, but it was different, too. We stopped just inside his bedroom door and pulled apart, both of us breathing fast and hard. I couldn't remember how long it had been since anyone had seen me the way he did.

I was made of feathers when he lifted me, but I became flesh when he laid me down.

It was a new bed, new sheets. The smell of fabric softener was the same, and my heart seized, going still before it lurched to life again. His mouth ate my gasp. He swallowed my breath.

I'd worn clothes he could ruin without me caring, but Austin didn't tear or rip anything from me. Kneeling between my legs, staring at me on his pillow, he only put his hand on my belly. The muscles jumped.

When he smiled I almost couldn't remember what it had been like not to love him, but I forced myself to. This was not going to be anything but what I'd intended it to be. I spread my legs a little as I inched the skirt up over my thighs.

Austin put his hands to the hem of my shirt and lifted it to run his fingers over the swell of my breasts. He looked me over as if he'd never seen me before, like he hadn't once spent long hours cataloging every inch of my skin.

I liked the way it felt when he looked at me.

When his gaze met mine, we both smiled, which was a relief. There had been a moment at first when I thought this might turn awkward. Either sentimental or angry. We'd fucked a few times after I left him, and it hadn't always been a good choice.

It probably wasn't a good choice now, but when he ran his hands up the insides of my thighs, and a finger underneath the elastic of my panties, I stopped worrying about it. I arched into his touch, my eyes closing in anticipation. He slid a finger along my clit, then another down to press gently at my opening. That's when he stopped.

I looked at him. "Austin?"

He opened his pretty mouth, but all that came out was a hiss of air as he pushed inside me. I groaned as he crooked his finger against my sweet spot. He used his thumb on my clitoris at the same time, the familiar double whammy that had always worked for me.

"You like that?"

"Yes," I told him. "I like that."

He hooked his other hand into my silk panties and eased them down one side at a time as he kept up the in-out stroking. His eyes left my face to watch the motion of his hand, and I was glad. I didn't want to watch him watching me.

He stopped only for a few seconds, long enough to pull his shirt over his head. I used the time to pull down the side zip of my skirt, and he helped me off with that, too. My shirt went next. We moved together, coordinated, until I lay naked on his bed.

"Take off your pants."

I returned his hard stare. We'd never spoken much during sex. Now we were practically reciting the Declaration of Independence. I toyed with my nipples, teasing him as he unbuttoned and unzipped. He wasn't wearing the loose boxer shorts I'd expected, but tight boy shorts cut high on his thigh.

"Nice underwear," I told him.

The old Austin smirk came back, and he stripped them off quickly before getting back on his knees again. His cock stirred, half-hard but rising, on his thigh. "Thanks."

"Did you put those on just for me?" I got up on my elbows to look at him.

Austin just raised a brow. "What if I did?"

It wasn't the smart-ass answer I expected, and consequently, I had no answer.

"Paige." His hand went stroke, stroke, stroke, and I was hypnotized. "Open your legs."

I did, because I wanted him there. I thought he'd use his hand, but Austin got on his belly on the bed, instead. He wriggled up between my legs before I knew it, his breath hot on my inner thighs and finally, at last, my cunt.

I cried out when he kissed me there, but stifled it with my fist. When he licked me, I drew in a breath that tasted of my own skin. It had been a long time since a man had gone down on me…since the last time I'd been with him, as a matter of fact.

His lips worked my rigid clit as he pushed a finger, then two, then three, inside me. Rough but not harsh. He found my G-spot and I convulsed around his fingers. Pleasure took my voice away.

I pushed my hips upward in lieu of command, and he fucked me with his mouth and hands until I gasped and trembled. Shaking, I looked down at him, nestled between my legs. Passion had hazed my vision, but everything became crystalline when he paused to look up at me.

"Don't come yet." Austin's voice had grown impossibly deeper over the years. Now it went lower still. His breath drifted over my hot, wet flesh and the motion of his lips tantalized me mercilessly.

He moved up my body and captured my wrists with his hands as he pushed mine over my head. My fingers curled around the wooden spindles as I stared him in the eyes. I wasn't the same girl he hadn't taken to the prom, and I wasn't the same girl he'd married. I was a different woman now. But I held the headboard anyway, watching him as he fumbled in his nightstand for the package of condoms and slid one on.

When he moved back over me, one hand on his cock to guide it inside me, I tensed. My eyes closed as he filled me. When he moved, I moved with him. It was easy to remember how.

He fucked into me slowly, then faster. He pushed up onto his hands to drive his cock deeper, and I took the pain of his thrusts and turned it into pleasure. My hands gripped the wood. His eyes never left mine, not even when he slid a hand between us to stroke my clit in time to his thrusts.

"Now," he grunted from between clenched teeth, "you can come."

I hadn't been waiting for his permission, but my body took it anyway.

"Say my name." His fingers left me and he pushed his face into the side of my neck. "Say it, Paige."

I tipped into the swirling oblivion of orgasm, and I gave him what he wanted with his name, if he could decipher it from the moan. But I also let go of the headboard. My nails raked his back as I came again, as hard the second time as the first. Harder, maybe, because I was bringing blood and he cried out as he pumped inside me as he came, too.

Austin shuddered. His arms slid beneath me, clutching me

tight. He burrowed his face harder into my skin. And he just held me that way for what seemed like a very long time.

I had to unwrap my legs from around his waist after a few minutes to ease the cramp in my hips, but I didn't unwind my arms from around his back. His weight on me was more comforting than claustrophobic. When he finally pushed himself off me, he only rolled to the side with one arm and leg thrown over my body.

Now he would sleep, I thought.

But he didn't. Austin moved to get rid of the rubber in a nearby garbage can, then slipped right back to where he'd been. His hand moved lazily up and down my body in smooth, flat strokes.

"Paige."

"Yes," I said after a second.

"I thought you liked it when I was a little rough." His hand centered over my contented cunt, his fingers dipping into my well.

I wasn't squeamish about post-fucking cuddles or anything leading up to a potential round two, but when Austin stroked my pussy, I put a hand over his to stop the motion. "Is that why you did it?"

He didn't look at me. His breath puffed hot on my shoulder and he kissed me. His lips pressed my skin. His fingertip settled on my clit and circled lightly. I'd had two orgasms and my body wasn't ready for another, or so I thought. As his hand moved, tension stirred inside me.

"Is it?" I drew in a breath but kept my voice even. "Austin?"

"Well, shit, Paige. Yeah. Of course." He sounded insulted.

I put my hand over his again, though what he was doing was starting to work. "Look at me."

He did. I hadn't noticed the shadows under his eyes before. Faintly blue, they made him look older. Well, he was. We both were.

"I thought you liked it rough, that's all."

"Did it look like I wasn't enjoying myself?" I didn't want to defend my orgasms to him. I didn't want to think he'd done something for my sake that he hadn't wanted to do for his own.

Pushing him off me, I got out of bed and gathered my clothes. I dialed the cab company and arranged for a ride home. Austin watched me without pulling up the sheets or making a move toward his own clothes. When I looked at him, his expression had gone inscrutable. That was as familiar as everything else had been, and I figured whatever glitch in his operating system had made him ask me those questions had been fixed.

"Why did you come over here?" he asked, loud in the quiet. "Really?"

I stepped into my panties and pulled them up, then zipped my skirt, too. "I came over here to do just what we just did."

"Just to fuck me?"

"Yes, Austin," I told him. "What else did you think I wanted?"

"Nothing." He rolled to grab the remote from the nightstand and I discreetly ogled his ass and the sweet backs of his thighs—places I'd bite, if I had more time. "Forget I asked."

"Are you getting pissy with me?" I straightened my shirt and ran my fingers through my hair to shake it into some semblance of order. "No, you are not. Are you? Seriously?"

"No." Austin, his jaw set, kept his gaze on the television. He punched the buttons of the remote so fast I knew he couldn't possibly be able to see more than a second or two of each program before moving on.

"Because I'll tell you what, if you're going to give me an attitude every time I come over here to fuck you, I'm not going to bother anymore." I stepped into my shoes. "That cake is baked."

Now he looked at me. "Huh?"

"That cake," I said carefully, "is baked. Done. Over. Finished."

"Iced?" One corner of his lips turned up, but only a little.

He was maybe the only person who'd ever really "gotten" me. It was why we fought so hard and fucked so good. He knew every button to push.

"Yeah. Iced."

He shrugged, looking back at the television, but his mouth still quirked. "If you say so."

"Austin." I waited until he looked at me. "Don't make me regret this, okay? You know what this is."

He shrugged again, the brief glint of a smile fading. His finger stabbed the remote as he cycled through all bazillion cable stations. I thought about kissing him before I left. I even took a few steps toward the bed, but when he turned to look right at me, I stopped.

"I'll let myself out. No, no, don't bother getting out of bed," I said, though he hadn't done so much as shift. "I'll do it."

I was already out the door and into the hall and at the head of the stairs when he called after me.

"That's not all it is!"

I stopped, my hand on the newel post of his stairs. There were half a dozen retorts, but none of them made it past my tongue. At the bottom, the smooth banister shoved a splinter into my palm and I muttered a curse as I plucked it free. That would teach me, I thought as I let myself out of his house and onto the street, where the cab was already waiting.

Chapter 05

Daylight teased the sky by the time I made it home. I paid the cabdriver and ignored the way he ogled my thighs when I stepped onto the curb. I didn't want to be sorry I'd gone to bed with Austin even though I'd said I wouldn't. The sex had been too good, as good as it can be only with someone who already knows you, but I'd started a new life, with a new job and a new apartment, in a new city. I wanted new habits, too, and Austin was definitely not one of those.

I wanted a man who'd gone to college. Who had a career, not a job. One who owned a car and paid bills on time and wore clothes that matched. A professional man, not one who smoked and drank and cheated, or one who'd run up the credit card and skipped out into the night without leaving a note. Not one who wrecked my car because he didn't have one of his own.

I wanted a man, not a boy in a man-suit.

You're unfair to me, Austin had accused me more than once. *I'm not like those guys.*

Those guys. The men my mother dated. No, he wasn't like those guys. At least not mostly. But I'd always been waiting for him to turn into one. Maybe he was right and I'd been unfair, but he'd done his share of shitty things even when he knew they'd hurt me. Hell. I'd done the same.

My heels sounded very loud on the marble tile as I passed the front desk, empty at this hour. I'd occupied the elevator alone, dressed to kill, more times than I could count on both hands. Tonight, because I knew I looked ridden hard and put away wet, a hand shoved its way through the doors just before they closed, and I had to share it.

"Thanks," said that man I'd seen before. "I'm too tired for the stairs."

He slouched, eyes half lidded, in the corner opposite and just behind mine. His shoulders lifted with a sigh that became a yawn, prompting one from me I hid behind my hand. He looked at me with a half smile. Conscious of the fact I was sure my lipstick was smeared and my eyeliner smudged, I smiled back. We both turned to face the front, but I felt the weight of his gaze on me, could see him looking from the corner of my eye. Unlike before, this time he wasn't too distracted to notice me. When I turned my face, just slightly, he was studiously watching the blinking white numbers showing the elevator's progress.

I had to bite my lower lip against a smile. He was seriously eye-fucking me. Who doesn't get off on being noticed?

It took a very long time, it seemed, to reach the first floor. He moved past me without touching me, but my skin prickled as though he had. He stepped out of the elevator and I let out the breath I'd been holding. I'd seen him twice now. Three times? It must have been the charm, because unlike all the others, this time he was the one who looked back.

"I missed you."

I'm already diving into Austin's arms when he says it. A week was too long to be away from him. His parents had taken him from me, stolen him to go to visit family for a funeral. At nineteen, he's plenty old enough to stay by himself, but they'd insisted he go along to pay his respects. I think it's more like they don't want us fucking our way through every room in the house while they're away, but I can't blame them. They'd have been right. I wouldn't have felt comfortable going along, even if they had invited me, but a week is an eternity in the summer when the only thing I have to look forward to is long hours with Austin's mouth on mine.

His arms slip around me, hold me tight, and his hands run down my back to grip my ass. Nobody's watching, and would I care if they were? I'm just so frigging glad he's home, it's worth the risk of parental discovery to have him squeezing me. His cock nudges my belly.

He really did miss me.

"I brought you something."

"What?" I already have my hands out, expecting a snow globe, a T-shirt. A magnet, maybe. Something he picked up in the Pennsylvania Turnpike gift shop.

Austin hands me a small box with a lid. Inside it is a package of paper, not note cards but stationery. I lift a page and hold it to the light. It's soft on my fingertips and has a faint design of flowers pressed into the paper. I give him a look.

How did he know?

"It reminded me of you." Austin gives an awkward shrug, as if his admission embarrasses him. "You like that sort of thing."

I do. Tablets and note cards and pretty papers. I always have, but this is the first time someone's ever noticed or given me something as pretty as this. "I love it."

"When's your mom getting home?"

My mom's been working weird shifts at the Hershey plant since she got pregnant. Because it's summer, her brother Lane is home from college and taking over the shop, and I've been putting in more than my share of hours there, too. I haven't seen her much. I'm not sure if she's avoiding me, but I know I'm trying not to hang around her too much. She's only got another month or so before she pops, and I can't even begin to imagine what's going to happen then.

"Late." I snuggle closer, my knee going between his and my cheek fitting just right into the place over his heart.

Austin pushes me so he can grin down into my face. "Good."

The apartment isn't big enough to make the chase much of an effort, but we manage to work up a sweat as I dodge his grip and duck behind the big wooden rocking chair to keep out of his grasping hands. Not that I don't want to be caught. Just that it's fun to make him catch me.

When he does, his mouth slants over mine, his tongue probing deep inside. He's got me so hot already. Hot for him. His hand goes straight between my legs, no fooling around now, and he cups my pussy through my thin cotton shorts.

The rocking chair, set in motion by our mock struggle, bumps my ass as we kiss. I grab the back of it to still it, then push Austin from my mouth and shuck out of my shorts. I'm wearing the tiny bikini panties he likes, but those go, too.

I lift my T-shirt up over my breasts, no bra covering them, and settle into the chair. I spread my legs. He's watching, jaw slack and eyes gleaming. He doesn't move.

He's eaten me out before, though I've never asked him to. It's always just...happened. But it's all I've been thinking about for the past week, his mouth and tongue and fingers fucking me until I come. Every night while he was gone I'd lie in bed, eyes wide open to the dark, and imagine him there with me. I'd pretend my fingers were his tongue, flicking my clit or sliding inside me, but it was never the same.

My friend Kira says her boyfriend won't go down on her. Not ever. He's all about the blow jobs but refuses to dine at the Y. He's a pussy about eating pussy. I'd break up with a guy who expected me to suck cock but wouldn't return the favor, but Kira says she's in love. I think she just doesn't know what love is.

Austin's friends, the guys from the football team and the men he works with at his dad's construction company, would probably say they don't go down on their girlfriends, either. I wonder how many are telling the truth? I wonder if Austin tells them about me, if men talk about their sex lives in the same detail I do with my friends. I wonder if he'd admit he makes me come with his face between my legs, or if he'd deny it.

"Austin." My voice is low and slow, almost not mine. His gaze jerks up. I put my hands on my inner thighs and open myself wider to his sight. "Use your mouth on me."

He's already on his knees before I finish. I gasp when his hot, wet mouth finds my skin. When his tongue strokes over my clit, I grip the arms of the chair and toss back my head, my back arching. It feels so good it almost hurts. The chair rocks me into his mouth again and again as he licks and kisses and sucks. When he puts a finger inside me, then two, I come hard with a strangled shout.

I look down at him. He's smiling, full of himself. I touch his hair and want to tell him how much I love him, but something about the way he's looking at me makes me suddenly shy. I want to close my legs, but his head is resting on my thigh and I can't without pushing him away.

"What?" I sound nervous, because I am. "What are you looking at?"

"You." Austin kisses my thigh.

I push him onto his back on the floor and straddle his legs until I can get his belt open and his pants down. His cock springs free, nice and thick. I take it in my hand and stroke. He's already got a little pre-come dripping, and I lean forward to taste him.

"Fuck!" His hips jerk and his hand tangles in my hair. "Paige, God."

"What?" I want to put him inside me, but we don't have any condoms handy and there's no way I'll go bareback.

"Nobody…"

I frown and sit back on my heels, my grip tightening on his prick. "Nobody what?"

What the hell did he get up to while he was away?

"Nobody does this like you," Austin says.

He thinks he's giving me a compliment, but I let him go and grab up my shorts. I make sure to grab my panties, too. Don't want to leave them on the floor for my mom to find. "Nobody, who?"

"Huh?" He lifts his head to stare, then sits when he sees my expression. "What's the matter?"

I stab the air with my finger. My throat is tight when I swallow, and I blink away the burn of tears. "Nobody does what like me? Suck cock? Nobody, who? Who else is sucking your dick, Austin?"

"Nobody," he says and must realize how it sounds, because he scrambles to his feet to come after me when I stalk down the hall to my tiny bedroom at the back of the apartment. "That's not what I meant, baby."

"Don't you 'baby' me." I grab my robe from the hook on the door so I don't have to try to get into my clothes while we fight.

His hands come down on my shoulders and turn me, reluctantly, to face him. "I just meant that the other guys, they tell me their girls don't do the stuff you do."

I guess that answers my question about if they talk about sex. I don't smile, don't lift a brow, just keep my face stony. Austin pushes my hair off my shoulders.

"That's all I meant. That nobody…that you're so great."

"Great at sucking cock?" I frown, even though I'm glad to know he thinks so.

"And other things." He teases me back toward the bed and I let him until we're both lying on top of the quilt my grandma made me.

Austin strokes down my body and kisses me. When his hand finds my pussy again, I know I'm wet from earlier. His fingers slide against me. His breath is hot on my neck as he pants. His thumb presses my clit and his fingers move inside, then out. Against my thigh, his cock presses hot and hard. He moves his mouth to my nipple and sucks gently, and though I came just a little while ago, desire gathers in my belly again.

"I missed you," he says again.

"Did you?"

Austin nods against my neck. It seems stupid to be angry with him now, or to worry about if he cheated on me while he was gone. I know he did, once or twice, when we were in high school. Hell. I cheated on him, too, if you want to count the times he thought we were on and I thought we were off and vice versa. But not since graduating, not since we both got full-time jobs and a full-time relationship.

He fumbles for the rubbers I keep in the box in my nightstand and puts one on. I could help him, but I'd rather watch just now. He rolls it on over his cock, his teeth clamped onto his lower lip in concentration. Then he moves up my body and centers himself before pushing inside me.

I groan; I can't help it. I fucking love this, the sex. His weight. His prick so hard and thick and long inside me, so long it hurts sometimes when he fucks me, but I like that, too. He's got muscles in his arms from all the heavy lifting and I grab one as he thrusts inside me.

I lift my hips to meet him and his belly presses my clit every time we move together. Orgasm doesn't build, it tears me down. I'm coming again when he starts to move harder and faster, and I know Austin's coming, too.

It doesn't always happen that way, that we finish together, so it's sort of magical and leaves me sleepy and contented and cuddly, after. He loops an arm around me when he's thrown away the condom. We lay on my bed, spooning, and his breath ruffles my hair.

"Paige," Austin says. "I want to ask you something important."

And then we're on the ocean, in a boat that's going down.

As the cold, dark sea closed over my head, the sound of the alarm bells ripped into my ears. I took a deep breath, even though I was underwater. I kicked, the tight clutch of the waves around my ankles becoming the tangled grasp of sheets around my feet as I opened my eyes and fumbled, without seeing, for the phone.

"What?" At this hour I couldn't be expected to be polite, could I?

"Paige?"

I blinked, not wanting to look at my bedside clock's numbers. It was way too fucking early to be up. "Arty. What's the matter? Where's Mama?"

"Mama's still sleeping. And Leo's at work," he added, though I hadn't asked. "I'm hungry."

"Make yourself some cereal." I stifled a yawn and pondered giving in to a hangover that wouldn't have bothered me with just a few more hours' sleep.

"There isn't any."

"No Cheerios? No Raisin Bran?"

My little brother, the only other sibling I'd ever actually lived with, made a familiar noise of disgust. "I don't like those kind."

"Then I guess you must not be that hungry." I was hungry, but didn't feel like getting out of bed at the butt-crack of dawn to fix toast. "Arty, it's too early to call me. What did I tell you about that?"

"Can't you come over and make me some pancakes?" His little-boy voice sounded very far away. I pictured him in his

Spider-Man pajamas, bare feet swinging because his legs weren't long enough to reach the floor. "Please?"

Maybe if I kept my eyes closed I'd fall back to sleep. I snuggled deeper under my soft blankets. "Buddy, I don't live there anymore. I told you that. I told you I couldn't just come over whenever you called."

Silence.

"But I miss you," Arthur said in a tiny voice.

I sighed. "I miss you, too, buddy. How about I come down and take you to the movies sometime soon?"

"When?" At nearly seven, the kid had been reading since he was four and could tell time on an analogue clock, a skill that sometimes stumped me. There wasn't much that slipped past him. "Today?"

"Not today, no. Maybe later this week."

"When? When?"

I couldn't think straight and just tossed out a day. "Wednesday?"

"Saturday. Sunday. Monday. Tuesday. Wednesday. That's a week!"

He sounded so dismayed I hated to laugh. Laughing, in fact, hurt my head. "Not quite. Five days."

"That's too long!" Arthur's voice pitched high enough to drill my tender ears.

"You've got gymnastics on Tuesday, and Monday I've got an appointment in the evening. Sorry, buddy. You have to wait until Wednesday. Besides," I said, offering an incentive against despair, "the new Power Heroes movie comes out on Wednesday. How about that?"

"Okay." He didn't sound convinced, only resigned. "But I'm hungry now, Paige."

"Cereal. Or have a snack from the drawer."

"Mama says no snacks from the drawer until after breakfast."

"Aren't there any cereal bars in the drawer?" I bit back another yawn. If I didn't get back to sleep in the next ten minutes I was not going to be a happy camper.

"Yesss..." Even Arthur knew where I was going with this, but he sounded like it might be too good to be true.

"Have one of those. They're cereal, right?"

"Can I tell Mama you said it was okay?"

"Sure." It wouldn't be the first time she'd holler at me for giving the kid permission to do something she'd have refused. On the other hand, this was the woman who'd allowed me to go to school in a pair of hand-me-down, slip-on Candie's shoes in the sixth grade and bought me my first package of rubbers in the tenth. She was a different sort of mother to Arthur than she'd been to me. "Now let me go back to sleep, okay?"

"Okay. Bye, Paige."

"Bye."

"I love you," my little brother said before I could hang up.

It wasn't the first time he'd ever said it, but suddenly the memory of how he'd smelled as a baby washed over me with enough force to push my eyelids open like snapped-open blinds. How his hair had been so soft against my lips when I kissed his little baby head, and how the heavy weight of him had filled my arms and lap. How I used to hold him while I watched hour after hour of bad TV, just because he was so small and sweet. Just because he loved me.

"I love you, too, buddy. I'll see you on Wednesday."

He had a seven-year-old's social graces and didn't say

goodbye again, just hung up. I put the phone back in the cradle of its receiver and my head back in the cradle of my pillow, but sleep had vanished and there was no getting it back.

With a groan, I looked at the clock. Almost eight. And I'd gone to sleep, what, just before six this morning? God. I was so going to pay that kid back one day, maybe when he was a teenager and prone to sleeping as late as he could…yeah. I'd wake *him* up.

Unfortunately, my revenge was far-flung and I was still awake. I stretched and sat up, waiting for the rush and boil of acid stomach or the pound of a headache, but aside from a gnawing hunger, I felt all right. At least until I heard the muted beep from my cell phone, which I'd left abandoned in my sparkly purse under the pile of my discarded clothes. I had to dig past my Steve Madden pumps to reach it.

Five missed calls.

Five? Crap. I thumbed the keypad to check out the numbers. I had voice mails, too, though without dialing in I couldn't tell how many. Kira had called me around 4:00 a.m. but hadn't left a message. That could be good or bad, depending. One was an old call from my mother I hadn't deleted. The other three were from Austin.

Triple crap.

The voice mails were from him, too, half an hour apart. The first two were brief "when are you going to get here?" messages. The last one had come in around six-fifteen, after I'd already gone to bed. It turned the corners of my mouth down.

"Look, I know I've been an asshole to you in the past." Then fifteen seconds of awkward silence, punctuated only by the soft in-out of his breathing. "I'm sorry. I just…I was a fuckwad, and I'm sorry. Call me, okay? Please."

A few more seconds of silence and he added, "Please."

Is there anything more simultaneously pathetic and arousing than a pleading man?

I couldn't bring myself to delete that message. I thought I might want to listen to it a couple-twenty more times. I thought I might want to get that statement, *"Sorry, I'm a fuckwad.—Austin Miller"* embroidered on a tea towel and wipe my hands with it.

It was the only time Austin had ever apologized to me for anything he'd ever done. I wasn't sure it meant anything now. Not after all this time had passed.

I didn't delete the message, but I didn't call him back, either. Instead, I hauled my sorry ass out of bed and stumbled to the bathroom where I peed for what felt like an hour and brushed my teeth and pulled my hair on top of my head in a messy ponytail.

I wanted to go back to sleep, but I knew better than to expect to be able to. I was up for the day now. My stomach rumbled and I took my last two slices of wheat bread from the fridge, where I kept it to prevent mold, and popped them into my toaster oven. I needed to hit the grocery store in the worst way, though the state of my finances meant it would be another week of on-sale tuna and ramen noodles rather than steak and lobster. Ah, well. There was nothing new about that. I'd grown up thinking Kraft shells and cheese was gourmet fare.

While my toast browned, I sifted through the pile of junk mail I'd brought in the night before. I tossed aside a few catalogs addressed to the former tenant. I thought of the note I'd had yesterday, the beautiful paper and the words written in that fine hand. What had it said to do? Make a list of flaws and strengths? I thought of it as I ate my toast dry because I had no butter or jam.

You will write a list of ten. Five flaws. Five strengths. Deliver them promptly…

From the junk drawer next to my fridge I pulled a yellow legal pad and a stub of a pencil with a point rubbed to softness by the creation of many lists. Chore lists, mostly, or grocery. I'd never used it to detail my flaws and strengths.

I tapped the pencil against my lips as I thought.

Proud
Stubborn
Independent
Smart
Curious
Determined
Conscientious

That was it. As far as lists went, it didn't feel complete, but I couldn't think of more than that. So much for the ten, I thought as I put away the pen and paper.

And the real question was, which had I written? Flaws or strengths? Couldn't they sometimes be both?

I looked again at the tablet on the table. It had made me think hard about myself, though it hadn't been meant for me. I hoped the person it was meant for had better luck.

Chapter 06

I finished my shopping just before noon. I had only two small bags of groceries, the bare minimum to get me through until payday. I'd left a few bucks in my wallet on purpose, though, for one reason. I didn't need a large coffee with extra cream and a gooey cinnamon bun, but I wanted them.

Located in the building adjoining Riverview Manor, the Morningstar Mocha teemed with people out for a caffeine fix. A few joggers, bundled against the cold, filled travel mugs at the small stand in the corner holding the sweetener packets and jugs of milk and bins of creamer containers. And in the corner, my corner, the seat I took because it was in the smallest table and I was usually alone, sat my elevator eye-fucking buddy, Mr. Mystery.

Was it synchronicity? Or serendipity? His wasn't the only familiar face there. I spied a few people from my building, one or two I recognized as Mocha regulars, and of course I knew the girl behind the counter. Her name was Brandy, and you couldn't miss her. She chewed gum like cud.

I deliberately tried not to stare at him while I ordered my coffee and bun, but he was still there by the time they arrived.

Still there when I'd dumped my mug full of sugar and cream. He wore a white, long-sleeved shirt beneath a black concert T-shirt and worn jeans that suited him nicely. His hair looked as if he'd run a hand through it a few times or just rolled out of bed. He had a large mug in front of him, still steaming, and a plate with the remains of a bagel slathered with cream cheese and lox. He was staring out the glass onto the street, empty but for the occasional weekend-traffic car cruising slowly past. In front of him sat a pad of legal-size paper, white not yellow, and in his left hand he held a thick-barreled pen. A worn leather bag rested at his feet as faithful as a hound.

The lighting inside the Mocha was golden and indirect, but late-winter bright sunshine shafted through the plate-glass window and across his face. I wanted to stare and drink in the fine-featured grace of him. The casual beauty. The crooked twist of his mouth as he bit down on his lip in concentration, the furrow of his brow. The way his hand curled around the pen caressing the paper.

Fortunately for me, he was still staring out the window, absently doodling, when two people in matching tracksuits slammed into me and knocked my coffee and cinnamon bun all over a couple, who looked as if they hadn't yet gone to bed, sitting at the table in front of me.

The fitness twins were very kind. They bought me new coffee and pastry and replaced the party-kids' bagels, soaked through by my spilled drink. They did it all with a fanfare that smacked a bit of "look at me, what a good person I am," but they did it. I didn't dare look at the man by the window until all the fuss and feathers had died down. When I did, finally, my fresh mug was burning my palm and my eyes had blurred from the dip in my blood sugar. I didn't want to shove the entire bun into my mouth, but a dainty nibble wasn't going to get the goods down my throat and into my stomach fast enough.

He glanced over at me as I was licking icing off my mouth. He smiled. I paused, coffee halfway to my mouth, and smiled back.

I thought for sure he'd say hello, but maybe without the allure of my fuck-me pumps all he could manage was the grin. Maybe he didn't recognize me as the woman from the elevator. Or more likely, he didn't care.

He got up, papers and pen already tucked away in his bag, garbage cleared from the table. He slung his arms into a plaid flannel shirt I hadn't noticed hanging on the back of his chair and eased the strap of his leather bag over one shoulder. He left the Morningstar Mocha without a backward glance, which allowed me to stare after him without fear of being caught.

He'd left a crumpled discard to the window side of his chair, on the floor. With a quick glance around the now-empty coffee shop to see if anyone would notice me being a total snoop, I vacated my seat and took the one he'd just left. It couldn't have been warm from his ass, or at least I shouldn't have been able to feel it if it was, but I imagined heat. I knew I shouldn't pick up the paper, or smooth it out in front of me. I knew, especially, that I shouldn't read it.

But I did, anyway.

I didn't learn the secrets of the universe. I didn't even find out his name. He'd mostly been scribbling and doodling, with a few chicken-scratch phrases I could read but didn't understand here and there on the paper. Looking over it, I should've felt dirty. I only felt disappointed. But what had I expected, a hand-written autobiography listing his education, career and medical history?

Still, I smoothed out the creases as I finished my breakfast and folded the paper in half. Then half again. And again, until finally I'd turned a legal-size sheet of paper into a palmful of secrets. It wasn't any of my business. I had no right to keep it. It weighed there as heavily as a handful of lead, and yet I couldn't manage to toss it into the trash.

I did wish, though, that I'd lingered over the coffee. Riverview Manor doesn't have a doorman, and the front-desk staff was there to accept packages and take care of problems, not keep anyone from entering the building. The building had security cameras in the elevators and on every floor, but no real means of keeping anyone out who wanted to be in.

Part of me wasn't surprised when I turned the corner of the hall to see Austin waiting for me in front of my door. Another part wanted to turn and run away. I lifted my chin instead, wishing again I'd at least bothered to wear makeup, though honestly he'd seen me look way worse.

"What are you doing here?" I bent to put my bags down so I could pull my key from my purse. When I stood, Austin's eyes were on my face, not my ass. Now, *that* surprised me.

"You didn't answer my calls."

I fit the key into the lock, but didn't turn it right away. "I meant, what are you doing *here?*"

"I called your mom."

I unlocked and opened my door and pushed it, but didn't go through. I turned to look at him. My irritation must have been clear on my face, because he held up his hands right away as though I meant to punch him. "My mother told you where I lived?"

"Your mom always liked me."

I blew a sigh that fluttered the fringe of my bangs off my

forehead and then pushed through the door. I left it open behind me, as much of an invitation as I could bear to give. He followed and shut the door. Softly, with a click, not a slam.

I put my bags in the kitchen and kicked off my shoes. Austin stood still and watched me without making any move to sit. He looked around the apartment with interest, then shoved his hands deep into his pockets and rocked on his heels while I took my time unpacking and putting away my groceries.

"Can I sit down?" he asked finally, when I'd made it clear I wasn't going to offer.

"Do you have to ask?" I kept my back turned as I sifted through the change from my wallet. I found a Wheatie penny and set it aside to put in my collection, then washed my hands thoroughly with soap and hot water. Money is one of the filthiest things a person can touch.

When I turned to look at him, he was still standing. We stared at each other across the expanse of my unimmense living room until I nodded. He sat the way he always had, legs sprawled, taking up as much space as he could.

I took my time cleaning the kitchen, wiping the counters and scrubbing the sink with bleach-infused powder. I even emptied the garbage pail and took the trash out to the chute at the end of the hall. I expected Austin to be restless or irritated by the time I came back, but he'd found a copy of a Robert Heinlein novel inside the pile of books and magazines thrown into the straw basket next to the couch and was flipping through it.

"It doesn't have any pictures," I said from the doorway.

Austin put the book on the coffee table. "This is nice."

He hadn't risen to the bait, though I'd made a point of pushing one of his buttons. "The book?"

"The coffee table," he said, still not rising.

"It was Stella's."

Austin nodded, like that made sense. "Glad I didn't put my feet up on it."

It took me an actual five seconds before I realized he was trying to tease me without pissing me off. He was actually just…kidding. I knew how to handle him trying to seduce me or piss me off. I didn't know how to take that.

"I miss you," Austin said.

The words were hard to hear, and I don't mean because he spoke too low, or mumbled. They were hard for me to listen to because I didn't know what to say. I didn't want him to miss me.

I sat across from him, instead. The recliner's springs sometimes poked through the faded material, though I'd tossed a fleece throw over it. One did now, and I winced as I shifted.

"I do," he said, as though my expression had been in response to his statement and not a coil of wire in my butt.

"Austin." Nothing else would come out.

He shrugged. I hadn't fallen in love with him because of his way with words. Back then it hadn't mattered if he spoke more with his hands than his mouth. Back then we'd both been young and dumb.

"You look good, Paige. This place," he gestured, "it's nice."

"Thanks."

His hair used to be bleached almost white by the sun, and he wore it so short I could see his scalp. When I ran my fingers through it, my nails scraped skin. Now it fell forward over his ears and forehead and was the color of wheat in a field, waiting to be cut. His eyes, moving over my face, made me think he was waiting to be cut, too.

I almost couldn't do it. I mean, the night before I'd let him put his tongue down my throat and his hands all over me. When the warmth of him wafted over me, I wanted to close my eyes at how familiar it was. How easy it would have been to take him by the hand and lead him to my bedroom.

I kept my eyes open, a lesson I'd been taught a long time ago but had taken me a long time to learn. "I don't miss you, Austin. Last night was a mistake."

"C'mon, Paige. Don't say that. We were always good together."

"We haven't been together for a long time," I said, not quite as evenly as I wanted.

"It's not just the sex." Austin leaned forward, too, his hands on the knees of his dirty denim jeans. A white spot had worn through just below his kneecap, not quite a hole, but on its way to becoming one. "I didn't just mean that. I can get laid anytime I want."

"I'm sure you can." I got up, my arms folded across my chest.

He got up, too. "I didn't mean it that way."

I wasn't going to bend. Not over the chair, not over the bed, and not over this. "It doesn't matter how you meant it. I think you should go."

"Same old Paige," he said with a shake of his hair. "Still hard as nails, huh? Hard as a rock. Can't ever give me a break."

"You don't need a break from me. Besides, you can just get laid whenever you want. Look, Austin," I said when it looked as though he meant to speak. "We can't keep doing this."

"Why not?"

I studied him deliberately until I couldn't hold in the sigh any longer and it seeped out of me like air from a nail-punched tire. "You know why not. Because fucking doesn't solve every problem. And we had a lot of problems."

He crossed his arms and looked stormy. I didn't point out the arguments we'd had about money, about religion, about monogamy. I didn't remind him of the nights he'd gone out for a few beers with friends and had come home smelling of perfume and guilt, or that it didn't matter whether he had or hadn't fucked anyone else, it was that he was content to choose a night with his buddies over staying home with me. I didn't bring up the times I'd said I was studying for school when I was really someplace else, with someone else.

"I just want you to be happy, Austin." I meant it.

He leaned back and frowned more fiercely. "You want me to be happy so you can feel better about yourself, that's all. So you don't feel so bad about what happened."

The truth of that stung me like a wasp, smooth-stingered and able to jab more than once. "I think you should go."

Damn him, he didn't. He moved closer and cupped my elbows in his palms so I had to uncross my arms to push him away or let him snuggle up close. I put my hands on his chest, but didn't push. His muscles beneath the tight T-shirt were hard and firm. He leaned, and I didn't pull away. If he'd kissed me, I'd have been lost, but if he'd ever thought he knew me, he proved himself wrong again. He didn't kiss me. He spoke, instead.

"I'm your husband."

I pushed my arms straight. His hands slid from my elbows along my arms and fell away at my wrists. I stepped back, my hand against his chest preventing him from following unless he pushed me, too. Austin looked for a second as if he meant to try it, but didn't.

"I have a folder full of paperwork that says otherwise," I told him.

"Okay, so not officially. But you can't tell me—"

"I can tell you anything I want, so long as it's true," I shot back.

"Can you tell me it's true that you don't miss me, too? Not even a little?"

"I miss fucking you," I said flatly. "The rest of it? Not so much."

Austin grinned and spread his fingers. "It's a start, right? I'll call you."

"I won't answer."

"I'll call again."

I pointed at the door, and he went. I waited until it closed behind him before I gave in to the urge to sigh. What is it about bad boys that make them so, so good?

I've known him since kindergarten. Austin. In my elementary-school class photos, more times than not, his freckled face is beaming from the row behind me. In one, we stand beside each other, our grins showing the same missing teeth.

In high school, we had nothing in common. Austin was a jock. I was a gothpunk girl with multiple piercings and a tattoo of a dragonfly on my back. We shared college-level classes and the same lunch period. I knew who he was because of his prowess on the football field. If he knew me it was maybe because I was one of the girls every boy knew, or maybe just because we'd been in the same school since we were five. We didn't say hi when we passed in the halls, but he was never mean to me the way some of the boys could be. Austin never called me names or made crude invitations.

In the fall of our senior year, Austin went down under a pile of boys pumped up with testosterone and fury. We won the homecoming game, but instead of riding in Chrissy Fisher's dad's 1966 Impala convertible, Austin took a red-lights-flashing ambulance to the Hershey Medical Center.

He recovered, nothing miraculous about it. His body, bones broken and skin torn, healed. Nobody ever said he'd never play football again. Austin simply never did.

Nor basketball, either, and in the spring, not baseball. By then his chances of going to anything other than community college had vanished along with the scholarship offers, but if he ever cared he wasn't getting a full ride to Penn State, he never said so to me.

And by then, he would have. By the time our senior year ended, Austin told me everything.

We were an odd couple, but nobody shunned us for it. I didn't hear whispers in the halls. No jealous cheerleaders tried to pull out my dyed-black hair, and no slick rich jocks tried to convince him he was better off without me. We didn't go to the prom, but only because we decided to stay home and watch soft porn and fuck, instead.

When I told my mom we were going to get married, she hugged me and wept. Her belly poked between us—she was pregnant with Arthur, then. If she suspected I wanted to marry Austin as much so I could move out of the house as for passion, she didn't say anything.

When we told his parents, his dad said nothing and his mother's eyes dropped to my waistband. She didn't ask me if I was pregnant, and she must have been surprised as the months of our marriage passed and my belly stayed flat, but no matter how she might have felt about the prospect of me as a daughter-in-law, the idea of a bastard grandchild must've been worse.

I wore a thrift-store wedding dress and Austin wore a suit of his dad's we'd paid the dry cleaner to take in. In pictures, my thick black eyeliner and my spiked black hair make me look pale, wan. Tired. Scared, even.

The truth is, I was happy.

We both were, I like to think. At least at first. Austin went to work for his dad's construction business, and I kept up work at my mom's shop. My granddad had died and it was hers, full-time, and now that she had Arty, she couldn't spend as much time with it, so I managed the shop.

We were happy.

And then, we weren't.

Chapter 07

When I was younger, the prospect of Sunday dinner at my dad's had so excited me or stressed me out I'd vomit. Never at my father's house—even when I was little I knew Stella wouldn't approve of a puking kid. I didn't puke anymore, but I'd never managed to get rid of the knots in my stomach, either.

I popped an antacid tablet now as I sat in my not-expensive-enough-to-be-impressive car in their half-circle driveway of stamped concrete. This was the fourth new house my father'd had in the past seventeen years of life with his second family. Before that he'd lived in a stately Georgian-style half mansion with his first family. He'd never lived with my mother.

Birth-order studies claim that an age difference of six or more years between siblings complicates the normal oldest, middle and youngest personality traits by also making each child an only. That's why, though I have five half siblings and an uncle who's more like a brother, I'm an only child. I've tried identifying with being the middle kid—but what it comes down to, in the end, is I'm not.

The door opened and Jeremy and Tyler ran out. They both

favor my dad, too. All of us look more like siblings than we were raised to be. I was fourteen when Jeremy was born, sixteen for Tyler. They're more like nephews or cousins than brothers. I'm not sure what they think of me, just that they're always glad to see me and aside from the fact they're spoiled brats who could use a good spanking now and then, I'm usually glad to see them, too.

"Hey, Paige." Jeremy at twelve no longer ran to clutch at my legs. He settled for a half wave with limp fingers.

Tyler, ten, was nearly as tall as me but squeezed me anyway. "Paige, c'mon, we're going to play Pictionary. Grandma and Grandpa are here already. So's Nanny and Poppa."

"And Gretchen and Steve, too, I see." I pointed to the two minivans that belonged to my dad's kids with his first wife.

"Everyone's here," Jeremy said somewhat sourly, and I gave him a glance. He'd always been a pretty upbeat kid. Today he scowled, blond eyebrows pinching tight over the smaller version of our father's nose.

I leaned back into my car to grab the gift, then locked my car. It was unlikely anything would happen to it parked in my dad's driveway, but it was habit. "Come. Let's go in."

I slung an arm around Tyler's neck and listened to him babble on about school, soccer, the new game system he'd found under the Christmas tree. He had never known Santa to disappoint him. I'd stopped trying not to be envious of that, even though I no longer believed in Santa Claus.

Inside, Jeremy slunk to a chair in the corner and sat with crossed arms, the scowl still in place. Tyler abandoned me to round up pens for the game. That left me to the socially torturous task of making nice with Stella's parents, Nanny and Poppa.

Like their daughter, they weren't bad people. They'd never gone out of their way to be cruel. I wasn't Cinderella. And I understood, now, what it must have been like to try to find a place in their hearts for their new son-in-law's children, and how awkward it must have felt. A hastily wrapped *Jumbo Book of Puzzles* and a prewrapped box of knit mittens would always fall short in comparison to exquisitely wrapped packages in shiny foil paper with matching bows, the contents new clothes or toys. I understood. Spending Christmas at my dad's had been last minute, haphazardly planned and rare. At least Nanny and Poppa had made an effort.

It seemed easier for them now that I was a grown-up, though it was more difficult for me. As a kid it had never occurred to me they wouldn't like me. Now I was convinced they didn't.

"Hello, Paige," George, also known as Poppa, said. "How nice of you to come."

He meant well, but the unspoken insinuation of surprise made me bite my tongue against the shout of "Of course I came! She's my father's wife!"

But, like Stella herself, I could never hope to impress them. I just wanted not to prove them right. So instead of shouting, I smiled.

"How are you?" I couldn't call him George, Mr. Smith sounded absurd, and I would never call him Poppa.

I'd been asking out of politeness, but he told me exactly how he was. For fifteen minutes. And I listened, nodding and murmuring in appropriate places, as though I cared. I didn't know half the people he mentioned, but he acted as if he thought I should. He never asked me about myself, which was fine, because then I didn't have to answer.

Finally, the game of Pictionary got under way. Gretchen's husband, Peter, begged off, volunteering to take care of Hunter, their three-year-old son. Steve and his vastly pregnant wife, Kelly, played, though, as did my dad and Stella, all the grandparents and Tyler. And me. Jeremy had disappeared. We split into teams, boys against girls.

"I'll sit out," I said when we'd counted up the teams to find the girls' side had an extra player.

"Oh, no, Paige, are you sure?" Stella protested, but not too hard. She liked things even and square.

"Sure. Not a problem. I'll go check on dinner, if you want."

Okay, so maybe I'd cast myself in the Cinderella role. Just a little. But it was a relief to get into the kitchen and set out platters of vegetables and dip, cheese and crackers. Decorative breads and soft cheeses with pretty spreaders that matched the platter. Stella loved to have parties.

I found the cold-cut platters in the garage fridge and brought them into the kitchen to put them out on the table, which was serving as a buffet. I startled Jeremy when I came back in, and he whirled, can of soda in hand, from the open fridge.

From the living room, the sound of laughter wafted. I set the platter of meat on the table. Jeremy and I stared each other down.

"You're not supposed to be drinking that before dinner," I told him.

"I know." His chin lifted. He hadn't yet cracked the top.

"I'm not going to tell you on you, kiddo." I turned to the table and took off the platter's plastic lid so I could get rid of the fake greenery around the edges. I knew how to make things pretty.

"Don't call me *kiddo*," he said.

I expected him to slink away with his stolen prize, but he didn't. When I turned to look at him, he was still playing with the can, shifting it from one hand to the other.

"Something up?" I moved past him to the big, mostly empty pantry, to pull out the fancy plastic plates and plasticware, the matching napkins.

"No." Jeremy shrugged and disappeared up the back stairs.

After that, the party really started.

It was easier for me with more people there. Stella's friends knew who I was, of course, and avoided talking to me so they didn't have to deal with the awkwardness of how to address their friend's husband's illegitimate daughter. My dad's friends knew me, too, but had fewer inhibitions for some reason. Maybe because I'd known them longer, or because they had no conflict of loyalty. Some of them didn't like Stella much, and maybe that was part of it, too.

Of my father's other kids, I saw very little. Gretchen, Steve and I had never been close, even though it wasn't my mother who'd finally won our dad away from their mom. Of course, their spouses weren't sure what to make of me, either, and it was easier for us to be superficially polite without trying to get to know each other. Their children were and would be my nieces and nephews, but I doubted they'd ever think of me as an aunt.

"Paige DeMarco, how the hell are you?" Denny's one of my dad's oldest friends. Fishing and drinking buddies, they'd known each other since high school. He'd known my mom, too.

"Hey, Denny. Long time no see."

"Yeah, and you a big-city girl now, too. How's it going?" Denny gave me a one-armed hug.

"It's going great." It wasn't an entire lie. *Most* of my life was going great.

"Yeah?" He tossed back the dregs of his iced tea. I guessed he was hankering for a beer, but Stella wasn't serving booze. Not that I blamed her. Alcohol always made a different kind of party. "Where you living at? Your dad said someplace along the river?"

"Riverview Manor."

There was no denying the pride swelling inside me at Denny's impressed whistle. "Nice digs. And your job? You're not still working with your mom, are you?"

"I help out once in a while, if she's got a big job."

Denny grimaced at his empty cup, but didn't move to pour more. "What's she up to? She still with the same guy?"

Questions my dad never asked. I was the only part of my mother my dad needed to know about. He'd never said as much, but I knew it.

"Leo? Yes."

"And that kid, how old's he now?"

"Arty's seven." I had to laugh for a second. "Wow. Yeah. He just turned seven."

"You tell her I said hi, okay?"

"Sure."

We chatted for a while after that. The party got louder. Stella reigned over it like a queen, even if she was claiming to still be only twenty-nine. When it came time to open the gifts, I thought about slipping out, but forced myself to stay.

Stella sat in the big rocking chair in the living room, her presents arranged at her feet and her closest girlfriend beside her getting ready to write down the name of every gift and its giver. Stella opened gift cards, packages of bath salts, certificates for spa treatments. Sweaters. Slippers. A new silk robe someone had brought from a trip to Japan. She oohed and aahed over each gift appropriately.

By the time she got to mine, my stomach had begun to eat itself. The harsh sting of acid rose in my throat, burning. My heart thudded sickly. I had to turn away to pop another couple antacids and sip from a glass of ginger ale, even though I knew the soda would ruin the effects of the medicine.

It's silly to hold on to the past, but we all do it. I was almost ten the first year I'd been invited to Stella's birthday party. The paint had been barely dry in their new house. Gretchen and Steven were living one week with their mother and one week with my dad and Stella. I, of course, lived full-time with my mom and saw my dad on an occasional weekend or holiday, a practice he'd only started after leaving his first wife.

I'd picked out Stella's present myself that year, using my allowance to pay for it. I'd bought her a silky red tank top with a lacy hem. It was the sort of shirt my mom would've loved and wore often, and she said nothing when she helped me fold it and wrap it in some pretty paper that had come free in the mail to solicit money for a charity.

I'd been so proud of that present. I'd been sure Stella, who wasn't nearly as pretty as my mom but who tried hard, anyway, would open it and put it on right away. Then she'd smile at me, and my dad would smile at me, and we'd all be happy.

Instead, she'd opened the box and pulled out the shirt. Her gaze had gone immediately to my father's, but men don't know anything about fashion beyond what they like and what they don't. She didn't put it on. She fingered the red satiny fabric and peeked at the label, her eyes going a little wider at what she saw. Then she put the shirt back in the box with a thank-you even a nine-year-old could tell was forced. I never saw her wear it, but I did find it in the garage a few years later, in the box of rags my dad used for cleaning his cars.

I wasn't nine years old any longer. I wasn't even a teen in too-thick eyeliner and a too-short skirt. I'd learned how to dress and how to speak, but part of me would always be my mother's daughter, at least in Stella's eyes.

"Oh, Paige, what a thoughtful gift." Stella lifted out the box of paper and opened it to pull out the pen. She wiggled it so the tiny tassel danced. "Very pretty. Thank you."

I let out a long, silent sigh. "You're welcome."

"Where do you find such pretty things?" Stella continued. She turned to face her audience. "Paige always finds the prettiest things."

That was it. Bells didn't ring, little birdies didn't fly around on rainbow glitter wings. She'd said thank-you, and I thought she meant it. That was all.

I still managed to slip away before the party was over. My dad caught me at the door. He insisted on hugging me.

"Thanks for coming." I'm sure he meant it, too.

I doubt there's anyone who does not have a complicated relationship with his or her parents, so I'm not saying I'm special or anything. Considering the circumstances of my birth, I'm lucky to have any sort of relationship with my dad. For the most part, at least, it's an honest relationship. Except of course when honesty is too painful.

"Of course I'd come," I told him. "Why wouldn't I?"

"Of course you would," my dad said. "Well, I'm glad you did. How's the new place?"

"It's great." With his arm still around me, I wanted to squirm away. "It's a very nice place."

"And the new job?"

The job I'd had for almost six months didn't feel so new anymore. "It's great, too. I like my boss a lot."

"Good. You're up on Union Deposit Road, right?"

"Progress," I told him. "Just off Progress."

"Oh, right. Well, hey, maybe I should swing by some day and take you to lunch at the Cracker Barrel, what do you say?"

"Sure, Dad." I smiled, not expecting him to ever follow through. "Just call me."

He kissed my cheek and hugged me again, making a show of making me his daughter. It was nice, in that way we both knew was shallow but served its purpose.

The moment I got in my car and the door to the house shut, my every muscle relaxed. I blew out another series of long, slow breaths and lifted my arms to let my pits air out. I'd be sore tomorrow in places I hadn't realized I'd clenched. I was already getting a headache. I'd made it through another big family event without anything going wrong.

Chapter 08

Some consider the body a temple. As such, it must be cared for appropriately so it may be used in the manner for which it was meant.

Beginning tomorrow, you will eat oatmeal for breakfast. Sweeten it however you like.

Today, you will consume three fewer cups of coffee, replacing them with water.

Today, you will extend your regular workout by fifteen minutes.

Today, you will focus a conscious effort on your cigarette smoking. You may smoke one cigarette only once every two hours. You will do nothing else while you smoke it. You will concentrate on my instructions. You will think of the word discipline *each and every time you light up.*

Finally, you will record your efforts in your journal and describe your thoughts and feelings in detail, particularly your thoughts on what "discipline" means to you.

"Do this in memory of me, and go in peace to love and serve the Lord," I murmured, mocking. "Wow."

The second note had been nestled amongst a scant handful of bills and charity requests, and it had slipped into my hand as though it had been written just for me. I hadn't meant to open it, but something about the smooth, sleek paper and lack of glue on the flap had been too tempting to pass up. Hey, it had been delivered to me, hadn't it? Even though the number on the front still said 114, not 414, and even though I knew better, I'd read it anyway.

I still had no clue what the hell it was, or meant. I turned it over and over in my hands, then read it again. I closed the card and stared at it, but I couldn't decipher its meaning.

Unless it had none. Maybe it was some sort of crazy new diet or self-help plan. I'd heard of a new plan that hooked members up with mentors. Sort of like a 12-step program for food addicts, it was supposed to help to have a buddy. It was the only scenario I came up with, but it didn't feel right.

I lifted the card again, looking closer for clues. I caressed the paper. It had the same rough edge, like someone had cut one large sheet of paper into smaller sizes. No signature, and delivered twice in a row to the wrong person. Some buddy.

I kept the card safely in my hand. My fingers curved around it and my thumb caressed the thick paper. I looked at it again, the single sentence.

Discipline?

I still didn't get it. I tucked the card back into its envelope, restraining myself from sniffing the ink. I wasn't the only person standing at the mailboxes, and I didn't want to attract that sort of attention. I found the mailbox for 114 and studied it, too. The brass numbers were stylishly weathered but not worn. There wasn't really any mistaking a one for a four or vice versa, even if the number on the card itself were smudged.

"Excuse me." The woman next to me gave me a smile meant to look apologetic but only looked annoyed. "I need to get to my box."

"Oh. Sorry." I folded closed the note and tucked it quickly into the slot for 114, wondering if by some luck it belonged to her.

She used her key to open a different box, though, and pulled out a thick sheaf of mail. Then she bent and looked through the hole to the office behind it, but the mail carrier had already moved down the row to the end. She straightened as she closed and locked her box, then riffled through her mail with a disgusted sniff.

"Nothing ever comes when it's supposed to." She didn't say it to me, but I nodded anyway.

"I wish my bills wouldn't come."

She turned and gave me an up-and-down look as her mouth twitched into a grimace masquerading as another smile. Her gaze took in my coat, the same cut and color as hers but not as nice, my legs, clad in nude hose, and finally settled on my shoes. They were the only part of me that seemed worth her approval, but she raised a brow anyway and just tossed off a fake little laugh as she stuffed her mail into her Kate Spade bag and turned on her matching pumps.

Bitch.

Oh, I knew what discipline meant to me, all right. Discipline was what kept me from popping her in the back of the head with the heel of my barely-passing-inspection shoes. It's what kept my chin high and my mouth fixed in a pleasant smile instead of turning down at the corners so the tears would stay burning behind my eyes instead of slipping out.

Discipline, or maybe it was pride. Or stubbornness. Whatever it was, I had enough to spare.

I waited until she'd gone before I crossed the lobby and pushed through the revolving door. Outside, gray and overcast skies echoed my mood, and the breeze brought the scent of cigarettes to me. I looked automatically, wondering if I'd see someone pondering discipline.

"Ari," I said, surprised. "Hi."

Miriam's grandson tossed his butt into the sand-filled can and shrugged his coat higher around his neck. "Hey, Paige."

"I didn't know you lived here."

He grinned. "I don't. Just dropped off something for my grandma, you know?"

I didn't know, but I nodded. "Tell her I said hello."

"Stop by the shop and tell her yourself," he suggested with a sweetly dipping smile.

It was nice to be flirted with, albeit without much heat. "I'll do that. Have a good day."

"You, too."

I looked back as I crossed the alley to the parking garage, and Ari was still looking. Maybe there was a little heat, after all. And what woman didn't like to be appreciated? I had a much bigger smile on my face than I had before, and it lasted me all the way to work.

I wasn't even close to being late, but I might as well have been because by the time I got to my desk, my boss had already piled a stack of files on it. It could have been worse. He could have been standing over my desk with the empty coffeepot in his hand. He did that, sometimes, though I knew he was as capable of making coffee as I am. More, maybe, since he inhaled the high-octane stuff like it was air and I limited myself to a mug once or twice a day.

Spying the empty Starbucks cup in the trash, I knew he'd already had his first dose of the day. I was safe a little bit longer. I could get the files ordered and put away without him breathing down my neck. I decided to put the coffee on anyway, though, just in case. There were many days I could predict my boss's every move, from the midmorning break when the bagel man came around, to his post-lunch trip to the bathroom.

Today wasn't one of those days.

"Paige. Listen. I need you to get those files taken care of, okay?"

I turned from the small bar sink, where I'd been filling the coffeepot with water. "Right, Paul. Of course."

Amazing how someone with only a community-college education could still deduce simple things.

"Good." Paul nodded and smoothed his tie between his thumb and forefinger while he watched me fiddle with the coffeemaker.

I hadn't yet figured out if Paul hovered because he expected me to screw up, or if he hoped I would. Either way, it didn't bother me the way it would have some of the other personal assistants on the floor. Brenda, for example, liked to brag how her boss, Rhonda, spent most of her time traveling and she barely had to deal with her. She also liked to brag that she'd worked for Kelly Printing longer than that Jenny-come-lately Rhonda anyways, and knew what she was doing, so why should she have to run everything by someone else when she could get her work done faster and better without interference?

I never told Brenda I found Paul's constant supervision more comforting than annoying. After all, if he never allowed me the autonomy to make decisions, I couldn't exactly be held accountable for anything that went wrong. Right? Even when Paul did his share of traveling, he never left without making me a sheaf of notes and lists…lists.

I thought of the cards I'd found. Two, now. Two misdelivered notes with explicit, mysterious (to me) instructions. I could still feel the sleek paper under my fingertips. I regretted not taking the time to smell the ink.

With the coffee set to brewing, I turned to face Paul. "Anything else?"

"Not right now, thanks." Paul smiled and disappeared back into his inner sanctum, leaving me with the cheery burble of the coffeepot and a bunch of files to herd.

This is what I knew about Paul Johnson, my boss. He had a chubby, pretty wife named Melissa who sometimes forgot to pick up his dry cleaning on time and two teenagers too busy with wholesome activities like sports and youth group to get into trouble. I knew that because I'd seen their photos and overheard his telephone conversations. He had an older brother, the unfortunately named Peter Johnson, with whom he played golf several times a year but not often enough to be good. I knew that because he'd asked me to make a reservation for him at one of the local golf courses and to call his brother to confirm the date. The request was slightly out of the realm of my professional duties, but I'd done it anyway. I also knew Paul was forty-seven years old, had earned his MBA from Wharton, attended church on Sundays with his family and drove a black, but not brand-new, Mercedes Benz.

Those were things I knew.

This is what I thought about Paul Johnson, my boss. He wasn't a tyrant. Just precise. He held himself to the same level of perfection he expected from an assistant, and I appreciated that. He could be funny, though not often, and usually unexpectedly. He gave every project his full attention and effort because it pained him to do anything less. I understood and appreciated that, too.

I'd worked for him for almost six months. He'd told me to call him Paul, not Mr. Johnson, but we weren't anything like friends. That was okay with me. I didn't want my boss to be my chum.

Though sometimes it felt as if all I did was make coffee and file, my job did actually have more responsibility. I had documents to proof and send, invoices to fill out and appointments to book. I did all this to leave Paul free to do whatever it was that he did all day long in his lush, swanky office. If hard pressed, I wouldn't have been able to tell anyone what, exactly, that was. I didn't hate or love my job, but it sure as hell beat working at a sub shop or being an au pair, which was what I'd done while looking for a job that would use my freshly minted degree in business administration. If I never slung another plate of hash or wiped another ass I'd be happy for a good long time.

There was another advantage to having a boss who needed everything just so. He was willing to do what it took to make sure he got what he wanted, whether it was leaving me a three-page e-mail of the week's work, or taking five thorough minutes to describe to me exactly what he wanted me to get him for lunch. Also, if he sent me out to get him some lunch, he usually treated me.

Today it was a pastrami sandwich on rye from Mrs. Deli. Mustard, no mayo. No tomatoes, no onion. Lettuce on the side. Potato salad and an extralarge iced tea with real sugar, not what he called cancer in a packet.

I met Brenda in the hall on my way back. She took one look at the bulging paper sack from Mrs. Deli and sniffed hungrily. She held a small, boxed salad I recognized as coming from the same guy who sold bagels in the morning. I'd had one of those salads once, when I'd forgotten my lunch and had been so desperate for food I'd been willing to use my laundry quarters.

"Gawd, Paige," Brenda said. "Lucky. I wish my boss would send me out for lunch. Heck, I'd like to just get out of this place for an hour."

Officially, we got an hour for lunch, but since our building was located in a business complex on the outskirts of the city, by the time you drove to anyplace decent for lunch, you'd barely have enough time to eat and come back. Rhonda might not hover over Brenda, but she was a stickler about office hours and break time. Everything has a trade-off.

"Let me just drop this off with Paul and I'll be right down."

Brenda looked at the box of sadness in her hand. "Yeah, okay. I've only got about forty minutes left, though."

"I'll hurry."

Paul's door was half-closed when I rapped on the door frame. At the muffled noise, I pushed it all the way open. He sat at his desk, staring at his computer monitor. The screen had dissolved into a rapidly changing pattern of expanding pipe-work, his screen saver, and I wondered how long he'd been sitting there.

"Paul?"

"Paige. Come in." He gestured and swiveled in his chair.

Careful not to spill or drip anything, I pulled his lunch from the bag one item at a time. It felt like a ritual, passing lunch instead of a torch. Paul settled each item onto his blotter. Sandwich at six, potato salad at nine, plastic fork and napkin at three. His drink went to noon, and he looked up at me.

"Thank you, Paige."

It was the first time since I'd started working for him that he hadn't lifted the bread to make sure the sandwich had been prepared properly or sipped the tea to make sure I hadn't mistakenly brought presweetened.

"Do you need me for anything else?"

He shook his head. "No. Go ahead and take your lunch now. I will need you back here by one-fifteen, though. I've got that teleconference thing."

"Sure, no problem." Taking my own sandwich, I headed down to the lunchroom to meet Brenda.

Since no clients saw it, the lunchroom had seen better days. The vending machines were new, but the tables and chairs looked as if they'd been salvaged from the garbage more than once. My chair creaked alarmingly when I sat, but though I poised, prepared to hit the floor if the rickety thing collapsed, it held. I unwrapped my food quickly, my stomach already rumbling.

"This weather, huh?" Brenda stabbed at her limp lettuce. "I wish winter would make up its mind."

"In another three months everyone will be complaining about it being too hot."

She looked at me with a blink. "Yeah. I guess so. But I wish it would get warmer. It's nearly March, for cripe's sakes. Though we did have that blizzard in '93, right around Saint Patty's Day. I hope that doesn't happen this year."

Under other circumstances we'd never have been friends. Not that I didn't like her, but we didn't have much in common. Brenda was older than my mom and had twin girls in college. She also had a husband she referred to constantly as "my sweetie," and whose name I hadn't even yet learned. I imagined him as a Fred, though, for whatever that was worth.

"We've hardly had any snow. I'm sure we'll be fine."

"I don't know how you stand it, honestly." Brenda, finished with her salad, had started casting longing looks at the other half of my sandwich.

I was pretending not to notice. I might only have been hungry enough to finish half, but the rest of it would be dinner tonight. "The lack of snow?"

She laughed then lowered her voice with a conspiratorial look around the empty lunchroom. "Gawd, no. I meant Paul. I don't know how you can stand working for him."

"He's not that bad, Brenda. Really."

She got up to get a snack cake from the machine. "Tell me that in another month."

"What's going to happen in another month?" I wrapped my sandwich carefully in the thick white butcher paper. Grease had turned it translucent in a pattern of dots and made it unusable, which was too bad. Butcher paper was great for coloring pictures. Arty loved it.

"Paul hasn't managed to keep an assistant for longer than six months, tops."

"I've been here for almost six."

"Yeah," Brenda said with the knowing nod of someone who's been keeping track. "And you can't tell me you don't notice he's a little…particular."

The days when a good secretary was unfailingly loyal to her boss had apparently passed. Even so, I didn't leap to agree with her. "I said, he's not that bad. Besides, it's not like he screams or anything if things aren't exactly right."

"He'd better not!" Brenda was already indignant on my behalf. "You're his assistant, not his slave."

I gave a small snort that tried and failed to be a chuckle. "Slaves don't get paid."

"Just remember this conversation in another month when you're groaning to me that he's become impossible. They all do, eventually," Brenda said. "He's gone through seven assistants already since he's been in our department."

"They all quit?"

"No. Some he fired." She raised a brow at me. "They were the lucky ones, if you ask me."

I checked my watch. Five minutes left before I had to rouse myself from my postlunch lethargy and head back to the office. Time for a snack cake, if I wanted to stuff my face with processed sugar, or a cup of coffee from the communal pot. I didn't want the calories or the germs. I did crack the top on my second can of cola, though.

"Why were they lucky?" I asked mildly, not so much because I cared, but to make conversation.

"The ones who quit had to put up with a lot more garbage, that's all. I heard the last girl he had went to work at some grocery store after she left here, that's how desperate she was to get out."

"That's pretty desperate." I stretched. As I started to get up from the table, pain sliced the back of my thigh.

Brenda startled at my cry. "What? What's wrong?"

I craned my neck to look over my shoulder, my leg stuck out behind me like I was a ballet dancer getting ready to perform some complicated dance move. My skirt hit just above the knee and I could make out the ragged line of a run in my stocking, but nothing else. "Something snagged me."

"It's the chair," Brenda said. "It's full of splinters."

I rubbed the spot still stinging and smarting just behind my knee. "I can't tell if it's in there or not."

"Shoot. I gotta run. Will you be okay?" Brenda stuffed her trash into the plastic box where a few scraps of lettuce still clung and tossed it all into the garbage can.

"Sure. Of course." Sort of like a bee sting, the pain had turned from sharp to a dull throb. I was more upset about the panty hose I'd have to replace.

In the bathroom I used the full-length mirror to check out my injury, but could still see nothing. I ran my fingers over my skin around the sore spot but felt nothing poking through. I didn't have time to keep searching, so I stripped off the ruined panty hose and went back to the office.

"Just in time," Paul said from the doorway between his office and my small work space. "I was beginning to think you weren't going to make it."

I looked at him sharply. "I'm hardly ever late, Paul."

"Oh, I know you're not." He glanced at his watch. "C'mon, it's time."

I pushed Brenda's warnings to the back of my mind. This was the best job I'd ever had, and while I never assumed it would be the best I'd ever get, I wasn't in any hurry to lose it.

My task during the teleconference was to type up the notes. Paul not only had notoriously bad handwriting but he was a hunt-and-peck typist. As he got settled into his chair, I picked up my AlphaSmart Neo, the portable keyboard/word processor I used rather than a notepad and pen. Paul might be a slow writer, but he could be a superfast talker, and typing was the only way I could keep up.

I couldn't decipher half of what they talked about. Profit

margins, balance sheets, long-range planning. I was ignorant, and fine with that. I didn't need to understand what they were saying to take it down. In fact, the less I knew the better, because my mind could wander while my fingers kept track.

Not so many years ago I'd have been expected to hover on the edge of my seat, pen poised over my steno pad while I took vigorous shorthand. Typing was so much easier. I'd learned shorthand in school, one of those skills they still found necessary to teach even if nobody would actually use it. The clacking of my nails, kept to a practical length, *tap-tapping* on the keys couldn't replace the sensual *scratch-scratch* of a pen sliding across paper, in my opinion, but typing was much faster, and being able to download the document directly into my computer for processing was better than having to retype it all.

The call ended abruptly, at least to me. I looked over the last few sentences and saw I'd actually typed the goodbyes without paying attention. God bless multitasking.

Paul sighed and leaned back in his chair. "Well, that's over. Thank you, Paige."

Brenda could say what she liked. Paul might be particular, but he was also very polite. "You're welcome."

I'd been sitting with both feet planted firmly on the floor with the keyboard on my lap. When I shifted to get up, the sudden flaring sting of pain from my invisible splinter surged so fiercely I gasped. The keyboard fell to the thick carpet with a muffled thump, and I bent to grab it at once, hoping it hadn't been damaged.

Paul had already rounded the desk. "Paige, are you all right?"

"Yeah, I just…I caught my leg on something earlier. I think there's a splinter."

The keyboard hadn't broken, thank God. I put it on the conference table pushed off to the side of Paul's desk. Warmth trickled down my calf and I strained to see it. Blood.

"You're not fine, you're bleeding. Stay right there. Don't move."

Paul's office had pale beige carpet. I assumed he didn't want me staining it, so I did as he said for the thirty seconds it took him to grab a handful of tissues from his desk.

He ought to have handed them to me so I could tend my own wound. Like compliments and free lunch, taking care of my boo-boo was probably a no-no. So why didn't I protest when Paul told me to put my hands on the table? Or when he knelt on that pretty beige carpet and slid the soft tissue from just above my anklebone all the way to the back of my knee?

I said nothing because no sound would come out. I didn't move because my fingers refused to do more than twitch on the polished surface of the table. I could see the faint shadow of my reflection in it, the startled O of my mouth and the curved arch of my raised eyebrows. But I didn't move, and I didn't speak.

"There," Paul said in a low voice. Through the tissue the warmth of his fingers pressed against my suddenly chilled skin. "I can see it. Stay right there, Paige. Let me find some tweezers."

I'd placed my hands slightly more than a shoulder width apart and far enough toward the table's center I had to lean forward just a little. I didn't want to know what I looked like, my skirt riding up the backs of my bare thighs and my face flushed.

"It's a big one," Paul said in a moment. "Hold still."

I pressed my lips down on a squeak trying to escape at the touch of the cold metal tweezers. Paul's hand curled around my knee, holding it still, while he probed and pulled.

I felt the splinter slide free, snagging my flesh, and the further slow trickle of my blood painting a line down my leg. I closed my eyes so I wouldn't have to see the blurred woman in the table, the one with my face looking as I'm sure lovers had often glimpsed, but I never had.

The soft press of tissue again slid up my leg as Paul wiped away the blood. I heard the crinkle of paper and his fingers smoothed something on me. An adhesive bandage. I could feel it pulling the soft hairs I never managed to shave. Then the stroke of his fingers along the secret place at the back of my knee, so swift I might have imagined it.

"All done."

I turned. Paul had already stepped away. In one hand, he held the tweezers. In the other, the shredded paper wrapper of the bandage.

I didn't strain or stretch to look at his handiwork. "Thank you."

Twin spots of bright color bloomed on his cheeks. "No problem."

Before he could say anything else, I grabbed up the keyboard and left his office with a nod.

Later, in bed, I would fall asleep thinking of two things. One was the smooth, expensive card and the beautifully written list. I wanted that paper, that pen, whatever it was.

And two, the feeling of Paul's fingers on the back of my knee.

Chapter 09

My Monday-night gyno appointment went as well as could be expected for an event that had my legs in the air and my ass exposed to the entire world. I weighed less than I had the last time I'd been to the doctor, which was good, and I found out I no longer qualified for the same reduced fees I'd been used to getting based on my income, but that was fine. I had insurance now.

"Wish I could lose ten pounds," said the nurse-practitioner when she read my chart and looked me over. "But I like to eat too much."

"Me, too. It just takes…" *Discipline* was the word that rose to my lips, and I was thinking of that note again. "Work."

She patted her round hips and belly and sighed. "Yeah, doesn't everything?"

Of course it did. You didn't get very far in the world thinking you could get away with anything less. But I didn't say anything else, just took my shot and paid my bill and went on my way.

I thought about it, though.

Discipline.

I thought about it on the drive home and up the elevator to my apartment, where I changed into a pair of black yoga pants and a formfitting white T-shirt with the words Frankie Say Relax in block letters across the front. It was a good conversation starter. On my feet I put a pair of trainers that had actually cost more than the Madden pumps and were the most expensive shoes I'd ever owned. I'd discovered I could deal with sore feet for fashion's sake, but not when I was trying to exercise.

Discipline.

Today, you will extend your regular workout by fifteen minutes.

I grabbed a cereal bar from my snack drawer and wolfed down the chewy jam center and crust as I cracked open a can of diet cola and drank it back in a few gulps, then filled a water bottle with ice and water from the tap. My shoes might be designer, but my water was generic.

I took the stairs to add a little extra to my workout, laughing at myself for obeying a command meant for someone else. My heels rang on the metal stairs as I took them two at a time all the way to the basement. I flung open the metal door, too, and it clanged against the wall. Riverview Manor has a nice, if outdated, gym, though it was hardly ever used. Not trendy enough, I guess. There was someone at the elliptical machine when I came in. He looked up but didn't speak around his huffing and puffing.

It was him.

Of course. Why shouldn't I have to sweat and strain next to the man, that handsome man, I kept running into all over the place? I drank back some water to give myself fortitude and hopped on the treadmill.

After five minutes my legs were screaming, and I shot him

a glance. His mouth had set into a tight, hard line of determination. Sweat ringed his armpits and neckline, but far from being disgusted, the sight of it made me go all tingly in my pink places. There's something so fucking sexy about a man who's working hard.

I saw him shoot me a glance, and his machine beeped, but he punched the button to go longer. Uh-huh. I got it. Bound by sweat and bad television programming, we worked out on neighboring machines and forced each other to keep going even when we wanted to stop. Well, I did anyway. It had become a point of pride to keep grunting and groaning my way through the treadmill's fifty-minute program even when I wanted to hop off.

The fact this guy had the body of a god and stopped briefly to strip off his shirt didn't hurt. Not one bit. Every time his abs and pecs rippled I thought about how his sweat would taste if I ran my tongue along the rim of his ribs and around the concave cup of his belly button. I tried to be grossed out at myself for thinking such crude thoughts but couldn't convince my traitorous body that wanting to ride his thigh was wrong.

I blamed the TV.

This time of night the only shows we could get on the gym's battered set were reality-TV shows, game shows or the music channel. The eye candy on the videos was nice, but it sure did put a girl in an interesting frame of mind.

As much as I might want to grab ahold of Mr. Mystery's ears and ride him like a roller coaster, random, careless sex was absolutely not part of my plan. Especially not with someone from my building. Guys talked. Even now, when women were supposed to be able to go after what they wanted with the same passion and lack of emotional commitment as men, guys still talked. Peanut-butter legs, easy to spread. Doorknob, everyone gets a turn. The good time had by all. I wasn't out to get a renewed reputation for having round heels.

Instead, I sweated and bit back grunts that would give away the ache in my thighs as I watched beautiful women with porn-star tits writhe on red satin sheets to the oompah-pah-oomp of some badonkadonk-donk hip-hop song.

Surreptitiously, I watched to see if he had any sort of reaction to the pseudofucking being played out in three-minute increments. His profile told me nothing. Staring straight ahead, I couldn't see if his shorts were bulging.

Silly, I told myself. Who got turned on in the middle of a workout? Too much blood was being pumped to other places for him to get a hard-on. Hell, I thought my heart was going to bust right out of my chest. There was no way I could spare any for my clitoris.

His treadmill beeped to indicate the end of his program. He slowed, grabbed his towel and wiped his face as he climbed off. He drank thirstily from his water bottle. When he bent to touch his toes, I groaned aloud. This guy's ass was like two cantaloupes in a silk bag.

He looked up with a small grin, as if he could read my dirty mind. I hoped he couldn't. No, damn, I hoped he could.

"You all right?"

"…fine…"

I was, in fact, almost a puddle of overexercised goo. My machine beeped a minute later, my program over. I wiped my face and drank water, too, but I didn't try any sort of bending. I'd have passed out.

He'd moved to the tension machine, but hadn't yet begun. He gestured to me, instead. "C'mere. Try this."

"Oh, I don't think so." I shook my head even as my feet followed the siren call of muscled thighs and an irresistible set of back dimples.

"You can't just do cardio," the guy said. "You need to do strength training, too. Tone up."

I thought about being insulted, but let's face it. When Adonis is critiquing your body, he probably knows what he's talking about. "Okay."

"Sit."

I did. He adjusted something in the back and pulled down the rods on either side so I could slip my hands into the grips. Across from us, the mirrored wall reflected him standing behind me as he explained how to pull the grips to move the weights.

With my feet hooked under the padded bench and my hands holding the grips, I was effectively imprisoned. He put his hands over mine the first few times to get me used to the rhythm. It was easy enough, working my arms, since my legs still trembled from the stint on the treadmill.

"Good job," my new trainer-cum-boyfriend said.

His tone suggested he might pat me on the head. Instead, he let go of my hands and put his on my sides. His fingers curved around my ribs just below my breasts. I drew in a sharp breath and didn't move at first.

"Keep going." In the mirror his eyes met mine. "Feel how the muscles in your abs are working, too?"

I couldn't feel anything but his fingers inching upward. My nipples stabbed through my sports bra and the thin, damp-with-sweat cotton of my T-shirt. Between my legs a slow, steady throb began with every pull and release of the weights. I couldn't see his body behind me, could only feel his heat. I could not feel the hard, long length of his erection pressed against my back, but suddenly it was all I could think about.

"Harder," my newfound fantasy man murmured almost directly into my ear as one hand slid down flat over my belly. "Feel your body work."

Oh, God. My mind insisted he was not hitting on me. My body, on the other hand, thrummed and vibrated and practically did the hokeypokey. I wanted to throw the left one in, the right one out and turn it all about.

I bit down on my lower lip, instead. He gave me an encouraging smile. His scent, body spray and hard effort cut through the gym's pervasive odor of mildew and cleaning products. My lust didn't show on my face. The mirror only reflected a sweaty, grouchy-looking woman whose hair had started sticking to her cheeks. Big wet rings spread from my armpits and sides, and I couldn't believe he wasn't disgusted. Maybe he was. He let go and stepped back with an approving nod.

"Add that to your routine," he said. "You'll see results in a couple weeks, I promise."

Ohhhhh, God. He really wasn't hitting on me. He was totally just trying to be nice and help me work off the extra inches nobody ever had on TV. He was the jock with the heart of gold being kind to the brainiac. Too bad this guy didn't know that in high school I hadn't been the brain.

"Thanks." I drank more water and wiped my face with my towel.

He wiped his chest and I forced myself not to watch. "You don't really look like you need to lose any weight, but it's always good to supplement cardio with weight training. Builds muscle."

I had a vision of myself in a bathing suit made from one

thin strip of fabric, tanned to orange splendor and oiled like an olive. It wasn't a pretty picture. "Okay, thanks."

Mr. Mystery grinned. He had dimples on his face, too. "See you."

He stuck his head into a tank top, then his arms, and pulled it down. Then he grabbed his towel and water bottle and headed out. I waited until he'd gone before I followed, not only because I wanted to ogle his ass but because I needed time to cool down. Literally.

My calves ached. My butt did, too. Now I could add my arms to the list after the workout I'd given them.

I wouldn't have thought I could still be horny after the thigh-crunching walk up the stairs to the seventh floor, but by the time I got into the shower, all I could do was think about his hands on me. Austin's hands, the stranger's hands…somehow it didn't matter, just that they hadn't been my own.

I scrubbed quickly, conditioned and moisturized. I even shaved my legs, though it seemed utterly unlikely anyone was going to be touching them, since I'd turned Austin down and Mr. Mystery had only felt me up a little bit. By the time I got out of the shower, my nipples had peaked into tight, hard nubs that defied me not to tweak them as I dried myself with a soft towel.

In my bedroom I shed the towel and stood in front of the bed. The lonely bed. It was king-size, and even though I never shared it with anyone, I still slept only on one side. Some habits are harder to break. I smoothed the quilt, then pulled it down to reveal the crisp, white sheets I'd paid too much for. It had seemed like a good thing to do at the time, spend money on fancy sheets for my new place. I'd regretted it the next time I was hungry, but that's the way it goes.

The window had nothing but a sheer curtain covering the glass, but I wasn't too worried about being seen. The parking garage across the street was the only building high enough to give anyone access to peep at me, and my apartment was set a little too far back to make it worth anyone's while. Still, the thought someone could be watching me had me covering my breasts with my hands for just a moment.

I cupped them, the weight familiar. I'd gotten tits in fifth grade but hadn't really grown into them until I was a junior in high school. I couldn't really remember a time when I didn't curve this way. I could recall being thinner, yes, but not flat-chested.

Under my palms, my nipples stayed hard, tight peaks. I wished for a man's mouth on them, but had to settle for licking my fingers and circling the hot flesh. A whisper, a sigh, a moan leaked from my throat. I saw the ghost of my reflection in the glass. Faint and insubstantial, nothing more to me than a slash of dark where my eyes should be and the white, curving shape of my body.

"I've been watching you." His dark eyes gleam and his mouth twists up into a smile I can't resist returning. He moves closer and I can smell him, warmth and spice, purely masculine.

He holds out a hand and I take it. His fingers are long and strong and entwine with mine so tightly I can't pull away. Not that I want to. I want him to tug me close, up against his body. I want him to put his other hand on my ass to press me against his crotch. And I want him to dip his mouth to stroke along my neck and settle his teeth briefly at the curve of my shoulder.

He licks me with a quick flick of his tongue and my nipples get hard and tight. He can see them through the soft fabric of my blouse. His lips part. He sighs.

I press my body to his and he kisses me. Hard. He backs me up against a wall and pins both my arms above my head with only one of his hands. When the other slides up my thigh, beneath my skirt, and finds me wet and ready, he smiles again.

Before I know it he's turned me. Pushed me. The bed's soft and my cheek presses onto the pillow. My ass feels cool in the breeze made when he flips up my skirt. His hand cups each cheek, maybe measuring, maybe just caressing. I don't know. I don't care. I push myself into his touch.

He blindfolds me. Darkness weighs my eyelids and I close them beneath the cloth. He ties my hands; excitement surges in every breath from my throat, past my lips. My tongue darts out and I taste sweat.

It's not that I can't move if I really want to. It's that I'm bound to his whim, that I'd have to fight and struggle against him if I want to get free. And I can, he hasn't tied me so tightly I can't.

I just don't want to.

His cock is long and thick. It fills me, all the way. I'm stretched from the inside.

I don't have to do a thing. He takes control, he sets the pace, and it's perfect. I don't have to direct him. He just knows. Every thrust presses something sweet until I cry out.

I ride the waves of pleasure. I lose myself in it. Up and over, writhing on his dick as he slaps my ass once, twice. It doesn't hurt bad enough to keep me from coming all over his prick and all over my hand.

It wasn't a unique fantasy, as far as fantasies went. What made it different from others I'd had was the man in it wasn't an actor or an anonymous quiltwork of features. It was Mr. Mystery, of course, and though my own hand had done the work, it had been his face that set me off.

And with that in my head, I went to sleep.

Chapter 10

The next morning I woke with a craving for oatmeal.

The power of suggestion, I told myself as I mixed water into the contents of the packet I found shoved way back in my cupboard, formerly ignored in favor of diet soda and junk food. That was all. But when the maple-syrupy goodness hit my tongue, I knew that wasn't all it was.

It had been a simple command. Eat oatmeal for breakfast. Sweeten it however you like. Straightforward and uncomplicated.

It had taken away the issue of what to have for breakfast, a problem I faced every morning as I rushed around trying to get ready and spent precious minutes staring without enthusiasm into my refrigerator. I didn't have to think about what to have, or waste time concerning myself. Eat oatmeal for breakfast, the list had said, and I did.

I'd eaten oatmeal every day as a kid. Sometimes for dinner, too. My mom bought it in bulk from an Amish market. Great huge tubs of big, rolled oats. Not the fancy kind with Benjamin Franklin or whoever he was on the front. The kind you had to slow cook. Funny how I hadn't thought about how easy, filling and tasty oatmeal could really be until I got that note.

Even though the mail almost always was delivered or in the process of being delivered before I had to leave for work, many times I didn't care to brave the crowd flocking around the mailboxes and just waited to pick it up after work. Until recently, I'd never had anything exciting to pick up.

This morning, though, I muscled my way through the crowd and pulled my mail from the box. My heart pounded as I flipped through the junk and bills. I had a postcard from my dentist reminding me I was due for an exam.

And a new note.

Today, you will be strong and know you are beautiful.

Wow.

I closed the card, returned it to the envelope, and slid it through the slot of mailbox 114. I didn't stop to hide what I was doing, not caring if anyone saw me do it, though at that moment the flock of tenants had flown away and I was the only one there. I peered through the glass window at the card in its cradle of other mail and wondered how such a simple command could have completely stolen away my breath.

Paul traveled often, so it wasn't unusual for me to go several days or a week without seeing him. On the days he was in the office, though, he never failed to come out to greet me when he heard me arrive, or if I'd managed to get to my desk ahead of him, he always stopped to say good-morning. But not today. I heard him muttering into the phone through his closed door, but he didn't come out. He had, however, left something for me on the desk.

A list.

It didn't tell me to be strong or know I was beautiful, but I couldn't stop thinking about that as I read the chores and tasks he'd left for me. He hadn't given me anything out of the ordinary. It was only my reaction that was different.

I would never have said we had a close relationship, but it was always cordial. On the day he'd taken out my splinter, it might even have gone beyond that to warm. Too warm for Paul, apparently, because he barely looked at me when he came out of his office around eleven, his coat on and his briefcase gripped so tight in one hand his knuckles were white. I sat up straighter at my desk.

Strong and beautiful.

"I'll be gone until about four."

He didn't need my permission, of course, so it was stupid to say, "Okay."

That was all he said. Tension like gum stuck to the bottom of a sneaker stretched between us. He wouldn't look at me.

This pissed me off.

I hadn't asked him to treat my wound. I hadn't made him touch me. And I wasn't going to sic him with a sexual-harassment suit or anything asinine like that, either.

He nodded, his gaze cutting away from mine. "Bye."

"Goodbye, Paul."

I could see the crimson creeping into his ears even from my seat at the desk. He didn't acknowledge me after that, just left. That pissed me off, too.

I hadn't become an executive assistant because I'd dreamed of it ever since I was a little girl. I became an executive assistant because nobody seems to have secretaries anymore. And because it was the cheapest and fastest business degree I could earn that would qualify me for a position in the range of salaries that would allow me to move the hell out of Lebanon and start a new life.

I never intended to stay at this level forever. I'd taken the job with Kelly Printing because of their employee-education program. I had to work there for a year before I could start taking night classes toward my MBA, a cost the company would partially reimburse if I qualified, and I'd make sure I did. I wasn't an executive assistant because I didn't want to be something else. Just too poor. And until today, I'd never felt bad about what I did, this one step up on a ladder that had many rungs.

The list he'd left hadn't been written with fine ink on creamy paper, just scribbled on the back of a paper already printed on one side in handwriting so fiercely indecipherable that reading it was like cracking code. It wasn't a long list but even so, it *was* a list and I looked at it for a long time.

That piece of paper, those numbered sentences, effectively broke my day into chunks. They provided a purpose, a path, a pattern. I didn't need Paul to give me that; I was more than capable of prioritizing my daily duties, and yet, staring at the instructions gave me a sense of accomplishment before I'd even completed a single task.

It surprised him, I think, when he came back to the office just after I should have left. I hadn't dawdled, but the list had been very long and some of the tasks I hadn't yet been trained for. I'd figured them out, though, my fingers *tap-tapping* on the keyboard as I filled in data spreadsheets and saved files and sent e-mails. I was shutting down my computer as he disappeared into his office.

I took my time gathering my sweater and water bottle. In a moment Paul reappeared in his doorway. Paul had not loosened his tie or taken off his suit jacket, not at the end of the day. He looked tired.

"Paige. I wasn't expecting you to still be here." He slid his gaze from mine in a manner so blatant I couldn't have missed it. "I got all the files you sent."

I could've let it pass, pretended something wasn't strange between us. Maybe I should've, but his attitude rankled. "Is everything all right? I mean, I did everything you asked for, right?"

He nodded, but when he spoke, his voice was gruff and he avoided looking at me. "I've been very pleased with your performance."

I thought of what Brenda had said, about how the girls never lasted long. Well, I needed this job and I'd be damned if I was forced out of it. I could find another job *if* I wanted, but it would be *when* I wanted. Not when Mr. Johnson decided to make me miserable enough to quit.

But there was more to it than that. Strength and beauty. Flaws and strengths. Lists. It was bound wrists and a blindfold and being told what to do without having to think for myself.

We stared at each other until he looked away.

"Thank you," Paul said. Then he went into his office and closed the door behind him.

The misdelivered note handwritten in fine ink on gorgeous paper wasn't anything like the one Paul had given me. So why, then, had they both become so inexplicably linked?

Kira caught me on my cell phone as I drove home. Our conversation didn't last long, and while she might not have felt the strain, I did. We hadn't been best friends for a long time, but like all my other old habits, Kira was a hard one to break.

Her call took my mind off Paul and the lists, but got me

thinking about Austin again. I wasn't sure that was an improvement. She didn't apologize for inviting him to the Pharmacy with us, but she didn't bring up Jack's name, either, so I guessed that was sort of a draw.

I let her talk on and on even though I didn't have much to say. She didn't notice, or ignored, my lack of replies, until finally she hung up before I could remember to tell her I still had her purse. Typical. Kira was always careless with what she had, no matter how much or how little.

At home when I wanted to drive for a while to clear my head, I could have my pick of backcountry roads, winding through cornfields and cow pastures and woods. I could drive for hours, literally, without crossing a major highway. I could open the windows and let my hair blow in the wind with the radio cranked up loud, singing along. I could lose myself on the ribbon of asphalt and make time stand still.

Not here. I could've found a rural road if I went out of my way, but it would've taken more effort to do it than it was worth. Instead, I suffered stop-and-go traffic through urban neighborhoods with my windows rolled up and my doors locked. Harrisburg wasn't a big city, but anyone who didn't think it had crime was a fool.

The song came on the radio just as I pulled into the parking garage. I'd just started listening to the public radio station out of Philly. The Cure had done a cover of Hendrix's "Purple Haze" with a lot of funky backbeat and some sort of weird *Star Trek* effect. It was an old song and not one the local stations played.

I was transported.

"You ladies here to see the guys, right?" The guy behind the counter gives us all a knowing wink as though he's seen our type before. "Bachelorette party?"

It's not. It's an anti-bachelorette party, a divorce party, I guess you could call it. I've just signed the paperwork dissolving my marriage to Austin. For the first time since I was seventeen years old, I'm a single woman.

I have good friends. I can be glad of that. Kira couldn't make it tonight, but I've got Nat, Misty, Vicky and Tori. Laurie and Anna made it, too. It was my idea to come to see the boys dancing at the nudie bar, but they all joined the band and jumped on the wagon as soon as I suggested it.

The bouncer leads us past a stage with two poles on it where two bored-looking girls teeter in slutty shoes and wiggle lethargically. There's nobody in the club yet, though there's seating for a couple hundred horny men. We follow the bouncer to a back room, all of us giggling like maniacs and more than a little nervous.

It's not what I expected. I'd seen the Chippendales dance, but this…this is a small room painted entirely black with a small stage in the center, a single, silver pole rising to the ceiling. A couple small tables and a couch I don't want to sit on ring the stage. There's no music. There's nobody.

Until the curtain at the back of the room parts and a young guy about my age comes out. He's got a sheaf of blond hair, fuck, like Austin, and the same build. But I lift my chin and act like I don't care. I don't care. I don't.

He's not alone. He has another guy with him. And believe me, they are not the Chippendales. The music starts, the heavy bass thumpa-thumpa *of some club song I don't really know. The boys, dressed in dark slacks and white shirts, ties, start to dance.*

Holy fucking shit.

I glance at Nat, whose eyes are wide. I look at Tori, who's grinning from ear to ear. Laurie puts her hand over her face and peeks through her fingers.

They dance.

I've never seen anything like it. I was expecting some sort of choreographed dance routine, some cheesy costumes. But not this. This is…I am…

Wow.

The taller, dark-haired guy strips out of his white shirt, takes off his cap and shakes his hair over one eye. He grins, fingers going to the white tie and slipping it loose from its knot. The blond's made his way around the room, which has filled with curious, giggling and hooting women and a few silent men. The dark-haired one, though, he turns on one foot and tosses his tie directly at me.

I know him.

Oh, shit, I know him. It's Jack, that guy Kira was so fucking crazy for. He's taller now, and his hair's longer, and oh, shit, shit, he's coming over to me with a look on his face that says he knows me, too. His fingers tug the buttons free on his white shirt and he slides it open to show off a lean chest and belly.

He's got his nipple pierced and tattoos all over his arm. He tilts his head and gives me a grin that sends a lightning bolt right to my pussy, and I wish I could pretend it didn't, but there's no hiding it. He has to see it, the way my mouth opens and my tongue slides over my lips.

More guys come out of the back and dollar bills are flying left and right, but all I can see is this one guy. This one grinding in front of me, taking off his shirt, undoing his belt, sliding the pants down over his thighs. I want to cover my face, afraid he's bare assed, but he clearly knows the benefit of anticipation and pulls his pants up again, leaving the zipper undone to show dark briefs beneath.

He's got a nice body, nothing like Austin's. He's lean and hard, though, and he smells like sex when he puts a hand on the back of the couch I didn't want to sit on but did. His face is close to my ear when he sings along with the lyrics of the song I'll never be able to forget now. He makes kissing the sky sound dirty and delicious.

When he nudges a knee between my thighs I open for him. He rubs his body along mine, but fast, not lingering. Then he turns. Gives me a sly-ass grin over one shoulder and toys with the waistband of his pants.

Other women are screaming, "Take it off!," but I can't do anything except stare. The song ends and slides into another and I'm sure he's done. He'll take the dollars and go into the back room.

But he does something else, instead. He gets on his knees, sliding across the floor on them until he ends up at my feet. And for that one moment, that instant, everything freezes for me.

I can't breathe. I can't blink. I stare at him on that dirty floor and our eyes lock. I've never wanted anything as much as I want to put my hand in the long silken darkness of his hair and pull.

And in the next moment he's up again, this time shaking his ass at the woman waving a five-dollar bill like she might fly away with it. The moment passed, but not the feeling. Not the memory.

Later, after the club closed, I fucked Jack in the backseat of his car while he whispered dirty, filthy things in my ear. We fucked a lot, but not for long.

He never got on his knees for me again.

The rap on my window startled me so much my hands flew up and knocked against my key ring. I stabbed at the radio, switching it off. Heart pounding, I turned to the window, expecting a gun.

I was shot all the same by the sight of the man's face beyond the glass. My neighbor, my workout buddy, Mr. Mystery. He frowned and leaned closer.

"Are you all right?"

I pulled my keys from the ignition and grabbed my purse,

then waited until he'd stepped aside before I opened the door. "Yeah. Fine. I was just…spacing out for a minute."

"Decompressing? Yeah. I do that, too. Sorry I scared you."

I could breathe again, but every nerve ending still tingled. This guy looked nothing like Jack aside from dark hair, but even that was nothing alike. I swallowed hard and fought not to smooth my hair, though I had a sudden fear of how messy it probably looked.

"It's okay. It's probably not smart to sit in the parking garage."

His smile crinkled the corners of his eyes. "No, probably not. You never know just who might be watching you."

Funny how that was supposed to sound like a warning but came off as a temptation. He shifted his bag over his shoulder and looked me over, seeming as though he might say something else, but satisfied himself instead with another smile. With a little wave he backed off and got in a car across the aisle. It was newer than mine, a dark blue hybrid, which told me that at least he was environmentally responsible as well as hot.

I waved, too, and watched him drive away. For a second or two the memory of Jack's face shimmered and merged with my mystery man's. It made me shiver and I put the thought from my mind. Jack had been a long time ago, and a different time. I was a different me back then.

Or so I thought.

Chapter 11

Though I'd checked my mail that morning, I couldn't resist peeking into my mailbox when I got home. Through the small glass window I expected to see nothing, so at first, that's all I saw. Then the black sliver of shadow on the mailbox's metal floor caught my gaze and my breath razored my throat as I sucked it in. I hid my cough behind my hand. There was something in my mailbox.

A Tenant Association flyer, probably. The T.A. was notorious for its enthusiasm for memos. But they usually came on half slips of cheap computer paper, the message printed multiple times on one sheet and torn in halves or thirds. This was not a memo from the T.A.

I pulled out the card, still not addressed to me, and looked around with sudden suspicion. I have never liked surprises. Not in parties, not in relationships, not in practical jokes.

I saw other tenants in the lobby and standing by the elevators. Some with unfamiliar faces moved past me toward the stairs to the basement. Nobody looked at me. If anyone was watching to see what I'd do, they were being very shy about it.

And why should anyone be watching? I'd passed the other notes along to the rightful recipient. Chances were good the person putting them in the wrong box didn't even know they'd gone through a different one first. Yet something about it seemed off. Who would keep making the same mistake over and over?

Unless it wasn't a mistake?

But I could think of no reason why anyone would be slipping me sexy little instructions. I looked around again. I tapped the card against my palm. I looked at the mailbox for 114. I peeked through its glass window, saw the magazines and letters inside and held the card to the slot.

I wouldn't read it. I shouldn't read it. I didn't dare read it.

I couldn't help it, I swear. I was thirsty and it was a drink of cold water; I was hungry and it was a loaf of bread. I had PMS and it was a bar of chocolate and a bowl of ice cream with peanuts and fudge sauce on top. It was the cherry on that sundae.

With a quick glance from side to side, certain no one was watching, I tucked the card into my bag and hightailed it to the elevator. My phone was ringing when I got to my apartment. The answering machine had just clicked on when I grabbed up the portable handset from the end table. My mom had already started talking.

"Paige. It's Mom. Call me—"

"Mom. Hi." The note, unopened and unread, burned my palm.

"Are you screening your calls?" She sounded amused.

I took a couple of deep breaths and stared at the number on the front of the paper. "I'm not screening my calls. I just got in."

This perked her ears. "Oh? Were you out?"

"Yes, Mother," I said. "Hence the just-getting-in part."

"Where were you?"

"Not on a date, if that's what you're hoping," I told her, just to poke.

"Too bad for you."

"Yeah, yeah. What's up?" I put the note in the center of the kitchen table where it could watch me and I it. I circled it, only half my mind on the conversation with my mother, so distracted by this new note I'd forgotten I needed to be angry at her.

"Does something have to be up for me to call my favorite daughter?"

My mom has always been almost more like an aunt or older sister than a mom. She was only nineteen when she had me, about the same age I'd been when she'd had Arthur. I'm not saying she didn't do her best. I'm just saying that now, when I'm in my twenties and she's in her forties, the age difference seems even less than it did when I was growing up and she was the only mom I knew who cared as much about the Backstreet Boys as I did.

"No, I guess not. But there usually is. Usually you just hit me up on e-mail."

Since I moved "so far away," anyway, and phoning me had become a long-distance call.

"Well, I don't have to do that anymore." She paused and I could hear the grin in her voice. "Guess where I'm calling from."

"Paris."

"No, Paige," my mom said as though I'd been serious. "My car! I'm driving to the mall!"

"You're talking and driving? Mom, you do know that's illegal in the city of Lebanon. You'd better hang up. You'll get a ticket!" Not to mention my mom's driving was haphazard even when she wasn't distracted by a phone.

"You're missing the point, Paige. The point is, I'm calling you from my own cell phone!"

"Ah." I should've guessed it was something bright and shiny that she'd called to tell me. "Congratulations. Welcome to the millennium."

She ignored my far-from-subtle sarcasm. "Leo bought it for me. Isn't he the sweetest?"

As boyfriends went, Leo was one of the better ones. Being older might have been part of it, though with his big beer belly and long beard there was no question he was as rough a biker as any guy my mom had ever dated. He still rode his Harley to work and sported a line of faded tattoos on each arm, but he was mellower than some of the younger guys she'd dated.

"That was nice of him."

"So now I can call you all the time! And text. I can text you, too, if I can figure out how."

"Oh, joy." I dug into the junk drawer for a pen and some paper and paused when I pulled out the yellow legal pad. My scant list of flaws and strengths stared out at me, and I forgot to speak.

"Paige?"

"What's your number?" I put that list aside and poised to take down the number.

"I.D.K.," my mom said airily.

"Huh?"

"I.D.K.," she repeated. "Geez, Paige. Don't you know what I.D.K. means? It means 'I don't know.'"

"I know what it means. I just didn't think you did. Besides, Mom, nobody talks like that out loud. It's just textspeak."

"L.O.L.," my mom said.

"M.O.M.," I said.

We both laughed.

"Also, listen," she said, but didn't say anything else.

"I'm listening."

"Guess who I ran into the other day."

"With your car?"

"You," my mom said, "are a smart-ass."

"I.D.K., who'd you run into?"

She paused. I waited for the sound of crunching glass and metal, but she must've just been pulling into a slot rather than ramming into a phone pole.

"Austin's mother."

Serendipity. It's not just the name of a mildly entertaining John Cusack movie. "Oh?" I couldn't manage a different response.

"She said to say hi."

"Uh-huh." As far as I knew, when her son and I had broken up, Mrs. Miller had been happy to see me go.

"Don't make that face at me, Paige."

"You don't know what face I'm making."

"I'm your mother, I don't need to see your face to know you're crunching your nose. You're going to get horrible crow's-feet that way."

"Around my nose?"

"And guess what she said?"

I waited while she dangled further information in front of me like cheese in front of a rat.

"She says he's moved up there. Where you are."

Well, at least I'd forgotten to keep staring at the note with hungry eyes. "Harrisburg isn't a foreign country, you know. It's only forty minutes away." I tried not to sound sharp, but failed.

My mother didn't care. When "going away" in the vernacular of the area means you're taking a trip to the store, forty minutes was an eternity. I was gone. Anyway, I'd already known about Austin.

Harrisburg was my place. Not his. He didn't belong here. He should've stayed in Lebanon, where his family lived and had always lived and would always live. He should've stayed there where every street could remind him of me and he could weep bitter, salty tears at the loss.

"Lemoyne," she said as though I hadn't spoken. "His mom said he got a new job with some big heating-and-cooling company. He's not doing construction with his dad anymore."

"Good for him."

"I'm sure I could get his number for you."

"I have his number." She was silent to that, because as far as she knew, Austin and I hadn't spoken since the day I'd walked out of our apartment.

"Fine. Be that way. I just thought you might like to know, that's all. He's got a good job."

"Depends on what you consider good."

This time, her silence was longer. "Well. When did you become such a snob?"

I sighed. "I'm not a snob. I'm just…trying to change things for myself. That's all."

There really was no better way to put it, and no way not to say it without offending her. My mother had everything I never wanted. Most parents want better for their kids, and I know my mom wasn't different. But there's always that sting when you realize what you gave someone hasn't been enough, even though it was your best.

"I just thought maybe you might..."

"What?"

My mom cleared her throat, a sure sign she was getting ready to pretend she hadn't done something to piss me off when she knew she had. "I just thought maybe he'd seen you. That's all. Been in touch."

"Stalked me, you mean?" Angry again, I paced the length of my living room and then around my kitchen table, and finally into my bedroom, where I stopped so I didn't have to make another round. "How could you tell him where I lived, Mom? You know I don't want to see him!"

"You know, Paige, once upon a time you'd have been mad at me for keeping him from you."

"Once upon a time was a long time ago," I said.

"I'm sorry," my mother said stiffly. "He called and asked if I could tell him where you were living. I didn't think you'd mind. You said yourself you had his number."

"Mom..." I sighed and pressed my fingers between my eyes to keep myself from completely losing my temper. "If I wanted him to know where I lived I'd have sent him a card."

"I'm sorry, Paige." She sounded sincere, but I knew her well enough to know she was sorry I was angry. Not sorry because she thought she was wrong. "I have to go. I'm at the mall."

"Okay. Fine."

"You know," she said suddenly, "it wouldn't kill you to come back home every once in a while. Arty misses you. Me, too."

I didn't suggest they come up to visit me. Even meeting

halfway would've taken her out of her comfort zone. "I'll be there tomorrow night, remember? Taking him to the movies? *Power Heroes?*"

"You could come on Friday, instead. Spend the weekend."

She might be able to know what my face looked like without seeing it, but I doubt she knew about the shudder crawling over me at the thought.

"I can't. Busy."

She didn't push it. "Okay. Fine."

We were so alike, sometimes it was scary. Which, of course, was one reason why I'd moved away. We hung up.

I stripped out of my clothes and headed into the bathroom, wishing the conversation could be washed away as easily as soapsuds down the drain. Growing up, I'd lived with my mom in a series of low-income-housing apartments, rented trailers and dilapidated houses owned by men who often seemed more interested in the way my mom cooked and kept house than anything else about her. There had never been enough of anything, but especially hot water for showers.

In the best of them, I'd been able to sneak a late-night shower when nobody else needed to use the bathroom, the washing machine wasn't running and nobody was cleaning dishes. In the worst of them, I'd sought the shower as a refuge from the shouting and the slamming doors, shivering under spray that turned frigid long before I was ready to get out.

I worked hard and sacrificed much to afford the smallest unit and cheapest maintenance package in one of Harrisburg's hottest new apartment buildings. Unlimited hot water might be wasteful, and I didn't care. I took advantage of it every chance I could.

By the time I came out dressed in a pair of stretched-out

fleece pants and a T-shirt that had been threadbare when I stole it from Austin's drawer, I felt better. I fixed myself a sandwich and a glass of cold milk, and I set it on the table. The note was still there.

It slid into my hands as though it had been made for my fingers. The same black letters stroked this paper with the same black ink, and this time, with nobody to see, I brought it to my nose and breathed in deep.

Fresh, good ink smells like nothing else in the world. I closed my eyes and breathed again. The paper still had a scent, faintly musky like cologne or perfume I didn't recognize. I sat to study it. Bold, heavy strokes of the pen carved the number on the front. No envelope, no name, no postmark to show where or when it had been mailed. Not even a fingerprint smudge to give me an idea of the size of the hand that had written it. The elegant handwriting showed no gender.

Without an envelope and stamp it couldn't have come through the mail, which meant someone had pushed it through the slot. The wrong slot, again. They'd taken the time to write the number on the front, but hadn't paid attention to the number on my mailbox. It wasn't a note for me, and I should not have read it. If I hadn't, everything would have been different.

If only I'd done the right thing.

Chapter 12

You will take your finest paper and your best ink.

You will write down in explicit detail your most erotic experience. It may be real or it may be fantasy, but you are to write it without error in your best handwriting, without blots or misspellings.

You will return this essay to me by Thursday.

The note listed the same post-office box as before.

I blinked and read the note again as heat rose in my cheeks. I closed it and put it aside. I shouldn't have read it. It wasn't for me.

I opened it again, read over the words in that fluid, beautiful hand that gave away nothing of its origin, and something twisted inside me. Finest paper and best ink. Already I could feel my fingers curving around the pen, could imagine the words unscrolling under the tip as I put my secret thoughts onto paper. I even knew the paper I would use. Creamy white, unlined, bordered in gold. It was the perfect sheet to use for writing something so intimate and explicit as had been demanded. I had only two sheets.

I folded the card carefully and slipped it back into the envelope, closing it up as tenderly as I might pull the blankets higher on a lover next to me in bed when I woke to a chill. I pushed it away from me on the table, and folded my hands while I stared at it. The mystery of *who* was sending these notes, these lists, had been overshadowed by the more intriguing enigma of *why.*

I got up from the table and pulled a glass of water from the tap, but even though I drank it back in a few quick gulps, more the way a practiced drinker will take whiskey than water, it didn't cool the heat rising in my throat to my cheeks. I turned, my back to the counter, and leaned. The note sat on my table. Not accusing.

Inviting.

In a long, long list of sexual experiences, what would I consider my most erotic? Not the first time I ever sucked a guy off, or the first time I came from someone's else's hand. Not the first time I ever fucked, either. All of those had been memorable. I'd had a lot of sex, a lot of it good. Quite a bit bad. I had a long list of experiences I could have written, but what was the one worthy of my finest paper? My best ink?

I busied myself with cleaning my tidy kitchen but was unable to put the list from my mind. The first few notes had been simple, if enigmatic, instructions. Eat oatmeal. Work out. Be beautiful. It had been something of a game, these suggestions implanted in my brain and leading me toward the choices I'd have probably made anyway even without the suggestions. But this...this was different. What had seemed harmless before had become slightly more sinister.

Also, a helluva lot sexier.

Late night.

The only light comes, flickering blue, from the TV in the corner. The sound's turned down low because it's not so important to hear what's being said as it is to see what's going on. I've seen this movie before, a few times, in pieces, but it's the first time I've ever seen it all at once.

He lifts his head from kissing me when it comes on, his hands stilling on my belly where they'd been wandering their way up toward my breasts. "Hot," he murmurs. "This movie is hot."

I push his face back to mine and take his mouth to keep his attention on me, not the TV screen. I open my mouth and legs to him, pulling him down on top of me. Pulling him close. My heart's open, too, though I haven't yet told him I love him. Those are words for prom pictures and class rings.

We don't have that, him and me. We have the backseat of his car, we have the space beneath the bleachers after school. We have the back row of the movie theater. We have the basement in his parents' house and this couch.

But when I hear the song, the one my mom plays over and over on those old mix tapes from her youth, I lift my head from his kisses to see what's going on. I know why she loved this song. She'd been a fan of Duran Duran in her youth, complete with fedora hat and bleached-blond streak in her hair, just like the bass player. John Taylor, the same guy singing this song. Well, not singing it. Chanting it, sort of. I knew she loved this song because he sang it, but until now, I hadn't known this was the movie it had come from.

The woman on the screen bites her finger. The slide show she's watching cycles through to another picture, but the movie doesn't show what she's looking at. Only her. She touches herself, her thighs opening, her head falling back in ecstasy as she makes herself come.

He watches me watch. His hand presses flat on my chest, over my heart. My breath had caught in my throat and I let it seep out, slow and silent, not wanting him to know I'd been holding it.

"Do you do that?"

I tear my gaze from the TV to look at him. "What?"

He jerks his chin toward the set. The movie's moved on to something else, but I know what he meant. "That. Do you?"

"Do I touch myself? Do I get myself off?" I hitch higher against the arm of the battered couch his parents donated to the basement. A cat had scratched it; a dog had lifted its leg on it. We'd fucked about a thousand times on its faded cushions, or maybe only ten.

He sits back. His shirt hangs open at his throat. I'd been the one to undo the buttons. The waistband of his boxers peeks from his jeans. Beneath the denim his cock had throbbed, hard and hot, moments before.

I know him now, though not as well as I will eventually. He doesn't know me very well at all and never will. Yet this is different, this coyness as he scrubs his hand over the brush of his hair and grins.

"Well. Yeah."

"Do you?" I pull down the bottom of my sweater and cross my arms over my stomach.

He laughs low. I've known him for years, since elementary school. I've watched him become a man. He sounds like a man when he laughs, all low and growly deep. Rough-edged.

"Well, yeah," he says. "All guys do."

"But you don't think all girls do, too?"

"I'm not asking what all girls do. Just you," he points out.

He knows how to work me. And, because I want to believe I'm the only girl in his thoughts, I answer his question honestly. Later we'll both lie.

"Yeah. I do it."

He clears his throat. "Really? I mean, you really—"

"Wank? Masturbate? Pet my pussy?" I guess I'm trying to shock him. Make him blush. He's not the blushing sort.

"Is that what you call it?"

"What do you call it?"

We're whispering, though his parents sleep a full two floors above us and we haven't bothered to keep our voices down about anything before. He leans forward and so do I. He smells faintly of cologne and more like fabric softener. His mother does his laundry. Mine doesn't.

"Jerking off, I guess."

"I don't call it anything," I admit. "I just do it."

"How often?"

I laugh, then, and look to the movie for strength. The couple in the film are fucking in what looks like a clock tower. Their hands scrabble at each other as they pull off their clothes.

"Whenever I feel like it!"

He laughs. "How often do you feel like it?"

I don't want to tell him about the nights I've spent with other boys' hands on me, revving me up without finishing me off. Or the blank-fronted books I sneak from the shelves of the family down the street who pay me to watch their kids while they go bowling. I've learned a lot more about sex from those books than I've ever learned from a boy. Until him, anyway.

"Do you feel like it now?" he asks when it becomes clear I'm not going to answer.

"Do I feel like coming now?"

He's used his hands on me, put his cock inside me, put his mouth on my mouth and on my body. I've come with him more than a few times. But not every time.

"Will you?" he asks. "While I watch?"

I don't know what answer to give. I only know I want to give him everything he asks for and some things he hasn't. I nod.

He sits back against the couch's opposite arm. I'm not sure he'll even be able to see me, painted in shafts of white and dark from the TV's glow. I'm not sure I want him to see me do this without a shield of shadows.

I've never done this in front of anyone, and at first I'm not sure how to start. In the privacy of my bedroom I'd have the door locked and soft music playing in the dark. I'd be naked, or wearing only panties and a T-shirt. Now I have to navigate the barriers of my jeans and sweater, underpants and bra. So I start by touching my breasts through the wool, not because I usually feel my boobs when I'm masturbating but because I think that's what he expects me to do, and doing it will buy me time to find the nerve to follow through with the rest of it.

The small noise that eeps out of his throat convinces me I made the right choice. My hands feel small on my breasts, which are fuller in my palms than in his. I can't remember the last time I touched them this way, cupping and rubbing, trying to tweak my nipples to points. The sweater is too thick for this, so I shift until I can pull it off over my head.

Another small noise from him, and I bite my lower lip. My fingers tiptoe over the slopes of my now-naked chest, over the lace and satin of my best bra. The one I bought from Victoria's Secret with my babysitting cash. The one I wear on every date. Beneath its expensive material and breast-lifting bands of metal, my nipples have gone tight and aching.

My palms slide on the smooth fabric. When my thumbs pass over those hard points, I bite harder. Soft flesh dents under my teeth. It doesn't hurt yet, but if I don't ease up I will soon taste blood.

I close my eyes because it's easier to be what I think he wants me to be when I'm not watching him watch me. And it gives me darkness, which I'm used to and prefer for this sort of thing. I feel my skin, softer than the bra that has been through lots of washings and, despite its cost, wasn't made to last.

I go away.

From this basement, which always smells a little of wet dog though his dog died years ago. From him, the boy-man watching me. Even from the TV and the movie in the corner that started all of this in the first place.

I go away to the place where everything feels good, and I don't have to think about anything but the whisper of my fingertips along my sides. Down across my belly, which will never be flat enough no matter how many crunches I do or lunches I skip. The metal button on my jeans isn't cold or warm, it's the same temperature as my skin. My fingers miss it in their first walk across, though the belt loops snag my touch.

I don't open the button at first. I slide my hand down the front of my jeans. My panties are already damp from the hour we've been on the couch. Sometimes, though I'd never dare tell him this, no matter what I'm about to share, my pussy gets wet even before we start kissing. Sometimes, when I'm in the shower getting ready to meet him, I do what I'm doing now with my hands, which is rub them all over my body and pretend they're his. Sometimes I spend the entire date—the movie, the dinner, bowling, whatever it is, waiting for it all to be over so we can get to this part. The couch, the backseat. His hands and mouth on mine. His cock inside me.

I gasp aloud when my finger finds the small bump at the front of my panties. I don't have room to stroke, so I satisfy myself with pushing gently. I use my middle finger. The fuck finger, he calls it. It's the one he uses inside me to get me ready before he uses his dick, but when he touches my clit he uses his first finger. Or his thumb, if I'm on top. I didn't come to his bed or his backseat or his couch as anything close to a virgin, but I don't want to think about who taught him how to do that.

I can always get off faster by myself than with someone else. I'm already close. Another gentle press of my finger pushes a shudder through me. My toes curl against the cushions. My hips lift a little.

I don't have room to do this right, so now I unbutton my jeans.

My zipper ratchets apart, tooth by metal tooth. My jeans open. I hook my thumbs into the sides and push them down, over my hips and thighs. They get hung up at my knees, and he reaches forward to grab a handful of denim and help me.

In my bra and also-best panties I lean back and give myself over to his scrutiny. I push my hands over my body, all the curves that scared and annoyed me when they started forming but I'm grateful for now. Boys like boobs and ass and even a little belly is okay if you have the rest of it, too.

He unzips his jeans, too, while he watches. Soon his prick is settled firmly in his fist and he pumps it slowly as he watches me caress my body with my hands acting like his. I have seen him do this before, stroke himself erect, give himself a few quick pumps now and then. I've never watched him finish this way. He's always done it in my mouth, or my hand, or in my body.

"Take off your panties," he whispers in a voice rough-edged with need.

I can't remember him ever saying that to me before. They've always just…come off. But now I slide the cotton and satin down to end up on the floor next to my jeans. I try not to think about the couch under my bare flesh, or wish we'd at least put down a blanket.

When he groans, I'm no longer distracted. I can't focus on anything but my hand moving between my legs and his moving on his cock. I'm wet and my fingers slip and slide. I push two inside myself, echoing the motion he's making. It's like my fingers are his prick, his fist my pussy. Our bitten-back moans come at the same time.

My clitoris is hard. Rigid. When I brush it with my fingertips I want to arch and squirm, thrust my hips. I want to fill myself deep with something hard. I want to ride his dick while my clit rubs his hard belly.

I want to come.

My hand moves faster between my legs. My other hand finds my nipples, which I twist and tug in time to the thrusting of my fingers. My knees fall open and my head falls back. The arm of the couch is unyielding, but I push against it anyway.

The couch dips as he moves closer to me. He's on his knees, his jeans and boxers tangled on his ankles. He stops just long enough to pull his shirt over his head, the sleeves going inside out as it flutters to the floor. Then his hand is back on his dick and his other is on my hip.

I stop rubbing my clit, thinking he's going to take over. That he means to cover me with his body and push up inside me. Every nerve is singing now, and I want that. I want him to fuck me, but he doesn't.

"Don't stop, Paige," he says. "I want to watch you."

So my hand moves back between my legs and my fingers still, going slower even though he's hand-fucking himself ever faster. I want to draw it out, make it last, build the pleasure.

My breath is coming in short, harsh pants and my hips are moving all on their own. I'm so close I could come only by thinking about it. I take my clit between my thumb and first finger and squeeze, just gently. Just softly. Just enough.

Everything contracts at once. My pussy, my ass, my clit. My breath bursts out of me in a cry that's too loud but I can't hold it back. This time when I bite my lip, I do taste blood.

My orgasm has taken over. I am steamrollered by it and left flat. I can't move, though my neck is killing me from the awkward angle and something sharp is poking me in the ass.

"Ah, God," he cries. "Ah, Paige!"

Hot wetness spatters my chest and belly. It pumps out of him in three hard spurts. The rest surges over his hand as it cups the head of his cock and he strokes a few last times. The scent of him fills me. The couch beneath me dips again as he leans to put his hand on the arm behind my head.

Crouching over me, his hand still on his penis, his face is lit by the television's moving shadows but I have no trouble looking straight into his eyes. His jizz is going cold on my skin and I'm afraid to move in case it drips off me onto the cushions.

He leans to kiss me with an open mouth, but no tongue. It's sweet and unexpected. I taste the salt of his sweat on his upper lip.

He pulls his shirt up from the floor and wipes me clean, which is also unexpected and leaves me uncertain how to react. He scrubs at the wetness on my bra with his sleeve, but it's too late. I can wash it, but there will always be a stain.

"You are so beautiful," Austin says when he kisses me again.

It's the first time he says it and this time, though later I won't, I believe him.

My fingers had gone stiff from gripping the pen. I hadn't thought about that night in a long time. Other memories had crowded it out. Worse memories, actually, that had made me forget there'd once been a time when I'd been young and in love.

"Discipline," I said aloud. I wasn't smoking, but the taste and scent of tobacco smoke filled my senses anyway.

What the hell was going on?

I gave in to the need to let my legs buckle under me then. I let myself fall onto my couch, where I curled into a ball and pulled the knitted afghan over my head. Through the holes the stark walls of my apartment glared at me until I closed my eyes.

I'm no prude. When other kids were watching *Aladdin,* my mom was working third shift and leaving me alone in the house from ten-thirty at night until eight in the morning. She thought I was asleep when she left, and it was true I was in bed. I never told her how anxious I was when she left, or how hard it was for me to sleep knowing I was alone in the house all night. I'd creep downstairs and console myself with hours of cable television. I saw a lot of things I probably shouldn't have, but it also taught me a lot.

Even so, these notes. The commands. What had seemed fairly innocuous at the start couldn't be confused for anything innocent now.

The lists had been specific. Detailed. And now, explicit.

What sort of woman wanted someone to tell her how to live her day? What sort of woman needed someone else to tell her to be beautiful, to be strong? What sort of woman craved the commands of someone else dictating her life?

I put my hand between my legs, on the damp cotton of my panties, and felt my clit pulse.

What sort of woman?

I thought I knew.

Chapter 13

Here's a funny story made humorous by time, since it wasn't funny when it happened. I was nineteen when my mom had Arthur, which means that when she got pregnant, I was eighteen. A senior in high school and screwing my brains out with Mr. Popular Jock.

My mom had always been up front about sex and protecting myself. Too up front, in my opinion, since my sex life was the second-to-last topic of discussion I ever wanted to share with her, the last being hers. Austin wasn't the first boy I'd fooled around with. He wasn't even the first boy I'd slept with, though the previous few times I'd had sex had been so unremarkable and meaningless I mostly forgot it had ever happened. I'd been on the pill for a couple years already, but I made him use condoms, too. There's nothing quite like being an illegitimate child to make a girl fear pregnancy. There was no way I was going to end up the way my mother had.

Still, when a condom broke I wasn't too worried. At least, not until my period was late. Not even a warning cramp to announce its pending arrival. I counted the days and when we'd had sex—easy enough to do because it was pretty much every time we were together, which by that point was almost every day.

I didn't tell Austin what I suspected. I didn't tell anyone. I went to the drugstore on the far end of town and bought the first pregnancy test I could find. I came home and drank a quart of water before I went to sleep so when I got up I'd have plenty of pee to use for that first morning urination. I read the instructions four times. I peed on the little stick and watched with my guts cramping from fear, not PMS, for the lines to show up. One or two? Safe or caught?

One line.

I hadn't been raised a regular churchgoer, but I got on my knees there in front of the toilet and I sent a prayer of thanks so fervent I was sure any God who'd listen would forgive me for my past sins. Then I wrapped the test in a handful of toilet paper the way I usually wrapped my tampons and shoved it to the bottom of the garbage can.

I got home from school to an empty house, my mom at work as usual. And, as usual, I was already flying through my homework and my chores so I could spend the rest of the time with Austin until she got home. When I went into the bathroom to clean it, my heart stopped. Literally. The world grayed out in that two seconds before it started to beat again, and I clutched the sink to keep from falling.

There on the counter was a pregnancy test. The same brand I'd used that morning. Only this one had two lines in the little window. A positive result.

This time when I got on my knees it wasn't to pray. I put my head in my shaking hands and concentrated on drawing in breath after breath. I could smell the bleachy cleanser I'd meant to use on the shower walls, which never wanted to come clean from the soap scum no matter how hard I scrubbed. I could feel my breath whistling through my fingers.

I got myself under control and onto my feet to stare again at the test. Hadn't I left enough time for the results? Had it turned positive after I'd thrown it away and gone my merry way to school, secure in my un-knocked-up state?

Had I been pregnant all day and not known it?

Normally I wouldn't touch the garbage without rubber gloves, but I dug through the layers of used tissues and Q-tips without even a gag, though my stomach had risen in my throat. I found the box I'd wrapped as carefully as the test, but before I could tear it open to reread the instructions to see if it was possible a test could turn positive later than the three minutes I'd given it. And I found, still wrapped tightly and hidden, the test I'd taken that morning. Which meant, of course, the one on the sink wasn't mine.

My thanks this time were louder and more fervent than they'd been that morning, but shorter. Because if it wasn't mine, that meant it was my mother's. I didn't want to think about that.

Thinking of this now, I pulled up in front of my mom's house. The one she'd lived in with Leo and Arty for the past three years, not one of the many in which she'd raised me. A brick row home sandwiched between two others and within a stone's throw of the railroad tracks, it wasn't anything like my dad's house. Yet inside the good smells of something baking tickled my nose instead of expensive scented candles, and the hug I got from my mom felt natural and not forced.

"Arty's upstairs getting ready," she said. "I told him he couldn't wear his Batman costume to the movies, but...well."

"I don't care if he wears his Batman costume."

My mom sighed and shook her head. "You're sure?"

Once upon a time I'd have been appalled at the thought, but distance seemed to have mellowed me. Or time, maybe. I shrugged.

"What's it to me if the kid's happy?"

I couldn't decipher her look, which only lasted a second as she turned to shout up the stairs. "Arty! Paige is here!"

"Where's Leo?" I'd always liked him, even if he did laugh too loud at truly stupid television shows and wear offensive novelty T-shirts.

Again with the look I couldn't interpret. "He's not home."

"Obviously." She didn't return my smile, but before I could ask her if something was wrong, Arty bounded down the stairs. "Hey."

"Pow!" Arty leaped in front of me with his hands on his hips. His brown eyes glinted from behind the mask. Clearly he'd had no intention of listening to our mom. "I'm Batman!"

"I see that. Are you ready to go, Batman?"

He launched himself into me, his arms and legs wrapping around me. "Yay! Yes! Yay for Paige!"

"Good luck with him. Today was somebody's birthday at school. He's had a lot of sugar."

"Oh, joy. Put a sweatshirt on, shorty. The movie theater might be chilly." I squeezed him back, tight. He smelled like baby shampoo and candy. I could handle even a sugar-infused Arty.

My mom tried to press a ten-dollar bill into my hand as Arty struggled into his jacket, but I refused to take it. "Mom, no."

"For popcorn."

"I said *no.*" I'd been taller than her since seventh grade, but looking down at her now it seemed strange to be staring at the top of her head. She'd starting graying early but had always kept up the color. Now I saw half an inch of white here and there along her part.

I noticed lines in the corners of her eyes, too, when she looked up at me. My mom had never looked old to me, I guess because she wasn't, but she looked tired. Her eyeliner had smudged a little as though applied by an unsteady hand, or as if she'd been rubbing her eyes. She did that when she had a headache.

"You okay, Mom?"

"Fine, baby." She pressed the folded bill toward me again, even though I jerked my hand away. "Take this."

"I said *no.* C'mon. It's my treat."

She frowned. I looked like my dad most every other time, but now I saw myself in her face. "Paige. You can't tell me that fancy apartment's not expensive."

"And I have a good job, remember? You don't have to worry so much. Really. I'm happy to take Arty to the movies. I'm fine."

With a sigh she tucked the bill into the pocket of her jeans. "As if you'd tell me otherwise?"

She had me there. I merely grinned and shrugged. She shook her head and bent to help Arty slide his arms into his sleeves. Considering how much Arty was bouncing up and down it was no small feat. I reached a hand to help her and she stepped back with a strangely defeated sigh.

"Let's go, let's go, let's go, let's go!"

"Chill, little dude. Chill," I admonished with a hard look at my mom. "You sure you're okay?"

"Just tired, baby. Go have fun. I'll see you when you get back. Not too late," she cautioned for Arty's benefit and not mine. "School tomorrow."

Arty, still bouncing, grabbed for my hand. "Let's goooooooo!"

Like me, my little brother looked like the man who'd fathered him. Personalitywise, though, he was almost entirely my mother. Nonstop chatter from the backseat kept me entertained on the ten-minute drive to the mall. Growing up, I'd had to go all the way to Palmyra to hit a multiplex, but now Lebanon had its own stadium-seating theater fancy enough to rival anything in Harrisburg. The prices were cheaper, too, a reminder there were some minor advantages to life in the town where I'd grown up.

Halfway through the movie, my phone vibrated against my thigh. I flipped it open with a sigh when I saw who it was from...ignoring the fact that not only did I recognize the number on sight, but that I had, in a fit of insanity, assigned it a photo. I shielded the glare of the backlight with one hand as I read it.

Where you @?

I didn't reply, just flipped the phone closed and slid it back into my jeans pocket. The movie went on and on. And on. And on some more. I never knew an hour and a half could last so long, but since Arty stared slack-jawed in wonder at the cavorting cartoon figures I figured he, at least, was enjoying it.

I blame the cartoons. If the movie had held my interest I would never have pulled out my phone again. I'd never have answered Austin's text. I know better now, but that's what I told myself at the time.

I'm watching a movie.

Cool. What movie? The answer came within seconds.

I tried not to be excited that he'd been waiting for my answer.

Something with elves and fairies. My eyes are bleeding.

You're with Arty?

I loved that Austin didn't abbreviate his texts. Yes. What are you doing?

Thinking about you.

Something brilliantly colored and loud happened onscreen, but I couldn't blame the sudden thunder of my pulse on that. I glanced at Arty, his mouth full of popcorn, his entire attention taken up by what was going on. I looked again at the phone. My fingers stroked the keys, but I didn't type anything. I didn't want this to keep going.

Or maybe I did.

What are you thinking about me?

"Paige," Arty whispered. "I have to go to the bathroom!"

"Now? Can't you wait five minutes? The movie's almost over." I looked at the jumbo-size drink in his cup holder. It had been the smallest size and still contained enough soda to float a boat. "Never mind. C'mon."

Arty squirmed. "No, no, I want to wait."

"Dude, you'll pee yourself."

The woman in front of us gave an annoyed glance over her shoulder. Since her own three kids had been bouncing out of their seats and talking over the entire movie, I wasn't really sure where she got off with the bitchface, but I ignored her to focus on my brother.

"No, I want to wait," he insisted, eyes glued to the screen.

With a sigh, I watched him squirm. He was totally going to wet himself, but I remembered what it was like to miss the best parts of a movie because of a teeny bladder. Not that this movie seemed to have any best parts.

My phone vibrated again, earning me another look from Mrs. Grumpy in front of me when I opened it to see another text from Austin.

I'm thinking about how good your hair always smells.

Once I'd stuck a bobby pin in an electrical socket. What can I say? I was young and dumb and it had seemed like a good idea at the time. Much like this text-message flirtation. Austin's message shot the same frigid-inferno tingle up and down my body, and I saved myself from gasping aloud only by biting my tongue.

I was saved from myself by the movie ending. Thanking God it wasn't one to have outtakes and jokes scattered throughout the final credits, I hustled Arty to the bathroom where he peed forever as he chattered about the movie. The weight of my phone in my pocket distracted me so much I forgot to make him wash his hands, a fact I remembered too late when he grabbed mine on the way to the parking lot.

"Paige, you're the best sister, ever. I love you!"

"Love you too, squirt." I ruffled his hair and helped him into his seat belt.

My phone remained silent, and so did I. Arty talked enough for both of us all the way home. By the time I pulled up in front of my mom's house, he'd relayed the entire movie to me, including dialogue, and I marveled at how he could repeat word for word eight minutes' worth of dialogue but was unable to remember his telephone number.

"Inside and get ready for bed," I told him on the front porch. "No fussing."

"Okay." He was off the moment he got in the door, up the stairs before my mom even made it out of the kitchen.

"He's sufficiently caffeinated now," I told her. "To go along with the sugar."

"Great." My mom's laugh sounded forced.

From my pocket, my phone buzzed.

Her eyebrows lifted when I didn't reach to answer it. "So I'm not the only one you ignore?"

I remembered then I was supposed to be angry with her about something. "It's Austin."

She didn't even try to hide the pleasure on her face. She pulled a pan of brownies from the oven and settled them on top of the stove, then slapped the hot pads on the counter. "I'm not surprised. You were crazy about that boy for so long—"

"*Crazy* being the operative word."

She turned to face me. "I said I'm sorry, all right?"

I eyed the brownies, then her. "What's wrong?"

"Nothing's wrong. Why would anything be wrong?" She rummaged in the fridge to pull out a bowl of what looked like fudge icing.

"Because you bake when you're upset."

She held out the bowl to me. "Taste this. Is it too sweet?"

"I don't want to taste that, Mom."

"Trying to watch your figure?" She ran a finger around the edge and tasted, then grimaced. "Is this too sweet? I think it's too sweet."

"What's wrong?" I asked more quietly this time, and this time, she put down the bowl to answer me.

"Leo moved out."

My mom had been with countless men during my lifetime. Some had been boyfriends. Some had been dates. Only a few had been live-ins, and out of all of them, Leo had lasted the longest. I didn't expect to be so surprised he'd gone.

"Why?"

"I asked him to." My mom waved a hand as she dug in the drawer for a rubber spreader.

Above us, the floor creaked as Arty ran around. I looked upward and said, "I'll go."

"Thanks, hon."

Upstairs, I wrangled my brother into the bathroom to brush his teeth, then into bed. I tucked him in tight and gave him half a dozen hugs and just as many kisses. I held him close. Now he smelled like popcorn and little-boy sweat, not candy.

"Go to sleep, monster."

He protested, yawning, that he wasn't tired, but his eyes were already closing as I ducked out the door. I stood in the hall for a few minutes, my own eyes closed. I'd never lived in this house, but it smelled the same as all the places I'd ever lived with my mom. Dust and chocolate brownies and, fainter, below it all, the subtle odor of never-quite-good-enough.

Downstairs, my phone vibrated again in my pocket. I clapped a hand over it to stifle the buzz, which sounded like a fly in a bottle. My mom had iced the brownies and wrapped up half the pan in aluminum foil for me to take along. She didn't mention the phone call, and I didn't try to refuse the food.

She hugged me on the way out the front door, her grip fiercer than usual. "Drive carefully, sweet girl."

My retort to that had been, "No, Mom, I plan on driving recklessly," but tonight I kept those words inside. I hugged her back as hard as she hugged me. She didn't have to be crying for me to know she was upset about Leo. The brownies had told me that.

"I'll call you tomorrow, okay?" I said into her hair, which smelled as always of Apple Pectin Shampoo.

She nodded. When she stepped away her eyes were bright but she smiled. "Sure, honey. Good night."

She stood silhouetted in the doorway until I drove away. By the time I reached the railroad tracks the light on the front porch had gone out. My car *bump-bumped* over the rails, taking me away from the house that hadn't ever been home.

My phone buzzed again as I pulled into the parking lot of the Manor. I flipped it open to read all three messages. All from Austin.

How was the movie?
Say hi to your mom for me.

I had to laugh at that. Oh, that bastard. He knew my mom had always loved him. More than his had ever cared for me.

And finally, Call me when you get home.

Chapter 14

I didn't call Austin when I got home. I didn't call him the next day, or the day after that, and though I tensed every time my phone rang, eventually I stopped worrying. He didn't call me, either.

The notes arrived every few days but never on a day when I might expect one. Only on the days I was convinced I'd be left without instructions, a list, a command. I read each and every one, committing them to memory before tucking them into the slot of 114, a mailbox that had become so familiar to me it was like stroking a lover.

You've done well. Treat yourself to your favorite dessert.

That had been a piece of key lime pie so decadent and rich I'd made sex noises while eating it.

You didn't return your essay in time. Clearly, discipline means nothing to you. Don't waste my time again.

A fit body deserves appropriate clothes. Purchase yourself an appropriate new outfit. Don't skimp on it.

A simple suit, navy blue to match my eyes but with a crisp stripe of summer green at the hem and on the buttons of the jacket. It was the first outfit I'd ever bought I also had altered to fit just right. Wearing it, I felt more than professional, I felt appropriate.

Go to the bookstore. Look at the aisle you don't normally browse. Find a book that looks good and buy it. Read it. Enjoy it.

I'd picked a book on the history of movies, trivia mostly, but also photos of stars from days past. I'd savored the glamour and taken to wearing my hair parted and over one eye like Lana Turner.

For days the notes had arrived in my mailbox, telling me what to eat, what to wear, what time to go to bed and what time to rise. I was a rat following a piper unseen, maybe to the cheese nirvana, maybe to a watery grave in a river. I couldn't tell.

I only knew that I didn't want it to stop.

I want you to be bare for me today, beneath those clothes you bought. I want you to feel the coarseness of denim, the roughness of wool, the sleekness of satin lining, on your bare ass. Every time you move, you're going to think of me and how I own you.

Voices echoed in the lobby and the elevator dinged, but nobody came down the hall to catch me, a thief, taking what I hadn't meant to steal. I pushed the card through the slot and bent to make sure it had gone all the way through. It would be gone when I came home, gone and read by the person for whom it had been meant.

Did she glory in them as much as I?

Did she deserve them, the small rewards of treating herself to a hot bath, a piece of gourmet chocolate, for completing the tasks? Did she force herself to another hour in the gym as punishment when she failed to follow the list exactly?

Or was it only me who looked forward to each day's commands?

Paul had left me another list. Along with the standard "copy the files" and "schedule the appointments" he'd added something interesting. Lunch. He'd underlined it twice. Like I wouldn't remember to eat?

Order from China King for delivery.

He'd added what I should order and in what amount, and what time I should place the call to ensure the food would arrive by the time he and his client returned. As if I couldn't figure all that out for myself.

Order enough for yourself, he'd added. At least he was being generous.

I tried to put the morning's note from my mind, but my thoughts were focused more on the fact I was bare beneath my skirt than anything Paul was having me do. His list was longer this time, more detailed, and while I enjoyed the new responsibilities and projects he'd left for me, I hadn't finished by the time the food came. I'd only just managed to collect it from the front desk downstairs and set it out on the small conference table in Paul's office when he and the woman from marketing showed up. Vivian Darcy. I'd seen her before, a tall woman with blond hair she wore in a sleek twist. She wasn't thin but dressed like she was and managed to carry it off. Her shoes cost more than my rent.

I had my own lunch, chicken and broccoli, to eat at my desk. Paul gave me little more than a glance and closed his door. I heard them laughing behind it. They were in there for a long time. When the door opened again, I'd finished eating and set back to work on the filing I hadn't managed to finish before lunch.

"Paige, bring me the advance proof packet," Paul said from the doorway. He'd loosened his tie and taken off his jacket and rolled up his sleeves. From behind him I heard the flush of water running in his private bathroom.

I nodded as he disappeared into his office, but a moment later my stomach sunk. I hadn't actually finished copying the packet. I'd known I needed to do it, it was part of my regular weekly projects, but it hadn't been on Paul's list. I also didn't want to admit I'd been distracted.

"Paul?"

They both looked up. She had pulled her chair close to his, their heads bent over what looked like a spreadsheet. She'd taken off her suit jacket, too, and her breasts pushed at the front of her silk shirt.

"I'm sorry," I said. "I haven't finished with the copies of that packet. It will take me about fifteen minutes, but I'll do it right now."

I'd been made to feel small before, but I hadn't expected the look both of them gave me. Different looks, neither pleasant. Hers was cutting, an arch of brow to indicate surprise but not too much, as though she'd expected as much from the likes of me. Hers I could deal with.

Paul, on the other hand, looked blank for the span of some

long seconds. Then he looked disappointed. "We need that packet now, Paige."

He didn't need to tell me I'd screwed up. I'd have liked it better if he had. I could have been angry, then, at being scolded. Instead, all I could feel was the vast wash of guilt for knowing I hadn't done what I was supposed to do.

"Ten minutes," I promised.

"No need to jump through hoops," Paul said. "Just get it done."

I did it in seven minutes, though it meant cheating and taking up all three copy machines at the same time. When I handed the packets, properly collated and stapled, one each to her and him, I didn't expect a reward.

I didn't get one. Not even a smile. Not even a terse thank-you. Both of them took the papers and bent back to their work without more than a glance at me, and I slunk out of Paul's office in disgrace.

My mood only lasted another ten minutes. I worked for a paycheck, not approval, and I'd never given him a reason to have any complaint about my work, not even in the first few weeks when I hadn't known what I was doing.

"Paige, can I see you for a minute?" Paul said when Vivian left, finally, at a quarter to five.

"Sure. Of course."

He stepped aside to let me into his office and gestured at the chair that had been returned to the front of his desk. I sat. Paul sat, too, and looked across the desk at me with his hands folded together.

"I wanted to make sure you were doing all right."

This wasn't what I'd expected. "I'm fine, thanks."

"The job's not overwhelming you?"

I had a bad feeling about where this was going. "No…."

"Good." Paul looked down at his hands, now clasped tightly. "Because I'd hate to think you were unable to keep up with the position, Paige."

One mistake in six months, and he was worried I couldn't keep up? I wanted to stand up and walk out, flipping Paul the bird. I might have, had he sounded sarcastic or condescending. He didn't. He sounded…cautious.

"I'm sorry I forgot the packet, Paul. It won't happen again." I knew it wouldn't. I might forget a dozen other tasks, but I wouldn't ever forget to copy the fucking proof packet again.

He still didn't look at me. His voice quiet but not soft, he said, "I hope you won't."

That was it. He nodded at me and I got up, and I went out to my desk to shut it down for the night. My fingers had gone cold and stiff and I mistyped the password I needed to log out three times before I got it right.

> *You will masturbate in the shower, but you will not allow yourself to come. Your orgasm is a reward for good behavior, and you haven't earned it. You will write, on your best paper and with your best ink, how you masturbated and how it felt when you stopped, and you will return it to me no later than tomorrow afternoon.*
>
> *Disobedience will not be tolerated.*
>
> *You said you wanted discipline.*

With shaking fingers and hot cheeks I passed the mailboxes without looking to see if the note I'd shoved into 114 was still there. I'd done what it said. Rubbed myself in the shower that morning until my breath came tight and close and my entire body tensed until I eased off. It had been close. I knew my body too well not to bring myself off within a few minutes. But I'd stopped myself, because unlike the intended recipient of the notes, I did know discipline.

I'd written the letter, too, describing how I'd touched myself with fingers slick with my saliva and tilted my clit against the spray of water until my thighs shook and my breath came hot and hard and fast. How I'd had to turn the water to cold to keep myself from getting dizzy as I rubbed and stroked. I'd used the finest paper in my collection, my favorite pen, and I'd taken such care with each letter, every stroke, that I was almost late for work.

I didn't give anyone the letter, of course. But I couldn't bring myself to throw it away. I put it in my nightstand, instead, tucked into the pages of the book on movie history.

The ache between my legs flared as I shifted the gears of my car, and as I walked, and as I turned in my desk chair to pull files from the drawer.

Paul was not out of the office today, but he hadn't come out yet this morning. Not even for coffee. Him hiding away with his door closed was not unusual, but him not at least calling out to me for a mug was.

Two weeks ago it wouldn't have occurred to me to think he was still angry with me for screwing up the files the day before. Two weeks ago I wouldn't have much cared. Now, I listened hard for the sound of his voice and stared at my computer screen without typing anything.

"Paige." Paul stood in his doorway. I'd been so preoccupied, I hadn't even heard him. "Can you come in here, please?"

I nodded, but was clumsy when I stood. I knocked a pile of folders, so the papers inside slid across my desk in a messy heap. Paul stopped me when I tried to gather them.

"Now, please."

I nodded again and followed him into his office. He didn't tell me to sit, so I didn't. I could tell nothing from the look on his face, which was carefully blank. Over his shoulder, I could see the red numbers of his clock radio, tuned to a station playing soft jazz. I swallowed hard, my nerves on fire.

"I think we need to have an understanding."

I said nothing, not trusting my voice.

Paul cleared his throat and folded his hands together on the desk. He didn't look at me. I couldn't look away.

"I believe I have a reputation for being…difficult. To work for."

"I don't think so." The pulse beat in my throat, forcing my voice to deepen.

He looked at me then, straight in the eye. His hands on the desk tightened inside each other as though he wanted to be holding something else, something precious, but was afraid he might drop it. I lifted my chin and met his gaze.

Without speaking, he unfolded his hands and pushed a piece of paper across the desk to me. Neither of us looked at the paper. We looked at each other.

I didn't look at it when I touched the tips of my fingers to the paper, nor when I pulled it toward me, or when I clasped it in my hand. I didn't look at it until I sat at my desk and laid it down in front of me.

The list.

I sat at my desk and looked at the list. It took up the entire sheet of ruled paper. It was insultingly long and infuriatingly detailed. He hadn't yelled at me yesterday, he'd done this instead, and it was infinitely worse than if he'd called me on the carpet.

It was also infinitely, inexplicably better.

Not only did the paper have the projects he needed me to work on today, but it contained detailed instructions on duties I'd been performing without supervision for months. He'd left out breaks for me to eat and use the bathroom, but every other minute of the day had been accounted for.

In high school I'd had a teacher who didn't like girls. I don't mean he was gay, just that for whatever misogynistic reason, he'd thought females somehow lesser creatures than males. Considering the boys in my class, I thought the man was an idiot, but at sixteen there's not much you can do about it but get through it. This teacher hadn't been impressed by good grades earned through hard work, and I'd had to work very hard for all my good grades. I've already said I wasn't the brain. Even so, I wasn't a bad student, and so when I got an A on my first test and this teacher, this man put in charge of young adults to mold them into something fit for future society, sneered and suggested I'd cheated off the boy next to me in order to have earned that grade, I learned a very important lesson.

No matter how hard you worked, there was always going to be somebody out there who thought you were a fuckup.

Part of me pictured myself storming into Paul's office, tossing the list on his desk and quitting in an outrage, but I knew there was no way I'd ever do it. I needed my job. I wanted it. I could put up with a lot more than a stupid list to keep it.

So instead, I did what I'd done in high school with that dumbass teacher who thought girls couldn't be better than boys.

I worked my ass off. It was a game, that day, going down

that list and completing each task on it. And as the day wore on and I finished item after item, my sense of accomplishment grew. I'd never realized, actually, how much work I accomplished in one day.

I'd never thought to write down everything I did. Looking at it at the end of the day, this job no longer seemed a mindless drone. I'd done something. A lot of somethings, as a matter of fact, and when I took that list into Paul's office with each item boldly checked off and my neat annotations in the margins, there was no hiding my triumph.

"Finished," I said and stepped back, waiting to see what he'd say.

But, unlike my teacher who'd have probably dismissed my efforts with a snide comment, my boss looked over the list, ticking off each item with the point of his pen.

He looked up at me. I'd never noticed how blue his eyes were before. Paul held the paper with both hands.

"Thank you, Paige," he said. "This is exemplary work."

"Thank you," I said graciously.

We did have an understanding, after all.

Chapter 15

Through the mailbox window I could see Alice, one of the women who ran the office. I could also see the thin edge of a folded note card.

I pulled it out with the tips of my fingers and held it by the edges so as not to muss the paper. All I had to do was bend, just a little, and slip it directly into the right box. But of course, I read it first.

You've failed at every task I've set you. Your reward and your punishment are in my hands. If you cannot learn discipline, this will end.

You have one more chance.

Today, between 5:00 and 6:00 p.m., you will visit Sensations. There you will purchase the item that most embarrasses you. You will pay for it with a credit card, so there will be no question that the clerk won't know your name. You will engage the clerk in pleasant conversation, so there is no way he or she will not know your face.

And tonight, you will use that item until you achieve orgasm. You will do this knowing it's not for your pleasure.

It is for mine.

I had to put my hand on the wall and close my eyes after I slid the card through the slot. The brass, cool under my palm, did nothing to steal the heat from my cheeks, my armpits. The inferno between my legs.

I hadn't been the one to fail. I hadn't been late with my essay on discipline. I hadn't even written one.

This note was not for me!

Yet there was no question in my mind I would do as it said. I had written the sexual fantasy. I'd read all the notes. Whoever was meant to find these and follow them, I had done it, too.

Looking back, I understand how much easier it would have been, how much better sense it would have made for me to simply complain at the office about the misdeliveries, to throw the notes away. To knock on the door of 114 with a note in my hand and say, "Make sure these stop coming."

I can't explain why I didn't, except to say, simply, I didn't want to.

I'd moved away from home to get away from my past and my life, and the life I didn't want to have there. I'd taken a new job, found a new apartment, tried to make new friends. I wanted to become someone new, but the truth is, I would never be new.

I would always be me.

Somehow, whoever was sending these notes knew that.

I slapped the note closed. I walked around the corner to the desk. I could see her through the office door and after a second she came out. "Alice? Did you see who put this in my mailbox?"

"Nope." She barely glanced at it. "It's not a religious tract, is it? We have a strict policy about that."

"No, it's not a religious tract." I kept the note close to my body so she wouldn't see the number on the front. "I just wondered if you'd seen who put it in there, that's all."

"No, sorry, hon." Alice flashed me a grin. "What is it, love letter?"

I laughed when heat spread up my throat. "No. Nothing like that."

"Wouldn't be the first time," she said. "Last year at Valentine's we had a bunch of anonymous notes coming and going. The T.A. wanted to ban people from putting notices in the boxes but then they realized if they did that, they couldn't deliver their newsletter, either."

The Tenant Association could be a little overzealous. "Maybe I'll get lucky next time."

"I wouldn't doubt it, hon," Alice said. "This place is a hotbed of lust."

She said it without so much as a blink and I had no reply. Seeing I wasn't going to comment, she gave me a nod and went into the back to finish sorting the mail. I looked down at the note.

I couldn't stop myself from opening the note one last time before I gave it back.

I was still thinking about it as I went outside and faced the sunshine for a moment. I knew I wasn't alone, but I hadn't expected an audience. When I opened my eyes, blinking, I saw Mr. Mystery watching me. He hovered over the sand-filled tube meant for disposing cigarettes, and when he saw me looking he stabbed his out with a furtive smile.

"Caught me," he said.

"And without a net," I replied. Clever.

He laughed and looked with unrestrained longing at the cigarette butts nestled into the sand. "I'm trying to quit."

"Good for you." It was a little surprising for someone as into fitness as he'd seemed in the gym to be a smoker. But appearances weren't everything, and I should know that.

"Eric." The hand he held out engulfed mine as we shook.

My name wasn't a prize, but I offered it like one. "Paige."

Eric shifted on battered hiking boots. Today instead of the long-sleeved T-shirt, he wore a faded black AC/DC shirt under an open plaid button-down minus a few buttons. His hair, long to his collar in the back, ruffled in the wind. A scruff of beard stood out on his cheeks and over his throat. Dark stubble. He looked tired and disheveled, but his hands were clean and his teeth white. The leather bag slouching by his feet wasn't cheap, nor was the watch tangled in the dark hair on his wrist. I noticed things like that.

He yawned, jaw crackingly, and rolled his neck on his shoulders. He looked out at the sunshine, across the street to the river. He looked around with a grin that stopped me in my tracks and held a finger to his lips. "Don't tell on me, huh?"

I laughed. "Your secret is safe with me. But it's a good thing you're quitting. Smoking is bad for you."

He hung his head before peering up at me through the fringe of his dark, shaggy hair. "I know. It's terrible. I started in college and just could never kick it."

"But you are now, right?" I stared down into the butt holder.

Eric chuckled. "Yeah. I'm trying, anyway. Hey, nice officially meeting you, Paige. Maybe I'll catch you later in the gym."

Was that a promise? "Oh, sure. I try to make it in a few times a week. After work."

He yawned again, adding a loud, drawn-out sigh. "Yeah, me too, but I'm just coming off a twelve-hour shift. I'm beat. I might see you, though. We'll work on some reps or something."

"Okay, sure." I managed to sound casual even as the thought of another round of Eric helping me work out sent my heart skipping in my chest.

He looked at the sand, the butts, then pulled a pack of cigarettes from his pocket and held it up. "One left. I should just toss it, right?"

"You should." But I could tell he wasn't going to.

I watched him tug the cigarette from the pack with his lips, crumple the package and toss it. He cupped the match he lit to shield it from the breeze and held it to the end. He drew on it. He took the cigarette from his mouth and licked the end, and I watched him with helpless fascination.

He looked up at me and stopped for a few long seconds before he smiled. "I know. Really bad habit. This is my last one, see? Then I'm done. Kicking it cold turkey."

I wasn't staring to get on his case but because watching his mouth work had been so damn sexy, and I was already feeling weak in the knees. "No. I mean, yes, it is. But it's not my business."

Eric drew in a long, slow breath and let out the smoke. The wind came and whisked it away and he closed his eyes briefly before looking at me again. He looked at the cigarette. "I know it's the best thing for me. I know it is. You ever have anything you keep doing even though you know it's bad for you, Paige?"

"Hell, yeah," I said without a second thought. "More than one thing."

We laughed together. His gaze caught mine. Maybe it was the sunshine reflecting in his eyes or maybe it was my own reflected heat, but I met it full on. He was the first to look away.

"See you," he said.

"I hope so," I told him, and he smiled.

I passed Sensations every day on my way to work. The building, nondescript and set back a bit from the main street, had suffered a fire not too long ago, but apparently the dancing girls and nudie film booths hadn't been damaged, because the parking lot was half full and I watched a stream of men go in and out the door for about fifteen minutes before I went in, myself.

I'd been inside that memorable night with a boy on his knees, and a few other times to buy joke gifts for wedding showers or birthdays. I hadn't been embarrassed then, giggling with my friends or feigning nonchalance while comparing the girth of dildos molded from actual porn stars' cocks. I wouldn't have been embarrassed this time, except the note had told me I should be.

I'd owned a vibrator I rarely used. I had slinky, kinky lingerie I never wore. I even had, someplace, a book of illustrated sexual positions, the corners of the pages folded to show which I'd done.

The clerk behind the counter looked up when I came in. I'd been expecting something different, not a hot, well-built guy with model-pretty features.

Now I was embarrassed.

It was akin to looking down between the stirrups at the gynecologist you were expecting to be fat and balding, someone's dad, and finding Brad Pitt, instead.

"Hi," he said. "Can I help you find something?"

You will find the one thing that embarrasses you the most, and you will use it until you achieve orgasm.

None of the plastic pricks or fur-lined cuffs embarrassed me. Hell, the anal beads and butt plugs had me squeezing my ass cheeks tighter, but they didn't embarrass me.

"Yes," I said. "I'm looking for something special."

He had a nice smile. Fuck. Really nice eyes, too.

"Something special? For a gift? Birthday party, bachelorette party, maybe?" He sounded as if he did this every day. Probably because he did.

"No. For me."

His gaze held mine for a second totally longer than necessary. "Okay. Well, maybe I can help you find what you're looking for."

A beat, a pause, one small breath in and out. A smile. "That would be great. Thanks."

The racks of cheap crotchless panties and feather-trimmed bras were toward the back. Victoria's Secret this was not. Not even Victoria's un-secret. None of these garments looked as though they'd stand up under one wearing, not to mention what would happen to them in the washing machine. I sorted through them anyway, my fingers toying with the hangers and making them clatter on the metal rack.

I held up a flimsy corset printed with a pattern of misaligned roses. My fingers itched touching the fabric, and I could only imagine how awful it would feel against my breasts. I held it up to me, anyway, and turned to the clerk. "How's this look?"

I expected him to say "good." Or maybe "hot." So when he frowned and shook his head, brows furrowed and mouth twisting, my self-assured position as a fairly attractive female in a sex shop plummeted to hit my toes.

"Not for you," he said.

I put it back on the rack and crossed my arms. I wished I'd had the time to change into jeans and a T-shirt after work instead of being stuck in three-inch heels and a skirt to my knees. I wanted pockets to shove my hands into denim to shield me from his assessing gaze. I hadn't dressed this morning for showing off and now he'd made me feel like I shouldn't want to.

Flirting is a funny thing. Earlier, talking with Eric, I'd no doubts I was the hottest bitch around. Right now I wasn't sure I shouldn't be ringing bells in a church tower.

"Come with me." He quirked a finger.

I almost didn't. The look on his face had left me feeling shot down. Embarrassed. And when I realized that's what it was, I nodded and went after him down through the narrow aisles of sleazy underwear and gigantic plastic pricks. Surrounded by a sea of tits, ass, pecs and abs, I tried to keep my eyes on the man in front of me, but I couldn't help comparing the jugs on one box of "Titty Twister, the Party Game!" with the boobs on a package containing a vagina molded from an actual porn star's pink parts.

He glanced over his shoulder as we stopped at the shop's far end. Through a doorway to his right I glimpsed the interior of the nudie bar. Even this early, girls wiggled and writhed on a small stage. Every few seconds a disembodied leg, foot clad in skyscraper heels, sprang into view. There must've been a pole I couldn't see.

"You wanna go check it out?" he asked.

I had been staring, and my cheeks heated, though I couldn't have said exactly why. "No, thanks."

His smile lit up eyes the color of toffee. "You sure?"

"I'm sure." I cleared my throat and gestured at the shelves he stood in front of. "You had something to show me?"

"Oh. Right. Yeah." He reached to pull a box toward him.

I stepped back, gaping, at the box in his palm. Not because it had been festooned with pricks and pussies, but because with its treasure-chest shape and small, hinged lid, it was a smaller version of the box I'd spied in Miriam's shop. It fit neatly in his palm with his fingers open to cradle it. Butterflies patterned the box's red satin.

"You know what this is?"

"No." I shook my head and closed my mouth.

He blinked, watching me closely. Then he crooked his finger for me to lean closer, and I did. I held my breath, waiting as he opened the box. I didn't know what I'd see inside. When I saw the small, stoppered bottle, I looked at him.

"Ancient Chinese secret," he said. "And I'm not talking about laundry detergent."

The bottle had clear plastic sealing it, so it couldn't have been too ancient. I had to squint to read the print and couldn't make out the words, but the picture on the front was a stylized butterfly. That didn't tell me much.

"It's orgasm-enhancement gel. For women. The ladies go crazy for it," he said, as if he was confessing.

An invisible yardstick slid down the back of my shirt. My shoulders came up, and so did my breasts, which finally got more than a disinterested glance from him. He didn't look long, but he did look.

"What's it do?" I asked.

He held out the box to me until I took it. "It helps women who can't come."

"I—" I had nothing to say to that. I tried, but the words stuck in my throat. My back went impossibly straighter, my shoulders squaring. I put my hand on my hip as I tried to hand him back the box.

He wouldn't take it. "You said you wanted something for yourself. You can't tell me you want a crappy piece of lingerie."

"I don't need this!" I shoved the box toward him again. "That's for women who need help!"

Maybe I was primed to be embarrassed. Maybe the idea had already been put into my head that I would find an item, as unbelievable as I could find it, that would embarrass me to buy. Vibrators that could guide missiles and ass plugs with horsetails on them hadn't made me blush, but this small bottle had turned my cheeks to fire.

I looked into his face. "This is for women who can't have orgasms, right?"

He shrugged and wouldn't take the box from my hands. "It's supposed to help."

"Do I…do I look like I need help? With…that?"

I have been checked out and dismissed by women who knew how to cut me down with no more than a glance, but I've never been so thoroughly dissected visually by a guy. Guys look. They find the parts they like and linger there and maybe they turn away if there's not much to hold them, but most often, in my case, they'll look again if for no other reason than I have all the right parts where they're all supposed to go.

This guy looked. And looked some more. He took me in from every inch and then went over them all again. When he settled, finally, on my face, he shrugged again. "Sweetie, fuzzy panties aren't going to get you off. This will."

The "sweetie" gave it away, but guessing he didn't like girls made me feel only marginally better about the fact he thought I looked like a woman who didn't know how to come. I closed my fingers over the box. I lifted my chin and blew out a slow breath that did nothing to cool my cheeks.

"Fine," I said through gritted teeth. "I'll take it."

At the register, he rang me up while he chattered about the dancers on the other side, and how on Monday nights they had "boys," if I was interested. He slipped the box into a plain brown bag and swiped my credit card, peering at my name like he wanted to imprint it on his brain.

I kept my head high, even though my signature skidded on the paper from the shaking of my hands. I was sure he'd question it, but that would've only added to my embarrassment, which was why I was here. Wasn't it?

In the parking lot, I took long, shallow breaths to clear my head. The brown bag, spotted with sweat from my palms, got tossed immediately into the backseat. I put my hands flat on the roof of the car and took another few breaths.

Night had begun to drift over the parking lot while I was inside. I hadn't thought I'd come out in darkness, but spring is tricky that way. You think you have another few minutes in the sun and you end up stubbing your toe because the twilight hides the rough spots on the pavement.

I needed a drink in the worst way, my throat so dry now I could concentrate on it and not my molten face. Sensations sat back from the road, but it wasn't alone in the strip of stores. A small Handi-Mart with a liquor license sold snacks, beer and wine coolers, probably to the patrons of Sensations' dance parlor.

I yanked open the door and heard the bell jangle, my attention focused on the row of refrigerators at the end of the shop. I stepped aside, though, for the woman pushing her way out of the door as I went in. Then I stopped as the door swung in to close in my face, and I pushed it open to call after her.

"Miriam?"

She turned and gave me a broad, white-toothed smile. "Hello, dear. So nice to see you."

I knew she had a life outside of her shop, that she lived in a house. Drove a car. Shopped for wine coolers, too, apparently, and bought gum and cigarettes. Even so, seeing her outside what I thought of as her natural environment stumped me.

"What…hi. Wow, I didn't think I'd run into you."

She smiled again and patted my arm. "Of course not, dear, why would you?"

I laughed. "I don't know."

"Will you be in to the store soon?" She tilted her head to assess me. At her throat she wore a tiger-print scarf tucked into the lapels of her sleek red coat. Damn, I wished I had her style. "I have some lovely new things. And that box is waiting for you."

I thought of the box I'd just purchased and what I was meant to do with it, and my voice went a little faint when I answered her. "Maybe I'll make it in this week."

"Good." She nodded and moved off. She walked slowly but without limping or using a cane, belying her age.

I watched her go for a little, then turned and went inside the store, where I added a six-pack of wine coolers to my bottle of water. I had a date with my hand and a bottle of Cum-Ezee.

Chapter 16

Why had I been embarrassed?

Naked and wet from my shower, I stood in front of my bed and opened the box lid. I pulled out the bottle, peeled off the plastic meant to protect me from God knew what. A glass bottle, it was heavy, and the stopper made of rubber reminded me of a nipple when I squeezed it between my thumb and forefinger.

I squeezed my own nipple with fingers slick from my own saliva. It stood up under my touch. Already my heart had begun beating a little faster, not so much from what I was doing but in anticipation of what I meant to do. I shook the bottle and held it up. Inside, clear liquid shifted, looking oily. It reminded me of those toys I made in elementary school out of plastic soda bottles, oil and colored water. I'd always liked to add glitter to mine.

This had no glitter, just an oily clear liquid that shone when held up to the light. I read the ingredients but could find nothing scary. Hemp oil. Was that even legal? Ginseng. Ginger. All natural ingredients, I thought.

My face flamed again. I didn't have a full-length mirror in

my bedroom, just the mirror on my dresser. From where I stood, only my torso reflected. I had no head. No legs below my upper thighs. I was nothing but my sexual parts.

Breasts. Belly. Ass. Cunt.

You will find the one thing that embarrasses you the most, and you will use it until you achieve orgasm.

Why had I been embarrassed to buy this bottle of liquid from a man who didn't even like women, and therefore shouldn't be blamed for not seeing how fucking sexy I really am? I shook it again and took the stopper out. It looked like a medicine dropper, but without the marks to indicate dosage. I squeezed the rubber nipple again as I pinched my own.

In the mirror, the woman did the same. I held out my fingertip, the dropper poised over it. The liquid, still shining, made a teardrop before it fell onto my skin. I rubbed it in with my thumb and waited. The slickness didn't dissolve and faint warmth filtered through my skin.

Why was I embarrassed to have a stranger think I couldn't have an orgasm? I let another drop fall onto my fingertip. I spread it on my nipples. This time, when I squeezed them, my fingers skipped and slid over my skin. My nipples, hard, now, warmed under the oil and my touch.

Lubricated, my finger slid across my clit like silk on satin. My lips parted. Air eased out. I touched myself again, finger circling, and waited for the heat. It came a second or two later, hotter than it had been on my nipples. I bit my lower lip with a hiss.

It was hard to tell if the oil had aphrodisiac powers or the effect was in my mind, but in the end, did it matter? I lay back on my bed, my legs spread, feet planted firmly on the comforter to make it easier to rock my hips into the seduction of my hand.

I rubbed my clit in slow, smooth circles, just the way I liked it best. The oil absorbed into my skin but left it slick enough I didn't need to add more. I let my fingertips explore the familiar dips and curves of my body, the soft, secret places that could bring me such pleasure.

My clit got hotter as I rubbed, and that seemed only natural, because heat and shame both rode the same bus to school, so far as I was concerned. Sweat pooled in my armpits and salted my upper lip. I licked it away, wishing it were someone else's tongue on my mouth. Another person's hand between my legs.

Why had I cared so much what a stranger thought of me?

I groaned and closed my eyes to push away thoughts of anything but the sensations building in my body. It was easier to pretend that way, to imagine I wasn't alone in my brand-new bed with the clean, new sheets that had never had another body in them. With my eyes closed, the whisper of my hand moving against my skin tugged my ears.

Why did I want so much to follow the commands of a stranger not even meant for me?

The oil slid from my fingertips down my labia and into the crack of my ass. I used my other hand to follow its path. I could probably come from this, in a minute or two, but I stopped, thinking of how it had been such a short time since last I'd done this. It didn't take a genius to figure out I was psyching myself out, losing my orgasm to too much thinking.

Or maybe I really was embarrassed?

She might not be too smart, but she's pretty enough.

One of Stella's friends had said it, not knowing I could hear.

I groaned. I didn't want to be thinking about my father's wife and her friends when I was trying to get off. Yet the hotter the oil on my clit got, the less interested I became in finishing what I'd started. I stopped trying.

She might not be too smart, but she's pretty enough. Just like her mother.

They'd laughed, but not as though they found the subject really funny. More like it embarrassed them. As a kid I hadn't understood why, exactly, just that it had made my stomach hurt to know Stella thought I wasn't smart, even if I was my mother's pretty daughter. As an adult, I figured it out. It embarrassed Stella to admit she'd married a man who'd been so swayed by some tart, he'd knocked her up and then had the compassion to make the bastard child a part of his life. Sort of.

To them, I wasn't Paige. I was some slut's daughter. Thinking of that, I understood something else, too.

I wasn't embarrassed by the fact a man I didn't know or like, a gay dude, for that matter, didn't want to jump my bones. No. What had been most embarrassing was not that he didn't want to fuck me, but that he'd believed I was something I wasn't.

I licked my mouth, tasted the salt of my sweat. I listened to the sound of my breathing still coming fast. I rolled to get the tiny bottle from under my ribs and tossed it into the trash can by my bed, and then I tucked my legs up toward my chest with my extra pillow in my arms, hugging the lover who wasn't there.

The notes started coming more frequently. Every morning before I left for work, or sometimes when I came home, there was another sleek card telling me how to go about my day. Sometimes the list was short, a sentence or two.

Listen to your favorite radio station today. Sing out loud.

Sometimes the instructions were lengthier. More demanding.

At eleven-thirty today you will stop what you are doing and focus on one thing in your life that makes you happy. For thirty seconds you will do nothing but appreciate this reason for joy.

I'd spent the entire morning waiting for eleven-thirty to arrive, half-afraid I'd forget and half-defiant, imagining I'd refuse when the time came to follow the instructions. I did, of course, helpless to resist in the same way someone who's told not to think of the pink elephant can do nothing else.

If there is someone in your life whom you've hurt, you must make a true apology.

That one had been easy enough. I hadn't seen Kira in weeks and arranged to meet her after work for coffee in Hershey, halfway between Harrisburg and Lebanon. She wasn't quite ready to forgive me.

"But can you blame me?" I asked over steaming mocha lattes. "I mean…Kira…it's Jack."

"Jack Rabbit," she said. "Yes. I know."

I raised a brow. "I'm sorry. It wasn't when you were even close to being with him."

She sighed, then, and shrugged. "I know. I guess I'm just pissed you got him and I didn't. But then, so what else is new?"

That wasn't exactly what I'd expected to hear. "Huh?"

She pretended to be very interested in her new beige manicure. "Just like every guy I ever liked, right?"

"What are you talking about?"

She leveled a look at me. "Austin?"

"What about him?"

Kira just stared, then looked away.

I had to laugh. I really did. "You tried to get with Austin? But you were mad at me for fooling around with Jack? What a hypocrite!"

Her eyes flashed. "You knew how I felt about Jack! It was different with Austin."

"How was it different?" I finished my coffee and picked up my purse to go, not because I was furious but because as I'd said not so long before to the very man we were discussing, that cake was baked.

"You left him! You didn't love him anymore." Kira grabbed up her own purse, too, glaring. "Not that it mattered."

"He turned you down, huh?"

Her expression was enough of a reply.

"That's why you were pissed off, isn't it? Not because I messed around with Jack, but because you tried to get together with Austin and he turned you down."

"He turned me down because he still wanted you," Kira said.

I didn't have an answer to that.

"And then you went and screwed around with him again anyway."

"Kira. I didn't know you wanted Austin."

But she couldn't have him, I thought, suddenly and surprisingly. Because he was mine.

"Whatever. Does it matter?" She slung her purse over her shoulder. "We shouldn't let boys come between us anyway, right?"

I didn't tell her the reason I'd apologized had nothing to do with our bond of friendship, which had been strained in times past. Sometimes you stay friends with someone more out of habit than anything you have in common. If not for the note, I might not have called her again at all.

"Right," I agreed.

"So, what's going on with you? You getting back together, or what?"

"Oh, God, no."

We walked to our cars, parked next to one another in the lot. I looked past her to the sidewalks overrun with shoppers attacking the outlets in search of bargains. When I was younger my mom had taken me to the real outlet stores, places that sold seconds and out-of-stock items. These stores weren't anything like that.

"Anyway. I think Tony's gonna give me a ring." She said this with less coyness than I was used to from her. "For my birthday. I thought maybe he'd get me one for Christmas, but…"

It seemed suddenly outrageous and unlikely to me that Kira could get married. "You want to marry him?" I hadn't even met him.

She gave me a level look. "Yeah. I think I do. I'm not getting any younger, you know."

It was such a cliché and yet fit her so well.

"Marriage isn't everything, Kira." I was trying to make her feel better, but she fixed me with another steady look.

"Easy for you to say, sure. Because you gave it up."

"That's not why. That's not what I meant," I added. "I just meant you shouldn't feel like something is missing. That's all."

"But something is. Hey, maybe you'll be my bridesmaid," Kira offered.

"Sure. Okay."

We parted with half a hug and brush of cheeks. I wondered if she'd really ask me. I wondered if I'd care if she didn't. I drove home, glad I wasn't her. Glad I wasn't missing something.

But I was missing something in my life, and those notes, those lists, gave me something I needed. One waited for me when I got back. My fingers shook a little as I opened it. What next? I wondered. What fantasy would I be asked to live out this time? I already imagined the paper and pen I'd use to write it, this time. This time I would write it.

Tomorrow you will wear a blue shirt.

That was it.

I think I bared my teeth before composing myself quickly. If someone was watching, I wasn't going to give him the pleasure of seeing my disappointment.

Tomorrow you will wear a blue shirt.

"Tomorrow," I muttered as I shoved the card through the slot of 114, "I'll wear whatever color shirt I damn well please."

I refused to think of it all the way up the four flights of stairs to my apartment, then all the way down again as I hit the basement for an hour's workout. I refused to think about the note and its simple, one-sentence instruction as I sweated and cursed at the television and its bounty of buxom, slim-hipped beauties on their mission to make all other women feel inferior. I refused to think of it in the shower as I lathered my body and deep-conditioned my hair and shaved my legs.

"Damn it!" I cried to my empty room as I stood in front of my closet.

I had no clean blue shirts.

I put on a soft pair of sleep pants patterned with grinning monkeys wearing Santa hats and twisted my hair up high, clipping it out of the way so it would be wavy when it dried. I turned the TV on, then off. I picked up a book and put it down.

"Shit."

I lay on my bed, arms crossed behind my head, and stared at the ceiling. The plaster had been laid in small, even swirls. There was a medallion with a metal cap in the middle in the ceiling's center. The former tenant had taken the ceiling light and fan when he left, and though maintenance was supposed to replace the original fixture, they never had. The metal reflected light from my bedside lamp and the window outside when the room was dark. Sometimes when I woke in the night I imagined it was the moon's bright eye somehow transported into my room. Watching me.

Was someone else watching me? Playing some sort of game? I got up on one elbow to look around my room and at my closet, where rows of shirts hung in every color but blue.

I got out of bed and riffled through my laundry basket to see what I could find. Blue wasn't my favorite color. I preferred white shirts for work, since any stains could be bleached. I did have a blue shirt, though it wasn't one I would've worn to work. The neckline dipped a little too low and the cut was a little too close. I held it up in front of my reflection and turned this way and that. Paired with a pair of black dress slacks, it would probably be okay. With a blazer over it. Sure.

And I needed to do laundry anyway, I told myself as I tossed socks and panties and towels into the basket to make a full load. If I did it now, I wouldn't have to do it later in the week. And there was nothing on the tube.

Yeah.

There was no getting around it. I was hooked on those lists. For whatever reason. Even if nobody was watching me. But if someone was, he'd know I hadn't obeyed.

Tomorrow, I would wear a blue shirt.

But first, I had to wash it.

Chapter 17

Riverview Manor had the highest line of efficiency washers and dryers, but never enough of them. Just another of the quirks of this supposedly high-end building, and one about which the T.A. had sent around many memos. Some of the units were supposed to have their own washers and dryers, which explained why the laundry room had been understocked. Whatever. All I knew was when I walked in with my laundry basket and found the room empty but for the scent of fabric softener and the hum of rotating dryer drums, it was a bonus.

I filled a washer with my clothes and the detergent, then took my empty basket and my book, one I'd found in an aisle I rarely browsed, to one of the hard wooden chairs along the wall. I promptly let out a small shriek as I realized I was not alone, after all. The man sitting there had his head bent, headphones on, so he hadn't heard my scream but the way I jumped must have caught his attention, because he looked up.

Eric looked up at me with a smile and slipped his headphones from his ears. I heard the tinny, faraway chant of a song I'd have known if I'd been able to pay attention to it, rather than him. His eyes, specifically, which were a deep, dark liquid brown.

"Hi," he said. "Sorry, did I scare you?"

"I didn't see you behind the washers." I set down my basket and put a hand over my rapidly beating heart.

"Yeah, the layout's not so great in here." He looked around, then shifted the papers off the chair next to him. "Sorry, though. You want to sit?"

I took the chair two spots away from his and pushed my basket to the side with my foot. He still smiled at me, so I smiled back. "Thanks."

"Fancy meeting you here," he said.

"Here, there. Everywhere." I tapped a finger against my chin, feigning thoughtfulness. "Are you stalking me?"

To my delight, his cheeks pinked. Just a little. But enough. "It would seem like that, huh?"

I shook my head and bent to pull a handful of laundry from my basket. "Missed you around the gym lately."

I looked up and caught a flash of something in his gaze. Guilt, maybe, though why Eric should care if I kept track of his workouts, I didn't know. He shrugged and ran a hand over his shaggy hair.

I stuffed a load of whites into the nearest washer as we spoke. I was conscious of my panties and bras among my T-shirts and blouses, but I didn't draw attention to them by blushing, even when I caught him looking.

Eric had a smile as slow and easy as honey dripping from a spoon. I wanted to lick it the same way. "Did you? Damn. I'm sorry."

We looked at each other, surrounded by the scent of fabric softener and moist, hot air.

"Were you…looking for me?" Eric asked. "For any reason in particular, I mean?"

Heat flushed my cheeks, and I answered with laughter and a duck of my head. Eric laughed, too, after a second. His voice joined mine like a duet, and when I looked up at him, his deep brown eyes were shining with good humor and undisguised interest.

"Were you?"

"Yes," I admitted. "It's not quite the same without you there."

"Sorry. Work's been insane."

I stuffed my quarters in the slot and dumped half a cup of detergent, then started the cycle. "What do you do, exactly?"

Eric leaned back in his chair. "I'm an E.R. doc."

Bing, bing, bing! We have a winner! Hot, funny *and* a doctor. My mother would be so proud.

"What's that like?"

He looked a little surprised. "Busy. But exciting."

"Saving lives and all that? Lots of pressure," I said, watching his mouth form the words as he spoke.

"Yeah," Eric said after a second or two of silence. A shadow passed over his face, but only briefly. "Lots of pressure. What do you do, Paige?"

I told him without making it sound as if I was at all ashamed of not being a doctor. If Eric wasn't as impressed with my career as I with his, his eyes didn't give it away. Neither did his mouth, which held on to his smile.

The conversation flowed as we washed, dried and folded our clothes.

"I bet that color looks great on you." He pointed at the blue shirt I'd pulled from the dryer.

I held it up in front of me. “You think so?”

“Yes. It matches your eyes.”

I’m hardly ever at a loss for words, but this time I only managed to swallow, hard, and say, “Thanks.”

He scrubbed the back of his neck with a hand and looked utterly endearing. “Too much?”

“No. I’d be a liar if I said I don’t like compliments.” To save myself from having to look at him just then, I bent to pull more laundry from the dryer.

“And you’re not a liar?”

Over my shoulder, I said, “No. What about you?”

I’d meant it lightheartedly, the way the entire conversation had been going. So when Eric didn’t answer, I straightened and turned to face him. The look on his face stopped me from speaking.

“I know where it was.” He snapped his fingers. “Where I saw you for the first time. It wasn’t the gym.”

I drew in a breath. My hands, full of warm, soft laundry, tightened. My tongue slid along my lips as I considered what to say. “No. It was the Mocha.”

“No. That’s not it. Have we ever met in the Mocha?” He laughed and covered his eyes with his hands for a second before looking at me again. “I’m sorry. I meet so many people, sometimes I forget where I met them. But believe me, I wish I did remember seeing you there.”

“We didn’t actually meet. I just saw you. You were sitting by the window, writing something. Very serious. You wouldn’t have noticed me, anyway. You were busy.”

“I should’ve noticed you, Paige.” His smile let me know exactly what he meant by that.

I laughed again. “But you didn’t. Because you meet *soooooo* many people. So. If it wasn't the Mocha, or outside by the smoking station—"

Again, that flash of something furtive and guilty in his gaze.

"And it wasn't the gym," I continued as though I hadn't seen it. "Where was it?"

His dark eyes gleamed again. "Outside the Speckled Toad."

My mouth opened, but I had nothing to say.

He snapped his fingers again and crowed, laughing. "Yes! I'm right, right? That's where it was? I knew you looked familiar!"

"I love that place." With my laundry in my hands, there was no chance I was going to leap into his arms, so I kept it there.

"Me, too." Eric's smile softened as he looked over my face. He seemed to be studying me harder this time. He nodded after a moment. "Yes. That's definitely it. A few weeks ago, right? You were going in and—"

"You were going out. Yes." I pretended to just remember now. "I guess that's why when I saw you in the Mocha I noticed you. You looked familiar."

It sounded like a much better story, said that way, and Eric's grin stretched wider. "Uh-huh. Wow. Small world, huh?"

"Infinitely."

I wanted to kiss him. I wanted him to kiss me. Instead, I bent to finish pulling the rest of the clothes from the dryer and into my basket. He was still staring when I stood, my basket in my hands.

"What are you doing after you're done with your laundry?"

"I thought I'd read my book…" I glanced at the clock on the wall, then back at him. "I have to work tomorrow. Why?"

"I was going to watch a movie. *Monty Python and the Holy Grail*. Have you seen it?"

"No." I drew the word out, slow, not wanting to jump to conclusions.

"Would you like to?"

I pretended to think about it, though inside I was already screaming out the YESYESYES of Sally's deli orgasm in *When Harry Met Sally.* "Are you asking me to watch it with you?"

"I am." He spread his hands at his sides. "How about it?"

"Sure. Why not? Just let me put this stuff away and I'll come over."

"Great!" He flashed straight, white teeth and all I could think about was how they'd feel denting my flesh. "Half an hour, then? Forty minutes?"

"Sounds good."

"I'm in one-fourteen," Eric said.

I dropped my basket.

Chapter 18

"Are you all right?" Eric had already gone to one knee to gather my scattered clothes while I did nothing but gape.

The world made one slow revolution as everything changed.

I recovered well, or at least well enough to keep him from checking my pulse and offering me CPR. I watched his strong, big hands slide along my clothes and put them back in the basket, and I didn't move. When he stood to hand me the basket, I took it.

"Fine." I sounded fine. I even managed a smile. I white-knuckle-clutched the laundry basket and kept my eyes pinned on his. "Let me just run this home and I'll meet you at your place, okay?"

We rode the elevator together, not in silence, though looking back it's impossible for me to remember what we talked about. I remember his voice, low and rich, and the sound of his chuckle when I made some small joke. I remember the sound of machinery whirring as we lifted and the way the cool breeze blew against my face when the door opened on his floor. I can recall the gleam in his eyes when he glanced over his shoulder, and the half wave he gave me as the door closed. But I can't remember what we said.

In my apartment I set my basket on the bed and pulled open the door on my nightstand. From inside I took the folded paper on which I'd written my most erotic memory, and the bottle of Cum-Ezee I'd retrieved from the trash before I emptied it. Without the notes and their commands, I wouldn't have either one of them. I looked around my bedroom, at the new clothes in the closet, at the books on the shelf. At the new me I'd become because of those letters.

None of them meant for me.

All of them for him.

The sound of my laughter stung my ears and I closed my mouth tight to keep it from escaping again. I looked at the jumbled mess of laundry in my basket and thought of Eric on his knees, picking it up. My heart thumped a little faster and my throat got a little drier.

All this time I'd imagined the intended recipient of the letters to be a woman. Not me but like me, at least. To discover they were meant for a man… I shook my head, my hair falling forward from the clip. I closed my eyes and pressed a fist to my lips. They'd been meant for a man. Did that mean the writer of the notes was…a woman?

God, that was so fucking hot I couldn't stand it.

My cunt bloomed molten heat and the seam of my jeans pressed suddenly on my clit as I let myself fall back on the bed. My nipples tightened, begging for a mouth and hands on them. I took my hand from my mouth and let it roam my body, though they did little to ease the sudden fire.

Minutes ticked by as I ran through the lists and pictured Eric performing the tasks I'd found so arousing. What memory had taken him so long to write he'd returned it late? What had he bought at the store that had embarrassed him? I thought of his basket, his laundry, and the blue shirt there.

I sat, my hair askew and clinging to my forehead in places. Sweating, I pulled off my shirt and jeans and ran the shower cold enough to make me hiss as I got in and rinsed off quickly. New panties, new bra, not so fancy as though it would look as if I was trying too hard should my clothes happen to come off. A fresh T-shirt, sleek-fitting, soft and flattering. My favorite jeans, the ones that gave me a round ass but kept my gut tucked up tight. The gut I didn't really have any longer, I had to admit as I checked out my reflection. Courtesy of those lists, I'd been working out more diligently than I ever had.

I swiped a brush through my hair and slid clear gloss over my lips. A dusting of powder finished me off without making it look as though I'd tried too hard. I grabbed a couple of packages of microwave popcorn and a big bowl from my cupboard, slipped my feet into a pair of flip-flops and tucked my key into my pocket.

My phone buzzed as I debated taking it with me. Now Austin called me? After so long silent? I put the phone on the table, flipped it the bird and locked my door behind me.

Eric hadn't changed his clothes, but I spied telltale wetness in his hair that told me he'd at least washed his face. Minty-fresh breath gave away the fact he'd brushed his teeth, too, and I hid a grin as he let me in. I hadn't been the only one assuming there might be more to this than watching a movie.

I did brace myself as I stepped inside his apartment, but on first glance I didn't see anything freaky. He gave me a quick tour. Living room, kitchen. His was a two-bedroom unit, and he used one for an office complete with shiny new iMac that had me salivating with envy. He didn't take me into his bedroom, but I caught a glimpse through the open door. His window overlooked the parking garage, same as mine, but he was closer to it.

I'd been half expecting a St. Andrews Cross in the living room. I think I was a little disappointed. Eric did have a lot of leather, but in the form of a modern black-and-chrome sofa and chairs arranged in front of a flat-screen television hooked up to a bunch of high-end equipment.

"You have a Wii. Sweet."

"Ever played?" Typical male, proud to show off his toys, Eric grinned and headed for the TV.

"Sure. Not for a while, though."

"Want to try a game of tennis? I know it's not the latest and greatest, but it's still fun." He held up the controller.

That's how we ended up playing video games instead of canoodling on the couch under a blanket, hoping our hands met in the popcorn bowl. Eric had a wicked backhand, and yet he let me win. We laughed a lot as we played, sharing the sort of random conversation that lets you get to know someone without treading into territory too intimate for a first date.

If that was what this was. I had my doubts. Brushed teeth aside, Eric didn't seem to have any intentions about putting any moves on me, if he ever had. It had been a long time since I read a guy wrong, but it wasn't impossible. When at last we collapsed together onto his slippery leather couch, Eric's smile didn't give me any clues one way or the other.

I was flummoxed, to say the least, my confidence shaken. I remembered the trip to Sensations, and how the clerk had set me back. I didn't get a gay vibe from Eric, and in any case, if he liked boys, why had he invited me over in the first place? No. Something was most definitely up and unfortunately for me it didn't seem to be his cock.

I excused myself to use his bathroom. And yes, I looked in his medicine cabinet. Anyone who says they've never done it is a liar or forgot to add the "yet" to the end of that sentence. I found shaving gel, ibuprofen, Tom's Natural Toothpaste and a jumbo box of condoms. In the cabinet beneath the sink I found toilet paper, extra towels and a few scant cleaning supplies. Like the rest of his apartment, Eric's bathroom was apparently kink free.

I shouldn't have been so surprised. After all, my own place wasn't decorated in early-medieval dungeon, either. And there had never been anything in any of the notes or lists to indicate he was into hard-core bondage or pain play, unless I'd been so focused on getting my own rocks off I hadn't read between the lines. Who knew what those notes had meant to him?

I had to find out.

He'd put the movie in the DVD player and was popping the corn in by the time I came out. "It's not too late, is it?" He gestured at the clock. "We kind of got carried away with the game. Sorry."

He shot me a sincere and slightly abashed grin. I wanted to pet him. I wanted to sit extraclose and whisper naughty words into his ear to make him blush. I wanted, I realized only a bit uneasily, to see him on his knees again.

"No. It's fine. Anyway, I'm in the mood for a movie."

"Great! Thanks for bringing the popcorn." Eric hopped over the back of the couch in a fluid motion and headed into the kitchen. "What can I get you to drink? Soda? Beer?"

"Soda's fine." I watched him pull the bag from the microwave and empty it into the bowl and grab two cans of Coke from the fridge.

"Coke okay?"

I'd never been with a man so solicitous. "Sure. Yes."

"A glass? Ice? I could slice up a lemon for you."

I broke down and laughed. "I could just drink it from the can."

"If that's what you like." Eric smiled after a minute, cans held high. "Saves me washing the glasses."

He brought the drinks and popcorn but waited until I sat before he did, too. I thought of Austin, who'd have been yelling from his place on the couch, feet up, to bring him a beer. This was a nice change, no doubt about it, even if it did leave me feeling more than a little off balance.

"Be right back." Eric hopped up and disappeared into the bathroom.

I took the chance to look around. He had framed photos on the end table and on the brick-and-board bookshelves that looked as if he'd made them himself but that probably came from Ikea. He was in a lot of the pictures, his arm slung around the shoulders of his companions. He'd done a lot of traveling it looked like from the backgrounds of his collection. I spotted the blue oceans of the Caribbean, Hawaii's lush greenery. In one he wore the whites of a cruise-ship crew-member and was sitting at the captain's table. Ship's doc, maybe.

It didn't look as if he had a girlfriend. Or a boyfriend. None of the people in the pictures were standing close enough or giving him goo-goo eyes. Eric was a puzzle, no question. But at least I could be fairly sure he was single.

"Ready?" If my perusal of his pictures annoyed him, he didn't show it.

I sat on the couch again, popcorn bowl balanced on my knees. "Sure."

There's nothing potentially embarrassing about *Monty Python and the Holy Grail.* Even the tiny reference to oral sex isn't really sexy. I'd seen the film half a dozen times but never in its entirety and never completely sober. And yet I had a hard time concentrating. Eric stretched out long legs next to mine. He had a deep, infectiously sexy laugh I couldn't help echoing even if the movie itself hadn't been hilarious.

It didn't last long enough. I'd forgotten the abrupt end. When he leaned forward to use the remote to click off the TV, a thin stripe of skin bared between his shirt and jeans, tempting me to run my fingers over it. I resisted…but only barely.

He caught me looking when he turned. "One of my favorites. Sometimes after a long day in the E.R., all I can think about is coming home and watching something stupid."

"I can imagine so. Sometimes after a long day at work I can't manage anything other than stupid." I grinned in sympathy. "And I'm not saving lives."

Eric's handsome face went still for a minute. "It's not the saving them that's the problem. It's when I can't. Sorry, that's a bummer."

"No, it's okay. There must be a lot of pressure." I watched him look away from me.

When he turned back it was with another smile, less convincing than his others. "Yeah. Well. I did a couple rotations on terminal wards. Pediatrics, too. That was worse, believe me. A lot worse. At least most of what I see is fixable. A few stitches, a cast, give out a script for meds. I'd rather face a roomful of broken bones and bloody noses than a terminal ward again."

"I can't even handle being sick myself, much less take care of anyone else." I shuddered involuntarily.

Eric dug into the popcorn bowl to scoop out a couple unpopped kernels, which he crunched. "Funny thing. When I was a kid, I was sick all the time. At least it felt like I was. Constant colds. Probably allergies, now that I think about it, but at the time, all we knew was that I always had a runny nose. I was the kid who always looked like he'd been squashed in the face with something nasty."

"Nice to see you outgrew it."

His smile quirked higher on one side, charming me. "Yeah. So anyway, I got older and decided I wanted to become a doctor, right? And my mom, you'd think she'd be happy to have her son the doctor, but all she said to me was, 'But, Eric, think of the germs!'"

"It's a good thought." I looked at the bowl of popcorn we'd shared and tried not to wonder if he'd washed his hands after work.

"But I haven't been sick in years. Nothing more than a mild cold or two. I think I immunized myself to everything when I was a kid, so I can't get anything now. In med school they called me Iron Man because no matter what we faced, stomach bugs, coughs, colds, flu…whatever it was, they usually got it and I never did."

"Wow. Lucky you."

He swirled those long fingers through the crumbs again, bringing them out covered with buttery salt. He licked them one by one as I watched. If I'd thought he was doing it on purpose to tempt me I'd have been annoyed, but Eric didn't seem to have any awareness about how he looked. Or of how my mind went at once to that dirty place.

"Yeah. Pretty amazing." He held out the bowl. "Want some more?"

I shook my head. "That's interesting, though. Why you decided to become a doctor. Was it everything you thought it would be?"

"It's not like I dreamed it would be. No," Eric said flatly.

I waited for more. It seemed there must be more, but no. His gaze went to the bowl in his lap. He swirled again through the popcorn and licked the tips of his fingers. He put the bowl back on the coffee table and looked up at me.

"It's an incredible amount of responsibility. It's a lot to handle, you know?"

I didn't, really. Not the way he meant. I thought of my own job and the lists from Paul, and how there really wasn't anything I had to be accountable for there. How I had nothing in my life I needed to take care of. How I never had. Even when I was married, what had I ever done but taken care of myself?

"But Monty Python makes it better?"

Eric laughed and ducked his head again for a moment before looking back at me. "I'm glad you liked it."

"It's a classic. What's not to like?"

Eric shrugged and leaned back against the couch, one arm stretched out along the back. His fingers could have touched my shoulder if he'd stretched half an inch more. Neither of us moved.

"Some of the women I've known…most of them, actually, don't get Monty Python. Don't like it." He shook his head. "So when you said you loved it, I wasn't sure you meant it."

I studied him. Many things had brought us to this point. Too many to discount as coincidence or chance. There was a reason I was here, I believed it in my gut.

"You thought maybe I was lying?" I didn't ease myself closer to him, but I turned my body in his direction. "Why would I do that?"

He laughed, self-conscious, and scrubbed the back of his head with a hand. "I'm not saying you're lying, no. Just that maybe you were—"

"Lying." I laughed. "To impress you, maybe?"

Eric ducked his head but shot me a glance. "Something like that. I don't know."

Today you will know you are strong and beautiful.

Advice meant for him, but I'd taken it, too. The difference was, I knew something of what he'd been doing and living the past few weeks, and he had no clue about me.

There was such power in that.

"You have an awfully high opinion of yourself, Eric." My voice came out different. Lower and sultry. It was the voice of a woman who had never believed she was anything but strong and beautiful, and I saw how he heard it.

He sat up straighter. It was subtle, but I noticed. "You're right. I shouldn't have assumed."

I wasn't sure what I saw in Eric's eyes, only that I wasn't ready for it. I made it different with a laugh and a pat to his arm. "It's okay. I'm just teasing you."

"Right." He laughed, too, but I glimpsed something like disappointment on his face, so brief I couldn't be sure it had been there.

I made a show of looking at the clock and getting up. "This was great, but it really is getting late."

He was up, too, seconds after me. "Right. Yes."

He walked me to the door, all prim-and-proper-like, and there I stopped and turned to face him. "Thanks for inviting me."

Now would have been a good time to kiss me, but he didn't do it. I didn't lean to kiss him, either, though I could have. I wanted to. I didn't believe for one second he'd turn me down. And I didn't choke, either, dithering at the last second about what he might think of me or whether he'd call me the next day if I gave it up to him tonight.

I didn't kiss him because I had the power to decide which way this went. Hours before I'd lain on my bed and touched myself, thinking it might be his hands. I thought of doing that now, when I went upstairs. How I'd undress myself and make myself come pretending it was his fingers and mouth on my tits and clit, my cunt and ass. Or maybe I'd think of Austin.

Hell, maybe I'd think of Brad Pitt.

I didn't kiss Eric because he was waiting for me to do it. I saw it in his eyes and the part of his lips, the cock of his hip as he leaned against the doorway with one hand up high and the other hooked in his belt loop. He wanted me to kiss him, but I knew about him what he didn't know about me.

I knew he wanted to be told what to do.

"Good night, Eric," I said.

And I didn't give him what he wanted.

Chapter 19

There was an actual voice-mail message waiting for me on my cell when I got home.

"Paige. It's me. I'm bored. Why don't you come over? Call me."

The call had come in only ten minutes ago, and I wasn't sure if I wanted to laugh or curse at Austin. It was after 10:00 p.m. on a work night.

"Your booty-call skills need improving," I said before he could do more than say hello.

"I knew you'd call."

"You know shit, Austin."

"What were you doing?" He sounded sleepy, and I hoped I'd woken him.

"I was on a date." It was only half a lie. It hadn't been an official date, but it had been with another man. It would infuriate him to hear it. He didn't have to know we hadn't even kissed.

"Couldn't have been a very good date if you're home already."

He had a point. "How do you know I'm home? Maybe I'm just only now answering my phone."

"Couldn't be a very good date if you're talking to me."

He had another point, but I wasn't going to concede it. "Why do you want me to come over? It's late."

"Is it?" He yawned. "I hadn't noticed. Anyway, you're still awake. And I'm up. Come over."

"I'm not coming over."

"You're not hanging up, either."

I gave him enough silence to make him think otherwise, but damn him, Austin knew me too well. He'd discovered patience, it seemed, whereas I'd lost mine. "If you were really that interested, you should've called me before now."

"I was giving you your space."

Phone clamped to my ear, I was halfway to my bedroom when his words brought me up short. He sounded sincere, and it killed me that without being able to read his face, I couldn't tell if he was putting me on. "How very Lifetime Channel of you."

"What are you wearing?"

"How very Playboy Channel," I said, and my breath hitched.

By the time I reached my bed I was already unbuttoning my jeans. When I lay back I cradled the phone against my shoulder to slide the denim over my hips. My panties came down, too, and I kicked them off. The comforter was chilly under my skin at first, but warmed quickly. I rolled, reaching for my nightstand drawer, and stopped with my hand on the knob.

"Are you naked? Tell me you're naked."

I found the small bottle of lube and my bullet vibrator, not the one that could land aircraft. I sat on the edge of the bed to pull them from the drawer, and I stared down at the evidence of what I meant to do in my palm before I answered. "I'm not naked."

"Liar." Austin's low laugh perked my nipples and parted my legs.

"I have a shirt on."

"I'm hard, Paige. And I'm naked."

I closed my eyes to see him better. "What makes you think I care?"

This stumped him for a second. In the past I'd been all about the phone sex. Sometimes we'd fucked more often on the phone than with our bodies. Before he could answer, I said, "Are you jerking your cock, Austin?"

"Y-yeah."

"Well. I want you to stop."

"Aw, Paige—"

"You can't just call me up and expect me to run right over and screw you, Austin. And you can't expect me to fuck you over the phone, either," I said, though I was thinking about doing just that. "We're not together anymore. Remember?"

"That never mattered before." He sounded sullen, and I pictured his frown.

I loved it.

"It matters now." He had to hear my voice dip low and breathy, and he knew me well enough to know what that meant. I just had to wait and see if he'd figure it out.

"Fine. I'm sitting here with my dick ready to go and I'm not touching it. Is that what you want to hear?"

I lay back again and twisted the end of the vibe to get it buzzing. Then I brought it to the phone and let him hear it. I took it away after a second.

"Shit. Is that your vibrator?"

"It is."

"Let me come over, baby. I can make you feel better than a vibrator."

"I'm hanging up on you now. And then I'm going to use this vibrator until I come. But you're not."

"Well...fuck," he said miserably.

"No." I laughed.

"What the hell am I supposed to do?"

I let the vibe tickle-tickle between my legs, then pulled it away to stroke with a finger, which I preferred over the mechanical. "You're going to take a cold shower and go to bed."

"What if I don't? What if just finish myself off right now?"

A low, slow groan seeped from my lips. "You'll do what I just told you to do, and maybe, just maybe, the next time you call me I'll let you come over and eat my pussy until I scream."

Dead silence greeted this. My eyes, which had been languorously closed, flew open. Too far?

"Uh..." Austin coughed. "Fucking hell, Paige!"

Apparently not.

"Good night, Austin," I said sweetly. "I'm going to get back to getting myself off now. Have a nice shower."

"Paige, don't hang up!"

But I did, because I could. Because there was power in that, too. And then I lay back and looked at the ceiling, my vibe still abuzz in my fingers, and thought of Austin. And Eric. And then some nameless, faceless stranger who would do everything I wanted him to do without talking it to death first or ruining it after with words.

My hands became his hands, running over my shirt and under to cup my breasts through the bra. Then under that to stroke and tweak my nipples. The vibe buzzed lower as I adjusted the setting and slid it between my legs, where I kept it clamped close to me by closing my thighs. I only wanted a tickle there, not a full-on buzz.

I'd used this vibe at the command of a note. I'd set it at the low speed and rubbed it on my clit and down over my lips. I'd rubbed it on my nipples, too. I'd brought myself close and eased off, then close again, but obeying the note, I hadn't made myself come.

What had Eric done?

Had he spread his legs in the shower, leaning forward with a hand against the wall while the other pumped his prick slowly? Did he bend his head beneath the spray, eyes closed, picturing some nameless, faceless woman on her knees sucking his cock? Or maybe she had a name. Had a face. Maybe he had someone who made him crazy the way Austin made me.

Or maybe he'd lain back on his bed the way I was, his hips thrusting upward into the cunt made of his curled fist. Maybe he'd spit into his palm to ease the way, or squirted a handful of lube. Maybe he stroked his balls at the same time as he stroked, twisting a little at the head and groaning at the pleasure.

I groaned, thinking of it, imagining how thick his prick must be. How his pubic hair would be dark like the hair on his head. In my head inches didn't matter. Length and girth were a matter of sensation, of how his cock would fill my hands and mouth and pussy.

I wanted something to fill me now but had only the bullet vibe and my fingers. My hips lifted, pressing my cunt into my hand. I didn't even need the lube, I was so wet. I sought my G-spot with one hand and stroked it, shivering as always from the gut-deep tingles that stimulation always gave me.

Austin had always loved to watch me make myself come. Sometimes we'd pretend I didn't know he was there as I sat at my desk or lounged in our apartment's old claw-foot tub. I could come sometimes more from the way he watched me than by what my hand was doing. Now I could only imagine his eyes on me.

I have a very good imagination.

Two men filled my head. One was jerking his cock but not allowing himself to spill over into sweating, moaning climax. The other watched me from a shadowy doorway as I licked my fingertips and swirled them over my hard, tight clitoris. One was dark, the other golden, and both wanted me.

I wanted both of them, too, and the realization washed over me as suddenly as my orgasm. Sweat tasted bitter on my upper lip when I licked it. My cunt bore down on my fingers and I came, hard. I opened my eyes as pleasure swarmed over me and swept me away. I shuddered with it, that pleasure, so familiar and yet so different, every time.

It was all about control, in the end, and I had it.

I didn't see Eric the next morning at the crush for the mail, but since I'd seen him every other place but the mailboxes I wasn't surprised. I held back for a lull, though, glad I did when I saw the familiar shape of a white note card waiting for me. I held my breath when I pulled it out, more aware than ever of how wrong it was for me to read it.

It didn't stop me. I shoved the other mail into my bag and slid the card from its envelope, my heart already pounding in anticipation of what I'd find today and how different it would seem now that I knew for whom the words were truly meant.

"No." My mouth fell slack with the sound of disbelief and I stared harder at the card.

I folded it shut as though it might change what I'd read, but as though they'd been written in flames, the words burned my fingers through the paper.

No. No, no, no.

This is your last list.

It couldn't be. It shouldn't be. It was not allowed to be!

You've done well, though I think you understand you need more work on discipline. Should you desire further instruction and encouragement, I might consider continuing your service to me. But only if I see a full commitment from you. You know how to get in touch with me.

Don't feel yourself worthy of more of my time. Only I can decide that.

Wow, and oh, no. I tucked the card back into the envelope and pressed it to my chest as I stepped aside to let the snotty woman who'd dismissed me several times before get to her mailbox. She gave me a curious glance, but something in my face must have looked formidable enough that she glanced quickly away.

I turned my back to the row of mailboxes with the note still clutched to me. I wanted to cry. Or puke. I wanted to put the note back and pretend I hadn't read it.

But instead, I did what I hadn't ever done before on purpose. I shoved it in my bag.

I was keeping it.

Paul wasn't in his office when I got to work, but that was fine. I didn't have time to worry about him this morning, or his lists that could never take the place of the one in my bag. I hadn't taken it out to look at it again, though I could remember each swirl and whirl of every letter and line.

I made the coffee and set his cup by the pot with the sugar and powered creamer already in it. In his office I lit the desk lamp instead of the overheads that gave him a headache, and I pulled up all the files he'd need to work on. I even set his radio, though not to the station he usually chose but one with alternative pop instead of the soft-rock channel he usually played.

I did all of this without a list and not because I feared what would happen if he came in and found none of it done. I did it, simply, because Paul needed these things in order to be productive. If my boss was being productive, he would have less time to hover over me, and simply put, today I would not have been able to stand hovering.

I fielded a few phone calls and settled some business by the time he breezed in with a frown.

"Paige, I need coffee, please."

I pointed to the counter. "It's all ready, Paul."

"Thanks." He said it offhandedly, then looked at the mug and back at me. "Thank you, Paige."

I nodded but didn't glance up from my files. I had a lot of work to do today and not enough attention to give him more than that. Most of my mind was still caught up in what I was going to do without the lists. Paul disappeared into his office and shut the door, and I let out the sigh I'd been holding.

Anger shook my fingers as I typed. What a fool Eric had been! He'd asked for discipline and from the start he'd made a mess of it! Turning in his essay late, not following the lists. Why had he bothered? Why had he wasted his mistress's time?

Because there was no doubt in my mind any longer the sender of the notes had been a woman all along.

Men weren't so eloquent. Men weren't so perfectly cold in dispensing their instructions even as they drew forth an emotional response. Only women could dig so deep and pull out so much.

I typed faster, making mistakes and going back to fix them because I'd be damned if I turned in faulty work and gave Paul a reason to judge me. From behind his half-closed door I heard the music swell, but he didn't change the station. The lights didn't come on, either. I concentrated on my tasks, but today they gave me no satisfaction.

Fuck!

I sat back in my chair, muttering. Nothing satisfied me, and I understood why. It wasn't only because the notes were going to end, it was because I'd solved at least half the mystery. I knew who the notes were for, if not who was sending them. And knowing, I couldn't stop thinking about it.

If I hadn't found out it was Eric, a man. If that hadn't changed my perception of what it meant to be on the receiving end of the lists. If. If. If!

"Paige?" Paul called. "Can I see you in here for a minute?"

He certainly could, though I doubted he'd be as thrilled with quiet, subservient little Paige as he'd been. I pushed back from my desk and stood tall in my expensive shoes. The list had told me to buy these shoes. This blouse and skirt. My armor, what I put on when I wanted the world to see me as who I wanted to be and not who they might think I was.

"Yes, Paul."

For the first time in many weeks, I didn't sit to talk to him. He had to tilt his chair back a little to look up at me. I noticed the difference, and I thought he did, too, because when he spoke he sounded a little uncertain.

"Thank you for setting up my office."

"You're welcome."

I thought he would say more, but Paul just turned his attention back to his computer and dismissed me with his silence. I had time to think of what it meant when I went back to my own desk, but I didn't care enough to bother.

When my cell rang just before noon, I almost didn't answer. I didn't want to talk to Austin, but it was my dad, an even greater surprise. I flipped open the phone and pressed it to my ear, though it wasn't my habit to take personal calls at work.

"Dad. Hi."

"How'd you know it was me?"

"I have caller ID, Dad. I have your number programmed into my phone." Not that I used it much.

He loved gadgets but wasn't particularly tech savvy. "Can't pull anything over on you, huh? What are you doing for lunch?"

"I brought a sandwich."

"How about I take you out for lunch? I have to be up your way today for a meeting. Stella's off shopping or something. It'll just be you and me."

My dad had taken an early retirement a year before, but though he'd suggested it a few times, this was the first time he'd actually invited me to lunch. We made plans to meet at a chain restaurant not too far from my office. I knocked on Paul's door to tell him I'd be leaving. He'd been concentrating hard on his work, and I had to knock twice before he looked up. He was going to get a headache that way, even without the overhead lights on.

"Paul. I'm going to lunch with my dad. I'd like to take an extra hour today. I can stay later, if you need me to."

He shook his head. "No, Paige. That's fine. Go enjoy yourself."

"Want me to bring you back anything?"

"No." He sighed and waved a hand at the monitor. "I need to get this done before I leave for Kansas next week."

"You have my cell number if you need me," I told him. "Call if you want me to stop on my way back."

Paul has a very nice smile he doesn't use half as often as he should. It doesn't make him into a movie star by any means, but it was easy enough to see why his wife had agreed to become Mrs. Johnson.

I couldn't remember the last time I'd gone to lunch with my dad. He usually managed to remember my birthday, if not the day at least the month, and major holidays seemed to trigger his memory, too, but with nothing on the calendar it was a bit unusual for him to ask me. He greeted me with the same hug and kiss as he always did, the one that left me feeling slightly strange though he never seemed to think so.

We both ordered the same thing, soup and salad. "Stella's got me on some sort of diet," he explained. "Says we both need to drop a few pounds. You look like you've slimmed down a bit."

"I've been working out." Leave it to my dad to compliment me while making me feel bad at the same time.

"We just got an elliptical trainer and a Bowflex. You can come over and use it if you want." My dad thickly buttered a roll already glistening with grease.

"There's a gym in my apartment building, but thanks." I didn't even take a roll, thinking of the word *discipline* and what it meant to me. I didn't point out how little sense it made for me to drive all the way to my dad's house to work out.

"You could stop by anyway some time this week. Check it out."

In the past I'd have given him an awkward laugh and shrugged off the invitation knowing that though he meant the offer, he wouldn't notice if I didn't take him up on it. Real invitations, the ones I was expected to take, came from Stella and always had. Now, though, something in the way he said it sounded different.

"Sure, I guess I could."

"Your brother's been giving us a bit of a rough time," my dad said.

Interrupted by the waitress bringing our soup, I didn't answer at first. My dad, as was typical of him, ignored the server, spilling his guts in front of a stranger when I'd have preferred the decency of a few minutes' wait. Ah, well, it wasn't my secret.

"Jeremy," he added. "He's been acting up in school, getting into trouble at home. Won't listen to a damn thing we tell him."

I didn't think pointing out giving in to your child's every whim was bound to catch up to you would be appropriate, so I made some sympathetic murmurs and wondered why my dad was sharing.

"He's been really mouthy to me."

"Kids go through stages, don't they?"

My dad gave me a fond smile. "You never have."

Choices. We all make them, sometimes more than once. Sometimes it's the choices we make over and over that define us, but more often it's the ones we don't.

"Kids who feel confident in their parents' affections can take the risk of acting out," I said calmly. "I gave my mom a helluva hard time growing up."

My dad's not a stupid man, though he is deliberately blind to certain things. He sighed. "Paige. I know I haven't always been there for you."

I lifted my spoon to give my hands something to do, but it clattered against the bowl and I didn't want to risk spilling the soup, so I put the spoon down. Of all the awkward moments we'd ever shared, this had to rank right up there with the top ten. Worse even than the year he'd noticed I'd started wearing a bra and announced it at one of Stella's parties.

Knowing he wanted me to say it didn't matter only made it harder for me to answer. I stared into my soup for a long, hard minute and felt his gaze weighting me. I wanted to make it all right for my dad because it would be easier then to pretend it was all right for me. But in the end I said nothing, silence more of an answer than words could ever have been.

"Could you come by?" he said after another half minute ticked by. "Jeremy has always liked you, Paige. He looks up to you like a—"

"Sister?" I looked up at him, then, and took pity on the man who was responsible for one-half of me.

"You *are* his sister. We've never tried to make you feel like anything less."

He wasn't going to apologize more, I could see that. I was pretty sure he hadn't really meant the first one. On the surface, sure, but not down deep. No where it mattered.

"I can come over. Sure. I'm not certain what you think I can do with him, though."

My dad's look of relief was genuine, anyway. "Just talk to

him. I asked Steven if he'd come, but he's busy with the kids. I knew we could count on you."

That, at least, was flattering and believable. "Sure. Thanks."

"Great." Just like that, things were okay again.

My dad slurped up his soup, then dug into his salad as he talked the rest of the meal about the trips they were planning for the summer. Again to the beach house he'd bought a few years back, and also to the Grand Canyon for a river-rafting trip. He invited me to come to the beach house if I could make it, and I said I'd try.

"Good," my dad said like that settled everything that had ever been strained between us.

In a way it had. I'd been honest with him, in some small way, which I'd never been before. We said our goodbyes and this time the hug didn't feel so strained. He patted my head, then pulled me closer for a second hug.

"You look so much like your mom," my dad said, which was untrue. "How is she, anyway?"

"Fine. Good." He never asked about her, but I wasn't going to act as if it was a big deal.

"Good." My dad hesitated. "Tell her…I said hi, and I hope she's doing all right."

"Sure, Dad. I will."

He looked at my car. "You get a new car?"

My car, a silver-gray Volvo, had seen me through three moves, multiple winters and road trips to the beach and back. It was the first car I'd ever owned and even though Austin had cosigned the loan he'd never put a cent toward it. It had been too much car for me when I bought it. It had been my debt and my work.

"No. Same car."

"Huh. Looks new."

I looked at it again. Lately all I'd been able to see were the scratches and dings. "Well, it's not."

"You had that when you and what's-his-name were together, didn't you?"

"Austin. Yeah."

"You see him at all?"

I gave him a hard look. The bright sunshine wasn't kind to him. I saw his years in the lines around his eyes and mouth and the sag of his jaw and the gray glint in his hair.

"Sometimes. Why?"

"Just that…hell. You were young. I should've told you not to marry him."

He was still my dad, despite everything, and I loved him. I think my hug surprised him as much as I surprised myself. "Dad, you couldn't have stopped me."

He laughed. "No. I guess not. That's one thing I'll say about you, Paige, you always knew just what you wanted and how to get it, and you never let anything stand in your way."

His assessment took me aback. What could I say to that? "Thanks."

"Give Stella a call, would you? See when's a good night for you to come over. She knows the boys' schedules better than I do. We'll give you dinner."

"You don't always have to feed me."

"I'm your dad," he said and tucked a twenty-dollar bill into the pocket of my jacket before I could even register he'd done it. "Call her. I'll see you later, kiddo."

I watched him go and turned back to my car to look at it with new eyes. Sunshine had made a mirror of the windows, and in it I saw a woman who never let anything stand in her way, who knew what she wanted and how to get it. My father saw me that way and suddenly, I could see myself that way, too.

Chapter 20

It's amazing how one small thing can change so much. I went back to the office humming under my breath. I'd have danced and scattered glitter if people did that in real life, but I settled for stopping at Starbucks to grab Paul a late-afternoon coffee and scone. He'd need one.

Tension creased his brow when I gave it to him, but he took the cup and bag gratefully as he pushed back from his desk. "Thank you, Paige."

Five minutes later, as my fingers flew over the keyboard, I heard the phone ring. Five minutes after that, I heard a thud and a curse, followed by the sound of water running in his private bathroom and more muttered cursing. I waited for him to call me, and when he didn't, I got up and went into his office without knocking.

Paul stood in the center of the room with a handful of sodden paper towels. He'd been using them to scrub at the coffee stain all over his white shirt, but all he'd managed to do was spread it. Small bits of paper towel clung to the fabric, adding to the mess. The harder he scrubbed, the worse it got.

The first three days I'd worked for Kelly Printing, Paul had been out of the office. He'd hired me, one of three people who'd sat in on the interview, but I hadn't known until I showed up that day who was going to be my boss. I'd assumed the thick sheaf of instructions left for me on my desk were because he wasn't there to start me off. I knew better now, of course, but looking back you always see things you didn't at the time.

The first day I'd come into work to find him actually in the office, he'd had this same look on his face. It was because he'd assumed I hadn't finished everything he'd left for me; when I showed him all the tasks I'd completed, he'd calmed down at once, and our routine had quickly become the way I've described it. So I'd seen the panicked look before, but not for a while.

"Stop." I didn't have to think about this. I took the paper towels from his hands and threw them in the trash. I went to the bathroom and pulled a handful of dry paper towels out, then dabbed at the wet spot on his shirt. "What happened?"

"I spilled my coffee," Paul said unnecessarily.

"I see that." I also saw there was more to it than that. I blotted the stain and scraped off most of the paper-towel flecks.

Under my hands, Paul's chest was firm. He radiated heat, though his face was dry and even a little pale. His hands shook a little as he held them out away from his sides to give me room to work. He was getting ready for a full-on panic attack.

"This isn't so bad," I soothed.

"I have a meeting to go to in five minutes, and Melissa forgot my dry cleaning again. So I don't even have an extra shirt." His voice went a little hoarse. "Damn it, why'd I have to spill coffee on myself now?"

"You wouldn't be the only person at the meeting who ever

spilled coffee, Paul." I stood back to assess the damage, then looked him over with a critical eye. "Did you bring a suit jacket today?"

"Yes. Of course."

"Wear that. Nobody will notice. It's a little warm, but you'll feel better." I patted his arm, and the muscles jumped beneath my fingers.

Paul shook his head slowly. "Paige…"

I let him trail off and didn't offer a response. We looked at each other. Without the harsh overhead lights, Paul looked younger. The lines in his forehead visibly smoothed as I stroked his arm.

It wasn't appropriate. If anyone had seen us, the gesture could have been misconstrued. At the very least, it might have started damaging rumors. But nobody saw us, and Paul gentled under my touch. After working for him for so many months, I knew what he needed.

It all fell into place. I thought of the day he'd put the bandage on my leg. How he'd taken such care. And of his lists, laid out in such detail to let me know exactly what he needed and wanted. I thought of how he'd owned to being difficult to work for, when in the end he'd made it so very simple for me to give him everything he needed I couldn't remember why I'd ever thought he was hard to work with.

And just then, I think we both understood.

He must have known before what he really wanted, and how hard it must have been for him to get it. Yesterday, too focused on what I thought I'd needed and wanted, I hadn't been able to see it.

"Put your suit jacket on, Paul. And go to your meeting. And tomorrow, instead of coffee, you'd better drink water until you can be less clumsy." I didn't say it lightly. I wasn't teasing.

I was testing.

He closed his eyes briefly and when he opened them, I saw relief and something else. A little shame. A little excitement. I felt the sting and swirl of it, too, but I lifted my chin and tried not to show it.

"Now," I said, "go to your meeting."

He put on his suit jacket and left.

There was nothing overtly sexual about what had happened. I didn't want to fuck my boss. Until today I wouldn't have believed he wanted to fuck me, either, beyond the fact that most men would like to fuck most women. Yet something had passed between us, something charged and tense and arousing.

Alone in Paul's office I had to bend and put my hands on his desk, my head down so I could catch my breath. I'd fainted twice in my life, and this didn't feel like that, the gray-red haze taking over my vision, the ringing in my ears. This lightheadedness was more like the breathless rush that comes just before orgasm, when every muscle clenches. When the body takes over and nothing the mind can do will stop the inevitable.

It was synchronicity again, or maybe serendipity. Like when you've never heard a word before and suddenly you see it in every book you read, or how you've been craving ice cream and the ice-cream truck rounds the corner just before you go inside. Three men, similar but different. I might not have noticed a few months ago, but now it was all I could see. The notes had done that. Opened my eyes to that need. Theirs and mine, too.

Last night, learning about Eric had rocked my world. This morning, discovering I was about to lose my lists had done it again. But now, just now, with Paul, I'd learned something so basic it had been with me all along. Only like Dorothy with the Scarecrow, Tin Woodsman and Cowardly Lion, I simply hadn't seen it. I thought of lists and notes and what they meant to me. And what I wanted.

And I knew what I had to do.

"Paige." Miriam gave me a broad, crimson-lipped grin. "So nice to see you. What can I do for you today? A gift for someone?"

"No. Today I came in for myself."

I looked to the shelf where the boxes of ink, pens and papers had been, but they were gone. Miriam came around the counter and saw me looking. She tugged gently on my sleeve.

"In the back. Come with me." She'd set the boxes on an eye-level shelf, each displayed with its lid open to show off the papers inside. "Not so many people will see these back here, but if they take the time to look, I believe they will be unable to resist."

I already knew the one I wanted. Red lacquer with blue and purple accents. The paper inside bore the watermark of a dragonfly, and there was enough to last a number of weeks even if I wrote a letter on it every day. The brush-and-ink set interested me less. I didn't intend to write in calligraphy.

"This one." I closed the lid and slid the small wooden clasp through the loop of ribbon to keep it shut. I turned to Miriam and stopped at the look on her face. "What?"

"I knew you would find something to write on that paper, that's all." She was already leaving the room and gestured over her shoulder for me to follow.

The box was heavier than it looked because of the marble stamper, also featuring a dragonfly, and the porcelain container of ink paste inside. Heavier, too, because of what I meant to do with the contents. The wood slipped against my fingers as I carried it to the cash register. I didn't want to let it go long enough for Miriam to ring it up and put it in a Speckled Toad bag, but I did.

I was sweating a little, my stomach and throat buzzing with anticipation. Colors seemed a bit too bright and sounds too loud. I was already thinking of a quiet room and candlelight, and the *scritch-scratch* of a pen on the paper. I already knew what I was going to write.

Miriam rang up my purchase and wrapped the satin box liberally in tissue paper, then slid it into a bag. She peered at me over her half glasses, her mouth pursed, and tapped the countertop with her crimson nails. "You need something else."

I was already spending too much. "I don't think so."

Miriam ignored me and turned to the glass-topped display case next to the counter. She leaned over to look at the Cross and Mont Blanc pens inside, each snuggled in its own cradle of velvet. She ran her finger over the glass, drawing my attention to each of the pens I'd lusted over since discovering her shop. There was a Starwalker rollerball pen in black and one in blue. There was a Meisterstuck Classique Platinum rollerball in classic black with silver accents. She even had one of the special limited-edition Marlene Dietrich pens I'd seen online that cost the earth.

"Mont Blanc doesn't call them pens, you know," she said in the reverent voice of an archeologist unearthing something precious. She didn't look at me as she unlocked the back of the case and ran her fingertips over the velvet. "They're referred to as writing instruments."

Her fingers closed on one, a slim black piece with the signature six-pointed star in the cap. She drew it out and laid it flat on her palm the way the jeweler had done with the diamond ring Austin had bought me. The pen in Miriam's palm wasn't quite as expensive as that ring, which I still had locked away in my jewelry box…but it wasn't much less, either.

I itched to take it, but shoved my hands in my pockets instead. "Yes, I know. I've been to their Web site."

Now her gaze, cool and amused, flicked to me. "I'm sure you have. You look at these pens every time you come in, Paige."

"They're beautiful pens."

Miriam pulled out a small square of velvet and laid the pen—the writing instrument—on it. Then she folded her hands and tilted her head to look at me over her glasses again. "Let me ask you something, my dear. Would a plastic surgeon operate on someone's face with a rusty butter knife?"

"I sure hope not." I grimaced.

Miriam smiled indulgently. "Would an artist try to paint a masterpiece with a box of watercolors from the dollar store?"

"If that's all the artist had, why not?"

"My point is, my dear, that in order to create real, true things of beauty, a person needs the right tools." She waved a hand over the Mont Blanc.

My soul strained toward it. "I'm not an artist."

"No?" Her perfectly plucked brows lifted in unison. "That paper says otherwise. Tell me you intend to use it for a grocery list, and I'll call you a liar. What's more, I won't sell it to you. It would be a sin not to use that paper for something special."

"I plan to use it for something special." My mouth curved into a smile on the words.

"Good. But what about the instrument? Don't tell me you plan to use a half-chewed pencil stub with no eraser."

I tore my gaze away from the Mont Blanc to look at her. "I have a nice fountain pen my dad bought for me for my college graduation."

I didn't tell her it tended to stain my fingers in addition to blotting the paper with ink. Miriam sniffed. Her fingernails ticktocked on the counter, timing the seconds before her response.

"It's not a Mont Blanc. Or even a Cross. Is it?"

"No. But it's what I have."

Miriam sighed and shook her head. "Paige, Paige, Paige. Pick up that pen and hold it."

I didn't want to—putting it down would be so much harder. But when Miriam pulled a piece of cream-colored paper from beneath the counter and slid it toward me, I did what she'd said. If you've never held a really good pen, you don't understand how the weight distributes itself so evenly in your palm. Or how the fit of it in your fingers makes writing even the longest documents easy. How the ink slides from the tip without effort.

I wrote my name.

"Oh…" I breathed and with reluctance, set down the pen. "It's so nice."

I'd put it down at once so I wouldn't be tempted to run away with it, but Miriam lifted it and held it toward me. "Buy it."

"I can't afford it." I hadn't even looked at the tiny, hand-lettered price tag attached to the pen's box still in the display case. I didn't have to see the numbers to know I couldn't buy it.

"Are you sure?" Miriam asked calmly. "You might be surprised."

"I doubt it, Miriam. I know what those pens cost."

"My dear," she said. "Aren't you worth it?"

Chapter 21

This is what I wrote on that expensive paper with my exquisite writing instrument.

The time has come to reevaluate our relationship.

You will send me your exact schedule, work and pleasure, for the next ten days. In addition, you will write ten things that excite you. You will send them in an e-mail to me at switch1971@gmail.com *no later than 6:00 p.m. the day you get this letter. You will include your cell phone number so I can text-message you my approval. Or not.*

Things are going to change for us both.

I'd stepped it up, but unlike my last interlude with Austin, I didn't wonder if it had been too much. I wondered, instead, if perhaps it hadn't been enough. There were several messages in my Inbox when I got home from work. One of them was from a friend from college, another from my mom. And the last was from an e-mail address I didn't recognize. Eric.

He detailed his schedule as I'd requested. Working twelve-hour shifts in a three-on, four-off pattern. I hadn't asked him what hospital he worked at, but he'd included varying drive times, so I thought he might fill in at several. His attention to detail pleased me. Clearly he'd done something like this before…but then, I was guessing he was more used to this sort of thing than I was. I liked his list of things that excited him even more.

1. *Standing in the rain*
2. *Roller coasters*
3. *Knowing I'm being watched while I make myself come*
4. *Serving a woman on my knees while she ignores me*
5. *Tacos!*
6. *Lingerie (on a woman, not me wearing it)*
7. *Being told exactly how to please the woman I'm with so I don't have to guess*
8. *Clean sheets*
9. Monty Python *on DVD*
10. *Lists*

Lists excited me, too. I loved that he had a sense of humor about it and was self-confident enough to show it. I also appreciated that he'd responded in time—5:55, by the time on the message. I didn't know if I'd have had it in me to punish him for failure.

I never wore leather and I'd never cracked a whip. I liked high heels, but the thought of using them to step on a person squicked me out big-time. I'd always thought of men who got off on "serving" women as pussies, though Eric had impressed me as anything but.

I didn't know how much of a mistress I was going to be, or how long I could get away with the impersonation. I could have pretended I'd taken this on for his sake—the thought of losing those daily lists had sent me into a mind-spin, after all. But I knew it was really for me. Those lists had given me something I hadn't known I needed.

Writing them, I discovered, fulfilled me even more.

This is what I left in his mailbox.

Tonight when you get home from work, you will eat your dinner. Then you'll shower. After that, you'll go to your bedroom and leave your curtain open.

When you jerk your cock, know that I'll be watching you.

"Cute shoes." The woman whose name I didn't know but whom I always seemed to bump into at the mailboxes sounded as if she meant it. "Enzo Angiolini?"

I looked down at the chunk-heeled pumps in classic black, tied across the top with a tasseled leather strap. I'd picked them up at the thrift store for three bucks. But yes, they were brand name and nearly brand-new. "Yes."

"Nice. I have a pair almost like it but in navy. I never wear them, though. I couldn't ever find anything to go with them." She gave the rest of my outfit a critical look. "I'd never have thought to put them together with a flared skirt and tapered top like that."

For months I'd agonized over what to wear to work each day and she'd looked at me as though I were something she'd scraped off the bottom of her enviably fashionable shoes. Today, caught up in thoughts of slipping Eric's note into the mail and what it would lead to, later, I'd thrown on the first outfit I'd grabbed. I looked at my shoes and swirled slightly to flare my skirt around my knees. My smile had nothing to do with her compliment, and I didn't thank her for it. Okay, so I can be a bit of a vindictive bitch. I never pretended otherwise.

I looked her up and down from the chiffon scarf she'd tied at her throat to her feet in the same pair of Kate Spades I'd seen several times already. "Really?"

One word. So many layers of meaning. She blinked rapidly, and then her mouth quirked into a grudging smile. We understood each other the way women do and men never will.

"They're having a great sale at Neiman Marcus next week. I'm on their preferred buyers mailing list and got a postcard about it," she offered.

"Thanks. I'll check it out." I waited until she'd gone before putting my letter in Eric's mailbox.

When I had, I leaned for a moment against the wall, my breath whistling through parted lips. Beneath the skirt she'd so admired, I wore lacy, silky lingerie. Sexy things to make me feel pretty all day, and to remind me of what I intended to happen later. As if I could forget, I thought with a secret smile I kept with me all day.

Paul noticed it. The smile, not the panties, which rubbed me deliciously each time I crossed or uncrossed my legs. He stood over my desk with a sheaf of files in his hands, but he waited until I looked up to acknowledge him rather than simply addressing me the way he had in the past.

Oh, how so much had changed in so short a time!

"You look nice today," he said.

In this era of sexual-harassment suits, in a time where I'm an executive assistant and not a secretary because of some misbegotten notion that a title means more than the job itself, his compliment wasn't really appropriate. I leaned back in my chair to give him a nice long look at my legs as I crossed them high at the knee. And he looked, Paul did, without pretending he didn't.

"What do you need, Paul?"

He offered the files. "These have to go out today."

I didn't take them. Power thrilled through me as he set them on the desk but didn't go. Was this a dangerous game? I didn't think it was so risky. I didn't even count it as flirtation, really. I had no intention of fucking my boss.

Of becoming my mother.

"All right."

We stared at each other. Paul cleared his throat and rocked on his heels a bit. I took the files and set them in a tidy pile in front of me to show him I would, indeed, get to them. Not at that instant, and I wasn't jumping through hoops to do it, but it would happen.

"Paige, there's something else I'd like to talk to you about."

I studied him for a second, trying to gauge what it could be about, then nodded. "Sure. What about?"

"Can you come into my office in about ten minutes?"

He asked as though he was afraid I'd say no, even though technically we both knew I didn't have a choice. "Absolutely."

"Thanks." He'd always been polite, but he was nearly dancing now with some hidden anxiety.

There were many things I knew about my boss, some I'd known from the start and others I'd learned only over time. When it all came down to it, though, I liked Paul very much. Whatever had his garters snapping, it was going to make it impossible for him to get some work done until it was resolved.

"Go get yourself a mug of coffee," I told him. "I'll send off these reports and see you in ten minutes."

I hadn't given him permission, and it was nothing he couldn't have decided for himself, but the relief in his eyes at my suggestion made me glad I'd made it. I flipped through the reports while he poured his coffee and made some notes about what needed to be sent where, then ducked down the hall to visit the restroom then make some copies so I could be back in time to meet with him.

He sat in a familiar slouch at his desk when I pushed open his door, but he turned his attention immediately to me. "Paige, hi. Would you sit down, please?"

I did, and watched his gaze flicker over my bared knees as I crossed my legs. "Is something wrong?"

"No. Nothing's wrong. I just...wanted to talk to you."

I waited. Paul drew in a breath and pushed back in his chair to run a hand over the top of his head. He'd taken off his suit jacket, but his tie was as snug to his throat as if it had grown there. He cleared his throat, and I waited another ten seconds for him to speak.

"It's about your performance."

I sat up a little straighter. "Yes?"

"It's past time for your first review."

I understood that. Kelly Printing, like most companies, gave annual reviews, but they also had an introductory probation period for all new employees. They'd told me about it when they hired me. Six months into the new job, you could be out on your ass if you didn't live up to expectations. It was hard to believe I'd been here that long. It felt more like forever, actually.

Again, I waited for him to speak. That was the thing with

Paul. He took his time with talk. I thought it was because each word that came from him had to mean something, like he had to weigh their worth before he said them. Unlike writing, you can't scratch out speech. Once it's said, there's nothing you can do to erase it.

"I just wanted you to know I'll be giving you the highest ratings, that's all. And recommending you for advanced training."

My pleased smile sat oddly on my face, which had been expecting to frown. "Really? Great. Thanks, Paul."

He seemed a little more at ease once he'd told me, though his fingers still toyed nervously with his pen. He rolled it onto the edge of the blotter, then off. It hit the desk with a sharp click.

"You're welcome. I've been very pleased with your work."

"I've enjoyed working with you."

He nodded a bit and focused his attention on the pen. "There are some opportunities available in-house. A good recommendation could…um…lead the way to some of them."

This was interesting news I wasn't sure how to process. "Like what?"

"Promotion opportunities."

I read the bulletin boards in the hall by the office mail every day. I saw the internal-job postings along with the memos on company policy and announcements about the holiday parties and picnics. Nothing there had caught my eye or sent me into spasms of excitement. I'd never considered applying for any of them. I still intended to get my MBA when they'd chip in to pay for it.

"Such as?" I leaned forward.

"They're looking for someone to start in a new entry-level marketing position in Vivian Darcy's department."

"And if I don't want to work for Vivian?"

For a moment, Paul looked pleased before he smoothed his features into studied neutrality. "It's something to think about. You can't be an assistant forever, Paige."

That was certainly true, and I was touched he cared enough to think so. "I don't plan to be."

"This could be a good chance for you," he said.

And that was true, too. So why did we both look so sad?

I knew from Eric's schedule that he'd be home around eight o'clock today. I gave him half an hour for dinner, another fifteen minutes for a shower. If he was as eager as I was to follow the instructions I'd left him, it wouldn't be more than that.

The black trench coat I wore wasn't meant to make me look like a pervert, though that's what I felt like as I entered the parking garage. I'd picked it to help camouflage me in the shadows, but I had toyed with the idea of going naked beneath it. I ended up putting on black jogging pants and a black T-shirt instead, not bold enough to go bare. I might have had I had a note telling me to do it, I thought with a smile as I climbed the second flight of stairs.

I came out onto a nearly empty level. At this time of night the spots taken up by daytime commuters would be vacant. But from this level I had a clear view across the street and into Eric's first-floor apartment.

The concrete wall hit me chest high, but I could lean on it to look across the street. At 9:00 p.m., night had already fallen. The orange lights of the parking garage lit the door to the stairs and hit every other pillar, but none was above my head and so I had no glare to distract me. The streetlights, too, were placed far enough apart they didn't interfere with my voyeurism.

I hadn't brought a pair of binoculars, but really didn't need them. The street between the buildings was one-way and narrow. I could have spit and hit his window. Inside his apartment, the lights went on.

My ears rang, and I let out the breath I'd been keeping prisoner in my lungs. He was there. This was really going to happen.

Everyone peeks. We do it all the time when we drive past houses at night with the lights on, in hotel rooms we can see into from across a courtyard, when we pass a half-closed office door. I'd never set out to spy in hopes of catching someone doing something naughty. I couldn't decide if the tension in my gut and tingling in my fingertips were from illicit arousal or self-loathing.

The former, I thought as the curtains in Eric's bedroom twitched and the light came on in there, too. I was more of a pervert than I'd ever imagined. Voyeurism had never melted my butter before, but knowing this would get him off, that this was a trigger for him, got my nipples hard and built an ache between my thighs I knew I'd have to alleviate with my own hand before the night was through.

He stood at the window for a minute or two, looking out for so long I wondered if he could see me. With the light inside his room and the dark out here, I didn't think so. I didn't dare move. Shielded by shadows, I drew in slow, even breaths and watched him stare out into the night. He didn't look as if he saw me, or anyone, though his eyes moved side to side, searching.

Finally, he turned and took a few steps toward the bed. He wore only a towel, his hair wet and slicked back. Water gleamed in silver droplets on the tanned skin of his back and shoulders. I wasn't quite close enough to see them run in rivulets down his spine and into the crack of his ass below the towel's edge, but I could imagine it. And did.

He hesitated, looking over his shoulder with a hand at his waist. I wondered if he'd ever thought so hard before about who might see him from outside. Though I kept my sheers drawn all the time, they wouldn't entirely block a peeper from getting an eyeful, but I'd never really believed anyone was trying to. I was sure I'd think of it every time, now, and wonder who might be spying on me when I thought I was alone.

The difference was, Eric knew he wasn't alone. I thought it would make it more difficult to get naked, knowing, even though he had said he liked it. That he wanted it. His shoulders hunched for a moment and then the towel was gone. Disappeared.

God, from the back he was magnificent. Broad shoulders, lean waist, smooth skin. His ass was tight and looked firm. A patch of dark hair furred the small of his back and drifted over his buttocks to get thicker at his thighs and legs. His arms, too, were covered in thick, dark hair. He half turned so I could see his chest and I grinned in delight. Hair there, too, dark and curling around his nipples, but not overpowering him. A woman could still find bare skin to kiss all over him, center her tongue on those nipples and flick them with her tongue until he cried out for mercy.

I had to grip the concrete wall to steady myself at my unwinding thoughts. Austin, blond-haired and fair skinned, had little hair on his chest and had taken to trimming his pubic hair. I didn't mind grooming, but I'd gotten used to seen a man without so much hair. Looking at Eric opened up something half-embarrassing I could only think of as…primal.

Eric lay on the bed, his cock in his hand. He stared at the

ceiling as he stroked, already half-hard. In the porn I'd seen the men had always yanked so hard on their pricks it looked painful. Eric didn't start off with a two-fisted yank. He ran a slow hand over his belly and thighs before gripping his cock, which he stroked just as slowly from base to crown and down again before repeating the journey.

I was mesmerized.

The head of Eric's bed was against the wall opposite his bedroom door, which placed the bed parallel to the window. Like the rest of his apartment, his bedding was simple, even stark. He'd already pulled down the black quilted comforter and blankets and now lay on the plain white sheet. He hitched himself a little higher to put his head on the pillow.

Did it make a difference, knowing he was being watched? I thought it had to. Why else would he take such time to show off? The bulge and flex of his biceps had me biting my lower lip. So did the flex of his calves when he bent his legs to push his hips upward.

I leaned forward too far, risking being seen, when his leg blocked the view of his gorgeous cock being stroked so slowly in that big fist, but as if he knew exactly what he was doing, Eric pushed that leg straight and bent the other, instead, keeping my view clear. His back arched as his head tipped back into the pillow. I wanted to see his face, but though I could make out the dark shadow of eyes and the slope of his nose, distance blurred his features a bit.

With a hand still on his erection, Eric reached with the other beneath his pillow to pull out a bottle. My lube came with a flip-top cap, but his had a squirt top, and he sprayed his hands and cock liberally before tucking it back under his pillow.

I didn't laugh because this was funny, but because this secret glimpse into his private sex life was so adorable, and told me a lot. He jerked off a lot and didn't bring women home to sleep over very often—people who shared their beds frequently didn't keep their sex supplies under the pillow. My earlier assessment had been right.

People and cars passed on the street below, but I didn't let that distract me from the show across the way. I heard the squeal of tires and rumble of an occasional engine as well as the hum of the parking-garage elevator, but nobody arrived or left on this level. Tucked against the concrete pillar with the wall in front of me and the night wind occasionally blowing the scent of the river over me, I immersed myself in what he was doing and wished I were with him.

I pressed my thighs together against the ache of arousal as I watched Eric stroking himself. Slow, then faster. I watched his prick disappear inside his curled fingers, watched how he added an extra stroke around the head and how he dipped lower every couple of strokes to give his balls some attention, too. I watched, and I thought of how I could get the chance to show him what I'd learned.

I couldn't hear him, but I could see his mouth open and watch his face contort with pleasure. His fist pumped faster, slick with lube, and his hips rose and fell to meet every stroke. If I were on top of him now, he'd be pushing deep inside me and my clit would be hitting his belly with every thrust. My cunt clenched as I watched, my clit hard and begging for more than the press of my panties against it. But I didn't touch myself. My fingers gripped the concrete, the pebbly surface biting into my fingertips and keeping me centered. Reminding me I was not in any place where I could risk shoving a hand down my pants and jilling off. I was risking enough standing here and watching. My body might crave the same sort of release Eric was giving himself, but my brain wouldn't allow me to act on it.

Later, I promised myself grimly as sweat lined my hairline and trickled down my spine, tickling like a tongue. Just a few more minutes and he'd be done, and I'd go home and finish this.

I licked salt from my upper lip and imagined it as the taste of him. My cunt clutched again empty, and I squeezed my thigh muscles. God, it felt so good I did it again. And again.

I watched him as he came, jetting his desire all over his flat, taut belly, and I came, too, without ever having touched myself. I coughed on the moist river breeze and scent of exhaust as pleasure ripped through me. My pussy spasmed, but I held still and quiet as the door from the stairs opened and a laughing couple came out and headed for their car.

I couldn't duck and couldn't hide, so I pretended to be talking on my cell phone, leaning casually against the hood of a car I didn't own. Orgasm still rippled through me as I lifted a hand to wave in response to their casual greeting, and I thanked the gods of kink I hadn't given in to full-out wanking in public.

They didn't even look toward the Manor, but I did. Eric had fallen back into his pillows, his chest rising and falling and a hand flung over his eyes. I'd already put his number in my phone, and now I entered a rapid text message.

Very nice.

Half a minute later his head turned toward the nightstand, and he rolled to his side to flip open his phone. He read the message and looked at the window. He got off the bed and stood at the window for a few seconds, his hand on the curtain.

I thought he mouthed "thank you," but then he pulled the curtain before I could be sure.

Chapter 22

It had begun.

I'd thought I'd known what it was to crave the discipline of an anonymous master who understood just what I needed and how to give it to me. With one short letter, one shorter text message, I'd become Pink Floyd. Dark side of the moon. I'd ventured into the unknown.

But was it, really?

In all my life, what had I craved more than anything? Control. Of my life, of my emotions. Of whatever situation I'd found myself in. The need for it was a weight I'd known a long time without acknowledging. It had been a huge part of the reason my marriage had ended, and even admitting it hadn't done much to change me.

Giving up some small measure of that control had been a relief. It had lifted the weight for a little while. Made it a little easier to bear, anyway. Because in the end, what had I learned but that I didn't want to give it up. I only wanted to learn how to use it, that desire.

After watching Eric make himself come, I went straight to my apartment. I sat at my table, desire an unrelenting ache in my belly. I opened the lid of my satin box and pulled out a sheet of the fine paper. I let it slide through my fingers. I put it to my face and smelled it, that inexplicably delightful scent of fresh paper.

Miriam had been right about my need for this paper, how if I bought it I'd find something important to write on it. She'd been right, too, about the pen. The writing instrument, I reminded myself with a smile. I wasn't a surgeon or even an artist, but that pen was perfect for this. Its weight shifted just right in my fingers as I put it to the paper. The ink scrolled every stroke without blots or skids or spots left blank. Now I only had to find the perfect words to write.

I knew I should do what my high school English teacher had called a "sloppy copy." None of the letters that had passed through me first had contained scratch-outs or misspellings. They hadn't exactly been poetry, but they had been neat and clean. My pen hovered over the paper as I thought of what I needed and wanted to say.

I was working too hard on it, overthinking. The sense of responsibility had pushed back even my arousal. I'd actually bitten down on my lower lip hard enough to sting as I thought.

I put down the pen and pushed back in my chair. I got up and poured myself a glass of orange juice that I sipped as I leaned against my counter and stared at the paper and pen on the table.

One thing I knew that Eric's previous unseen mistress had never seemed to grasp. He had a sense of humor about all this. It might also satisfy him sexually, and he might crave the hand of command as much as I briefly had, but in the end, he was no leather-masked pussy boy slavering to lick a woman's boots. He was not a cliché, and I couldn't make this one. I wouldn't.

It was already more than that, to me, and had been from the first moment I'd taken the words meant for him as my own.

Juice finished, I paced. The first note had been easy, written on a whim. The second hadn't been much harder. Now, though, now...I wanted so much for it to be perfect I was paralyzing myself. In the end, I thought of his sense of humor and the list he'd written. I took my pen, and I put it to the paper.

Have tacos for dinner.

"Paige!"

I'm not the blushing sort, but heat flooded me when I turned and saw Eric waving at me from the elevator. I paused at the Manor's big glass front doors to hold one open for him, and he followed me out into the spring-breezy morning. "Hi, Eric."

"Going for a jog?" He wore black track pants and a tight black T-shirt that showed off his biceps.

I looked down at my sneakers and workout clothes, then up at him with a grin. "You'd think so, wouldn't you?"

"I guessed wrong?" He put a hand over his heart and staggered a step. "Don't tell me you're going to the Embassy Ball."

"Nope. But I don't jog. I can manage a fast walk, though, if you're up for it."

"Fast walk it is," he said agreeably.

"I don't want to hold you back." I faked adjusting the tie at my waist to give my hands something to do while I watched his reaction.

He didn't give me much of one, just a shrug and an easy smile that lit his dark eyes. "Nah. I used to run a lot, but it's hard on the knees. A fast walk can give you a good workout too without being so tough on the joints. I see a lot of injuries from people pushing too hard. I don't want that to be me."

We crossed Front Street to the sidewalk just beyond. The Susquehanna River was running high with the last of the winter's melt and a few days of rain. It swelled, greenish brown, high up the concrete steps that had been set into the bank. Halfway across on City Island, I saw the bright red-and-white stripes of the bathhouse awnings at the public swimming beach. I'd dip a foot in that water. Maybe. But there was no way I'd ever swim in it.

"Left or right?" Eric said as he stretched one long leg, then the other.

Left would take us toward downtown and eventually, the highway, but we could walk down along the river if we wanted instead of up here. Right would take us past residential neighborhoods and the line of mansions that had once been private homes but now mostly housed offices. Oh, and the Governor's Mansion, which for some reason never failed to fascinate me. I guess it was because such an important building seemed out of place right out there in the open, where anyone could stand in front of the fence and look in. I felt the same way about the White House the one time I'd been to D.C.

"Right." I nodded that way and watched him stretch. I made an effort at doing the same, but since I never stretched before any workout, it was half-assed.

Eric eyed me with a grin but made no comment. "Ready?"

"Sure."

There had been a heyday of walking when I was around eight or nine. We'd been living in a cluster of trailers, too few to really be called a park, with my mother's then boyfriend, Bob. My mom had been laid off from her job in the packing department at the Hershey factory, and for the first time I could ever remember she'd formed a group of girlfriends who did the sorts of things moms did on television. Lunches where they dished over their men, and trips to the mall where they walked and shopped but hardly ever bought anything. Though my mom had never carried an extra pound and wouldn't until after she had Arty, they'd formed a group to walk around the neighborhood to help get in shape. It was more an excuse to get away from us ever-present kids as they gossiped, but I'd often watched them from the concrete front porch as they passed by on their rounds and wondered what made them laugh so loud.

There was no laughing as Eric and I walked. I'd set the initial pace, but his legs were much longer and we ended up walking faster than I usually did. Pride kept me from asking him to slow, and I didn't have breath left for chatter. We passed office buildings and finally, Green Street, where Harrisburg went from city to neighborhood most drastically. We passed bikes and other joggers, most heading the opposite direction. I was glad for the pace that made talk impossible. Eric didn't seem the chatty type, anyway. Arms swinging, he didn't walk so much as lope along the sidewalk.

Somehow I didn't care about the sweat ringing my armpits or dripping down my cheeks. I hadn't bothered with much makeup either, and no woman looks her best in sweatpants. With any other man I'd have been cataloging my flaws and wishing I'd at least swiped my lips with gloss, but with Eric it simply didn't matter.

Because I knew he had made himself come at my command, and it didn't matter what I looked like or wore. I had power over him. He didn't know it, but I did.

It took a lot of the pressure off in a major way. I didn't have to worry if he liked me or what he was thinking. I could find out any time I wanted, just by writing him a note. And if I decided I didn't like him, this never had to go beyond a walk along the river.

"How far do you want to go?" His question came close on my thoughts, startling me.

I looked at my watch, calculating the distance we'd gone and how long it would take to get back. I was going to my dad's supposedly to watch the boys while he and Stella went to some charity fund-raiser, though I knew my real task was to figure out what burr had gotten into Jeremy's britches. Still, it was only lunchtime. The sky had still been slightly overcast when we left, but now the sun had come out. The first really good weather of the spring. I didn't want to waste it.

"Another half a mile." I swiped the back of my hand across my face. "And I need to stop for a drink, too."

"Fair enough."

We walked on, slowing. The sidewalk ended just ahead as the bank fell off much harder down to the river. Across the street were a couple of restaurants.

"Let's stop at Taco Bell," I said suddenly, unable to resist.

Eric gave me a quick glance, but though I sought a smile or some sign he was thinking about the last note I'd left, I saw nothing to give it away. He nodded, though, and when there was a break in the traffic, we headed across to walk on the other side of the street.

The pause had slowed us both, so by the time we crossed

the parking lot to the restaurant I was cooling down. The sun, so fiercely bright, had gone behind some clouds again, and the wind off the river whipped us. It felt good, though, drying my sweaty face. Eric held the door open for me. Once again, the gesture from anyone else wouldn't have given me a second thought, but I wondered if he'd done it to be polite or from some other, secret need.

I was going to drive myself nuts thinking of this stuff, so I shoved it aside as best I could and concentrated on the menu board. It had been so long since I'd been to Taco Bell they'd added a whole list of new items. I'd practically lived off fast food for years because it was cheap, but nothing up there really looked appealing even when I figured in the fact I'd walked all the way here and would walk back.

"Go ahead," Eric offered.

I ordered a large diet cola and there was a moment of awkwardness when he insisted on paying and I tried to stop him but ended up conceding with a laugh. It was nice, that gesture. I hadn't expected it.

"A soda's not going to break me, Paige." Eric flipped a twenty at the cashier, who stared at it suspiciously and did some strange things to it with a marker.

"Thank you, anyway." I took the drink, which I hadn't realized was going to contain enough soda to fill a fishbowl. The sweetness and carbonation hit the back of my throat in a bubbly, fizzy splash of utter joy.

Following me to a table toward the front, Eric laughed at my sound of delight. "That's the sigh of a true addict."

I lifted the humongous cup. "Is it that obvious?"

He waited for me to sit before he did. Pleasure, not exactly sexual, purred through me. I could definitely get used to this.

He set his tray on the table and took the seat across from me. Our knees bumped.

"Only to a former caffeine addict." He unwrapped his taco and spread out the paper with his fingertips. "You sure you don't want anything to eat?"

"I'm sure." The greasy meat and cheese might look good but I knew I'd pay for it later. My stomach couldn't handle that sort of junk anymore. I had the notes to thank for that.

Eric contemplated the taco. "I love tacos. They're life's perfect food."

I laughed and sipped my drink. "If you say so."

"You don't like tacos?" he asked, still not biting into his food.

"Oh, I love Mexican food. Just not from Taco Bell."

"So why did you want to stop here?" He pushed some stray lettuce into the taco shell.

I was caught, though he couldn't know it. "I like the extra-huge drinks."

Eric nodded as though what I'd said made sense. I excused myself to use the restroom. I wasn't eating anything, but I still wanted to wash my hands and face after the walk. My phone vibrated from my pocket and I pulled it out to find an unexpected picture text message.

A taco.

No message, just the photo, but I knew it at once as the one in front of Eric. I fell back to lean against the stall's metal wall, my phone clutched to my heart. I wanted to dance. I wanted to laugh. Then I washed my hands quickly and patted my face with a wet paper towel. I hesitated only a minute before typing a reply. Fast food will rot your guts. Next time when I give you a reward, I expect you to treat yourself to something worthwhile.

The words felt stilted without my paper and pen and the luxury of time. Standing in a public bathroom that reeked of disinfectant, it was hard to conjure up an image of myself as a wickedly commanding mistress. Yet there was no denying the thrill rippling through me when I hit the send button.

Eric had finished his taco by the time I got back. If he thought anything of how long it had taken me, he didn't mention it. He balled up his wrapper and tossed all the trash as I picked up my cup.

"We could start back," I said just as his phone erupted in a jangle.

"Excuse me," he said and waited the bare half second for me to nod my assent. He flipped open the phone and his eyes scanned the message. He smiled and tucked it back into his pocket. "Ready?"

"Can we go back a little slower?" I lifted my cup.

"Sure." Eric rolled his head on his neck then patted his stomach with a grin. "If you want."

The darkening sky and sudden chill breeze kept us from dawdling, but the conversation made the time pass just as fast as if we'd been running. I forgot for a moment or two, listening, that I was deceiving him and that I knew his secrets. Eric had a great sense of humor and was smart. God, was he smart, but not in the way that made me feel stupid. He talked about a lot of subjects, always leaving room for me to comment. And he listened, really listened to my answers. By the time we got back to the Manor the first drops of cold spring rain were spattering, and I was half in love with him.

"I need to go in," I said at the front door. "Thanks for the soda."

"I'm going to head down the other direction. Get another

mile or so in. It's my day off," Eric explained. "I need something to work off some of the stress, you know?"

I could help him with that, but I couldn't exactly say so. "Sure. See you around."

He waved and left me at the door. Upstairs in my apartment, I stripped out of my clothes and ran the shower, where I scrubbed away the sweat and thought about Eric. I had the unfair advantage, no doubt about it. I tipped my face into the spray, thinking of his smile and laugh, and then the stroke of his fist on his cock. I knew things I had no right to know.

I couldn't decide if I liked him better because I knew, and I had no way to tell. I'd noticed him before I found out. Maybe that meant it was fate. Or coincidence. Or stupid, dumb luck. Maybe if I hadn't put two and two together I'd have already forgotten about him. Or at least fucked him.

But I hadn't done either of those things, so I did this, instead.

Your time is no longer your own. Every minute belongs to me. No matter what else you're doing, I expect your thoughts to be of how your actions would please or displease me. To this end, I expect a full accounting of your evening from 6:00 p.m. until midnight. Hourly, you will text your whereabouts to me and your activities of the past hour.

Chapter 23

"You have our numbers, right?" Stella was running late, as usual.

"Yep."

I'd arrived on time with a handful of gossip magazines I'd picked up to get me through an evening of watching the Cartoon Network or listening to Tyler's commentary on his latest video game. My dad had promised me dinner but that meant a couple of frozen pizzas already heading toward burned in the oven.

She hopped on one foot to slide the strap of her shoe higher on her heel while she fumbled with an earring at the same time. The woman was incredibly coordinated. She got both ends of her situated and put her foot down, then looked at me. "Have you lost weight?"

I looked at myself. "I guess so. Some."

Stella did a slow circle around me, staring. "You look good. That skirt is nice. Ann Taylor?"

Leave it to Stella to look at my ass and see a brand name. She didn't need to know I bought it at the Salvation Army. "Yes."

"Nice. I have a great bag that would go with those shoes, too. Let me go grab it."

"Stella," my dad broke in. "We're going to be late."

Stella fixed him with a look that put him in his place. "Vince, really. It's ten minutes away. Let me just run up and grab the bag for Paige."

My dad followed her with a fond look as she ran up the stairs. He always looked at her that way, as though he was granting her every wish and it made him happy to do it. It probably did. I sometimes wondered if he'd ever looked at my mom that way.

"Where are the boys?" I asked him.

He waved a hand toward the den. "In there, somewhere."

"Have a good time," I told him just as Stella reappeared with a truly monstrous purse.

She handed it to me with a beaming smile. "Here. Won't they match just perfectly?"

I looked at my pointy-toed boots and then at the bag. They were both black but that was where any matching I saw ended. The bag sported several huge gold buckles, and the straps had been braided with gold lamé. Tassels dangled. That purse had more bling than Flava Flav's mouth.

I thanked her anyway, but she held the purse back when I reached for it. Stella shook her head slowly and eyed me. She put the bag on the kitchen table.

"No. You know, that's not really for you, after all. It's not really your style, is it, Paige?"

I was too surprised that she thought I had a style to disagree even for politeness. "No. Not really."

"Stella. Time." My dad tapped his watch.

She sighed. "Oh, well. I thought it would look so cute with those boots, but honestly, Paige, you've got a much…cleaner…style. Now."

It wasn't the cleanest of compliments, but I smiled anyway. "You'd better get going."

In a cloud of perfume and the jingle of jewelry, she finally allowed him to pull her away. I walked them to the front door and closed it after them, but it took me until I reached the kitchen again to realize something. Even a few months ago, Stella's compliment would have had me buzzing with resentful gratitude. Now…it wasn't that I didn't care. It was more that it didn't matter.

My phone buzzed against my thigh and I pulled it out with a smile.

Just showered. Am eating a turkey sandwich. Have a video to watch. I'm alone on a Saturday night.

He might be expecting an answer, but that wasn't part of the plan, so I put my phone back in my pocket and turned my attention to my own dinner.

"Paige!" Tyler bounced into view as I opened the oven and pulled out the pizza, cheese overbrowned. "Guess what!"

I set the pizza on the special marble trivets Stella had ordered from Italy when they redid their kitchen. "What."

"I got all the way up to level seventeen on Windago Diamond! C'mon, come and see!" Tyler tugged at my hand still covered in the hot mitt.

"Give me a minute, Ty." Together we studied the pizza.

He made a face. "Do we have to eat that?"

"I thought you loved pizza."

He leaned forward. "But it's gross."

"Yeah. Sorry, kiddo, it's what your mom left."

He sighed and leaned on the counter. "Can I have peanut butter and jelly?"

Wow. If the kid was giving up pizza in favor of PB & J that was pretty bad. "What if I take you guys out? Want to go to Jungle Java or someplace?"

They had pizza there, overpriced and not much better than the one Stella had left. At least it wouldn't be burned. And yeah, it was a little selfish of me. If the boys were running rampant through the playground or in the arcade I could sit and read my magazines in as much peace as the constant noise would allow me.

"Yesss!" Tyler pumped his fist in the air. "Jeremy, c'mon, let's go! Paige is going to take us to Jungle Java!"

One young boy shouldn't have made so much noise, but he was going to be tall like our dad, and his feet were already bigger than mine. Tyler thundered into the den with me at his heels. We found Jeremy sullenly thumbing the controls of the game hooked up to the big-screen TV in the corner. He didn't even glance up when Tyler bounded down the two steps to the sunken room and flew onto the couch to bounce his brother.

"Get off, retard!" Jeremy shoved Tyler hard enough to roll him onto the floor.

"Hey!" I shouted before either of them had the chance to get into it. "Shut up, both of you. Cut it out, or you can stay here and eat your mom's shitty pizza."

Two pairs of wide eyes looked at me. I knew it was the language, but it had worked at getting their attention. I gestured at the TV.

"Turn that off and get your shoes on. Let's go."

"Jungle Java blows," Jeremy muttered as he pushed past me.

I caught him by the elbow. He stopped, refusing to meet my eyes. He stood almost as tall as me, but he didn't pull away.

"They have a whole new arcade section." Normally his attitude would have tempted me to tell him to get over himself. Whatever was bugging Jeremy had spilled beyond his parents and was slopping onto me, but I thought of what I'd been like at twelve and gave him a break.

He shrugged and wouldn't give me his face while his brother rocketed past us blabbing a mile a minute about what he was going to play and how his friend from school had spent his tickets on a really cool neon light for his room, and…and…and…

"Can it, shorty. Get in the car." I watched them both head out the front door, Tyler still blabbing and Jeremy maintaining his unusual silence.

Once we got to Jungle Java, I had to physically restrain Tyler from running across the parking lot. "Dude. Chill. There are cars here."

He lunged like a racehorse trying to get out of the gate. "Hurry up, Paige! God!"

"God," I mimicked him, but moved them both inside where I forked over twenty bucks in tokens for each of them and ordered a large pizza and soft drinks.

"Wow, Paige. You're the best!" Tyler goggled at the tokens in the special plastic holder that clipped to his belt.

Jeremy took his without comment, but held back until I'd let his brother loose in the arcade. "Thanks."

Forty bucks wasn't anything for me to sneeze at, but I'd thought to them it would be chump change. Their gratitude surprised me. "You're welcome. Go have fun. I'll be right here."

Jeremy nodded and stalked off toward the arcade. Jungle Java was reputedly adding a laser-tag section to the rear, but so far nothing had started. For a little place that had started off serving coffee and hosting an indoor playground for toddlers, it had really grown. I'd taken the boys here a couple times when they were younger. It was hard to believe Jeremy would start middle school in the fall. It was hard to believe a lot of things time had changed.

My phone rang and my heart leaped, but it wasn't the next text from Eric. I'd set my phone to vibrate for texts, and it wasn't yet time. I took the call anyway.

"Austin."

"How'd you know it was me?"

"I have caller ID, dork."

He laughed. "So that means I'm in your address book, huh?"

I didn't want to admit it.

"Paige? Do you have me in your phone?"

"Yes, but only because you keep calling me all the time." Around me harried mothers squawked at their kids and I cupped a hand over the mouthpiece.

"Where are you?"

I sighed. "Jungle Java."

"You got Arty?"

"No. Jeremy and Tyler."

Austin was silent for a few seconds. "Can I come over?"

A screaming child ran by me with his mother in hot pursuit. The clerk brought the pizza to my table and I craned my neck to motion for my brothers to come and get their food before it got cold. Both of them saw me but ignored me. "Little bastards."

"Huh?"

I'd heard what he said, but pretended I hadn't. "Austin, I have to go."

"You haven't returned any of my messages." Austin didn't sound pissed off, but I went immediately on the defensive.

Some tunes just don't change, you know?

"Sorry. I didn't know I was beholden to you."

"Paige, you're not. I'm just saying…I thought maybe we were past some shit. Christ. Why do you have to beat me up?"

"You called me," I pointed out. "What do you want?"

"What do I always want when I call you?"

"I'm busy," I said flatly.

He didn't take offense at that, either. "I can be there in, like, ten minutes."

"In ten minutes the pizza will be all gone and the boys will have burned through their tokens."

"Seven minutes."

"Austin…" I sighed and gestured again, standing to make sure Jeremy and Tyler couldn't ignore me again. "Why?"

"See you."

He hung up before I could say anything else, but then my phone gave its tell-tale buzz and I pulled it from my pocket to read the next update.

Halfway through *The Life of Brian*. Thinking of ice cream.

Again, I didn't reply.

Just the fact he was obeying me had my mind whirling with all sorts of possibilities. Distracted, I was too busy handing out soggy pizza and supervising refilling drinks to think about Austin. It wouldn't be the first time my high school boyfriend turned ex-husband had promised to meet me someplace and didn't show. So when I saw a familiar wheat-gold head moving toward me through the crowd, all I could do was sit back in my seat with half a slice of pizza oozing grease all over my fingers.

"Austin!" Jeremy's face lit for a few seconds before he remembered he was supposed to be furious with the world. He slumped down and raised a limp hand. "Hey, man."

"Hey." Austin gave Jeremy the same languid greeting but slid into the booth next to Tyler. "Shove over, kid. Give me a slice of that pizza."

Tyler had been in the middle of a long description about the games he'd already played and the tickets he'd earned. With fresh ears to bombard, he turned to Austin as though he'd last seen him yesterday instead of more than three years ago. I shook my head and laughed as I finished my slice. Tyler had been just a bit older than Arty when Austin and I split up, and even while we were together, my dad's boys hadn't spent much time with us. Yet both of them had gravitated toward him the same way Arty did. Austin, an only child, had been a good big brother.

I rarely spent time regretting our divorce, but watching Austin with the boys guilt flashed over me. There were other women to replace me, but his relationship with my younger half siblings had been taken from him, too. His glance caught me looking, but I didn't look away.

When the boys went back to the arcade, Austin convinced me to put away my magazines and join him in playing Skee-Ball. He was better than me, racking up the points while tickets flooded from the slot. I didn't get as many points, but I had fun trying. When I tossed my last wooden ball and managed to get it in the ten-point hole, I turned with a whoop to find him staring at me.

"What?" I said, self-conscious about pizza-sauce stains on my face.

"What's going on with you?"

My phone buzzed and I took it out. "Nothing," I said as I flipped it open to read the message.

Done with the movie. Ate ice cream. Considering reading but not sure what. Thinking of getting into bed. So far, very dull night. Sorry.

I pushed my phone deep into my pocket and bent to tear off my tickets. "It's getting late. I need to get the boys home. Let's go cash these in."

Austin stopped me with a hand on my elbow. "Paige."

Around us the noise level never fell below earsplitting, but I heard him clearly. I raised an eyebrow and looked at his hand. He took it away.

"Can we talk?"

I searched the crowd for the boys. "It's late, Austin. I should have the boys back before my dad and Stella get home. I didn't leave a note or anything and they'll be worried."

"I could come with you."

I'd been half turned from him, but now I gave him my full attention. "To my dad's house? Are you nuts?"

For a man who'd been underinvolved in my life, my dad had been furious with Austin when he'd learned we were splitting. A lot of that was because of me. I hadn't told my dad the whole story. Hadn't told anyone, really, just let them make their own assumptions. My mom was the only one who'd seen through my silence and guessed the truth. Not that I felt judged by it. She'd never mentioned it. I just knew she knew.

"Your old man still got it in for me?"

"He's not a fan. Jeremy! Tyler! Let's go!"

Tyler ran toward me with his tickets trailing behind him

from his hand. Jeremy followed with his fisted tight. Before they could say a word I tore my string of tickets in half and handed each a section.

"Go get your prizes and shake your moneymakers. I have to get you home before your mom and dad."

"Here. Take these, too." Austin gave them each half of his tickets, too.

They knew a good thing when they had it and ran off before I could change my mind. I turned to Austin. "You didn't have to do that."

"What am I going to do with a bunch of junky prizes?" He shrugged. "They're kids."

"It was nice." I sounded grudging, and he shot me a grin.

"I can be nice."

I rolled my eyes. "Goodbye, Austin."

"I can't come with?"

"To my dad's house, no." I held up a hand. "And no, not later, either."

His glance fell to my pocket. "You have a boyfriend now, or what?"

Nothing happened to the noise around us, but silence still fell over me. I opened my mouth to reply. Nothing came out. I tried to think of what to say, but my mind stayed blank.

"You can tell me if you do." Austin's eyes didn't make me believe his words.

"I don't have a boyfriend, Austin. Jesus. Is it any of your business?"

I'd always been able to turn around his accusations, but he wasn't having it this time. His blue-eyed gaze pinned me in place as easily as his hands on my wrists had done more than once. He shrugged.

"Or is it just another fuck buddy?" He paused, slim golden brows furrowing.

"No," I said coldly. "And watch your mouth. There are kids around."

Austin's gaze traveled up and down my body before settling on my face. I couldn't tell from his expression what he thought. I didn't have to guess, though, because he told me.

"You've changed, Paige. A lot."

"People change."

He leveled me with a steady look. "Yeah. They do."

And with that, he turned on his heel and walked away.

Chapter 24

"Austin!"

Heads turned. He stopped. He waited until I caught up to him, which was more than I'd expected. Maybe more than I deserved.

"Why do you care?"

It wasn't the question I meant to ask, but I wasn't really sure what I'd meant to ask. I clamped my mouth shut on other words, softer ones. I bit my tongue until I tasted blood.

"Why don't you?"

"I care," I said in a low voice, conscious we were surrounded by a hundred pairs of eyes.

"Paige! Can I go play—"

I cut Tyler off by jamming my hand into my pocket and pulling out a palmful of coins. "Go. You and Jeremy go. Don't leave this building."

"Wow." Tyler took the coins from my hand and looked from me to Austin. "Thanks, Paige!"

"You're good to them," Austin said when Tyler had gone.

"That's me. Sister of the year." I led the way out the glass front doors to the concrete outside. I wished for a coat, though my chill came from deep inside and not even an Eskimo parka would have helped.

We stared at each other until I looked away.

"What do you want from me?"

There wasn't anything wrong with Austin's question, but it made my stomach twist and turn. "I don't want anything from you. That's the point. Isn't it?"

"Jesus, Paige!" The doors opened and a mother holding two kids by the hand pushed her way through. Austin stepped aside to let her pass and we waited until she'd halfway crossed the parking lot before he spoke again. "Why not? Why the fuck not?"

"I don't know!" Again, not what I thought I meant to say but once the words came out I had no others.

He stepped closer to me. Taller. Broader. I couldn't decide if I was intimidated or turned on.

"What will it take to convince you I'm different?"

"What will it take to convince you I'm not?"

We weren't shouting, but my throat hurt as much as if I'd screamed. Austin's face worked. He stepped closer still.

"What do you want? Do you want me to jump through hoops? Is that it? Is that what you want?" He studied my face and must have seen something in it, because all at once his shoulders slumped. "What kind of man does that?"

Helplessly, I thought of Eric and the mingled heat of shame, fury and desire mingled with despair. "Some men would."

Austin tossed his hands in the air and made a noise that had a depth of meaning, even without words. This time, when he walked away, I watched him go and I didn't call him back.

The car ride back to my dad's was quieter, thank God, as Tyler wound down. We made it home to a message on the answering machine telling us they'd be home later than expected. I sent Tyler upstairs to brush his teeth and get into bed, but I held Jeremy back. It was proof of how much Tyler was worn out that he barely argued.

"Sit." I pointed at one of the bar stools pushed up against the kitchen island. "Want a soda?"

"I'm not supposed to."

I'd already pulled out two from the fridge and pushed one toward him. "Yeah, yeah, save the innocent act for your mother."

We both cracked the tops of our cans. From upstairs came the rush of water and some thudding footsteps, then some singing. I laughed. Jeremy rolled his eyes.

"So," I said after I took a long swig. "What crawled up your ass and died?"

"Nothing."

I understood sullen. "Dad says you've been giving him and Stella a hard time. And that you even got into trouble at school. What's up, dude?"

"Did Dad tell you to interrogate me?" Jeremy sneered and didn't even open his soda.

"Ooh. Mr. Vocabulary."

He scowled and hunched over the island. "Why can't he just leave me alone?"

"Because he's your dad."

Jeremy had the same color eyes as my dad. As me. Blue edged with gray. Now they'd gone dark with his anger. "He's your dad, too!"

Of all the things he could have said, I wasn't expecting something like that. "Yeah. So?"

He shrugged violently and hunched forward again. I

leaned on the island across from him and waited. Jeremy had used to be a lot like Tyler, mouth going a mile a minute. I could wait him out.

"Don't you ever…hate him?"

He'd voiced his question so low I almost missed it, but I didn't lean closer to hear better. I pushed back, instead, stunned at the vehemence in his tone. "Hate Dad?"

Jeremy lifted watery eyes to me. "Yeah. Don't you?"

I had absolutely no idea what any of this was about, but I kept my voice gentle. "Why, Jeremy? Do you?"

He ducked his head again. Twelve was tough. Not a kid anymore, not a teen. I'd given my mom her first gray hairs when I was twelve.

"He always tells us family is so *important.*" He spat the last word and I heard the snurfle of snot.

I grabbed a couple tissues from the box on the counter behind me and passed them over. Jeremy grabbed them and tucked them against his face, still bent into the circle of his arms. I drank some soda while I thought of what to say.

"Family *is* important," was all I could come up with.

Jeremy looked at me again, though his tears had to be embarrassing. "He was married before my mom."

"Yeah. I know. To Gretchen and Steven's mom. But that was before you were born, guy."

"But not," Jeremy said in a voice laced thick with disgust, "before *you* were born."

He'd only just now figured it all out. Well, I'd known it younger than twelve and it hadn't made it any easier for me to know my father had been married to another woman when he had me. I was three before my dad really started making an effort to see me, his first marriage already over.

He was dating Stella by then. I never really knew him with anyone else.

"My mom..." Jeremy shuddered and swiped at angry tears. "She's the reason he got divorced from Gretchen and Steve's mom. Isn't she?"

"I don't know, Jeremy. I never asked. It's not my business. And, really, not yours." I didn't want to come off hard on him. I understood. But I also knew it wouldn't change anything for him to be angry over it.

"If family is so important, why did he do that?"

I sighed, at a loss. "I don't know."

Jeremy scrubbed at his face, the tears gone. His bright eyes were shaped like Stella's though they were my dad's color, and he looked like her when he frowned that way. "He cheated on his first wife and had another baby, and then he did it again! That's not putting family first. That's not treating them like they're important!"

Of all my dad's kids I'd thought Gretchen or Steven might have had the most to bitch about. After all, their lives had been turned upside down and torn apart by their dad's infidelity. Mine hadn't been all strawberries and cream, but it had been all I'd ever known. Jeremy and Tyler had lived the lives of princes from birth.

"What are you worried about?" I asked him quietly. "That he'll do it again?"

He didn't have to answer with words. I reached across the island and took my half brother's hand. In my pocket, my phone buzzed, but I didn't reach for it.

"Your dad loves you. And he loves your mom. Crazy like."

Jeremy let me hold his hand but didn't squeeze my fingers in return. "Did he love your mom, Paige?"

I let go of his hand. "I don't know. That's between them."

"And it doesn't make you mad?"

I shrugged. "It used to, I guess. But what can I do about it? I'm a grown-up now, kiddo. I have to do my own thing. At least I know my dad, you know? Some kids never do."

He nodded finally and wiped at his face again with the grimy, shredded tissue. "It makes me so mad, though."

"It's okay to be mad. Maybe you should talk to him about it, though, instead of being bad in school."

Jeremy looked stricken. "He'd tell Mom that I know!"

I didn't point out that it wasn't just our dad who'd done wrong. Stella had known what she was doing, or at least I'd always assumed so since she wasn't a woman who ever did anything by accident. I just patted his hands and washed my own before I finished my soda.

The sound of the garage door opening had us both on our feet. Jeremy hopped up the stairs without a word from me, while I dumped his can in the sink and stashed the can in the recycling bin. By the time my dad and Stella got in the house, silence reigned from upstairs and I was flipping through a back issue of some home-and-garden magazine.

"How did it go?" Stella bustled into the kitchen and stuck an aluminum swan in the fridge. "You got our message? The fund-raiser had only the tiniest hors d'oeuvres and we were starving, and since you were here, well, we just decided to treat ourselves to a nice dinner out."

"No problem. I took them to Jungle Java."

Stella raised a brow. "That junky place?"

My dad had come in behind her and let out a long, loud belch. "What junky place?"

Stella rolled her eyes. "Paige took the boys to Jungle Java."

"Yeah?" He looked at the clock and yawned. "That place is still around?"

I got the not-so-subtle hint. "Yeah. They're upstairs, but I'm not sure if they're asleep."

Stella sighed. "Did they bring home a bunch of junk?"

I grinned unapologetically. "Absolutely."

She gave me a second glance, then a small smile. "I'm going up to say good-night. Are you leaving, Paige?"

"Yeah." I glanced at my dad, who was rooting around in the fridge for something.

"Vince! We just ate!"

"I need a drink," he said and came out holding a bottle of designer water.

"Fine. Good night, Paige. Thanks for watching the boys."

"No problem."

My dad and I turned to watch her head up the steps. I thought he'd ask me about Jeremy since that was the whole reason I'd come over in the first place, but he didn't. He drank his water with a sigh and tossed the empty bottle in the trash. Then he pulled out his wallet and handed me a fifty-dollar bill.

"For watching the kids," he said.

The paper, crisp and sharp edged, rubbed my fingers. "Dad, I don't need this."

"Jungle Java isn't cheap."

"I wanted to take them."

"Take the money, Paige," my dad said amiably enough. "I'm sure you can use it."

I straightened my shoulders and folded the bill in half, then shoved it in my pocket. "You don't have to pay me for watching the boys. I'm doing all right."

My dad laughed. "I'm sure you are. I'm not paying you for anything, I'm just being your dad, okay?"

"Well, then. Thanks." Gratitude stuck in my throat but I forced it out.

My dad had periodically tossed me some money over the years. Never enough. Never when I needed it. It would have been better if he'd done right by my mom and given her child support so I could've had the stylish jeans in middle school or the warmer winter coat. I'd have appreciated that more than the occasional twenty or even fifty dollars, or the sudden flurry of birthday gifts three weeks late and all in the wrong sizes.

"Do you want to go to lunch with me next week?" He yawned again, and I started toward the front door.

"Sure, Dad. Call me."

"I will," he told me at the door and gave me a hug and a kiss on the cheek. "Drive safe."

It was so fatherly it felt foreign. Driving home, my phone vibrated against my leg again, but I didn't pull it out until I got to the parking garage. Two messages waited for me.

In bed. Not tired. What should I call you?

And the second, Still not sleeping.

I hadn't forgotten how I'd looked forward to every note. I'd imagined the sender, my secret commander, crafting each word with the intent of forcing me one more step along a path so curved I couldn't see the end. I'd never thought about how difficult it would be to come up with detailed lists every time, or how it felt to hold someone so firmly in my command.

There were limits. There had to be. I'm sure I'd have found them had the notes kept coming, pushing me harder, or if they'd ordered me to do something so foreign to me I couldn't manage it. I didn't think I'd have committed a crime or done something against my personal code, like have bareback sex with a stranger, or taken drugs.

I didn't know Eric's limits, or how far I wanted to push him, but the thought sifted heat all through me. I thought for another few moments, then got out of my car. It wasn't terribly late, not for a Saturday, but the parking garage was quiet. Across the street I could see a few lights on in apartments, though many windows were dark. Most of the Manor residents would be out and about until much later.

By the time I got to the front doors, I was already tapping out a message. Grinning, I tucked my phone, set to silent, back in my pocket. It was a risk that might not play out the way I'd planned, but it was a good risk.

If you're not sleeping, you should put your time to good use. Go to the lobby. Greet the first person you see. If it's a man, you will engage him in whatever conversation you want. But if it's a woman, you will find a way to serve her. Not to please her, and not to please yourself. To please me.

It was a lot of typing, but the fact it took longer meant he had to wait longer for it. I was already in the lobby, which was still empty. All I had to do was wait.

I caught sight of my face in the mirror above the fireplace nobody ever lit. Blond hair slicked back in a high ponytail, blue eyes smudged with gray liner. The sun had brought out some freckles and my lips still could've used some gloss, but overall, it wasn't a bad picture.

I turned my face from side to side, envisioning heavier

makeup and a leather suit replacing my workout clothes. A whip in my hand. Spike-heeled boots. None of that appealed to me any more than being on my knees with my hands tied had ever turned me on. I swiped a hand over my hair to take care of the wisps falling over my face. I didn't look like a dominatrix. Was that what I was?

It was too soon to be insulted Eric hadn't even asked for my phone number. We'd had two pseudodates but no indication he had any sort of sexual attraction to me. So far, all I knew was that he got off on being ordered around by someone he didn't know, and that I liked him very much.

And that I could make him like me.

Chapter 25

"Paige. Hey."

I'd tried to time my "entrance" just right, grateful nobody else was coming in or out of the building so they couldn't see me lurking by the front door trying to catch a glimpse of the elevators. I'd managed to linger long enough I was the only person in the lobby just as Eric came out of the elevator. He looked around and lit up when he saw me. Relief, maybe. Gratitude.

I wanted it to be desire.

"Eric. Hi." I'm no actress, so I didn't bother pretending I wasn't happy to see him. "What's up?"

"Oh, just…" He didn't quite stammer, but he did trail off with a shrug and a smile. "I have the night off. Couldn't sleep."

I looked at the big clock on the wall opposite the fireplace. "It's only eleven-thirty. It's still early."

"Yeah. Well, I have to work early, so I was trying to be good."

I'd never been afraid to go after what I wanted, and I'd decided I wanted him. "Were you?"

I watched his throat convulse as he swallowed, and I drank in the sudden gleam from his gaze. I knew what he'd been told to do, but now I was watching it happen and my body reacted. My nipples went tight and I sighed silently at the friction of my panties against me.

"I was trying," he said.

Flirting is a dance, even when you're standing still.

"But not succeeding?"

His small smile called my attention to his perfectly full lower lip. "I guess not."

"Bad boy." I didn't coo or purr the words. I didn't have to.

Eric's dark eyes flashed. "I guess I am."

The difference in how he looked at me was subtle, but I'd been watching for it. I knew what he was supposed to do and wondered how he meant to do it. But just then I also wished I hadn't pushed him toward it. Me.

"Well, it's late," I said to tease. "I'd better go upstairs. I'm starving."

Eric dogged my steps toward the elevator. "What are you hungry for?"

I let his question turn me. "Ice-cream sundaes."

"I have ice cream. And hot fudge. And I even have those disgusting cherries."

I smiled at the good luck. "Yeah?"

"Yeah." Eric nodded slowly, his glance going over my shoulder when the elevator doors opened. "Want to come up to my place? I'll make you one."

I back-stepped toward the elevator and he followed as though I pulled him on a string. Or a leash. "Now, why would I do that?"

"Because ice cream's more fun when eaten in pairs?"

I laughed at his answer. “All right. All I have is diet fudge bars, anyway. I’d rather have a real sundae.”

He followed me into the elevator and watched me push the button for his floor. The elevator could hold and had held ten people at a time. We had plenty of room but he stood next to and slightly behind me, so I was aware of his body heat and the soft sound of his breath.

We barely had time to talk on the short ride to his floor and down the hall to his apartment, and I didn’t bother with small talk. Eric, to my relief, didn’t try to force the chatter, either. In five minutes he was unlocking his door and ushering me inside by stepping back to allow me to go through first.

“Such a gentleman,” I said.

He paused after he shut the door. “I try.”

Again, we stared at each other. I was used to men who made the first move. Eric didn’t move, so we stayed still, both of us looking.

“Ice cream?” I prompted over my urge to taste his mouth.

“In the kitchen.”

He pulled out a chair for me and settled me in it like a queen before bustling around to pull out a couple cartons of ice cream from the freezer. He set them on the counter, then grabbed a jar of fudge from the cupboard and put it in the microwave. From another cupboard he pulled real ice-cream-sundae glasses, and from the drawer two long-handled spoons.

“I had no idea,” I said as he turned. I waved at his preparations, searching for the words that would keep me on top, but found none.

He grinned. “I like ice cream. What can I get for you? Chocolate, vanilla or mint chip?”

"A scoop of each?" It had been ages since I'd eaten ice cream. "Extra hot fudge."

"Whatever you want." Eric's simple words felt anything but simple.

He brought two sundaes, heaped high with ice cream and oozing with hot fudge, to the table. True to what I'd come to expect from him, he served me first before taking the chair across from mine. He waited until I'd tasted my ice cream before he even lifted his spoon.

"Good?" he asked.

I could only make a murmuring happy noise as my taste buds, so long denied, practically sang. When I scooped a mouthful of hot fudge, my low, throaty moan was louder than I'd intended. Eric stopped with his spoon halfway to his mouth.

I swallowed sweetness. "It's good."

He finished his bite, and I watched his lips close over the spoon. I watched, too, as his tongue came out to lick away the drops of ice cream that had dripped onto his hand. Caught up in my lustful fantasy of what he could do to me with that tongue, I dropped my spoon.

Both of us looked to where it had clattered to the floor. I didn't move. Eric looked at the spoon on the floor, then up at me. And then slowly, carefully, he slid from his chair to his knees in front of me. The spoon clicked on the tile when he reached for it, and I saw his hand was shaking, just barely.

He looked up at me. "Let me get that for you."

This was the second time since we'd met he'd been at my feet. This time he was there because I'd put him there, though he didn't know it was me. My heart leaped, the thudding almost painful under my ribs. My breath lodged in my throat, and though a thousand words swirled around in my brain, not one of them would come out of my mouth.

When the heat of his hands cuffed my ankles, I drew in another breath on top of the one I hadn't yet released. I'd changed into a summer-weight black skirt, the cut loose and fabric soft on my bare legs. It hung just past my knees, but sitting had pulled the cloth tighter and higher on my thighs. The pressure of Eric's breath shouldn't have been strong enough to move the fabric of my skirt, but I felt it move on my shins as he exhaled.

He didn't look at me as he slid his long fingers slowly up my calves. They reached the soft skin behind my knees and I let out another slow sigh. When he reached the hem of my skirt I thought he'd stop, but Eric, head still bent, his eyes on only he knew what, pushed the material up and over my knees. He leaned forward to press his cheek to the inside of my knee. I froze. Our breathing sounded very loud in the silence.

When I didn't move or protest, Eric gave his head a half turn. His breath blew hot on my skin. I tensed, my hands clutching the arms of the chair, but my knees opened for him and my head tipped back just a little.

He kissed the inside of my knee with parted lips, and the brief wet press of his tongue teased my flesh. I looked down at his thick dark hair and wanted to sink my fingers into it. Instead, I clutched the chair arms tighter as Eric nuzzled higher onto my thigh.

He would be able to smell my arousal, I knew it, could feel my panties getting damp. His mouth moved higher as his hands moved up over my knees and rested there. My next breath turned to syrup in my lungs and gave me no air.

I could see his eyes, closed, the dark lashes so long they cast shadows on his cheeks. Each feathery kiss followed the next, a micron's distance apart. He would never reach my pussy at that pace.

The only sounds had been our breathing and the squeak of the chair as his movements rocked me gently in it. Now I heard the low but unmistakable sound of Eric's groan. I felt it, too, in a puff of hotter air and the wetness of his kiss higher still but not high enough.

I looked down at his hunched shoulders and the big hands pushing up my skirt. At his dark hair, the fringes tickling my thighs. At the sweep of his lashes and slope of his forehead, all I could glimpse of his face.

What the fuck was I doing?

One hand found its way to his hair and I lost my fingers in it, relishing the springy coarseness for only a moment before I tightened my grasp and pulled his head up. His eyes opened, blurred with lust. His lips, moist, parted as he focused on my face.

I could not do this. Not like this. Not because I didn't love him, or because he wasn't my boyfriend, not even because we hadn't even had an official date. I'd done more with men I'd never even seen again. And not because I didn't want his face between my thighs, making me come on his tongue, because I wanted it so much desire left me light-headed.

"No," I said in a grinding voice, because this wasn't fair.

Not to him, and not to me.

Eric pushed away from me at once and I released my grip on his hair. He didn't get to his feet but rocked back on his heels, his expression stricken. "I'm sorry. Paige. I don't know what made me think that was okay. I'm sorry."

With shaking hands, I pushed my skirt to cover my knees. I swallowed against the lump in my throat and tried to breathe slow and easy so I wouldn't embarrass myself by fainting or something stupid. I couldn't meet his eyes.

"Paige, I'm so sorry." Eric's voice broke on my name and he cleared his throat but didn't say anything else.

Would he have gone to his knees for me had he not been doing as I'd ordered?

The chair screeched on the tiles as I pushed to my feet. None of my muscles wanted to cooperate. They wanted me back in that chair, my legs spread wide with Eric's face between them. I shook my head at myself, but Eric misunderstood.

"Please…I'm really not a jerk." He stood but didn't reach for me. "I shouldn't have done it. But I was…"

I found my voice. "You were what?"

"I was taken by you." His curiously old-fashioned phrasing sounded just right. "I like you, and I thought…I was stupid. I'm sorry."

I could have said it was okay, but it wasn't, and not for the reasons he'd have assumed. "I'm going to go now."

He nodded and went at once through the living room to the front door, which he didn't open. By the time I got to him I was able to breathe, though my muscles still felt loose. Eric stepped aside, giving me plenty of room. We didn't look at each other.

"Thank you for the ice cream," I said formally. Stiffly.

"You're welcome."

He held the door open for me, but I didn't look at him as I went out.

I left no note, no list the next morning. Courtesy of the schedule he'd sent me, I knew Eric would be off to work before I roused myself from bed, but that was just an excuse. I was awake and could have run down to make sure he had something to keep him smiling all day.

I hadn't slept much, just tossed and turned, so when the phone rang I picked it up on the first ring. "Hmm?"

"Paige?"

"Arthur." I sighed. "What did I tell you about calling me so early?"

"But I'm hungry," he whispered. "And Mama won't wake up."

I yawned. "You know what you can have. You don't need to wake her up."

"When are you coming over again?"

I hadn't really thought about it. "I don't know, buddy. How's school?"

"My teacher says I shouldn't talk so much in class."

"Your teacher is probably right."

A shuffling squawk came through the phone, then a voice. "Who is this?"

"Mom. It's me."

"Oh. Paige. Hi, honey." Her relief seemed way out of proportion to Arty's early morning dialing. "What's wrong?"

"Nothing's wrong. Arty called me."

"What's wrong with him?"

"Nothing that I know of. He calls me a lot on Sunday mornings."

"He does?" She sighed. "I'm sorry. I'll remind him he's not to use the phone without permission. He's been…well, he's been calling Leo."

I yawned again, blinking. "So?"

"Leo doesn't live here anymore," my mom said flatly.

"But he was like a dad to Arthur." I got on one elbow to look at the clock. Gad-awful early. Silence told me I'd said the wrong thing. "I'm sorry, Mom, but it's true."

"Arthur is not Leo's son," she said after another half minute. "I haven't said Leo couldn't see him, but he can't go calling whenever he wants to. He's not my boyfriend. And he's not Arty's dad."

My mom had had a lot of boyfriends. She hadn't bothered to tell me all the reasons why she'd broken up with each of them, though I had been subjected to the ranting and raving on occasion when one had really pissed her off. When I got older, she'd shared more, though I'd never asked her to. Now I waited for some revelation about Leo, some reason that had turned her against him, but she didn't give me one.

"Arty! Get out of the snack drawer! Have some cereal!" She sounded tired and cranky.

I knew how that felt. "I'm going back to sleep, okay?"

"When are you coming down?"

I told her what I'd told Arty, adding, "I've got stuff going on."

"We'd like to see you. Me and Arty. You could come for the weekend, Paige. We could make fudge."

"Mom…"

"Don't say no. Just think about it, okay? We miss you. I miss you."

There wasn't anything to say that wouldn't hurt her feelings, so I sighed. "Okay. I'll check my calendar."

"I have to go. Arty just spilled the milk."

"You know what they say," I tried to joke. "Don't cry over it."

"I'm not crying," my mother said in a stone-edged voice I never heard from her.

Then she hung up.

Chapter 26

The flowers came the next day, a bouquet of thirteen red roses tied with a thick satin ribbon and adorned with baby's breath. They were delivered early, too, the card in my mailbox announcing I had a package at the front desk tucked in amongst the bills the way not too long ago the notes had appeared. It set my heart to racing the way those notes always had, but the flowers sunk my guts to my shoes.

"Someone has a special friend," Alice said when she handed me the bouquet with a knowing grin. She leaned closer. "I knew it wouldn't take you long, hon."

I paused with the flowers in my hand, not daring to hold them too tight unless there were thorns. "For what?"

"To get one," Alice said. "A man."

Being unable to speak is different than not having words. I hate not knowing what to say. I goggled at her like an idiot and pulled the flowers closer to my chest. The look on my face set her back a step, her ready smile fading.

"Pretty flowers." It was the woman from the mailboxes stopping to pick up her own package. "From your boy-friend?"

"I don't have a boyfriend," I said shortly for her benefit and Alice's. "I don't know who these are from."

If they shared a look it was behind my back, because I turned away to pull the card from between the stems. It was a printed card, not handwritten. Three words.

I'm sorry. Eric.

Austin had given me flowers once or twice, sad and scraggly bouquets picked up from the grocery store. He'd picked me flowers, too, from his mother's garden and put them in a beer mug for me to find on our kitchen table when I got home from school. These were my first roses.

I didn't have time to put them in my apartment before I headed off to work, so I took them with me. I didn't have to worry about getting them into water right away because each stem was capped in a small plastic tube, but I arranged them where I could see them from my chair.

One minute I smiled to look at them. The next, I frowned. Eric shouldn't be apologizing to me, but it was sweet he had. And he'd done it without prompting.

"Paige, I—" Paul stopped in his doorway. "Pretty flowers."

"Thanks." A mouse click saved my document, and I looked up at him. He had a paper in his hand. A list, for which I held out my hand.

He didn't hand it over. Paul held it in both his hands and rubbed the paper back and forth in his fingers. He looked again at my flowers.

"Is there something you need, Paul?"

Paul cleared his throat and folded the list in half, then half again. "Vivian has asked for a meeting with us today to talk about the possibilities of your promotion. We're getting lunch ordered in. At eleven."

He said it like I had a choice, as though he weren't my boss. He folded the paper again and tucked it into the pocket of his gray suit pants. Today he wore a pale pink shirt with a maroon tie and looked very pulled together.

"I'm not sure I really want to talk about a promotion with Vivian."

Paul nodded and gave me a small smile. "It can't hurt to listen to what she has to say, Paige."

He was right, so I nodded and turned my attention back to the computer. Paul waited a couple seconds, then left me. I stared for a while at my computer but couldn't make much sense of the words on the screen.

At ten-fifty, Vivian click-clacked into the office on her expensive high heels. She carried an immense mug, the sort you buy at the convenience store and use for refills on fountain drinks. It looked out of place against her high-profile suit and jewelry, but she clutched it like she'd kill anyone who tried to take it.

"Paige." She nodded. After a second she remembered to smile, too.

"Vivian." I didn't get up from my desk, though I did take my hands from the keyboard. "Paul said you wanted to meet at eleven. He's in his office. I'll be in when I'm finished with this last file."

My smile stretched the corners of my mouth, but I didn't feel it in my eyes. Vivian took a long, gurgling swig from her mug and went into Paul's office without more than a swift rap of her knuckles on the door frame to announce her arrival. My victory was small but mighty. She couldn't complain I wasn't being prompt, but I'd made it clear I wasn't going to be rushed, either.

I'm not a fan of scary movies, especially the kind where the girl knows there's something awful in the basement or attic but goes in anyway, armed with only her ear-piercing screams and a wooden spoon or something. Facing Paul's office felt that stupid to me. I knew what they wanted to talk about, and I knew I didn't want to discuss it.

I liked working for Paul, even if I was "only" an executive assistant. It wasn't, frankly, all I intended to be. Not forever. But for now. Moving into another position, working for another person didn't appeal to me even though I knew it should, but I didn't want to work for Vivian Darcy. I didn't like her, and I didn't think she liked me, which made her sudden interest all the more disturbing.

Despite all that, at 11:00 a.m. exactly I pushed away from my desk and knocked on Paul's door. They were laughing, their heads bent together, when I knocked, and they both looked up. Paul put distance between them at once, pushing back in his rolling chair. Vivian didn't move. Her mug rested with familiarity on the edge of Paul's desk.

I hadn't brought him coffee but he still sipped from a venti Starbucks cup, so I figured he was all right. I took the chair in front of the desk but kept it back far enough that my knees didn't come close to the wood. I crossed my legs, watching her, not him, and she gave me a level stare in return.

"So. Paige." Vivian's smile didn't warm me any more than it ever had, though I thought she'd put more effort into it. She tucked a short blond curl behind her ear with French-tipped fingers and didn't say anything else.

I smiled, too.

Paul cleared his throat after a few seconds and leaned his elbows on the desk. "Paige, Vivian's been working with the marketing department to create some entry-level positions. The idea is to get expansion going on, starting from the ground up. They're looking to hire in-house, people they feel will be an asset to the department."

"And you feel I'd be an asset to your department?" I watched her face carefully as she answered.

Her gaze flicked so briefly toward Paul and back to me I was supposed to miss it. She might not even have known she looked at him first, that's how fast it was. But I didn't miss it.

"Oh, yes," Vivian said. "Absolutely. Paul's spoken so winningly of you."

Seriously, what the fuck? Aside from the fact I was pretty sure she hadn't used it correctly, who ever says "winningly"? Except, of course, a woman who's trying to find something flattering to say to a woman she doesn't really like.

And then I understood it.

Paul and Vivian were fucking. They were very good about hiding it, more discreet than a lot of interoffice couples I'd come across. But there it was, the truth slapped down on the desk between all of us like a gauntlet. They were lovers and her dislike for me had nothing to do with anything as simple as my clothes or education. It was all about my blond hair and blue eyes and the size of my tits and ass. She thought I had her on the run.

"I haven't seen the jobs posted on the board," I said without bursting into sudden laughter.

Vivian looked at her gigantic mug but resisted drinking from it. "They're not going up for open applications until after we've interviewed the people we have already prescreened. We'd really like you to consider an interview."

I didn't know much about how human resources works, or the hoops anyone's required to jump through in the name of being politically correct, but that didn't sound quite right to me. At any rate, I nodded as though it made perfect sense. Paul smiled and looked back and forth between us.

I couldn't look at him. Not because I'd figured out Vivian thought he and I might be having a fling but because I was convinced *they* had. And it wasn't any swinging of my moral compass toward judgment, either, but more about the fact I didn't want to believe he had such bad taste.

"Can I ask you why you prescreened me? Aside from Paul's recommendation." I knew my smile for him had to be a sliver in her skin, but I didn't care. "I don't have any background in marketing. I have a business-school degree from Harrisburg Area Community College."

"There's a certain amount of on-the-job training we're expecting to provide."

I'd spent enough time around people who couldn't stand silence to understand how powerful it can be. I nodded instead of speaking, even to murmur what could be construed as consent. Vivian looked at Paul, but he and I had already established our lack of need for speech to communicate.

She cleared her throat to draw his attention and then drank, at last, from her mug. "Paul has spoken so highly of you, Paige, and your background can only help you. This is a great opportunity."

"Could you explain why?"

Her lips parted, and she drank again instead of answering me right away. When she put the mug down on Paul's desk the sloshing from inside had lessened considerably. She looked at him again with her brow furrowed. Clearly, the fact I wasn't jumping up and down for joy to leave behind my dreary life as a secretary for the bright, shiny world of junior whatever-thefuck confused her.

"You'd be salaried, not hourly," she said. "And of course, there'd be more responsibility."

I kept my eyes on Paul. "I have plenty of responsibility."

We all laughed, though she didn't sound amused. She drank again and her mug rattled with the unmistakable sound of emptiness. She put the cup down with a final-sounding thud.

"This would be different," she said flatly.

The men I knew were more often insensitive rather than purposefully cruel, obtuse rather than inattentive. Paul was more in tune than most and, smile fading, he turned to her. I wondered if he'd only just now figured out her real reasons for wanting me out of his office.

The silence went on long enough to make it officially awkward. Then Vivian stood. "Excuse me a minute."

I was surprised she'd lasted as long as she had. My kidneys would have been floating. Neither of us said anything as she went into Paul's bathroom and closed the door firmly behind her.

He turned to stare at me. "Paige."

"Let me just get something straight, Paul. This isn't even an interview for the new position. I'm interviewing for an *interview* for a job I've been preselected for, right?" I leaned forward and caught his gaze with mine.

Paul hesitated, then nodded. "Yes."

Back straight, chin lifted, I sat back in my chair and recrossed my legs. From the bathroom I heard the sound of running water. I kept my expression neutral, though I had no doubt he could tell my mood even through the steady monotone of my voice.

"Then I deserve to know exactly why I've been selected and why I should consider it," I told him. "You can't expect me just to jump up and down for joy because someone's offering to take me away from all this."

Paul opened his mouth but before he could speak, I added, "I happen to like the job I have, Paul. Very much."

"I'm glad," he said quietly, and before he could say more, Vivian came out of the bathroom.

I took petty pleasure in seeing that she'd splashed water on her skirt and silk shirt. She'd run a damp hand through her haircut, too, to settle it into place, and I could see the edges of her makeup had run a little bit along her cheeks. She didn't know I didn't want the man who wasn't even hers, but the fact she was worried he might want me settled the power between us, and I was on top. We both knew it.

"If you could describe the job to me, that might be helpful," I told her. "And we could set up a time for an interview."

The conversation had turned upside down and Vivian didn't like it, but it would have been difficult for her to react without looking like a bitch, or worse, stupid. We gave each other a matched pair of fake smiles with Paul the prize between us. I stood and looked down on them both.

"I'll get back to work, Paul."

He nodded. I left. Behind me I heard her soft exhale and the murmur of their discussion, but I couldn't tell if she was castigating me or if he was defending me. I didn't really care, either way.

Vivian Darcy didn't intimidate me anymore.

Chapter 27

My heart skipped all kinds of beats when I saw the note in my mailbox, but I didn't have to read the signature to know it wasn't from Eric's original anonymous mistress. I didn't have to know who she was to know she'd never have sent a note on anything less than the finest, and this was a piece of blue-lined, loose-leaf paper, the sort you can buy three packs for a buck during the back-to-school sales. I gave it a surreptitious sniff anyway, and caught a hint of cologne under the scent of cheap ink.

Eric had a doctor's stereotypical scrawl. *I hope you like the flowers.* His signature was mostly unrecognizable but for the E at the front. I folded the note and tucked it into my bag, then headed up to my apartment where I unfolded it and laid it on the kitchen table so it could stare at me while I made my dinner.

I had a few options. I could ignore the note, and the flowers, which I'd brought home and finally put in water. I could send him a text or leave him a note commanding him to pursue me…or ignore me. As I made my simple meal of pasta with olive oil and garlic and a tossed salad, I kept sight of the note and the flowers, and by the time I'd eaten and cleared away the dishes, there seemed only one real choice of action.

I knocked on his door ten minutes later. I'd brushed my hair and slid gloss along my lips, had changed from my work clothes into a pair of jeans and a cute T-shirt with a fitted sweatshirt. I'd brushed my teeth, too, just in case. When he opened the door I didn't want the first thing he noticed to be a wave of garlic breath.

"Paige!" He sounded pleased and only a little apprehensive. "Hi."

"I came to thank you for the flowers," I said without making a move toward the door.

I hadn't yet decided where I wanted this to go, but I was sure I knew how I wanted it to happen. I didn't want this to be forced by an unseen hand. I didn't want to wonder if I was competing against myself.

"You're welcome. I hope you liked them."

"They were beautiful. Nobody's ever given me roses before," I said, and Eric looked surprised.

"You're kidding."

I shook my head. "Nope."

"Well, that's just not right." He laughed a little and stepped aside, subtly, without making it seem as though he was inviting me in.

I'd learned the benefits of silence, but I also knew when it was time to speak. "Can I come in?"

I saw his hesitation, as subtle as the not-invitation had been, but then he stepped farther aside with a smile. "Sure."

He brought me a glass of iced tea and we sat on his couch facing each other from either side. I could've stretched out my arm and still not been able to touch him. He'd brought a glass of tea for himself, but he set it on the coffee table and didn't drink it while I sipped without quite tasting.

"About the other night," I said. "I just wanted to tell you, Eric…you don't have to apologize."

"No, I was out of line," he began, but I cut him off with a raised hand.

"No. It was fine. I was surprised, that's all." I sipped tea and then put my glass down, too. It settled onto the table with a clink.

"Paige," Eric said softly. "I was surprised, too."

I believed him, though it meant I was no longer on solid ground. I studied my hands, clasped loosely in my lap, before I looked at him. Tension bloomed between us and I wanted to lean toward it, and him, but I held myself still so as not to give myself away.

"Would you let me take you to dinner?" Eric did lean, just a little.

I had hooked up, hung out, made out and had a few unmemorable one-night stands. I'd been married and divorced and both purposefully and unintentionally celibate. But, like the roses, being asked out on a date was a first.

My phone, which I'd shoved into my pocket, buzzed. I didn't miss the way Eric's eyes lit up or how he reached automatically for the iPhone on the table behind him, or the faint look of disappointment when he realized it wasn't a message for him.

I'd have let it go but Eric looked expectant, so I pulled it out and flipped it open.

Where you @?

The sigh came out before I could stop it. I deleted the message. Eric didn't ask, but I offered, anyway.

"From my ex," I explained. "He likes to keep in touch."

"Do you like him keeping in touch?"

I'd have asked the same question if it had been him getting the call, but I'm not sure I'd have been as good at keeping any hint of jealousy out of my voice.

"I've known him since high school. It's sort of a habit."

"Ah." Eric sat back a little.

When my phone rang a moment later, I ignored it in my palm and didn't answer it. I looked at him, instead. "I'd love to go to dinner with you, Eric."

It should have been enough, the promise of that date, but it wasn't. Along with the other myriad lists commanding he relate to me just about everything in his life, I left him a pair of my panties, worn, tucked into an envelope and a note detailing exactly what he was supposed to do with them. And I wanted pictures. They were waiting in my in-box when I got home from work that night. A series of shots taken in close-up of his prick, his fist, the soft cotton of my panties clutched tight around the shaft.

I was halfway in love.

I could've found a thousand pictures just like them on any Internet porn site, true, but all my breath disappeared when I opened them. He'd done this for me. Because of me.

Powerful stuff.

Dinner was, if you'll pardon the pun, anticlimactic after that. He took me to a nice new Mexican restaurant where we drank margaritas and listened to a very good mariachi band while we shared first-date stories as though he'd never been on his knees in front of me.

He kissed me in the elevator when it reached his floor. One

small, sweet kiss, lips closed. A hand on my waist. A gentle squeeze. When the door started to close, he laughed and hopped off through. He watched me as it shut, until the last thing I saw was his smile through the crack.

When I got home, my phone rang. It wasn't the expected text from Eric relating the details of the date, though I had left him a list of topics I wanted essays on. It was the other man in my life, the one I couldn't throw away and didn't want to keep.

"I'm downstairs. I just wanted to tell you, I'm coming up."

"Oh, no, you're not." I cradled the phone against my shoulder and looked in the mirror. I'd been unbuttoning my shirt but now I stopped. "I'll meet you at the Mocha in fifteen minutes."

"No way!"

"Way," I said firmly.

Silence as neither of us gave in. Well, silence as I waited for him to refuse so I could hang up. Austin sighed, finally.

"Fine. I'll meet you there."

I didn't change my clothes. I wanted him to see me all dressed up and wonder why. Yes, it was bitchy. Yes, it was unnecessary. But I was hardly going to toss on a pair of grungy sweatpants and a pair of sneakers to greet him. It didn't matter that Austin had already seen me at my worst.

You might imagine the audience for caffeine would diminish after nine at night, but not in the Mocha. People hunched over their refillable mugs, mainlining high-powered flavored coffees and clutching at specialty drinks as they chatted in small groups and played board games. Soft music, something indie and folksy that would make my ears bleed if I paid too much attention to it, drifted out of the speakers.

I spotted Austin right away. His faded denim stood out from

the rest of the skinny jeans and flat-ironed-hair boys, and he didn't wear a speck of guyliner. His hair had grown long enough now to pull back in a ponytail at the nape of his neck. He was carrying two big cups.

When he saw me, his face lit up, so much the way it used to that my heart hurt. I swallowed hard against the rush of memories threatening to topple me right then and there. He handed me a mug and gestured toward a love seat set toward the back of the shop.

"Sit?"

He asked, didn't tell, so I nodded. "Sure."

I had time to compare first-date awkwardnesses as he followed me. My dinner with Eric had been thick with tension, but with Austin at my back all I could think of was how uncomfortable it felt to not know what to say. I sat and warmed my hands on the cup, which was almost too hot for comfort.

"You look pretty."

"Thanks."

We both sipped. Austin put his mug on the table and dug in his pocket for something he held out to me. "Here."

I didn't take it at first. "What is it?"

He held it out again. "Just something they were giving out at the bank when I signed up for a new checking account. Made me think of you."

"Is it money?" I took it, not money but a small clear plastic bottle.

Hand sanitizer, the bottle imprinted with the bank logo. Just a small bottle, only enough for one or two uses. I clutched it in my palm and didn't know what to say.

"I thought you'd laugh," Austin said when I didn't make a sound. "Shit, Paige. I'm sorry. I just thought—"

"I know what you thought. Why you thought it." I tucked it into my bag.

"It's just…you know. Your thing."

He did know me. I hadn't believed he did. Maybe I hadn't wanted to believe.

"Thank you."

More awkward silence.

When he finally spoke, it was in a man's voice and not the familiar voice of the boy I'd fallen in love with. It helped, a little. Made him more of a stranger than he was, so I could keep him just far enough away not to leap into his arms.

"Paige," Austin said. "I just wanted to tell you that I'm really sorry."

I didn't know I was going to touch him until it was too late to pull back my hand. His hair was soft beneath my fingers, and I let them drift over it and down to tug the ponytail he'd never have worn in high school. "Shit happens."

He laughed and looked down. "Yeah. Well, with us, a lot of shit happened, huh?"

I took my hand away and shrugged. "We were young."

"Young, dumb…"

"And full of come," we finished together, quoting one of our favorite movies.

It felt good to laugh with him. It had been a really long time since we'd sat like this. Beside me, his thigh was big and warm. The love seat dipped from his weight, forcing me to sit closer whether I wanted to or not. I thought I might want to.

"I just wanted to tell you that." Austin shifted to face me.

A smart-ass, snotty reply rose to my lips, but didn't come out. "You don't have to apologize. We've been divorced for years."

When he reached for my hand, I shouldn't have been surprised. It was the perfect moment, after all. Soft music, expensive hot drinks, the scent of cheap body spray wafting from the gaggle of out-too-late teens in the corner and the rise and fall of their laughter all wove a John Hughes–film mood. It was the perfect time to have my ex-husband kiss my knuckles, look deep into my eyes and say, with utmost seriousness,

"So, I didn't jerk off the other night. Just like you said."

I yanked my hand from his. "Austin!"

"What?" He looked genuinely confused. "You said not to."

"I know what I said." My heart became a bird, my ribs the cage it beat against.

He sat back, frowning, and crossed his arms over a chest I couldn't help noticing was broad and muscled under his T-shirt. "And?"

I frowned, too. "I thought you were trying to be nice."

"I am being nice! I bought you coffee!"

"You asked me here to get me into bed!" I'd turned heads with my raised voice. I stood and glared down at him. "That was the only reason?"

Austin looked guilty. Then he shot me a cunt-seeking missile of a grin. "That's not the only reason."

I jerked my chin at him and flipped my hair. Yeah, very high school, but we had a history. "Fuck you."

"I'm hoping."

I didn't want to smile or laugh, so I bit down on my tongue. Hard. "It's late. I have to work tomorrow. Good night, Austin."

I was gone before he could register the fact I meant it. What Austin didn't know was that it wasn't that I didn't want to take him to bed and screw the living daylights out of him. I wanted that very much. But there was a part of me, small though it was, that knew this couldn't be good for either one of us.

We had history, and a past, and all of that meant he knew how to push my buttons just right. It didn't mean we should keep pushing those buttons. Like Def Leppard said, it was time to stop treating each other like an act of war.

I made it all the way to the sidewalk before he was out after me. Austin grabbed my elbow and I turned to face him, my mouth already open to say something cutting. He stopped it with his tongue. He walked me up against the bricks, hard on my back. Him hard on my front.

I pushed him away. "I'm not that easy."

He pulled me closer and kissed me softer. "You could be. I know you could be."

"Austin…" His name eased out of me on a sigh. "This isn't a good idea. Can't we just be friends?"

"What? Are you shitting me?" His hands gripped my waist, but he wasn't pressing me against the wall anymore.

I sagged against him, my head in the place it fit just right on his chest. "No. I'm not."

His grip tightened on me, then released. I mourned the loss of his body when he stepped away from me, even though I knew it was for the best. Fucking like tigers had its place, no doubt, but I didn't think I could keep surviving the scars.

Austin smoothed my hair off my forehead and hovered his mouth over mine without kissing me. "Fine."

"Yes?" I refused to let myself feel miffed. It was what I wanted, after all. To stop the constant game of catch and release we'd begun so many years ago.

"If that's what you want. If it's all you want."

I stepped out of his embrace. "I think it's better for both of us, Austin. If we…you know. Move on."

"If that it's what you want," he repeated. "I'll do whatever it takes."

I blinked slowly. "What's that supposed to mean?"

He shrugged and looked around at the night before looking back at me. "It means I'll do whatever it takes. Whatever you need. What you want. I'm your guy."

"Austin," I said warningly, but he held up a hand.

"It's stupid not to have you in my life, Paige. We've known each other too long and too well to just throw that all away. I told you that when you left me."

"That was a long time ago."

"It hasn't changed." He shook his head and shot me a smile. "So. Friends? Fine."

"Whatever it takes?" I said warily. "Uh-huh."

He leaned to kiss me again, and this time I let him. He hit my cheek with his lips, his kiss chaste and demure. He didn't even grab my ass.

"I'm going home," I said.

"I'll walk you."

I pointed down the block. "You don't have to. I can see the door to my building from here."

"I'll walk with you anyway."

He did. We didn't speak. He didn't try to kiss me again, or come upstairs. He didn't shake my hand, either.

"I'll call you," Austin said, and I had no doubt he would.

Chapter 28

Not everything is meant to last forever, no matter how much you want it to. I'd married young. Too young. And I was grateful we'd both figured out our mistake while we were still young, before we had kids, before we'd tied ourselves together for a life and had none left after we fell apart.

I'd married him for the right reasons. I'd divorced him for the right reasons, too. Hadn't I?

I'm watching him, and he doesn't know it. I wish he could feel the burn of my gaze from across the bar, that somehow my eyes alone could make him turn, but Austin's too busy paying attention to the game and his friends and even that brown-haired whore shaking her tits every time he glances at her. I can't necessarily blame him for looking. They're like two beach balls shoved into a tiny tank top. But I don't like to watch him looking.

It's another late night for him when he should be worried about getting up early in the morning, and another late night for me studying for tests I know I'll pass but don't know if passing will matter in the end. School's been going on a long time, longer than I imagined it would when I decided to go. Money's tight and even community college costs a lot when you have to pay rent and buy food and pay off a car, too.

I only stopped here because I knew if I went home and he wasn't waiting for me I'd be furious. We'd fight and then we'd fuck, and I'm getting tired of that. I'm tired of him telling me what to do and making me feel like shit for doing anything else. I'm beginning to think this whole marriage thing was a bad idea, but after only two years I don't want to give up. I don't want everyone to laugh behind their hands and point and whisper. Mostly I don't want to give him up just so Miss Big Tits and Bad Extensions can get her claws into him.

At home I shower and toss my clothes into the hamper, and I'm making myself a sandwich when Austin comes in. He doesn't act drunk, but when he kisses me I taste beer. I turn my face to give him my cheek.

"What, you don't want to kiss me? Fine."

I hate it when he sulks.

He steals half my sandwich and tries to tell me about his day, and all I want to do is go to sleep so I can get up early and be at the shop to make the next day's deliveries. We need the money I'll earn. I have another tuition payment due.

I'm not listening to him, but I'm watching his mouth move. His lips glisten with oil from the sandwich. His tongue swipes across them. It's late, I'm tired and annoyed, but later when he comes to bed I think of the swipe of his tongue on his mouth and I roll over to face him.

It's easier to fuck him in the dark, when I can pretend he's got a different face and so do I. When we can be different people in a different place. I can forget I'm supposed to be in love with him and just fuck him like he's a stranger and I don't have to ever see him again in the morning.

Austin did call me, but he seemed to have meant what he said about agreeing to just be friends. I hadn't forgotten what it was like to hang on the phone with him for hours, in the dark, revealing every second of the day just to have a reason to keep talking. Our current conversations were shorter than that, but they reminded me of back then.

Things on the Eric front were more complicated. I'd seen him a few times since our dinner date. Another dinner, out to the movies, walks along the river. Things like that. Conflicting schedules had made it impossible to see him all the time. Besides, I wasn't "that" girl. The one who took one date and turned it into a marriage proposal.

We were moving slowly, slowly. Glaciers. And that was fine with me. I'd seen interest flicker in his eyes, watched him watching my mouth when I spoke. Felt his fingers tighten in mine as we walked.

I knew he was waiting for me to make the first move, or to be told to make one, himself. I wasn't quite ready to do either. As Paige, I was enjoying the whole taking-it-slow thing.

As his anonymous mistress, on the other hand, I had complete control of his life.

Each day I sat at my kitchen table with that Chinese box open in front of me, my pen stroking that thick, creamy paper with the touch of a lover. I didn't come from the writing. Not quite. But each note I wrote put me into a state of heightened awareness of every piece of me. My fingers, closing around the pen. My palms, caressing the paper. The inside of my wrist, my elbow, forearm pressing the table as I wrote. My thighs, touching beneath my skirt.

I didn't come from writing the notes, but it was almost as good as if I had.

I told him what to wear. What to pack for lunch. He had, at last, given up smoking. I ordered him to buy me lingerie, and I gave him the size but allowed him to choose. I had him send it to the post-office box I rented from a branch close to my office. I expected something in black. Crotchless, maybe, or at least with fishnets. The soft, baby blue satin and lace pleased me.

I let him stroke himself to orgasm for that gift.

It was time for something more now. I wasn't sure how I knew this, just that I did the way I knew each day when I went in to work how to gauge Paul's mood and keep him focused on work so he didn't hassle me about the job with Vivian.

What frightens you?

I tapped the pen against the paper, then my lips.

I want to know what makes your palms sweat but gets you hard at the same time. What frightens you because you want it so badly?

It wasn't a question I'd have been able to answer without a lot of thought, but that was the point. To make him think. I sealed the note in a matching plain envelope and ran it down to the mailboxes. Eric was working another twelve-hour shift and I knew he wouldn't get home until after I'd gone to bed, but I didn't want to get up early to deliver it, either.

I went online to pay bills and make some changes to my Connex account. I hadn't been on it in weeks and had a page of friend requests to approve and friends' list entries to scroll through. Nothing terribly interesting, since the people I knew from home were still doing what they'd been doing when I left.

Even so, I got sucked into watching a series of "ghost-sighting" videos and "true alien abductions," and so I was awake when my phone hummed and a new text message came through.

I'm afraid of being owned.

Not of being "pwnd" which was something else altogether.

I sat back, the computer forgotten, my heart thundering in my ears and my mouth tasting something like honey all at once. It was the sweetness of anticipation. Expectation.

He was afraid of being owned.

So that's exactly what I gave him.

I found it in one of the kiosks in the center of the mall. It sold hair barrettes of tooled leather, belts, along with necklaces of cord and beads. And there, hanging unobtrusively on a rack with a slew of others that didn't even turn my head, was the bracelet.

Flat black leather about an inch wide, fastened with a snap. It was the sort worn by teenage emo or skater boys and could be tooled with any number of phrases or designs.

"Help you?" The boy in skinny jeans and high-tops leaned around the kiosk to catch my eye.

I lifted the bracelet. "I'd like this."

He looked at me through the fringe of his long bangs. Bangs on boys. There was a fashion statement I was helplessly squishy over. "Want something on it? A name or something?"

He flipped open a rack of designs to show me my choices. I looked through rows of stylized hearts, flowers and fonts. I touched a simple, elegant alphabet.

"I was thinking…the word *slave.*"

That perked his interest. "For you?"

I laughed. "Oh, no."

"Sweet." He gave the word two syllables.

"You think?" My fingers stroked the stiff leather. It would circle his wrist like a cuff.

I tested it on my own and noted how the edge cut a little into my skin when I shifted. Not enough to hurt, but I knew it was there. I handed it to Emoboy, who took it over to the machine that stamped the letters. Idly, I flipped through the rack of designs while he fiddled with buttons and adjusted the bracelet inside the grips holding it still.

Then I saw it. "Wait."

He looked up, one finger on the button that would start the machine. "Huh?"

I gestured for him to come over, and he did, and I pointed at the picture on the menu. "I want this, instead."

He grinned, then nodded. "No problem."

It took him a minute to adjust the settings and another for the machine to stamp the leather. When it was done, he handed it to me with the black leather scarred into the design I'd chosen. A rose, the stem and thorns made of barbed wire.

Simple. Elegant. And far more subtle than the word *slave,* which didn't feel right, anyway.

"Here you go." He handed me a bag with the bracelet inside. "Enjoy it."

Enjoy wasn't exactly the word I'd have chosen, but I took the bag with a smile. Our hands touched, and he grinned. He knew nothing about me, but he thought he did. And I discovered I didn't care.

I don't think there's a woman alive who doesn't understand how the right clothes can entirely change a situation. Under my simple summer skirt and casual T-shirt I wore the bra and panties Eric had bought for and sent to his mistress. The lace and satin clung to my skin and reminded me with every step how it felt to be desirable.

Of course, none of that showed on the surface. I met him in the lobby as had become our habit on these semi-dates, and he greeted me with a smile and a half hug. He wore a long-sleeved Henley shirt, but when the sleeve rode up I saw the flat leather strap of his bracelet. The one I'd sent him. The one that marked him as mine.

"Ready to go?" Eric held the door open for me and we both went out into the warm spring evening air.

"Starving," I said. "I had my windows open and could smell the funnel cakes all the way upstairs."

He patted his stomach. "We'll stop there first."

All along the riverfront, stands had been set up for the first summer festival. Some sold handmade arts and crafts, others boasted displays from local companies. Some had games, the prizes cheap things like water bottles emblazoned with the names of banks and restaurants. As summer festivals went, it was one of the less glorious, but all that really mattered to me was the food.

Stall after stall of greasy, delicious fair food. Corn dogs, ice cream, French fries and vinegar to go with them. My stomach let out a loud, obnoxious rumble as we crossed Front Street to get to the sidewalk on the other side and headed to the left to walk about a quarter mile to reach the rows of booths. Music from one of the local radio stations blared from a huge boom box set up on a trailer. Morning-show personalities handed out T-shirts, mugs and key chains as we passed.

"Do you want something?" Eric asked as I stepped aside to let a mother pushing a double stroller pass on her quest for free junk. "T-shirt?"

"No, thanks. I don't listen to that station. And besides, it doesn't matter if it's free if I'll never use it."

"Mind if I grab one? You can never have too many T-shirts."

"Go ahead." I looked at the crowd surrounding the boom box and estimated how long it would take him to get his shirt, then down the rows to the line for funnel cakes. "I'll get in line for the funnel cakes."

We parted and I pushed my way through the crowd. The prizes might be cheap and the food overpriced, but nobody seemed to care. Kids carried balloons in ice-cream-covered fists and couples walked hand in hand. I got in line behind a couple with matching tattoos on their wrists, a pair of joined hearts. As I watched them whisper and giggle, their fingers linked, their eyes for nobody else, envy rolled slowly over in my gut.

Against my skin, lace and satin once again reminded me how it felt to be wanted. Craved. Obeyed. None of it did me any good standing here in the setting, early spring sun, with a ten-dollar bill clutched in my fist and nobody there to hold my hand.

I looked back through the crowd for Eric but caught only a glimpse of what might have been the top of his dark, curly hair. The crowd around the boom box had grown and the DJ standing on a small platform with a microphone in his hand was now announcing some sort of contest. The line in front of me was moving faster than I'd expected and I placed my order and walked away with a paper plate of hot fried dough covered in powdered sugar before the DJ was even done drawing a winner.

At first look they were just another couple, she in tottery heels better suited to a pinup-model calendar than a stroll along the river, and him in faded, baggy jeans and a T-shirt that showed off the muscles in his arms. The reddish sunlight turned his blond hair auburn, and I blamed that as the reason that I didn't recognize him at first, but the real reason was that with another woman on his arm, Austin had become a stranger.

She, on the other hand, recognized me right away and let out a squeal that could have cracked a mirror. "Paige!"

Kira. With Austin. My Austin? My teeth clenched, grinding, in instant reaction, and I couldn't force a smile. Our eyes met, his and mine, and while I don't know what mine revealed, his showed me he didn't like what he saw. His expression changed, and I recognized him again.

"Hi." I kept my voice even when I looked at her.

She slid her hand down his bare arm, her fingertips lingering on the inside of his wrist before diving down to capture his fingers. Austin didn't pull away, but he didn't tighten his grip, either. I noticed, and so did she, but Kira was good at getting what she wanted. She curled her fingers into his, instead.

"Are you here alone?" Acid didn't drip from her tone. She sounded genuinely curious.

And who knows, maybe she was. We'd already established high school was over and our rivalry should have followed suit. I'd fucked Jack once upon a time, and now she was fucking Austin. Tit for tat, literally. I should've let it go.

"No. I'm here with a friend." The way I said *friend* made it clear that's not what I meant.

Oh, I knew the tic of Austin's jaw, the slow narrowing of his eyes. Kira might be fucking him, but she didn't know him. Not the way I did.

She leaned into his arm, and I couldn't get a handle on if

she was being affectionate or cunty, if she was always that way or if she was trying to work my nerves. I guessed the latter.

"A boyfriend?" She pushed too hard.

Austin took his hand away to reach for my plate. He grabbed off a hunk of now-cool funnel cake and ate it. Powdered sugar coated his lips and he licked each finger slowly, his gaze never leaving mine.

"Help yourself," I told him. I held the plate out to her. "Want some?"

Kira wasn't the sharpest tool in the shed, but there wasn't really any way she could've missed Austin's look. She shook her head. "No. I can't eat that stuff. I'd have to exercise for a week."

"Paige, you been exercising for a week?" Austin shoved his hands in his pockets, down deep, and the jeans sunk lower on his hips to show a strip of tanned belly beneath his T-shirt.

"No. I'll take my chances." I tore off a piece for myself and bit into the heavy sweetness, then licked sugar from my fingers, too.

It wasn't nice, what we were doing to her, but it wasn't my fault she wasn't very good at it. It wasn't my fault he still wanted me even after all this time. I looked again for Eric and spotted him being handed a T-shirt. In a minute he'd be heading this way. I didn't want to introduce Eric to Austin.

"Austin and I were going to watch the barge concert. Do you…do you want to come along?"

I gave her a real look then, my once-upon-a-time best friend. She didn't try to reach for Austin again, and the corners of her mouth and eyes drooped. I remembered how once we'd practiced putting on eyeliner in her mother's bathroom, and how Kira had been the one to teach me how to use a tampon when my mother had been inexplicably too embarrassed.

She'd punched a guy in the nuts for hassling me and lent me her favorite lipstick without a second thought. She wanted Austin, and I knew I should let her have him since I didn't want him anymore.

So, I did.

Chapter 29

"Another time." I spotted Eric closer now, his T-shirt dangling from a front pocket. "I'll catch you guys later."

I left without a backward glance and hurried through the crowd to get to Eric before he got to me. "Hey."

"Hey." He looked at my half-eaten funnel cake. "Is it good?"

"You can have some." I'd lost my appetite for it.

With a shrug, Eric took a piece and chewed it. "These always smell better than they taste."

I risked a glance over my shoulder, expecting to see a sea of strangers. I saw Austin, his face tight, and Kira, staring up at him. "Yeah. Listen, do you mind if I bug out? I've got a killer headache all of a sudden."

Eric's brow furrowed, and he reached to rub the back of my neck. The gesture, automatic but casual, ought to have made me feel better, but I wanted to cringe away from his touch. He gave my neck a gentle squeeze and let go. "Sure, no problem. I'll walk back with you if you want."

"I don't want to ruin this for you." I didn't look behind us again, just started moving back toward the Manor. I dumped the funnel cake in the first garbage can I passed.

"Nah. These things are the same as that funnel cake. I'll walk you back."

I was already walking, but I shot him a glance. "Are you sure?"

"Paige, really. Not a problem. Oops, watch it." Eric reached to steer me away from a puddle of something I hoped was spilled fruit smoothie and not something grosser.

His fingers gripped my arm just hard enough to keep me from stumbling, and my heart thumped harder at the pressure. Lace and satin pressed my skin beneath my clothes. He held on a little longer than necessary but let go sooner than I wanted him to.

In the lobby he checked for mail even though he'd stopped to peek in the box on the way out. I knew how he felt when he found nothing but the Tenant Association newsletter, but he turned to me with a grin anyway.

"Looks like they're planning another barbecue. If it's anything like last year's the beer will be warm and the food cold."

"I wasn't here last year," I reminded as he crumpled up the paper and tossed it in the trash.

"But you'll be here this year, right?" he asked as we both headed for the elevator. "How's your head, by the way?"

"Oh…I'll be fine. I'm just tired." The lie slipped easily enough off my tongue, and though Eric gave me a curious look he didn't press me about it.

When the doors opened on his floor he hesitated before stepping off, and I wondered if he'd meant to kiss me or shake my hand. "I'll call you, okay?"

I nodded and smiled and watched the doors close behind him before I let the smile slide from my face. My jaw ached from clenching it. When I got into my apartment I ran a cold shower and let the icy needles pound my skin until envy swirled down the drain around my toes.

I blamed the tears on the sting on my scalp as I yanked a comb through my hair, but when I looked in the mirror I couldn't avoid my frown. So I turned from the mirror and pulled on a lightweight summer nightgown over my bare, damp and chilly skin.

Jealousy and the funnel cake rested heavy in my stomach, so I boiled water for tea. The headache I'd made up became real, though I nipped it quickly with ibuprofen. I grabbed up the novel I was reading and had just settled on my sofa when the knock came at the front door.

Expecting Eric, I didn't bother looking through the peephole. So when I saw Austin framed in the doorway, all I could do at first was stare. Then I took a step back to let him in.

His mouth was on mine before either of us said a word. My book fell to the floor in a flutter of pages, and I kicked it to the side as Austin stepped me back toward the couch. I put my hands up between us and pushed him away before he could get me there.

"What the fuck are you doing here?" I swiped the back of my hand across my lips, smearing the taste of him.

Austin licked his mouth and swallowed, his gaze flicking around the room. "Is he here?"

"You're lucky he's not. You can't just come in here and attack me like that."

Austin scraped a hand over the top of his hair, then cupped the back of his neck briefly, his head bent. He closed his eyes, brow furrowed. I stepped back when he opened them.

"He's not here," I said. "But you should go."

He shook his head.

"Austin," I whispered. "You need to go."

Again, he shook his head. Only an arm's span held us apart, but it might as well have been a mile. My nightgown swirled around my knees as I turned. I was very aware of the pull of cotton on my skin. The lingerie Eric had sent me had reminded me of how it felt to be desirable, but under Austin's eyes I didn't need something outside me to know how it felt for him to want me.

"Paige. Please." His voice snagged, rough and broke. "Let's stop pretending—"

"I'm not pretending anything." I crossed my arms but kept my back toward him.

Slow, rolling cramps clutched at my belly. When we were married, Austin had put me to bed with a heating pad when my cramps were bad. He'd rubbed my back, too, and gone at night to get me ice cream, no matter how late.

"He's not your boyfriend. Is he? That guy?"

"Is Kira your girlfriend?" I turned on him then.

"Hell, no."

"Are you fucking her?" I advanced a step to poke his chest, and Austin retreated a step.

"No!"

I laid my hand flat on his chest over the steady thumping of his heart. I had to tip my head to look at his face. "*Did* you fuck her?"

He shook his head, just once. I pinched his nipple only half as hard as I wanted to. He didn't wince, though his tongue crept out along his lower lip, leaving it glistening. The bead of flesh pebbled between my fingers, and I rolled the pad of my thumb over his shirt, so soft with the nipple so tight and hard beneath.

"Did you fuck her?" I repeated softly.

"I didn't fuck her, Paige. I swear it."

He groaned when I pinched his nipple again. When I slid my hand under his shirt to find his bare skin Austin didn't stop me. I hadn't expected him to.

My breath hitched at the feeling of his skin under my palm. I curved my fingers to let my nails bite into him for a second, then dropped it to his belt buckle. I tugged it hard enough to move his hips, then let him go.

I stepped back. "He's not my boyfriend. But that doesn't mean you can just keep coming over here and expecting me to let you in my bed."

He pulled his shirt off over his head and dropped it to the floor. I'd traced those ribs with my teeth and lips and tongue. I knew the hollow of that belly and the taste of his skin. I knew the heat of him.

He put his hand to his belt and undid the buckle. Then the button. When he notched the zipper down one tooth at a time, I bit my lower lip. When he shoved the denim over his hips and down the thighs I'd spent hours nibbling, my headache disappeared.

He stepped out of his jeans and pushed his socks off, too, along with his briefs, and stood naked in front of me. Austin was proud of his body and had a right to be. He wasn't fully hard, and I remembered the times I'd taken him in my mouth to get him erect.

"Fucking won't change things," I warned him. Austin shrugged and moved toward me, but I held up a hand to stop him. "No."

He frowned and made as though to speak, but again I stopped him. My voice surprised me, husky and low and utterly, without-a-doubt, in charge.

"Go to my bedroom, Austin."

He took a hesitant step, then another, while I stayed still. He watched me bend to lift his jeans, the long denim legs dangling while I yanked the belt from the loops. Austin's eyes grew wide when I wrapped the leather around one palm.

"Paige, what the hell?"

"Go to my bedroom," I repeated and pulled the leather tight between my two fists. "Get on my bed, on your knees, facing the headboard. Put your hand on it and wait for me."

I'd known this man for half my life. I'd seen him take hits on the football field and stand up for me in a bar brawl. I'd seen him cuss out men on the construction site who weren't pulling their weight, and I'd listened to him share rowdy, dirty jokes with his friends. He'd balked at cooking and laundry because those were "girls' work" and we'd had screaming fits about separate checking accounts when we were married because "women whose husbands took care of them right didn't need their own money." I knew he would never let me tell him what to do.

I didn't know him as well as I thought I did.

Chapter 30

Austin, without another word, turned and went to my bedroom. I heard the creak of the headboard when he grabbed it and of the mattress as he shifted his weight. Then, silence but for the sound of my heart beating fast in my ears and my breath trying to get unstuck from my throat.

I hadn't wasted money on frilly decorative pillows for my bed, and I'd covered it with the worn quilt my grandma had made for me when I was born. The headboard of slatted wood had seen me through childhood and high school, and I'd taken it from my mom's house to the apartment I'd lived in after leaving Austin. We'd fucked in my bed but had never shared it. My hands had gripped the wood where his now clenched, but his never had.

He turned his head when I came in, then looked back at the wall. His head bent, shoulders hunching, and I admired the play of muscles in his back and thighs. His feet dipped furrows in my bedspread as he pushed down with his toes.

I had to lean in the doorway to keep from going to my knees at the sight. My fingers gripped the wood as the cool metal of his belt buckle bit into my palm hard enough to hurt.

The sting of it pushed my blood faster through my veins. The leather dangled, brushing my calf.

When I slapped it lightly against my palm, Austin tensed but didn't take his hands away. He didn't look at me. The muscles in his back and ass went tight, then released, and I drew in a slow, silent breath.

Austin stayed in the place I had told him to stay. This man could put me up against the wall with one hand. He could break me, but he wasn't doing what I told him to do because he wasn't able to say no. He wasn't afraid of me.

He trusted me.

That trust almost broke me more than his hands ever had. It turned me upside down and inside out; it filled me up so I couldn't imagine ever having been empty. I stood in the doorway watching him give himself to me for whatever I wanted, and the leather slid through my suddenly slick fists with a sound like a whisper.

My feet moved even though I couldn't feel the floor. When my knees hit the bed and I got up on it, the mattress shifted. Austin gripped the headboard tighter, his head turning. I saw the flutter and shadow of the long lashes I'd always envied on his cheek.

"Paige…"

"Shh." I moved closer to kneel behind him, between his ankles.

The cotton of my gown brushed his skin and I watched, fascinated, as gooseflesh broke out on his back. Again he bent his head. I could see his hands, the knuckles white. I couldn't see his cock until I moved a bit to the side, and then I bit my groan into silence so he wouldn't hear and know how much the sight of him erect aroused me.

I had always been the one urging him to pin my wrists. Pull my hair. I had taken him down paths he followed eagerly but only because I led him there. Now I folded his belt in half to make a loop of it, and I ran the flat side of it down his spine and over his ass.

I followed it with the flat of my hand and reached between his legs to weigh his balls before I ran my finger along his perineum, up the crack of his ass and onto his back again. Austin shivered at the touch, but didn't move. He didn't speak.

Looking at the leather against his skin, I drew in a small sip of air. My world spun so much I had to clutch his shoulder. My nails dug into his skin, and Austin made a small noise.

I didn't want to hurt him. Not really. I didn't want to beat him, or raise welts on his flesh. I wanted to collar and leash him. I wanted to own him.

I tapped his ass with the strap, not hard enough to call it a slap. "Spread your legs wider."

His knees slid on my sheets and the headboard creaked. Austin leaned forward until his forehead rested against my pale green–painted wall. Those big shoulders hunched. Those big hands gripped. The muscles in his ass flexed.

My hand found the familiar length and girth of his prick. I stroked him gently a few times before withdrawing. I drew a finger along his balls and ass crack again. I put a hand on the back of his thigh to feel the tension there. I put a knee on either side of his calf and pressed myself along his back.

I couldn't reach his ear, but I kissed the smooth expanse between his shoulders. I bit him softly where his wings would be if he were an angel and smiled at the sound he made. I pushed my cotton-covered crotch against his bare ass. He made another noise when I gripped the hem and pulled it to my hips so my bare crotch touched his skin.

I always shaved my bikini line, but I hadn't short-trimmed my pubic hair in a while. Now the fluffy curls brushed him as I moved my hips from side to side. It must have tickled, because Austin shivered again.

I shivered, too. With my cheek pressed between his shoulder blades and my cunt aligned with his ass, I reached around to stroke him. Without lube my palm skipped along the silken skin of his prick, up and down. Austin pushed forward into it anyway.

"Do you like that?"

"What do you think, Paige?" His voice, harsh and low, sent another shiver through me.

"I want to hear you say it." My heart was trying to leap out of my chest, and all I could manage was a whisper, but he heard me.

"I like it when you touch me. Yeah."

"Like this?" I twisted my palm over the head of his cock the way I knew he liked it.

"Yeah, like that…" he groaned.

I dropped the belt. It was a prop and I didn't need it. Wasn't going to use it. If I couldn't leash and collar him with my words, then I didn't deserve to have him. It hit the floor with a thunk of metal. Austin didn't even look at it.

I molded myself to his back and closed my eyes. His skin smelled like nothing else in the world but Austin. No cologne or soap could take the place of it. I breathed him in, and in the darkness behind my eyelids, I lost myself in remembering the way it had always been.

It was a little different now. He jerked when my now-free

hand slid between his legs to cup his balls, and when my thumb pressed his anus in gentle counterpoint to each stroke of his cock. His body tensed and he muttered a small exclamation, but it didn't sound like it was of protest, and I kept on what I was doing.

Stroke, stroke and press, press in time to the slow, subtle bump of my cunt against his ass. I imagined filling him the way he'd filled me so many times. Austin shuddered, his groan sounding desperate. His cock swelled impossibly in my fist. The tender, secret muscles of his ass tightened under the pad of my thumb, and his balls contracted. Subtle signs of his impending climax I'd never noticed before.

"Do you want to come?" I asked him, certain of the answer and surprised by his reply.

"No…not yet. Please." The word slipped out on a sighing moan and he took a hand away from the headboard to put over mine and stop my stroking. "I want to f— I want to make love to you."

I kissed and nibbled his back for a second before I pulled away and spread myself out on the bed. "Use your mouth on me first."

Austin looked over his shoulder, the side of his mouth I could see tipped up. "Yes, ma'am."

He was teasing me a little, but I liked the sound of it anyway. "Less talking, more licking."

Austin turned, still kneeling, his prick in one fist. He let go of it to hold his weight as he moved between my legs, but he didn't dive straight into my pussy the way I expected him to. He brushed kisses over both my knees, first, then up my ticklish inner thighs. His nose nuzzled my cunt before his mouth did, but when his tongue found the tight bud of my clit, I wasn't quite ready for the shock of sensation.

My fists clutched the quilt as my back arched. "Oh, God."

Austin murmured against my cunt. His lips and tongue and teeth formed words I couldn't understand. He teased my clitoris with small, sweet licks and opened me with his fingers to stroke me inside, too.

Everything about it was perfect. I didn't have to tell him what I wanted or what I liked. He already knew.

In moments my orgasm built, ready to spill, but I didn't beg him to hold off. I lifted myself against his mouth, urging him to move faster. The world faded away until nothing remained but the tension coiling in my belly, the pleasure of his mouth and hands on me, the soft sigh of his breath as he whispered my name.

I went over. Slip-slide-fall and up again, desire blocked out everything else. The world crashed, and Austin was with me all the way when it did. His mouth eased off while his hands cradled me until the leap and jerk of my muscles stilled.

But if I knew Austin, he knew me, too. With less than a minute for me to come down, he moved up my body to take my mouth. His fingertips found my clit again and circled. He took me to the edge within seconds. His cock nudged me a moment after that.

I'm on the pill but I'm not stupid, not even for Austin. Not like that, at least. "Condom."

He reached a long arm to yank open my nightstand, even though I hadn't said that's where I kept them. He pulled out the long string of them—the same ones I'd bought a year ago when I was thinking about having lots of random sex with strangers. I never had gotten around to it. I'd only ever used them with him.

It was tricky, him putting on the condom without leaving my clit, so I helped him out by using my own hand in his place.

He rolled on the rubber and moved between my legs. Breathless, I put a foot on his chest to keep him from sliding inside me.

"No," I said.

My fingers were wet when I took them away from between my thighs. That was what he'd done to me. For me. I held out my hand and he took it to help me off my back. I pushed him gently until he sat and I gripped his cock to hold it still as I slid onto his lap.

Chest to chest, groin to groin and then, mouth to mouth. My arms went around his neck and held the back of his head. We kissed, hard but slow. Our tongues fought. He tried to move, but without my cooperation could only rock upward a tiny bit. Even when his hands gripped my hips, my legs wrapped around his waist and I held my body stiff and still except for the kiss.

He let out a shuddering sigh. "Paige…"

I rocked my hips and squeezed him with my internal muscles, but said nothing. I looked into his eyes. Austin blinked and swallowed.

"Fuck," he said. "Just…"

"I like it when you say please," I told him.

He blinked again. I watched his throat work as he swallowed. My fingers twisted in the hair at the nape of his neck. I watched him give in to me.

"Please," Austin said, and I came just from the sound of his acquiescence.

His arms tightened around me as I shook with it. His mouth found mine again. This time when he started to move, I gave him what he wanted. I moved with him, not against him.

His hands slid down beneath my ass to lift me higher on his cock, and I countered with a downward thrust and a roll of my hips that twisted me on him. I lost my grip in his hair and had to settle for clutching at his back. My nails dug furrows he'd notice later, but just then he only moaned into my mouth.

I couldn't come again, but it didn't matter. Austin could, and did with a grunt. His fingers bruised my ass and I didn't care. Our bodies smacked and slapped, and my bed shook. I bit his shoulder and he shouted and thrust so deep inside me it hurt. I didn't care about that, either.

Blinking, tasting sweat, I opened my eyes and looked into his. I felt the jump and play of muscles in his thighs and belly and arms. Austin shivered a little, but I didn't think it was from the cold.

I unwrapped my arms from his neck and tried to do the same with my legs, but he clutched me close. "Don't go yet."

The fucking was done. We used to spoon sometimes after sex, in the bed we'd shared. In the dark. That was when we talked the most, after the fucking was done.

I didn't want to talk to Austin now. With my body sated, my mind wanted to block out the feelings he always brought up in me. I pushed at his chest, and he let me go.

I went to the bathroom before he could say anything else. I turned on the shower and got in without waiting for it to heat. Austin didn't come into the bathroom until steam had veiled it. I heard him use the toilet, then run water in the sink. I heard him fill my glass and set it down a moment later. I waited for him to open the curtain and come in, but though I was prepared to tell him to get out, Austin left the bathroom.

He was dressed and sitting at the small desk in my corner by the time I came out, wrapped in a towel. He was too big for my chair and that desk, another old piece I'd inherited from my grandma. He was too big for me.

He looked up when I came in, and I saw he wasn't just sitting there. He held my cell phone in one hand, the screen flipped open. I hadn't heard it ring.

"What are you doing?"

Austin slowly closed my phone and set it on the desk. He stood. He was too big for my room, too.

I wished I'd taken the time to pull on my robe. A towel didn't seem adequate protection against the way he was looking at me. I grabbed for my nightgown, but it had tangled in itself when I threw it on the floor, and I couldn't easily slide it over my head.

"You got a message," Austin said. "While you were in the shower."

"Since when are you allowed to listen to my messages?" I yanked the cotton into place and tugged it over my head. With it covering my face, I closed my eyes, wishing when I opened them I'd discover this was all an inconvenient dream.

"A text message," he said.

I yanked the nightgown down on my shoulders and glared. "Since when are you allowed to read my messages?"

I stalked to the desk and grabbed up my phone but didn't look to see who'd called. I cradled it to my chest, though, the metal chill through the cotton. Austin didn't move.

"Well?" I demanded. "What the hell, Austin? Who the hell do you think you are?"

"Apparently, I'm nobody," he said.

I'd braced myself for anger, or accusations. A message from Kira or my mom wouldn't have bothered him. It had to have been from Eric, though I hadn't told him to send me anything.

"I have to ask you, Paige. Is that what you want?" He gestured at the phone, but since I didn't know what the message had been, I couldn't answer.

I refused to look now. "You'd better leave."

Austin shook his head. "Answer me first. I think I deserve an answer."

"I don't owe you—anything." My voice tore on the last word and I shut my mouth tight to keep from breaking totally.

"Is that what you want?" he asked again, lower now.

To my horror, I saw he wasn't angry. Austin was close to tears. I'd never seen him cry, not even when the dog he'd had since toddlerhood had died. I'd watched him bury that dog without a tear. But now…now, he was almost weeping.

I had done this to him.

I didn't need to beat his ass with a belt to hurt him.

I felt like the worst kind of bitch.

"Is it what you like? Is it what you need?" He looked helplessly at the headboard, where his hands had left no marks. I looked, too. We didn't need scratches in the wood to remember how he'd clutched it.

"I…think…I don't want to talk about this," I gasped out around tears of my own.

Austin had seen me cry plenty of times. If my tears moved him, he didn't show it. "Talk about it to me. I want to know."

He paused, moved forward. Reached for me, though I backed away.

"Please," he said.

I shook my head and covered my face with my hands, so I didn't see him getting on his knees in front of me. I only felt the thud as he hit the floor and the warmth of his hands as he grabbed my hips. I couldn't look, not even when he pressed his face to my pussy and whispered my name, his breath hot through the cotton. I didn't want to feel the wet of tears against my skin. I wouldn't look, not even when he inched the fabric of my nightgown into his fists and kissed my belly, then my thighs.

"Tell me," Austin said. "Is this where you want me?"

A strangled sound launched itself from my throat. I tried to take a step back, but his hands held me in place. He kissed me again, slow and lingering. Heat and wet against my cunt. Heat and wet against my thigh as he turned his face to press against me there.

"Because I'll do it, if it makes you happy, Paige. I'll get on my knees for you any time you want it. I'll let you do what you want. If you tell me what you want me to do, I'll do it. Whatever it takes, remember? Just…tell me. Please."

"I want you to shut up and go," I said as best I could without breath. It had stuck in my throat, too, my world spinning dizzily as I tried to draw in more air. "Just go, Austin!"

"If that's what you want." He stood and his hands slid up my body to pull me closer to him.

My nightgown fell back down, but it was no protection against him. His belt buckle pressed my belly. The denim of his jeans scratched my bare legs. I had my hands between us, pushing at his chest, and he snared them both in his. Too late, I realized I would have to look at him now.

"I love you," Austin said. "Don't you know that?"

I opened my mouth and he kissed me until I turned my face.

"You don't want to know it," he said.

"We've been through this before," I whispered. "It doesn't work with us."

"I want it to work. Things are different now. Aren't they? I'm different." He paused and tugged me half an inch closer. "You're different. You know you are."

But I hadn't wanted him to know.

"We weren't all bad together," he said.

I looked at him again. "We weren't all good together, either."

"I want to be with you. Not just to fuck you once in a while. Again, serious. You and me. I'm willing to try."

I almost said yes. But then I said no. "Leave."

"Whatever it takes," Austin said, and kissed me until I couldn't breathe.

I didn't walk him to the door. I waited until I heard it close behind him before I looked at the message on my phone. It was from Eric, as I'd thought.

If I were with you right now, I'd be on my knees for you. Your slave. I'd worship you. I wish I could be with you right now.

It's easy to look back and blame a lot of things on circumstance, and I could blame what had just happened with Austin for my response to Eric. But I'll own what I did. I answered him.

I think it's time we meet in person.

Then I wiped my face and refused to cry anymore.

Chapter 31

"Paige, I need you to come and stay with Arty next week while I go away for a few days." My mom, for once, didn't start with any sort of preamble.

I didn't stop to think about why she was asking, just that she was. "Stay at the house?"

"Yes." She sounded tired and cranky. "I need you to be here to get him on the bus in the morning. He has that after-school program until you can get home from work."

"What time does he get on the bus?" Already I was calculating excuses, thinking only of the torture of having to stay in my mother's house for any length of time.

"Eight. Plenty of time for you to get to work. And it's only five days, Paige. Sunday through Thursday. I should be…I'll be home on Friday."

Her assumption that I'd put my life on hold to do this rankled. I was already in a bad mood from my fight, if you could call it that, and I did, with Austin. My mind was on other things, like meeting Eric and telling him the truth about me and his unknown *her* and what would happen.

"Where are you going?" I asked. "It's not like I can just drop everything, Mom."

"I'm going away for a few days. To a spa," she said defensively. "Some me time."

I gritted my jaw and turned off the heat under my pan of reheated spaghetti. I wasn't hungry for it, anyway. "You couldn't have let me know sooner?"

"They had a last-minute opening. Don't argue with me about this, Paige."

Her tone, the one she'd used often on me as a child, set my teeth on edge even more. I dumped the pasta onto a plate and slammed it onto my table, but I didn't sit to eat it. "What if I can't?"

My mom's voice cracked. "You have to. I don't have anyone else to take him, and he loves you. You're his sister. I need you to do this for me."

The tremor in her voice slammed a door on my anger. "Is this about Leo?"

"Why would you say that?"

"Because you lived with him for five years, Mom, and you guys just broke up. You have to be upset."

"I am upset. Very upset." She paused. "Yes, it's about Leo. He…he's taking me away. To try to work things out. It's last-minute because he just got the time off and this place had an opening. So we're going. I know it's late notice, Paige, but I don't have anyone else to ask."

I still wasn't happy, but I was the last person to stop anyone from trying to repair a relationship. Helping out my mom might, in some way, redeem my lack of effort with Austin. Or not. In any case, I sighed and pulled out my calendar from my purse. "What days, again?"

She told me. "You could come for the weekend, you know. Friday night. We could spend a few days together before I go."

"Don't push it," I told her. "I've got stuff going on, Mom. I can't just pop over and hang out and get home in ten minutes."

"You think I don't know that?"

Shit, now she was crying. What was wrong with me, that I made people around me so upset? "Mom. C'mon."

"I miss you, Paige! I'm sorry! I'm sorry I don't have a big, fancy house like your dad does," she said more meanly than I'd ever heard her in my life. "I'm sorry we don't meet your standards. But it's what we have, and you didn't turn out so fucking bad, did you?"

I might have shouted back at her, except I was tired of fighting. With Austin, with her. With myself. So I said nothing and after a few moments of tense silence, my mom cleared her throat.

"I need to leave the house by 8:00 a.m. on Sunday. Be here before then, please."

I held back a groan and reconsidered staying over the night before. Which would be worse, a Saturday night in my mom's house in Lebanon, or having to get up at ass-crack o'thirty in the morning? "Fine. I'll be there."

"Thank you," she said stiffly, and not like my mom at all. "Arty will be thrilled."

That was the saving grace to it all. That my little brother would be happy to see me. I didn't miss living in Lebanon, and I didn't miss living with my mom, but I did miss being close enough to see them more often. I'd spent a lot of time taking care of Arty when he was a baby and a toddler. He was as much my child as he was my brother.

"See you then." I didn't quite manage to sound happy.

"I love you, honey," my mom said, and like the bitch-brat I was, I hung up without answering.

Austin didn't call me, and I sure as hell didn't call him. Eric didn't call me, either, a fact that pleased me less. I knew why—I'd nudged myself out of the top spot in his pecking order. It would have been funny if it wasn't also sort of sad.

It did prove one thing, that whatever we had, or almost had, it wasn't exactly what he was looking for. The question I couldn't stop asking myself, though, was could I give him what it appeared he wanted, full-time? And would he want it from me when he found out it was me?

Most of all, did I want to become in real life the woman I'd created in those letters?

I took my pen. I took the paper, the soft, fragrant, special paper. I only had a couple sheets left. Maybe I wouldn't need more.

My mom said she'd be back Thursday, a week from today. I had Eric's schedule for the month. He worked that night, as well as the following Friday and Saturday. Sunday, then. A little more than a week. That would give me plenty of time to prepare.

You will reserve a room at the Harrisburg Hilton for Sunday night. When you check in, you'll leave instructions for the second key to be left for me, under the name Rose Thorn. You will be in the room and ready for me no later than three-thirty. You will bring with you a bottle of your favorite lube, a box of condoms and a copy of your medical records guaranteeing your clean bill of health. Once inside the room, you will shower and shave and smooth your skin with lotion. I want you clean and smelling of lavender and mint. You will wait for me wearing only the bracelet I gave you. Kneel by the bed. When I come in, you may address me at once and show your appreciation of my presence by kneeling at my feet.

It didn't sound quite right. My words lacked a certain rhythm and delicacy, but they were all I had. Eric liked flirting with public displays of his submission, and he'd have to give up some of that to the clerk to whom he gave my name. But he'd be outing me, too, and I wasn't sure how I felt about walking up to a perfect stranger and calling myself Mistress anything. Still, I guessed it was time to try to find out if I could play this role for real.

"You gonna try for that new position?" Brenda had snuck up on me, not difficult to do since I was lost in swirling, deep-purple thoughts of fucking and sucking. I didn't think that was the new position she meant.

"I don't think so." When in doubt, stall. It took me a minute to figure out what she did mean, but then when she cast a pointed look at the bulletin board on the wall behind me, I turned. I scanned the papers tacked there and nodded. "Oh. The marketing position? No. I already said I wasn't interested."

This gave her pause. "They just put this up about ten minutes ago, Paige."

Okay, so Brenda hadn't been one of their preapproved applicants. I pretended to look more closely. "Oh, *that* new position. No. I don't think so. I'm happy where I am."

She made one of those noises people make when they don't believe you but don't want to come right out and say so. “I think I might go for it. The salary is a lot better, for one thing. I bet the benefits are good, too.”

“It’s a lot of responsibility, Brenda.” Together we left the bulletin board to head down the hall toward our respective offices, but paused in the hallway crossroads. Maybe if I was lucky Brenda would stop to summon a demon and I could avoid further awkward conversation.

This early there wasn’t much traffic, not even toward the copy room or the break room, which always had customers. She shrugged and shifted her purse over her shoulder.

“I think I could handle it. Don’t you?” Her eyes narrowed. “They’re looking for a few people, I heard. Not just one.”

I laughed to put her at ease. “I’m really not interested in it.”

Some small tension I wouldn’t have noticed had it not been so obvious when it eased lifted her shoulders. “I’m going to do it. My sweetie says I should, anyway. He says he wouldn’t mind retiring a few years early.”

That seemed like the last reason for her to take a new job, but I kept my mouth shut. “Good luck.”

“Thanks.” She nodded and headed off, pausing for a moment more. “Lunch, today?”

“I can’t. I’ll have to work through so I can leave early.” I didn’t explain further, though I could see her curiosity.

Paul, of course, was in the office when I got in. I dropped my sweater and purse on the rack and powered up my computer, then moved to the coffeepot to get that started. The scent of coffee usually brought him out from the cave if he hadn’t already caffeinated on the way to work, but since I needed to talk to him anyway I fixed his cup and rapped on his door.

“Paul? I need to—” I stopped just inside the door, at first convinced he wasn’t in there, after all.

He'd pulled the blinds down all the way instead of just half. The overhead lights, as usual, weren't on, but the table lamp wasn't on, either. The only light came from the blue-white shine off the computer monitor. I blinked, my eyes adjusting, and the gleam of Paul's eyes made me realize he was, indeed, sitting at his desk. He wore his suit coat, his tie tight to his throat, his shirt startling and white in the room's dimness. He reached at once to turn on the table lamp when I entered, but not even his smile could convince me nothing was wrong.

I didn't spill the coffee, but I did set it down so hard on the corner of his desk that I sloshed it over the rim. I went around the corner of the desk and knelt in front of him as he turned in the swivel chair to stare at me. I reached for his hands before I knew it, and he took them, his fingers strong and warm and heavy in mine.

"What's wrong, Paul?"

"I can't make these figures work," he said calmly. Solemn. His fingers tightened briefly, a twitch.

I squeezed back, gently. "Do you need me to take a look at them?"

"No," he said. "I just need to sit here for a few more minutes to get them straight. Okay?"

Whatever this was, it wasn't normal, but it didn't feel wrong. He trembled briefly, the twitch of his fingers echoing in his entire body before he stilled. I saw the effort in his eyes, what it took to stop himself from shaking.

I had known since the first week I worked for him that Paul needed more attention than any other boss I'd ever had. I'd been warned, but for the wrong reasons, and we'd gotten along more than fine. Great. We'd made an understanding. I didn't know what was wrong with him right now, but it didn't really matter. I had to take care of him.

"Do you want me to call your wife?"

He blinked and sighed. His shoulders hunched. "Paige, I'm just so very, very...overwhelmed."

I looked past him to the computer, where a few windows spread out across the screen. I stood and reached past him to click them all closed, one by one, until all that remained was the plain blue wallpaper and tiny icons of his desktop. Paul didn't move until I moved back to lean against the desk. Then he swiveled his chair away from me.

In profile, he looked older than he had before. He was a man who wore his age in the lines of his face and his frown, and in his heavy sigh.

"I just need a few minutes," he said quietly.

"How long has this been going on?"

He looked at me then and managed a smile. "A long time. My whole life."

"Do you take meds for it?" I kept my voice soft, and if the intrusive question offended him he didn't show it.

"Yes."

"Aren't they working?"

Paul sighed, but smiled a little broader. "Not today, I guess."

"Can I help you?" I asked without reaching for him again, though I wanted to run a hand over his hair and cup his cheek. Something small and soft to comfort him. The way my mom used to touch me when I was upset.

"You've helped me so much, you don't even know." Paul took a deep, long breath and squared his shoulders. "Just having you here has been such a...pleasure, Paige."

I smiled at his hesitation. "Uh-huh."

He rumpled his hair, and some of his tension eased with that simple act. He took another slow breath and let it out. He looked at me with naked eyes. "I find, sometimes, knowing that you're there with my coffee is enough to keep me on the right track. You never balked, Paige. Not at anything I asked you. You never made me feel like a tyrant for needing things a certain way."

"Of course not."

He half lifted a brow. "Others did."

"I know they did."

We shared some silence.

"You really know me, Paige," Paul said finally. "I'll be sorry when you leave."

This time I did reach for him, if only to give his tie a gentle tug. "I'm not going anywhere."

The cough interrupted us, and we both looked toward the door. I didn't drop his tie, not at first. Not when I saw it was Vivian, her blond hair freshly styled and her brows as high as her heels. I let Paul's tie slide from my fingers as slowly as I stood.

"I brought those files to go over, Paul." She didn't come into the room.

"I thought you were going to call me first," he said.

She and I both looked at him. I couldn't see her face, but I knew my mouth had dropped a little. Paul, as a rule, wasn't mean. Not even close. And he'd pretty much just spanked her, and not in the good way. I wanted to laugh, but settled for a smile he returned.

"I can come back in fifteen minutes," she said coolly. "Would that suit?"

"How about twenty? Paige and I were in the middle of a meeting."

She left without saying anything, and his shoulders tensed again, but he took another long, slow breath. When she'd gone he ran a hand over his hair again and let it cover his eyes for a minute. When he looked at me, though, his smile seemed genuine and the horrific blank look in his gaze had faded.

"She's going to think we're fucking," I said in a low voice. It was perhaps an inappropriate thing to say, but we'd moved beyond the pretense of formality.

He nodded. "She might."

"Is this going to be a problem for you?"

Paul didn't even look at the photos of his wife and family, though his mouth tightened. I wondered if I'd been wrong about him and Vivian. "It might be a problem for her. But not me, no."

He paused. "It could make a difference when she's your boss, though."

"I already told you, I'm not applying for that job."

I went to the bathroom to get a wet paper towel to take care of the coffee dripping on the desk. When I came back, Paul had moved the mug, contents half gone. He'd pulled out a pad of paper and his pen rested on it, though he wasn't writing. I wiped the spots and tossed the paper in the trash, then leaned over his shoulder to look at the list as yet unwritten.

"Start with your e-mail," I said. He wrote it down. "Then sort through the mail in your in-box. Take care of what needs done with those things."

He wrote that down, too, and the rest of the instructions I gave him.

"Send me home early," I added, and he looked up, the scratching of pen ceasing. "I have to be able to pick up my little brother from the after-school-care program every day this week. I'll need to leave by three, all right? I'll go without a lunch break and come in earlier if I have to."

Paul slowly wrote down, *Paige leaving early,* and looked up at me again. "No, you don't have to. Just make sure your work's done." Another pause. "As if I need to tell you."

I leaned closer, just a bit, to say in a low voice, "Write it down in a list for me. It will make you feel better."

I left the office with Paul's chuckle ringing in my ears.

Chapter 32

"Can we have macaroni and cheese for dinner? Please?" Arty clung to my hand like the monkey I'd always called him, then lifted his feet off the ground, so I staggered from his sudden weight.

"Cut it out." I shook him off and set down my overnight bag.

The living room smelled like my mom's perfume and something else. Old Chinese food, maybe. I'd have to do a search. My mom had been known to set down a container or plate next to the couch while she watched TV and forget about it. Arty tossed his shoes, coat and book bag onto the floor by the front door in an amazing one-two-three slingshot move I wouldn't have believed possible had I not seen it in front of me. He was already off and running toward the kitchen when I called him back.

"Pick that stuff up!" I pointed.

"I need a snack!"

I happened to know they fed him at his after-school program, because my mom had told me how great it was not to worry about him being hungry when she picked him up. "Have a piece of fruit."

Arty stopped in midleap, so fast he skidded on the worn carpet in the kitchen doorway. "Fruit?"

"Mom doesn't make you eat fruit?"

He made a face like I'd asked him to eat dung. "But I wanted a Doodle."

I had no fucking clue what a Doodle was, but it didn't sound pleasant. "Fruit. Or some crackers. I'll make dinner in about twenty minutes, just let me get settled in."

Arty grumped and groaned and stomped, but came back out in a minute with a box of cheese crackers. He hurtled himself into a beanbag placed close enough to the TV he could have read Braille on the screen, and turned on cartoons loud enough to make me wince. He wasn't happy to scoot back or turn it down, but he did. I tried to ignore the crumbs spewing from his mouth with each guffaw.

I took my bag up the narrow stairs and down the dark, close hall to the room at the back of the house. My mom had taken the front room, overlooking the street, with a panel of four large windows. Arty's smaller room was between hers and the bathroom. The room at the end should've been a nice den, a sewing room, a playroom, but for some reason nobody in the house used it.

There was a bed, at least, a creaking twin bed that matched one of the dressers I'd inherited from my grandma. The sheets were clean, and the bedspread, and my mom had laid out clean towels for me, too. I set my bag on the rickety, spindle-legged chair I'd never have dared sit on, and I collapsed onto the bed. The ceiling had cracks in it, and water damage. One high, narrow window had a blind but no curtain. That would be pleasant in the morning.

"Paiiiiiiiige! I'm hungry!"

The wail drifted up the stairs and I heaved myself out of the bed to holler, "I'll be right down!"

When I yanked the door opposite the foot of the bed, though, all I did was chip a nail on the knob. The door stayed stubbornly shut. Not the closet, then. It must have been the door to the attic. I tried the one next to the dresser, revealing a set of wire hangers I used to quickly hang my work clothes for the next couple days. Then it was downstairs to the kitchen, which looked as if it had been cleaned in preparation for my arrival.

Which meant my mom had wiped down the counters and cleared out the sink, but the floor was a little sticky in front of the fridge and crumbs coated the table. When I was younger, it had never occurred to me that other people stored leftover food in the fridge or the freezer. When we got pizza it often stayed out on the counter until it was gone. Sometimes she put it, still in the box, in the oven until we remembered to take it out and throw it away. My mom cooked but haphazardly, so spaghetti sauce had always made Rorschach blots on the stovetop and stiff noodles stuck to the ceiling where she'd tossed them to see if the pasta was done.

When I was in elementary school, I'd come down with food poisoning. To be fair, it wasn't my mom's fault. I'd spent the day with my dad at his country-club pool, where they fed me extravagantly on fries and hot dogs instead of making me eat the peanut butter and jelly sandwich my mom had packed for me. I brought it home and ate the sandwich later that night for dinner. An hour after that, the world began to spin. An eternal half hour after that, I started to puke.

I had a morbid fear of food gone bad after that. I wouldn't eat anything I suspected, even vaguely, of having turned.

When I opened my mom's fridge and saw the containers and jars, all potentially swimming with bacteria, my stomach clenched tight in protest.

"Let's go out to eat, okay?"

I didn't have to say it twice. My arms filled with squirming little boy as Arty tried to squeeze the breath out of me and mostly succeeded. I put the kibosh on McDonald's, but conceded to Wendy's, where he thought he tricked me into letting him get a Frosty, when really I just wanted an excuse to get one for myself.

Inside the restaurant, Arty launched himself across the room. "Leo!" Arty seemed incapable of using a voice at anything less than a shout, but Leo didn't seem to care. He patiently let Arty leap all over him, then looked at me over the top of Arty's head.

"Hey, Paige."

I stuttered for a second. "What…hey. What are you doing here?"

He lifted his bag of food. "Getting dinner."

Arty had settled back down to the toy he'd found in his kids' meal bag. Leo was hesitating, but I gestured at the table, and he sat. "It's good to see you, Leo."

"You, too. What's been going on?"

Of all my mom's boyfriends over the years, Leo was the one I liked the best. He'd never tried to be my dad, and he hadn't forced friendship on me, either. Maybe it was because I was already grown up and moved out of my mom's house when they started dating.

I glanced at Arty, lost in his own world of ketchup-firing French-fry cannons. "I thought you and my mom were going away together."

Leo's eyes never left mine, though his mouth set into a hard line centered in his bushy, biker beard. "Obviously, we didn't."

"So where did she go?"

He shrugged and looked away. "That's between you and your mom, Paige."

Another guy? It had to be. Why else would Leo look so…lost? And on a man his size, with that beard, the tattoos and the denim biker vest, lost wasn't a look I'd ever expected to see.

"I gotta run," Leo said and leaned across the table to ruffle Arty's hair. "Take care of the kiddo."

"Of course." I watched him head out and turned back to Arty. "Where did Mama say she was going?"

"To a spar," he said.

"A spa?"

"Yeah, that's what I said. A spa. She's going to get a message."

I sighed. "A massage?"

He grinned, showing the gap between his teeth where he'd lost one. "Yeah."

"Alone?"

"I guess so." Arty shrugged.

It wasn't like I could really expect him to know more, but why had she lied to me?

I woke, disoriented, when a small hand tugged my arm. Expecting Arty, I sat up and fumbled for the light next to my bed, but there wasn't one. I blinked until my eyes focused, but my brother wasn't hovering over me. The touch I'd felt had come from nothing.

I sat straight up, the blankets I'd tucked so carefully around me fighting against me now. At the foot of my bed stood two small children, both about Arty's age, clutching each other's hands. Pale, white children I didn't need a lamp to see because they both gleamed in the darkness. Pale children with empty black holes where their eyes should've been and blood dripping from their ragged fingertips. Behind them, the attic door gaped wide.

I waited for the blood to start pouring out of the door like it did in *The Shining,* but all that happened was they stared. And stared. The pounding of my heart became a roar and I did the only thing I had the courage to do. I closed my eyes, then clapped my hands over them, too.

Nothing happened until I heard a small voice whisper, "Take care of us."

Then I screamed, and screamed and screamed…until I sat straight up in bed to the sound of my phone ringing. The attic door was still closed. No ghostly children were begging me to adopt them. The room wasn't even that dark, lit as it was by the light from an outside streetlamp through the window.

I stumbled out of bed and dug in my purse for my cell. My heart had started pounding again, but for a different reason. I got all kinds of texts and calls in strange hours, but this one felt wrong, and I didn't recognize the number.

"Ms. DeMarco?"

"Yes, who's this?"

"This is Dr. Phillips at the Hershey Med Center. I'm sorry to call you so late, but your mother's surgery has had some complications—"

I had to blink twice to make sure I wasn't still dreaming and even then I wasn't convinced. "I'm sorry, hold on a second. Her surgery?"

"The breast-reconstruction surgery had some complications," he explained patiently, probably used to waking people up to give them bad news. "She's running a high fever and has been hemorrhaging."

My mother had gone and got herself a boob job. I gritted my teeth. "You're her plastic surgeon?"

"Yes. I've been working closely with her oncologist, Dr. Frank, since your mother was diagnosed."

I was still stupid. "Wait a minute. Her oncologist? I thought she was having her breasts done."

"Your mother had a double mastectomy," the doctor said. "With a planned reconstruction. But as I said, there are complications."

I sagged against the headboard. "What kind of complications?"

"Can you come to the hospital?" he said. "I think you should."

Chapter 33

Leo probably hadn't even gone to bed yet when I called him to come sit with Arty and get him on the bus in the morning. He was there in fifteen minutes. I should've been relieved to see him, but I was angry, too.

"You knew?"

He nodded. "She told me a couple months ago. When she told me to leave."

"Months? She knew for months and…she didn't tell me?"

Leo shrugged. "She didn't want to worry you, Paige. Hey, don't look at me like that. You know your mother. And she broke up with me because of it."

He didn't have to tell me that was worse than being kept in the dark. "I'm sorry she did that. Why would she?"

Another shrug. "She said she didn't want to be a burden."

"Did you try to convince her otherwise?" The question was a little mean, but Leo took it in stride.

"I love that woman, and I love that boy up there." He pointed. "Hell. I even took a shine to you. I was hoping she'd reconsider once she had the operation and she saw I didn't care about the size of her tits."

There wasn't much point in belaboring the discussion, so I left him at the house. The drive to Hershey was shorter than the trek from Lebanon to Harrisburg, but it was along a two-lane, rural highway and I had the bad luck to be stuck behind someone adhering strictly to the speed limit. By the time I got to the med center, my stomach had twisted itself into knots and I'd sweated big rings under my arms. I parked in the lot and headed into the lobby, where I managed to decipher the signs to find my mom's floor. I took the elevator with a pair of chatty nurses and a worn-looking older man with a baseball cap pulled low on his head.

It was just past 11:00 p.m., not the darkest hour of the night or anything, but even so the floor was dim and quiet. The nurses talked softly at the desk. I'd never been to the ICU before. I wasn't happy to be here, now.

"Alicia DeMarco?" I rested my hands flat on the counter to keep myself from biting my nails. "Her doctor called and said she was being moved here?"

The nurse consulted a chart. I thought there'd be trouble with visiting hours, but she just smiled and told me the room number and pointed the way helpfully. My knotted stomach twisted tighter. If my mom was really fine I thought they'd have made me wait until morning, which would've annoyed me since I'd made the trip, but would've meant she was going to be okay.

I didn't have that reassurance now.

She looked small in the bed. Pale without her many layers of makeup. Her hair not teased or even combed, just pulled back from her face in a high ponytail. She was sleeping. Machines beeped and something squeaked by in the hall outside as I just stared.

Her breath rattled and I jumped at the sound. When I crossed to the bed, I couldn't be sure I'd wake her. I didn't know if she could be woken.

Her eyes fluttered open when I sat in the chair next to the bed. "Paige."

"Hi, Mom." I scooted closer. Under the covers her chest rose higher than looked right. I couldn't avoid looking.

"Checking out my new rack?" My mom's voice cracked and she drew in a slow, pained breath.

"Why didn't you tell me?"

I waited for a long few minutes for her to answer. Her eyes closed. I thought she'd fallen back to sleep, but then she licked her lips and coughed.

"Hurts like a bastard," she said.

I didn't ask her again. There'd be time for questions and accusations, and I had no doubt there'd be plenty of both. My mom opened her eyes. Then she closed them again, only to reopen them a second later. She smiled. "Paige."

I moved to the chair next to her bed and took her hand. "Mom. What the hell's going on?"

"Language," my mother cautioned, and looked at the plastic pitcher on the nightstand. "Can you pour me some water? I'm dying."

Alarmed, I stopped halfway to grabbing the pitcher. "Mom!"

"Shh," she said.

"Mom. You're not dying."

"I'm dying of thirst. Give me a drink, for God's sake." She frowned. "Am I going to have to ring for a nurse?"

"No." I poured and held it up for her to sip, but she waved me away with an irritated sigh.

"I can do it."

I watched her sip delicately at the water, and I watched as she spilled it all down her chin to wet the neck of her hospital gown. When I took the cup away, I handed her a tissue from the holder next to the pitcher. She blotted her mouth and held the tissue to her nostrils, one then the other, before crumpling it in her fist.

"I know you think I should have told you what was going on," she said.

"No shit."

"Paige." My mom gave me one of her looks, but it left me unaffected. She sighed again. "I didn't want to worry you."

"How long have you known? Mom, my God." I wasn't thirsty, but I poured myself a cup of water anyway to give my hands something to do. Then I remembered I was in a hospital, the air afloat with who knew what sorts of noxious germs, and I put the cup down.

My mother watched me from dark-shadowed eyes. Without her makeup on she looked so much younger. Prettier, even, despite the circles and lines of fatigue etched at the corners of her eyes. She'd never have gone out in public like that, but I liked seeing her without so much paint covering her face.

"For a few months. I found a lump one day and went to have it checked out. They did a biopsy. It was cancer, so…" She gestured with her fingertips at the room.

"But why didn't you tell me?" I didn't mean to whisper, and the way I clutched at her hand surprised me. I bent forward to press my forehead to her hand in mine, and that surprised me, too. "I'd have helped you!"

"I didn't want you to worry," she repeated. "And you are helping me. You're taking care of Arty. Where is Arty?"

I felt hot, feverish, my mom's hand cool on my skin the way it had been for countless childhood illnesses. Only, she was the sick one this time, not me. "He's at home with Leo."

"Oh."

At my mom's small voice, I looked up. "You told him."

She nodded after a pause. "I had to. He wanted to know why I didn't want to be with him anymore. He wouldn't believe me when I said it was someone new."

"You didn't. Oh, Mom." I shook my head. "How could you do that to him?"

She yanked her hand from mine with an unexpected strength. "Don't you judge me, Miss Smarty. You're not exactly the best judge of how to make a relationship work, are you?"

My jaw dropped, but I closed it with a click. "What's that got to do with anything? Leo loves you. You love him."

She shrugged. "I wasn't going to wait and see if he still loved me when I was sick and losing my hair. When I was—" She snapped her mouth closed into a tight, fierce line, her lips sewn shut against whatever it was she refused to say.

"But you could've told me." I sat back in the chair, a million miles between us. "Unless you think I would've stopped loving you, too."

A single tear spilled out of each of her eyes and slid in twin silver tracks over her cheeks. "I didn't want you to worry, baby, that's all. This was something I thought I could manage on my own."

Her eyelids fluttered closed again. "Paige, I'm tired now. Let me sleep."

I wasn't close to being finished, but even I couldn't push her right now. I stood and patted the bedcovers. "I'm going to see if I can talk to a doctor or something. I'll come back tomorrow, okay?"

Her words stopped me in the doorway, a chill skittering along my spine.

"Take care of him."

I shuddered at the vision of eyeless children with torn and bloody fingertips. I turned, but of course it was only my mom in her bed, her eyes closed but her mouth moving.

"If anything happens to me, Paige, you need to take care of Arty. Promise me."

"I promise." It was the only answer to give, really, whether I thought I could honor it or not.

She smiled. Then I heard a familiar soft snoring and knew she'd fallen asleep. I left and went back to the nurses' station, where a woman in a starched uniform told me she'd page Dr. Frank and he'd meet me in the lounge when he was available. I followed her directions down the hall and around the corner to find the lounge decorated in early American Depression, worn couches in shades of beige and brown, and abstract art in the same colors on walls in the same tones. I felt like I'd walked into a giant box of chocolates, which might have been the look the designer had been going for. We were in Hershey, after all.

I perched on the edge of the couch but jumped again at once when the doctor entered the room. Dr. Frank turned out to be tall, with a head of wild, dark hair and a strong grip. "Paige DeMarco?"

I nodded and he smiled as he let go of my hand. "Your mom's going to be fine. Her blood pressure's stabilized and we managed to stop the hemorrhaging. It was touch-and-go there for a while, though, I won't kid you. And she'll have to stay in the hospital a bit longer."

I'd thought I was okay until the floor jumped up to try to smack me in the face, and Dr. Frank's big hands eased me onto a couch, where he put a hand on the back of my neck and pushed my head between my knees with the practice of a man used to dealing with fainters.

"Breathe in through your nose, out through your mouth," he said.

I tried, but my hands were shaking and each breath I took whistled through my nostrils in a way I found utterly distracting. It worked, though, because in a minute or so I no longer felt a red haze threatening to cover me. I looked up.

"Sorry."

He shook his head. "It happens. Your mom really is going to be fine."

"She didn't even tell me she was coming in," I told him. "I had no idea. I'm just a little…can you tell me what's going to happen now? With her treatment, I mean."

So he sat beside me and laid out the plan of treatment for my mom, how long it would probably take and what she'd have to do, and what I could do to help her. Her reasons for choosing a reconstruction right away instead of waiting for chemo treatment, the way I'd thought it was always done. He explained everything to me, more about breast cancer than I'd ever wanted to know, and I still didn't quite understand it all. It was worse than I'd been expecting, only because up until a few hours ago I hadn't known anything was wrong with her. My shock must have shown on my face, because he patted my shoulder.

"There's nothing you can do for her right now. Why don't you go on home and get some sleep." He paused. "Do you have anyone who can come get you? You don't look like you should be driving."

I nodded without really thinking about who I'd call, already pulling out my phone, and he patted my shoulder again. He left without saying much more, but what was there to say? My mom had breast cancer, she'd almost died, she'd probably be fine, but she was still going to need treatment. It was a lot to absorb, and I was glad he hadn't stuck around to baby me through it.

I flipped open my phone and pushed the Contacts button to bring up my list of names and numbers. I didn't want to call my dad, I hadn't quite made up enough with Kira, and Leo was with Arty. If I went home to Lebanon, I'd need a ride in the morning to get my car. If I got a ride home, I could take the bus to work and pick up my car later. I saw two names in a row, one after the other. Two names, but only one choice.

He came right away. I wasn't even ashamed that I hadn't even doubted he would. It was simply something I knew I could ask, and he would give.

The lobby doors parted and he walked through. The air disappeared around me. I opened my mouth to speak, to breathe, and could do neither.

I loved him.

I hadn't known it, or wouldn't admit it, but now I couldn't do anything but feel it. Love was like a punch in the gut, but I didn't double over. The world tipped up again, the floor a rocking, rolling platform that had decided to throw me off it. I didn't fall because he was there to catch me. The smell of him blocked out the scents of bad coffee and exhaustion and bad news. I breathed, and he filled me.

It was Austin.

Chapter 34

Of course, like an idiot, I didn't tell him I loved him. I let him drive me home and I took him upstairs, where he hesitated in the doorway until I pulled him close and shut the door behind us. When my mouth found his, he sighed and his arms went around me as tight as I liked it.

We'd never been shy about fucking on the floor, a table, the couch. Against a wall. But this time I took his hand and led him to my bedroom, where I pushed him gently until he lay on the bed and I crawled up over him to kiss his mouth and face. Straddling him, I rocked against his denim-covered crotch until his cock swelled inside his jeans, and then I slid my body down until I could kiss him there.

My lips left a wet mark, and through the thick material I could feel his hardness. I pushed my hands under his ass to lift him closer to my mouth as I rubbed my face on his thigh. I unbuckled his belt and pulled down the jeans and his boxers. I took him in my mouth, and he made a sound like coming home.

I let the smell and taste of him fill me up the way it always had, and I stopped trying to pretend it wasn't anything more than this. My hands found the weight of his balls, the length of his cock. My mouth sucked, fingers stroked, lips and teeth and tongue moved along him all the ways I knew he liked it best.

He was moaning in minutes, his hips thrusting upward. I took it all, his cock down my throat as far as I could, and when he came, I took all that, too. He fell back, panting, onto the pillows, and I crawled up him again to kiss his mouth. Then I tucked myself up next to him in the place that had always been mine.

He was quiet for a while, and I didn't want to talk. The rise and fall of our breathing timed itself to each other. I put a hand on his chest to feel the thump of his heart. Austin put his hand over mine, and our fingers linked.

I fell asleep that way and woke to light outside my window and a soft stroking between my legs. I didn't open my eyes. If it was a dream, and it might have been, since the entire night felt so unreal, I didn't want to wake. The stroking hit me just right through the soft material of my pajama bottoms and panties. I shifted, just enough, and Austin paused to pull the fabric over my hips and thighs.

The bed dipped when he settled back between my legs. At the first puff of his breath I let out a sigh. When his lips brushed my already erect clitoris, I put a hand over my mouth to hide my smile, and when he sucked gently on me, I bit down hard on my skin to keep in the groan.

Austin ate my pussy like it was his last meal on earth, and I gave up to the pleasure without hesitation. Aside from murmured yes or two, I gave him no instructions. I didn't have to. He didn't need me to guide him, because he already knew how to do everything I liked.

I came softly, a slow and subtle rippling of my cunt under

his tongue rather than a full-out blast of climax ripping me apart. It was good that way. Smooth.

He moved up my body and looked into my eyes as he slid inside me. So wet he had no resistance, I couldn't hold back my cry of delight when Austin's cock filled me. He gathered me close. His every thrust rubbed my clit and I wrapped my legs tight around him to keep him close enough to bring me off again. We came within seconds of each other, me without words and Austin shouting my name in a passion-strangled voice.

He rolled off me, and I didn't jump out of bed to get in the shower, or even to grab a cloth from my nightstand. Boneless, sated, I didn't want to move. Fragile, too, because I couldn't look at him. I was afraid of what I might see in his face.

It was probably too late for us, and love really didn't conquer everything. We'd tried to be together and hadn't made it work. It hadn't hurt for years, but that didn't mean I didn't remember how much it had.

"I'll drive you to work if you want. Pick you up after. We can swing by and get Arty and go visit your mom. Get your car."

I studied my ceiling as Austin's warmth trickled down my thighs. "You don't have to do that."

"I know that."

I turned my head to look at him. "What about work for you?"

He yawned and stretched. "That's the benefit of being the boss."

I sat. "Since when are you the boss?"

"Since I bought the business," Austin said with a strange look. "What's the big deal?"

"You just never told me, that's all."

"Paige," Austin said. "You never asked."

This changed things, and I didn't know why. I got out of bed and stripped out of my pajamas, tossed them in the hamper and got into the shower, where I contemplated my stubbled knees and underarms and thought about the ways life could sneak up on a person.

Just yesterday, Austin was eighteen, captain of the football team, apple of his mother's eye. My boyfriend. A day after that he'd been my husband, and for a while but not too long, my enemy. And now…now he was a man who owned a business and was there when I needed him.

Yesterday I was a scrappy, tough-punk girl who had no money and wore too much eye shadow. Yesterday I was young and stupid and thought love could take care of everything else. So who was I today?

Austin joined me in the shower and I soaped his back. He soaped mine. He used my razor to shave his face and cut himself in a few places. I didn't make him breakfast, but I did make him coffee. It was the nicest morning we'd had together in a very long time.

Even so, I braced myself for him to question me about "us" when he dropped me off at work, but Austin didn't say anything. He only kissed me and tweaked the single strand of hair escaping from my braid. He waved as he drove away, and I stood at the front doors and watched him until he was gone.

Paul didn't ask my reasons for why I'd changed my mind about the job working for Vivian. If he had, I'd have told him the truth. That even though I hoped I wouldn't ever have to take custody of my brother, I had to be prepared in case I did.

And that I was meant for more than being a secretary, even if I'd never believed being a secretary was being less of anything.

"Do you want me to call her?" He was already reaching for the phone, but put it back in the cradle when I shook my head.

"I'll just walk down and talk to her." I smiled at him, even though my insides were hopping like rabbits on crack.

Paul nodded and sat back in his chair. We didn't say anything at first, just looked at each other, but we didn't need words to share our thoughts. In some ways, Paul would always be more than a boss to me, which was even more reason why it was time for me to move on.

"Paige, I just want you to know…" He hesitated, and I gave him the time he needed to say what he had to say. "I've really enjoyed working with you."

"Me, too, Paul."

"And I wanted you to know, too…that if not for you, I don't think I'd have made it through the past couple of months."

I shook my head. "You're giving me too much credit."

"Maybe." His tone said he didn't agree, but he wasn't going to fight me on it. "I just wanted you to know, though, that every day I knew I could come in here to work and find everything the way I wanted…no, needed it…every day I faced knowing I didn't have to worry about anything because it would all be done…I appreciate that."

He could've offered me a raise, a better computer, more vacation time. He could easily have kept me, then, just by asking. Paul could've kept me without much effort, but he didn't.

He let me go.

"I'm not sure there are any slots left in the program." Vivian, for all her bravado, couldn't meet my eyes when she spoke.

She toyed with her files, her pen, the pad of paper on her desk where she'd ostensibly taken notes during my interview, but where she'd really only scribbled and doodled. "I'm afraid you should've applied sooner, Paige."

"Vivian," I said calmly. "I know why you wanted me to take part in the program."

She looked up, her eyes narrowing. "Oh?"

I nodded and let it sink if for a minute before she spoke again.

"Your qualifications are average," she said flatly. "But you come highly recommended."

I happened to be confident my qualifications were not merely average, but I didn't push her on it. "I'm also the best candidate you have for this program."

"You can't know that."

It was only a guess, but her answer told me I was right. No matter how much she'd wanted to get me away from Paul and under her thumb instead, she also had to hire candidates who could do the work. I also knew this was an in-house program, open only to current employees, that even if it was "better" than being an executive assistant, it was still considered entry level, and I could've counted all the people working there who'd be interested in applying. I didn't care if it was arrogant to say I was the best choice. It was true.

Vivian cleared her throat and put down her pen. "What does…Paul…say about this?"

I didn't miss the way she lingered on his name. "He's very supportive of me."

"And you'd be willing to leave him?"

"I wouldn't be sitting here if I didn't intend to take the job."

Again, she cleared her throat. I wanted to feel sorry for her, but nobody had made her start an affair with a married man. Knowing Paul the way I did, I doubted he was even the one to initiate it. Hell. Even if he had, anyone with two brain cells to rub together should know better than to poach.

"I'll let you know," she said finally.

I knew better than to poke. I stood and offered my hand, which she took as though the gesture surprised her. "Thanks for your time."

"I'll let you know," she said again.

"I'm sure you will."

She opened her mouth as if she meant to say more, but closed it abruptly. Without another word she bent back to her work and I left her to it. I passed Brenda in the hall, and she gave me a squinty look.

"Were you just talking to Vivian?"

"Yep. Is that where you're going?"

She nodded. "I hope she hires me, Paige. This is my second interview for the program." She paused. "I thought you said you weren't interested."

"Things change," was all I said.

Brenda nodded. "Yeah, I guess they do."

"Good luck," I said, and meant it.

"You, too," she said, but probably didn't. "Though I'd be—"

She stopped. I waited.

"Brenda?"

She shook her head, then gestured me closer. "It's just that…well, you know. I didn't think Vivian would want to work with you because of you know what."

I kept my expression neutral. "No, what?"

"Paul," Brenda whispered harshly. Her eyes glittered.

"What about him?"

"She…and him…you know."

"I really don't," I said calmly. I wasn't about to give her the satisfaction.

"Don't you? Because everyone knows they are…?"

I studied her, wondering if she and her "sweetie" ever did it doggie-style.

"Or were…?" Brenda lilted, waiting for me to respond.

"Not a clue what you mean, Brenda."

She frowned, maybe unwilling to go there. "Oh, okay, if you hadn't heard. But people are saying it, so I thought you knew."

"What would that have to do with me, anyway?"

Brenda looked uncomfortable. "Well, you have lasted longer than any of his other assistants."

I raised an eyebrow.

"Not that I think you and Paul," she said. "You know."

I lifted my chin toward the bathroom at the end of the hall. "I have to run. Good luck with the interview."

She nodded and turned on her heel. I watched her for a moment before I went into the bathroom, where I ran cold water in the sink and dampened a paper towel to press to my forehead and against the back of my neck.

I wasn't my mother, but nobody here knew that. Months ago I'd have been sick to my guts thinking anyone believed I was fucking my boss, but now it simply didn't matter. I knew the truth. So did Paul. Paul, who I was leaving.

I didn't need to use the toilet, but I went into the stall anyway. I put the lid down and crouched there, my head in my hands. I took a deep breath, but the scent of ammonia and those nasty pink toilet cleaners overwhelmed me and I covered my nose and mouth with my hand. I tried to catch a whiff of Austin, but could only faintly smell the lotion I'd smoothed on this morning.

I could remember, though. How he smelled. How he felt and tasted, and not just because of last night and this morning. From before.

Austin's behind me, his breathing heavy like he'd just run up the stairs. He's got his hand wrapped in my hair, tipping back my head so it's hard for me to swallow. His prick jerks inside me, but he's not thrusting right now. He's close to coming.

I am, too.

"Pull it," I tell him. "Harder."

His fingers tighten but he doesn't pull. "I don't want to hurt you, Paige."

I want him to hurt me. He's bigger than me. Stronger. He holds my heart in his hands every day and doesn't break it, at least not very much. But I want him to hurt me now, in this moment, when my cunt is clutching on his cock and I'm ready to burst into an orgasm that will blind me. I don't know why. I just want it, and I want Austin to be the one to give it to me.

"Pull my fucking hair!" I grit out the words around a groan.

His fingers tighten as he pushes inside me, then pulls out, but he doesn't do more than tug. This boy has tackled other boys on the football field hard enough to break their bones and knock them out. I know he could pull my hair harder than he is.

He fucks into me smoothly as his fingers find my clit and his other hand releases my hair. My head falls forward. On my hands and knees I can put my head down and look under my body to see where he's joined me. Instead, I bury my face in the pillow and lift my ass in the air, push harder against him, force him to slam his body into mine.

It does hurt, but hurts so good. Pain and pleasure are mingling. I've read about this but never understood it, even though it made me creep my hands into my panties and stroke myself into coming as I read. But it's not quite enough, it's not what I really want. Or it's not enough of what I want.

I pull away, leaving Austin muttering a complaint. I roll onto my back and hold him off me with a foot on his chest. His cock is huge and wet from me, and I think about taking it in my mouth. Right now. He'll taste like me, and I shudder at the thought as my fingers move to cover my cunt. I press my palm against my clit and pleasure jolts through me.

I get out of bed and he follows when I crook my finger. We've fucked in the living room before. I stand in the cool air with the windows open and without blinds, showing me off to anyone who might look through. We live on the third floor, which make voyeurs unlikely, but I'm still aroused at thinking we might be giving someone a show.

Austin smiles and moves toward me. Step and step and one more, and my back hits the old plaster walls we've never painted. His hands fit my hips just right. His knee nudges my legs apart, and his thigh presses between mine. He kisses me.

"What are you doing?" Austin says, laughing.

"Fuck me." My voice shakes.

His brow furrows for a minute, but only that briefly. Then he's got his hands under my ass and has lifted me, my legs around his waist, my back against the wall. His mouth seals mine before I can take a breath, and I can't breathe. His kiss steals my air.

My heart beats fast in my ears and the world rushes around us. Austin fucks me and I try to take another breath but his lips are closed tight over mine, his tongue fucking my mouth the way his prick fucks my pussy. I'm drowning in him. In this. In us.

I break the kiss with a gasp and now I understand more about the allure of pain. "Put your hand on my throat."

"What? No." Sweat gleams on his forehead.

"I want you to do it, Austin."

Both of us can barely speak, our bodies using all their energy for the fucking and leaving little for conversation. I dig my nails into his shoulders and rock my hips, getting closer. I close my eyes. I want him to do this, give me what I want. What I think I want, anyway. What I want to try.

"Put your hand on my throat!"

"Fuck...Paige..." He's getting close, and soon it will be too late. He'll come, I won't.

My eyes open and I bear down on him, my legs around his waist. "I want you to do it!"

"I don't want to hurt you—"

"It's sexy," I argue.

He'll have to put me down soon. He's got me braced against the wall, but even Austin isn't that strong. I bring his face to mine and kiss him. And then I make him give me what I want.

"If you don't, I can find someone who will."

"What?" His eyes fly open, the pupils wide and dark. He's so close he can't keep his hips from moving, even though he wants to stop. I see it in his face. "What do you mean, you'll find someone—"

"Maybe I already have. Did you think of that?" The lie, cruel, pushes from my mouth.

I see him thinking about it, as best he can anyway with the blood pooling in his cock and orgasm clouding judgment. How things have changed lately. How I've wanted different things...and where I might have learned to want them. From who.

He doesn't know about the books I've found, ordered from overseas, or the Internet chat rooms where people address each other as Master and Mistress or Slave. Austin doesn't know this part of me that wants to explore.

"Maybe I've been—" pleasure chokes me "—fucking around."

"Have you?" He's angry in an instant.

Oh, how well I know him.

I don't answer, but my head tips back again. My eyes close. I'm going to come. My back skids suddenly along the plaster as Austin shifts.

"Paige! Goddamn it!"

"Put your hand on my throat," I whisper.

And Austin does.

His hand can't close all the way around my neck, but it's big enough to come pretty close. We move together, sliding as sweat makes us slick and fucking leaves him unsteady. Something rips into me. A nail left from a picture knocked off the wall when once I slammed a door. I can't cry out, I can't breathe, he's done what I asked and taken my breath again.

Austin's fingers close tighter and my fingernails dig deeper and we both come at the same time. Only after that does he put me down, his hands shaking, and then sink to the ratty tied-rag rug that always manages to slip out of place on the dirty hardwood floor. I don't quite fall, but I collapse into a crouch.

My back stings. Hot blood drips steadily down my back, over my ass and down my leg. I sip in the air and wait for the world to stop rocking and my body to stop pulsing. It seems to take a very long time.

He won't look at me.

He gave me what I wanted, but it's the last time I'll ask Austin for anything for a long time. I move out the next day, letting the bruises on my neck and stitches on my back speak when I will say nothing. He gave me what I wanted, what I needed, but the price was high.

Too high.

Someone came into the bathroom and entered the stall at the far end. I couldn't stay there, holding back sobs and trying not to breathe. I washed my hands and face again, and looked in the mirror to be sure nothing was out of place. I went back to my desk and got back to work, wishing for a list to take up all my attention so I didn't have to think about the past.

I was really going to leave Paul. Move on. Move up.

But what about the rest of my life? Was I going to move on and up from it?

Chapter 35

"Thanks for taking me." I gathered up my purse and sweater while my dad pulled into the spot next to my car. "I appreciate it."

"No problem." He drummed the steering wheel with his fingertips and stared out the window at the hospital. "So. Your mom's in there, huh?"

I sat back against the leather seat of his BMW and nodded. "Yes. She has breast cancer, and there were complications with the surgery."

He flinched, his cheeks paling. My dad swallowed hard. His fingers stilled and gripped the wheel. He didn't look at me. "How does she look?"

It wasn't exactly the question I thought he'd ask, and it annoyed me. "She looks like someone who's sick and who almost died. How do you think she looks?"

"I meant how is she," he said, but I didn't quite believe him.

"You could go see her yourself." I knew he wouldn't. My parents weren't enemies, but in my entire life they'd never been anything like friends.

"Yeah. Yeah, I could do that." He licked his lips, then

turned to me with a bright, hard grin. "I don't think she'd see me, do you?"

"I don't know." I shrugged. "Maybe you could just send her flowers."

The easy way out. He nodded and hunched forward, looking upward to the hospital building as though he was trying to pick out which window was hers. Her room was on the other side, but I didn't mention that.

"Thanks again for the ride," I said.

"You know, I did love her, Paige. Your mother. I'm sure she's said otherwise—"

"She's never said, either way." I shifted, my hand on the door handle. I wanted to escape this conversation before it happened, but I didn't get out.

"She hasn't?" My dad looked surprised.

"She never really talked much about you at all, Dad."

This didn't make him very happy, and his eyebrows beetled down. I caught a glint of silver threads in them, too, against the blond. He sat back in his seat and turned toward me.

"She had to have said something. I mean…I'm your dad."

"She never gave me details," I told him as gently as I could. "It really wasn't my business, was it?"

Not to mention how squicky it would be to hear details about the affair that had resulted in my birth. I'd known my whole life who my dad was, and that I only saw him sometimes. That he had a couple other families more important than mine, and that he always had more money that somehow never made its way into my mom's wallet the way it should've. But I hadn't ever asked for details, the wheres and whys and whens. I'd assumed she loved him. I'd never considered that he might have loved her.

"I did, though. Love her." My dad cleared his throat. "You look like her, Paige. So much now."

He hadn't seen her in years, and I looked like him, but I smiled. "Thanks."

"She was so beautiful, you wouldn't believe it. She knew just how to make a cup of coffee, too, my God, that woman was a wizard." He drifted into memories, no longer seeing me.

I wasn't impressed with his recollection. She was pretty and made good coffee. Nice. What about she was smart, kind, generous, funny? That she made a wicked meat loaf and could stretch a budget so thin you could see through it, but still come up with the cash for a new pair of sneakers or a birthday cake.

"My first wife didn't really understand me."

I groaned. "Oh, Jesus, Dad. God."

I got out of the car and slammed the door. I didn't want to listen to his crock-of-shit explanations for why he'd fucked his secretary, knocked her up and left her to raise their kid alone. I didn't want to hear his reasons for being unfaithful. Maybe if he'd married my mother, if the story had become a fairy tale with a happily-ever-after, with me, their pretty princess, in a white dress and white patent-leather shoes with a pony and a clown at her birthday party, I might have cared. I might have listened. But as it was, I turned my back and tried to leave him behind.

My dad got of the car, too. "Paige!"

There had been few occasions when my dad had to raise his voice tone. I'd always been so terrified he'd stop loving me, I'd never misbehaved. My feet stilled automatically, but I didn't turn.

He caught up to me and reached for my arm, but didn't grab it when I glared. "Paige. Wait a minute."

"Dad, really. I have to get inside. I promised Mom I'd stop by and I have to get home to take care of Arty."

He looked blank.

"Arty. My brother." I didn't add the "half." "He's in an afterschool-care program, but I have to get back in time to pick him up."

He looked up again at the building, then back at me. "I don't think I'd better go in there. But will you tell her I asked about her?"

"Of course." I paused, then decided not to hold back. "You know, Dad, she's been laid off from the factory for the past couple months. I don't know what her insurance is like, but I'm sure she could use some money."

"Did she tell you to ask me that?"

I'd been annoyed before, but now his quick suspicion pissed me off. "No. She wouldn't. But you have it, and she needs it."

My dad shoved his hands into his trouser pockets and looked at the ground. "How much does she need?"

"How much can you spare for someone you say you loved?" I shot back, not caring if I made him mad.

He looked up at me. "You really don't know the story, Paige."

"I don't have to know it, Dad."

We faced each other over cracked concrete and neither of us moved. My father sighed and stretched his neck back and forth, then tossed up his hands. "If I give you a check, will you give it to her?"

"Yes, sure. Of course I will."

He eyed me, then leaned back into the car and fumbled around before pulling out a checkbook. He scribbled hastily and tore it off, then pressed it into my hand as though he was afraid he might change his mind and take it back. I didn't look at it, just tucked it in half inside my palm. My dad could be generous, but I didn't want to know, just then, if he'd made me proud or disappointed me.

"And tell her…tell her I was asking about her. Okay?"

"Yes, Dad."

"How about you? You need anything?" He held up the checkbook, but I waved it away.

"No. I'm fine. I'm going to be getting a new job."

He looked impressed. "Oh, yeah?"

"Yeah. I'm going to be in a new marketing program."

"Will they give you a raise?" He didn't wait for an answer. "It's about time they recognized your potential at that place. Gave you a step-up."

"Nobody's giving me a step-up. I interviewed, I'm qualified. It's not a favor, Dad."

"Of course it isn't." He tucked the checkbook into his jacket pocket. "I didn't mean that it was."

I straightened my shoulders. "I'd better get inside."

My dad held open his arms as if he expected a hug. I gave him one, stiff armed as it was, and he kissed my cheek. He squeezed my shoulder.

"I'm proud of you, Paige. You should know that."

I shrugged and smiled and left before he could get sentimental. When I gave my mom the check, she stared at it for a long time before she unfolded it. She blinked rapidly when she saw whatever he'd written, then folded it tight again and handed it to me.

"Would you put that in my purse in the drawer, there, hon? I'll have to get you to run it to the bank for me later." Her voice still sounded hoarse but her color was better, and she was sitting up. She'd brushed her hair and held it back from her face with a pretty headband.

"Aren't you surprised at all?" I put the check inside her wallet and closed the drawer.

"At what? That you were able to shame your dad into helping me out? Or at how much he gave?"

"Both?" I didn't ask her how she'd known I'd been the one to force his hand.

My mom smiled and patted the side of the bed. "Come here, Paige."

I did.

"I never told you why your dad and me never made it."

I sighed. "Mom, I really don't care. I know all the experts would say it traumatized me for life."

"Hush," she ordered, and I fell silent. "Me and your dad, when we met…well, it was really good. Right off the bat. I knew he wasn't happy at home, and not because he told me. I'd had plenty of guys tell me all about how their wives didn't understand them, or how their marriages had been over for a long time before I came along. I knew what I was looking at. It wasn't your dad who came after me, Paige. I went after him."

"Mom. I really don't want to know."

"Well, I want to tell you," she said. "So shut up and let me do it, or I swear I'll come back and haunt you if I die."

"Stop. You're not going to die for a long, long time." I told her and squeezed her hand.

"So I fell for this guy so hard it was like someone had snuck up behind me and shoved me down a flight of stairs. I just thought he was the handsomest, most special, smartest… sexiest…"

I grimaced. "Okay, I get it. You were into my dad."

"Oh, no. Not your dad," my mother said. "Denny. Me and your dad used to go out after work sometimes for drinks. He needed to get away from home, for whatever reason, I guess it was because he wife was a full-on bitch, but whatever. Me and him and Dennis used to go out after work and just hang out."

"Denny?" I shook my head, thinking of my dad's longtime buddy. "But…you and dad…and…wait a minute. Denny?"

"Oh, sure. Denny." She gave a happy sigh. "He was so handsome. I was crazy about Denny."

"But what happened?"

"Well," my mother said, "as it happened, Denny wasn't as crazy about me. I caught him stepping out on me with some whore he picked up at the Downtown Lounge on dollar draft nights. What with one thing and then another, with your dad not happy at home and me brokenhearted about Denny, we sort of just turned to one another."

I got up from the bed and paced the narrow corridor between it and the wall. My world had done its share of flips over the past couple days, but this had stood me on end. I finally sat in the chair and linked my hands together.

My mother had been watching me patiently. "You all right?"

"I'm fine."

Her laugh trailed off into a cough, and I gave her a drink. "Paige, I'm sorry. I know you had some idea in your head about me and your dad, but it's time you knew."

"He said he loved you!" I blurted.

"Well, I was pretty damn good," my mom said. "Don't men always think they love a really good lay?"

"Oh, Mom." I shook my head. "Was that all it was? A mistake?"

"No. It was the best mistake I ever made," my mother said with a smile. "Because I ended up with you."

Chapter 36

It was silly to be shy around Austin, but I was. He'd seen every part of me, the best and worst, and that should've made me more comfortable with him than anyone else. That was the way it had been when we were together, but now...now things had changed and I was still not sure what that meant for either one of us.

He wasn't pushing, for once. He called to ask me about my mom and to see if I wanted to meet him for dinner. He didn't say it was a date, but that's what it felt like it had to be on a Saturday night. I told him I was busy, that I was tired, I told him a bunch of excuses and he listened to each one with a soft "mmm-hmm" but no protest.

"Tomorrow, then," Austin said.

"I have plans tomorrow," I told him, and he was silent. "But...Austin, I'll call you."

"Okay, Paige. You do that."

He hung up, and I wondered if I'd lost him. I dialed him after five minutes, and when he picked up, I said, "I told you I'd call you."

He laughed. "You changed your mind?"

I thought of a hotel room and a man on his knees. "I do have plans tomorrow. But I will call you. Okay?"

"With that guy?"

I should've known calling him back would lead to a conversation I didn't want to have. "Yes. Eric."

"Does he treat you right?"

I laughed. "Oh, Austin."

"I want to know."

"He…it's not really…like that."

Austin grunted. "Then what's it like?"

"I can't explain it to you." I sighed. "Listen, I'm really wiped out. I'm going to go take a hot bath and read a book and go to bed."

"No dinner?"

He could be persistent, and charming, and I loved him. Suddenly, I loved Austin with everything I had inside me. More than I ever had, years before, when I was young and stupid and had no idea what it meant to love someone.

I knew now, because I'd had it and lost it. And then I was crying, a hand over my eyes and swallowing hard to keep him from hearing. But Austin heard me, anyway.

"Paige? What's wrong? Is it your mom?"

I couldn't tell him. Not until everything else had been taken care of and I'd done all I needed to do. I couldn't tell Austin I loved him without knowing for sure I could let him love me.

"I have to go," I said, but didn't hang up. I even loved his breathing, the familiar in-and-out of it. I wanted to hold on to it for a minute longer.

"Paige," Austin said in a low voice. "Remember what I said."

Whatever it takes.

I remembered.

"I have to go, Austin. I'll call you. Later."

I hung up that time. I wanted to cry. And then I did.

"Paige. How nice to see you again. What can I do for you today? Something pretty for a friend? Something nice for yourself?" Miriam's warm, crimson-painted smile didn't urge an answering grin from me.

It wasn't her fault. I felt as white and thin as paper held to a too-bright light. I felt ready to tear.

"Something for me." I already knew what I needed, but before I could head for the back room where she kept her files of writing papers, Miriam came around the counter.

"My dear, you look awful," she said without any pretense of diplomacy. "You sit down and have some tea right now. Or better yet, come here."

She gestured and I followed. She took me into a back room marked Private and sat me down in a spindly but comfortable chair in front of a polished wood table. I sat gratefully; my knees were a little shaky. She didn't pour me tea from a pot, but she heated water in a small microwave and gave me my choice of tea bags from a small container.

She didn't ask me to reveal my secrets. Not that I would have. I didn't know Miriam all that well, and though she was old enough to be my grandmother she'd never acted like one. I was glad for the tea, though. She passed me a cookie from a tin, too.

"Sugar helps," she said.

I nibbled. "With what?"

"With everything!" Miriam laughed an entirely sexy laugh

and I could easily imagine her as the 1940's pinup girl she must've been. "There, now. Your color's coming back."

Apparently I hadn't just felt like paper, I'd looked like it, too. "Thanks, Miriam. But I have to get going. I have an… appointment."

"Ah." She nodded and smiled. "And you need something special for it, yes? Something special to write on?"

I swallowed sweetness but tasted bitterness. "Yes."

"I have just the thing." Miriam held up a finger and got up from the table to pull down a large album from one of the shelves.

Covered in what looked like leather, the album opened to reveal sheets of paper, all types, each bound inside the album with thin strips of metal that held the pages together without punching holes. Several loose pages fluttered as Miriam turned the pages, carefully touching only the edges. I moved closer to look at what she offered. I'd seen lots of fine papers, many of them from right here in this shop, but the pages in this book were beyond fine. They were exquisite.

"Handmade papyrus," Miriam said with a reverence some people used for jewels. "This is linen-textured parchment cut from an antique book bound in the 1700s. And this one was just so lovely I had to have it."

She tapped a page of plain white, slightly glossy paper. "Doesn't look like much, but it holds the ink in such a way…"

She sighed and shook her head, still turning pages and catching a few more that floated free. "I know I have something in here just for you. I keep this only for the most special occasions."

"You don't even know what I need it for." It sounded like a protest, when I didn't mean it to. My fingers itched to caress those papers. To find exactly the right one.

"Gram?" Ari poked his head through the curtain. "I delivered that letter for you—oh, sorry. I didn't know you weren't alone."

Miriam waved a hand. "It's all right. Paige, would you excuse me for a minute? I need to go take care of something."

"Sure, of course."

"You go right ahead." Miriam put her hand on my shoulder as she passed, as though for support.

Greedy, I was already pulling the book toward me, but I paused when she touched me. I looked up. She was a tiny woman, and though she stood and I sat, we were still nearly eye to eye. She cocked her head to look at me.

"You'll find just the right thing. You always do. I told you, Paige, you have a knack for knowing just what someone needs." With that, she squeezed my shoulder and left me there.

She was right, I thought, my fingers already flipping the album back to the beginning so I could start with the first page and savor each one. I was good at knowing what people needed, and how to give it to them or how to help them take it. Too bad I didn't know how to do the same for myself.

And then, there it was.

I found it in the middle of the album. A heavy, cream-colored card of high-grade linen. Expensive stock. The sort of paper I coveted and hoarded but never actually used. A slightly rough edge along one side. Custom cut, I could see, from a larger sheet. Not quite heavy enough to be a note card, but too thick to use in a computer printer.

Shall we begin?

He'd been coming out. I'd been going in. Days later, the first note arrived.

Hi, Ari. What are you doing here?

Delivering something for my grandma.

With shaking fingers I pulled the paper from its binding.

Wow, I didn't think I'd run into you.

Of course not, dear, why would you?

I no longer had to wonder who'd sent that first list. The one that had changed my life. Miriam, it seemed, knew what I'd needed.

Now I knew what I had to do.

The right clothes make all the difference.

I wore a black pencil skirt with sheer, blackfoot seamed stockings and a garter belt. A white shirt, fitted, with buttons and long sleeves. Underneath, I wore plain white lace panties with a matching bra. Black stiletto pumps. In shoes so high it's impossible not to walk as though you're fucking the world with each step.

I looked like a mistress, finally, even if it wasn't the vinyl-catsuit and flogger-wielding sort. I felt like a mistress, too, which was probably more important. I'd put this outfit on like armor, a shield, and there was no mistaking I turned heads.

I loved it. I don't think there's a woman alive who doesn't relish that power of knowing any man she passes would get on his knees for a taste of her. Even if it's all mostly fantasy, it was one I was capable of delivering, and I had no doubt there were at least a few I passed along the street who would've gladly given me what I wanted just because I demanded it.

I was a few minutes early, but not too many. The lobby of the Hilton was done in subdued reds and golds and browns, the carpet clean but worn in places that turned the floral pattern into something more geometric. Paneled wood walls turned it into a gentlemen's club missing only men in cravats and top hats smoking cigars. The elevators were off to the left while straight ahead past the front desk were couches and chairs set up in conversational groupings and doors leading to conference rooms. I took a seat in a far chair half hidden by a tall potted plant that turned out to be plastic.

I saw him. He didn't see me, but then Eric wasn't looking for me the way I'd been waiting for him. Besides, I'd planned it that way.

He went to the desk. I could see his grin from where I sat, could tell by the way he pushed his too-long hair out of his eyes again and again he was nervous. He had an overnight bag slung over one shoulder.

He looked so beautiful. The hair, the eyes, the long legs and broad shoulders. I thought of him with his hand on his prick, coming at my command. I thought of him on his knees, his mouth on my knee, my thigh. My cunt.

I thought of the bracelet that marked him as my responsibility.

I thought of a lot of things as I watched him head for the elevator and punch the button. I thought of even more as I watched him wait for it to arrive, its progress from the top floor taking forever and marked with a *ping* and the floor number lit above the sliding doors. I got to my feet in my armor, with my shield. The plastic plant blocked the view a little, but he could've seen me, had he looked.

Eric didn't look around. He bounced on the balls of his feet. His bag slapped his side and he let it slide from his shoulder to grab the strap. The elevator pinged but didn't open, stuck on the third floor. I heard him mutter something. I stepped away from the plant. The elevator opened.

Sometimes, you turn back.

And sometimes, you walk away.

I watched him get into the elevator and the doors closed behind him. I watched its progress up and up, the lit numbers showing me exactly how far he went. Then I turned on my high, spiked heel and went to the front desk, where I pulled a letter from my black clutch purse.

It was an explanation, short but firm, and a final list of commands for Eric to follow. He would be disappointed, but something told me he'd be relieved, too. Some things are better left in fantasy.

I handed it to the clerk. "Would you see that the gentleman who just checked in under the name Rose Thorn gets this note, please? It's important."

The staff at the Hilton are well trained, and this boy was no exception. Or maybe it was the clothes and the way I said the words, as though I had no doubt he would jump to do my bidding without even the snap of my fingers. He nodded and took the paper from me. He looked at the blank front and then at me, and nodded.

"Absolutely, ma'am."

"Right away," I said.

"Yes. I'll do it myself." He looked to the girl beside him, who shrugged, not at all taken in by any of this.

He didn't peek as he walked away, and no matter what he might have done the moment the elevator closed behind him, I would never know.

It was done.

Austin opened the door after I'd knocked three times. He looked me up and down, his mouth slowly curving. He opened the door, wide, and stepped back to let me through. I didn't miss the way he leaned toward me as I passed him, or the way he breathed me in.

I stopped in his living room and pivoted to face him. "Austin."

"Paige," he said patiently.

I took a breath so deep it lifted my shoulders, and I dropped my purse. It hit the floor and bounced, but neither of us looked at it. When I opened my arms he came into them, and when I kissed him, he kissed me back.

"I want you," I said.

I showed him how much with my hands and mouth.

"I'm sorry," I told him.

Austin kissed me harder.

"I love you," I told him.

It was not the first time, but I didn't want it to be the last.

Austin gathered me close and breathed into my hair, his big hands hot and restless on my back. "I love you, too."

Sometimes, you turn back.

Sometimes, you walk away.

And sometimes, you find the place you're meant to be, and you stay there. You find a way to make it work.

Whatever it takes.

★★★★★